SPEARCREST SAINTS

Audentes

Fortuna

Iuvat

Copyright © 2023 by Aurora Reed

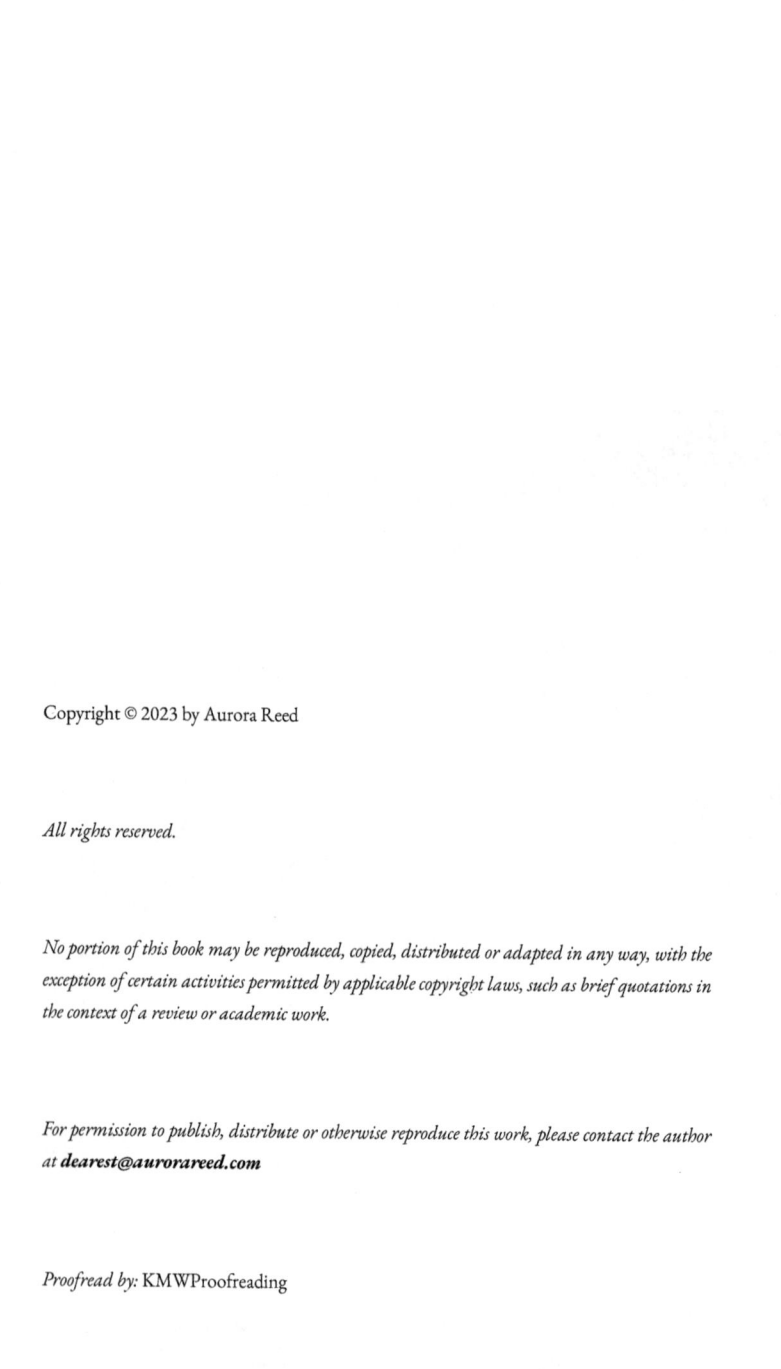

All rights reserved.

No portion of this book may be reproduced, copied, distributed or adapted in any way, with the exception of certain activities permitted by applicable copyright laws, such as brief quotations in the context of a review or academic work.

*For permission to publish, distribute or otherwise reproduce this work, please contact the author at **dearest@aurorareed.com***

Proofread by: KMWProofreading

CONTENTS

Author Note	VIII
Dedication	X
PART 1	1
1. White Rook	2
2. Sacred Duty	11
3. Marble Egg	16
4. Glass Coffin	23
5. Necessary Beauty	30
6. Promethean Myth	38
7. Summer Ball	46
8. Alone Together	54
9. Ice Queen	60
10. Staghorn Fern	65
11. Sweet Dreams	71
12. Elusive Angel	76
13. Left Hand	84
14. Defunct Philosopher	92
15. Perfect Parallels	98

PART 2 — 107

16. Porcelain Doll — 108
17. Blackwood Triptych — 114
18. Spearcrest Wolf — 122
19. Thrown Gauntlet — 130
20. Broken Goddess — 137
21. Fear & Fate — 144
22. Poetic Analogies — 151
23. Adored Adversary — 160
24. Green-Eyed Monster — 171
25. Glass Armour — 179
26. Oleander Promise — 186
27. Sibling Negotiation — 196
28. Anti-Ophelia — 202
29. Open Wound — 209

PART 3 — 219

30. Lucky Mouth — 220
31. Black Doberman — 228
32. First Edition — 237
33. Dauntless Dreams — 245
34. Pirate Lover — 253
35. Prison Cell — 263
36. Sage Lace — 271
37. Complete Combustion — 280

38. Sunshine Scandal	288
39. Bishop Blackwood	294
40. True Saint	301
41. Inexplicable Dread	310
42. Last Assignment	318
43. Gone	324
PART 4	329
44. Brutalist Patriarch	330
45. Ugly Truth	339
46. Primrose Cottage	347
47. Arm's Length	353
48. Debt Incurred	360
49. Friendly Fire	368
50. Beautiful Nemesis	375
51. Effective Method	382
52. Sublime Fools	390
53. Luminous Sound	396
THE END	403
Dear Reader	404
Acknowledgements	405
Annotation & Study Guide	406
About Aurora	408

Author Note

Dear reader,

This book takes place at the fictional private boarding school **Spearcrest Academy** and is set in the **United Kingdom**.

Speacrest Academy is a **High School and Sixth Form**, so students are aged **12** to **18**. If you are a US reader, I've included a little comparison guide of US and UK school years for reference.

UK High School (also known as Lower School) Years

Year 7 = 6th Grade

Year 8 = 7th Grade

Year 9 = 8th Grade

Year 10 = 9th Grade (Freshman Year)

Year 11 = 10th Grade (Sophomore Year)

UK Sixth Form/College (also known as Upper School) Years

Year 12 (Lower Sixth) = 11th Grade (Junior Year)

Year 13 (Upper Sixth) = 12th Grade (Senior Year)

The main characters in Spearcrest Knight are all in <u>UK Year 13 (US Senior Year)</u> and <u>18 years of age</u>.

I hope this guide makes sense and helps you during your time within the hallowed halls of Spearcrest Academy.

For Danni—my real-life dark academia darling.

SAINTS

Chapter 1

White Rook

Theodora

My voice is locked inside my chest, and my father holds the key.

It's always that way when he's around, although he's not around much. I see him maybe once or twice every few years. He's a busy man, and he lives in Russia. He's involved in politics, though I'm sure he's not a politician. I don't know because he never talks about work. He never talks about much at all.

And since I'm being educated in England, where I live with my mother and grandmother in their ancestral home, my father and I rarely see each other.

Sometimes, I wish I saw him more often. Part of me is just a little girl who wishes her dad would spend time with her and hold her when she's sad or scared.

Most of the time, I wish I never saw him at all.

When he comes to visit, my father always brings gifts. Perfect gifts for perfect little girls. Dolls, dresses, jewellery, all packaged beautifully in pastel paper the colour of sugared almonds, bound with thick satin ribbons.

The receiving of the gifts is a ritual: I must take the box and thank him, I must sit at his feet in the parlour and slowly pull on the ribbon to undo the bow. I must lift the lid and delicately set it aside, then push aside the tissue paper, which crinkles like desiccated skin underneath my fingertips.

Finally, I must lift the gift from its pastel coffin and widen my eyes and say, "Thank you, Papa."

That's the hardest part. Because during the entire ritual, my voice is a marble egg in my throat, suffocating me.

It happens every time my father is near, and his dark eyes are fixed on me, and his hard face is set in that permanent scowl of his. All it would take is a smile from him for the egg to melt and my voice to become my own again.

But my father never smiles.

So I swallow and swallow, trying to shift the marble egg—it doesn't. It never does. When I speak, my voice comes out strangled and warbling, like I'm about to cry.

Except that crying isn't allowed. Crying would draw my father's wrath as suddenly as the awakening of an angry god. Crying would shatter the ritual, which would end suddenly.

"I must accept that God did not give me a son," my father would say. "But I refuse to accept that God would give me such a weak child."

There lies the key to my father's dissatisfaction. He only ever had one child with my mother, and he's a pious man, too pious for divorce or affairs—so I am his only child.

Not a son, strong and bold and proud. But a scared, weak little girl who can hardly bring herself to speak without weeping.

If I don't cry, and manage to thank him without the trembling of my voice breaking into a sob or a whimper, then my father looks at me and gives a tyrant's nod.

It's how he signals that the ritual is over, that my performance was good enough, and that I may retreat. I carefully replace the gift in its box, pick it up, stand and leave, walking calmly when I would prefer to run.

When I get back to my bedroom, I open the closet set into the wall and place the new present on top of the old ones where they live, all untouched in the darkness.

My father's anger spins a web of fear around me, a mantle I can never shake off. It makes talking in front of him difficult, it makes my stomach squirm with nausea when he's near, and it fills my sleep with dark nightmares.

But it teaches me things, too. How to appear like the perfect daughter, how to turn myself to ice so that no emotion can seep through.

How to lock my tears up deep inside and never, ever let them out.

I'M ELEVEN YEARS OLD, and the summer is almost over. My father came from Russia to visit my new school with me. He has a list of demands and rules he wishes the headteacher to know before I start my secondary education.

In Russia, my father is surrounded by staff: cleaners and cooks and drivers and bodyguards and secretaries and accountants. They do whatever he says. When he comes to England, my father thinks everybody is staff.

Even people that don't work for him, like waiters in restaurants and police officers and teachers. Even, apparently, headmasters.

Spearcrest Academy—my new school—is like a place from a storybook. I hold my breath when I first see it, eyes wide, like Alice arriving in Wonderland or like a Pevensie entering Narnia.

I try to take it all in—the sight of it, the feel of it. Red bricks and façades feathered with ivy. Pines and firs and spires, all pointing straight into the blue sky—*siniy* blue—the blue of the Russian flag.

The headmaster's office is in the largest building, down a long corridor with the floor tiled like a chessboard. The walls are lined with portraits of students in dark uniforms, their mouths proud straight lines, unsmiling arrogance. Pins glimmer on the lapels of their blazers like dragon scales.

My eyes move from portrait to portrait, and my chest swells. I picture myself in one of these frames, my mouth a straight line, my dark blazer glimmering with badges.

One day, in the far future, the headmaster will gesture to my portrait and tell another eleven-year-old girl, *This is Theodora Dorokhova. During her time at Spearcrest, she was the best student. When she spoke, everybody listened because everything she said was worthy of being heard.*

My father, walking ahead of me, doesn't so much as glance at the portraits. His strides are long and imperious. I look at the back of his head, the dark, gleaming hair, the stiff neck. He wears a black coat over a dark suit. His silhouette is the silhouette of a stranger.

The headmaster, Mr Ambrose, greets my father at the door of his office. Mr Ambrose is the same height as my father, a big, imposing man, but his green-brown eyes are kind behind his gold-framed glasses, and his brown skin is deeply lined around his mouth and eyes as if his face is used to generous laughter.

He shakes my father's hand and turns to me, asking me in a kind and soothing voice to take a seat in the waiting area outside his door. My father follows Mr Ambrose into his office without casting me another look. The door closes.

I take a seat facing away from Mr Ambrose's office. For the first time, I notice there is somebody else sitting in the waiting area.

A boy my age.

As soon as I notice him, he takes up the full space of my attention. I couldn't say why.

I watch him surreptitiously at first, pretending to look at the old black and white photographs of Spearcrest on the wall above his head.

He is sitting very straight—his posture is excellent. He's wearing dark corduroy trousers and a dark jumper, even though the weather is still warm. His face is very serious, like an adult's. He wears his frown in his thick black eyebrows and on his lips, which have the softness of flowers but the severity of stone. His hands are on his lap, fingers laced together.

I straighten in my chair. Mine is blue felt, his is green. Between our seats is a table of glossy brown wood, and there is an enormous plant in the corner, underneath a window. A ray of daylight unspools like a ribbon of pale gold from the window, making the wood shine. The daylight doesn't touch me, but it falls fully on the boy.

In a moment of carelessness, I meet his gaze. He's looking straight at me. Unlike me, he's not looking by accident. He's looking with purpose and concentration, the way one might peer at the page of a book to decipher its words. I blink and hold my breath, disconcerted.

The boy leans forward, extending his hand across the table.

"Hello. My name is Zachary Blackwood. How do you do?"

I take his hand and shake it. My father is in the room next door; he might not be here right now, but he's too close for me to have the key to my voice. It's balled up tight and hard, the marble egg heavy in my chest.

When I speak, my voice trembles like I'm about to cry. "Hello. My name is Theodora Dorokhova. How do you do?"

Speaking to him is difficult, but now that we are engaged in a conversation, I'm free to look at him properly.

His hair is black, his tight curls cut close to his head. His skin is smooth and brown, the warm brown of acorns in autumn, and his eyes are brown too, almost luminous, framed by thick, curly eyelashes. His features still have the softness of boyhood, but there's a grim austerity to him that reminds me of the painted saints in my father's house in Russia or the ones in the gilded frames inside Smolny Cathedral, where my father took me when I visited him in St Petersburg for my ninth birthday.

The saints seemed to have an intense sort of conviction that made them look both full of power and devoid of joy.

This is what Zachary Blackwood looks like.

It's how he speaks, too. Earnest, ardent, cheerless.

When I tell him my name, he nods very seriously. We shake hands like adults and break apart, both straightening in our seats.

"I'll be starting here in the autumn term," Zachary Blackwood announces. "Spearcrest Academy only accepts the best of the best, so it's a great honour."

I nod. "I'll be starting in the autumn term, too."

Zachary narrows his eyes for a moment and tilts his head. He searches my face without trying to hide what he's doing as if he's both assessing me and wishing for me to know I'm being assessed.

"You must be quite clever then, I suppose," he says finally.

I want to tell him I am, but I have a feeling Zachary won't believe me unless I offer up some sort of evidence.

"I achieved the highest scores in the eleven-plus exams in my school," I tell him.

He nods. He sits very straight and very still. I'm impressed by the way he doesn't bounce his leg or pick at his fingers or tap his armrest. It took me years to learn to sit well, to avoid fidgeting. *Stop wriggling like a little worm on a hook*, my mother would say with a tut. Did Zachary have to learn, too, or was he born calm and still and already perfect?

"You must read a lot, I suppose?" he says. It sounds like both a statement and a question at the same time.

"It's my favourite thing to do."

We stare at each other. Zachary Blackwood. The significance of his name is changing with every passing moment.

At first, it was Zachary Blackwood—a name that meant a mysterious boy with a serious face.

Now, it's Zachary Blackwood—a name that means a challenge.

Because Zachary's face is still very serious and calm, but there is a new shadow in his frown. He's measuring me, weighing me up, placing me across him on a scale.

Just like the black and white tiles on the floor, Zachary has a chessboard in his mind. He is figuring out which piece I am. A pawn that won't make it through the game? A clever knight who slips and slides across the board? Or a useless king who must be toppled?

I've already worked *him* out.

He is the white rook. White, because he made the first move. I never play the white side anyway—starting first puts you at an advantage, but it forces you to be assertive, make more decisions, take more risks. The black side is the dark horse—you're always on the back foot, but your moves are also more informed.

Rook, because he moves directly and powerfully. A major piece—but not quite a queen. He's too straightforward.

"Well, I've just finished *Animal Farm*," Zachary declares. "Maybe you've heard of it?"

"I liked it well enough," I answer. "It was the shortest book I read last year."

Zachary's eyebrows quirk slightly upwards. He doesn't look surprised—he looks offended.

"Short? Just because it's short doesn't mean it's not an important book."

"I know very well how important this book is."

"Are you sure? Maybe you've not heard about the Russian Revolution."

My hands curl into fists. I feel my voice go icy and hard, the way it does when I'm debating in class against a student who is resorting to dirty tricks to scrape a victory. "I didn't read the book thinking it was just about animals if that's what you're suggesting."

Zachary gives a stiff shrug. "I just thought your comment about the book being too short maybe suggested that you didn't quite understand the writer's message."

"I never said it was too short," I reply in my frostiest tone. "I just said it was the shortest book I read last year."

"Well, I suppose when you think about it, most books are longer than *Animal Farm*," Zachary concedes with no grace whatsoever. "Even a book like *Peter Pan* is longer."

"What do you mean by 'even a book like *Peter Pan*'?" I ask with narrowed eyes. "What's a book like *Peter Pan*?"

Zachary gestures with one hand. "Oh, you know. Children's books."

"What's wrong with children's books?"

He lets out a short laugh. "For one, that they are for children."

"Children shouldn't read?"

"Everybody should read."

I raise my eyebrows and ask in a dry tone, "But five-year-olds should read books for adults?"

Zachary is quiet for a moment, watching me with the intense, solemn expression of the saints in Smolny Cathedral.

"I apologise if I offended you," he says with almost over-the-top politeness. "I didn't mean to."

"You've not offended me," I snap.

We stare at each other. There's a little smile at the corner of his mouth. I immediately understand why.

Zachary Blackwood's apology, like his questions, is just another way of testing me. He's still measuring himself against me, and one thing is clear.

His apology was an attack; my angry response was the blow he landed.

Now, he thinks he knows there's a chink in my armour—he thinks he knows where he can strike to hit.

But I learn fast. Any chink in my armour Zachary finds once, he won't find a second time.

That's my promise to myself and the first rule I set for the long chess game we are going to play over the next few years.

Chapter 2

SACRED DUTY

Zachary

THEODORA DOROKHOVA IS GOING to be the most important person I meet in Spearcrest.

I know it the moment I see her take a seat on the blue felt chair across from me, the moment her eyes sweep over me to watch the painting on the wall above my head. Her gaze brushes over me like starlight, like it's almost too remote for me to feel it.

I watch her intently, sensing her importance.

She's small and very pale, her skin almost see-through, like white fabric that's been drenched in water. She's wearing a blue cardigan with long sleeves, but I already know that the insides of her arms will be a map of blue veins. I don't need to worry about seeing it—I'll see it someday.

Her hair is light, too, the palest gold, like sunlight in the winter. It's long and tied back from her face in neat plaits. Everything about her is delicate and fragile, like a porcelain doll. Her eyes are big and vividly blue. She's not beautiful yet, she's barely even pretty, but she's going to be.

She's going to be one of the most beautiful girls in the world.

I know all this because she's special.

I can tell from her eyes when our gazes finally meet, and from the way her voice quivers when she tells me her name. Theodora Dorokhova. Even her name is special. I repeat it in my mind after she says it. When I'm alone later, I'm going to say it out loud, the way I do when I'm reading a book and I find a particularly satisfying sentence. Too satisfying to keep in my head, so I have to speak it, so I can taste the words and feel their weight and texture on my tongue.

We speak, and the more I speak to her, the firmer her voice becomes.

The quiver of her first sentence fades away. She speaks with perfect diction, with a smooth cadence. Her voice is far more expressive than her face. Does she know this?

Our conversation is a test.

There's a reason I'm seeing this girl right now, a reason she wasn't at the summer school days when I met the other students who are going to be in my year. There's a reason we meet like this, today, when I've come in on a random day because my father is meeting with the other governors.

There's a reason I'm the first person in Spearcrest to meet Theodora Dorokhova.

When our conversation transforms from a discussion into an argument, I decide it's time to relent. I apologise for having offended her, even though I know she's not offended.

She replies that I've not offended her. Her voice is hard and cold. It has the satisfying texture of icicles, sharp but smooth.

I've angered her, I think, but it's hard to tell. I hope I have. I have the feeling handling Theodora Dorokhova isn't going to be like handling other people our age. Handling her is going to be like handling an adult—like playing chess against a greater opponent, not a lesser one.

She'll be good at concealing her true feelings, I'm guessing. She'll wish to fight me without stepping on the battlefield, to gain her victories without appearing to be in the skirmish at all. She'll want to compete with me without ever acknowledging me as her rival.

She's going to be difficult and rigid and cold, like a thing of steel.

And that's why she's going to be the most important person here. Because I'll never be able to become the best I possibly can without being properly tested and challenged. Heroes don't become legends without fighting some great opposing force.

Theodora is going to become that great opposing force.

"What's your favourite book, then?" I ask her.

I'm not smiling at her—I don't need her to know her importance yet. Like an enemy kingdom, I'm better off making sure Theodora never sees attacks coming. I need to keep her as unprepared as possible, on the back foot. I need to make her slip up, scramble, rally. Her failures will become my victories.

"My favourite book is *Peter Pan*," she answers. Her voice is pleasantly sharp. I want to press it against my skin and see if it'll draw blood. "What's yours?"

I don't have a favourite book. Most of the time, when I read, I'm forcing myself. Forcing myself to get through dense prose, pausing every five minutes to look up words and references. I never read books that are easy to understand—I wouldn't respect myself if I read the novels and comics my peers are reading. Magic and teenage spies and superheroes.

I read because I am the son of Lord and Lady Blackwood, and that means I must be better than everybody else. My superiority demands superior intellect. So I read, but never for pleasure.

"My favourite book is *The Count of Monte Cristo*."

It's only a half-lie. I liked *The Count of Monte Cristo*, and the story is one I think about often. What's not to love about the doggedness of vengeance? But it's also an enormous book, and now Theodora Dorokhova won't be able to look down on me for reading short books.

She smiles—a small, restrained smile, but the first I've seen on her face.

It's an odd thing, her smile. It holds light but no warmth, like the cold gleam of moonlight.

"Oh," she says, "I've actually—"

Then the door to Mr Ambrose's office opens, and Theodora's voice dies like the extinguished flame of a candle.

The smile dies with it.

A man precedes Mr Ambrose out. The man Theodora arrived with. I can only assume he's her father, even though he looks nothing like her. Dark hair, hard eyes, and the sort of brutal, unpleasant strength of a big ugly factory.

Theodora looks up at him, her mouth still open. Her blue eyes are full of an expression I can't read or comprehend. I would have guessed fear if it didn't seem so unlikely to me that someone could be so afraid of their own father.

Mr Ambrose says goodbye to the man, then smiles at Theodora. "Goodbye for now, Theodora. See you on the first of September."

She returns his smile, except it's not really a smile. There's no light in it, not even the cold gleam of moonlight. It's just a dull stretch of her lips.

"Come," the man commands without looking at her.

He walks away. Theodora stands. Her fingers are curled around the ends of her sleeves, gripping the wool tightly. She hurries after the man without a word.

"Nice to meet you, Theodora," I say to her as she walks past me.

She turns and looks at me in surprise. Her eyes widen but she says nothing. Then her gaze slides off me, and she disappears around the corner.

"Is she very clever, Mr Ambrose?"

Mr Ambrose turns to me with a strange smile. "Very clever, Zachary. Just as clever as you are."

I nod, his words confirming the solemnity I feel, the sense that Theodora is special.

"Is that man her father?" I ask.

Mr Ambrose nods slowly, casting one last glance down the corridor. "Yes, he is." He gives me a sudden smile. "When she arrives in September, I'd like you to make her feel welcome, Zachary. Help her settle in, make sure she's okay—look after her. Can you do that?"

"Of course, sir."

"You promise?"

"I swear it, sir."

I say it like a vow—it feels like a vow.

The weight of it settles on me like the blade on the shoulder of a knight. Mr Ambrose has just given me a sacred duty—a task too important to give anybody else. It's an obligation and an honour, one I'll never abandon or fail.

Chapter 3

Marble Egg

Theodora

My father doesn't speak until we're in the car.

We sit at the back, side by side, and my entire body is tense with anxiety. The partition that separates us from the driver is closed, leaving us isolated in the dull silence of the car. The engine is barely a hum, a low murmur around us, emphasising the silence. Outside the blacked-out windows, the landscape is drained of colours, the blue of the sky dulled to a dim grey.

I sit and stare out of the window, forcing myself not to fidget. My father would notice immediately—he'd take it as a sign of weakness, a sign of inferiority.

"Do you know why I'm sending you to Spearcrest Academy?" he asks.

His voice is deep and harsh. Like me, my father was educated in England, but he still has a thick northern Russian accent from living and working in St Petersburg and Moscow.

I don't answer. My father doesn't ask questions he wants answers to. In English class, I learned that the term for this is a rhetorical question.

My father's questions, like his presence, only ever require silent obedience from me.

"I'm sending you there because I wish you to receive the best education possible. I wish you to be clever, well-spoken, sophisticated. You are my daughter—you bear my name. What the world sees when they look at you is an extension of me. Like my cars or my houses. I buy my cars from the best manufacturers, and I have my houses designed by the best architects. It is the same as sending you to the best school."

I already know all of this, I want to tell him. *I already know I must be the best because you only possess the best.*

I couldn't say so if I wished. I'm sitting stiff and straight, little more than an object at his side.

"Now let me tell you some reasons I do not have for sending you to this school."

There is a darkness in his voice like the heavy black clouds before thunder splits the sky. He pauses because he is about to arrive at the point he wants to make, and it's important I pay attention to it.

"I am not sending you to this school so that you may grow up to be a whore."

He spits the word as if it's venom in his mouth.

"I am not sending you to this school so that you may sit and preen for the attention of boys and men. You are Theodora Dorokhova—your reputation is mine. I would not have it said that I am a whore anymore than I would have it said that you are one. Do you know what a whore is?"

My voice is so hard and heavy in my throat I can't even swallow. I curl my fingers around the sleeves of my cardigan, holding on tight, hoping I'm not about to suffocate. There's a burning in my eyes like I'm going to cry, but I know I can't allow it to happen.

I've already drawn my father's anger—my tears would only tip him into fury.

I shake my head no.

"A whore is a woman who gives herself to men. There are many ways to be a whore, Theodora, but only one way to be pure. You must never let a man touch you, not in any way, not until you are married. Do you understand?"

This time, I nod. My nod says the things I can't.

Yes, Papa, I understand.

I must be exactly what you say I must.

It is the only way I might remain safe from your anger.

My father turns his head to look at me. I don't want to look at him; meeting his gaze is a painful act, like touching fire. But if I don't, his anger will grow.

So I look up at him; I pray to all the saints in all the cathedrals to help me keep my tears locked away safe and tight inside my chest.

I endure my father's gaze for as long as he needs me to.

"That boy you were speaking to," he says. "He might be the son of a nobleman or a billionaire—it does not matter. Like you, he will marry when he comes of age. He will do his duty for his family, for his name. But before this, he might wish to taste freedom, to learn what he likes. Him—and all the boys here. They are all like you, but you are not like them. Men have more freedom in this world—it is not fair, and if you had been lucky enough to be born a boy, you would not have to endure this injustice. If you were born a boy, I would not have needed to speak of this with you. Because boys—men—cannot be ruined in the way women can. Do you understand?"

I nod. I have a vague idea of what my father is saying. He's spoken of it before—as has my mother.

They are speaking of pregnancy. At eleven years old, I can barely imagine such a concept. At eleven years old, it's not a fear that would have ever occurred to me.

But it's a fear that's very real in my parents' minds.

"You will be in this school until you are a woman grown," my father announces with finality. "In that time, Theodora, you will remain the good girl you have always been. You will not throw your attention on everybody that seeks it. You will not date, as others in your classes might do. You will not kiss or touch boys or give yourself to them in any way. You must promise me, Theodora. Promise me you will do what is right, even if it's difficult. It is the only thing I ask of you."

I try to swallow, but the marble egg in my throat is so big that I can only swallow with a big, loud gulp. The noise is almost too loud. My father's eyes narrow.

"Promise me. Now."

I promise, I try to say. The words remain stuck. I look at him in panic.

I know he wants me to speak, but I can't. I wish I could. I would make him his promise, and I would tell him the other things stuck in my throat.

I'm not a whore. I'm just a girl. I was doing nothing wrong. I only spoke of books with Zachary Blackwood. I did nothing wrong. He spoke to me first. I'm not a whore, and I never will be.

"*Say. It,*" he bites out.

His arm shoots out, gripping my arm so tightly that a noise of pain squeezes its way out of my throat. I force my voice out after it. "I promise, Papa."

My voice is barely above a whisper. But it's enough for my father. He lets me go, shoving me away from him like a disgusting thing.

"Good. Break this promise, Theodora, and I will punish you for it for the rest of your life."

On my first day at Spearcrest, I stand with the other Year 7 students outside the assembly hall, waiting for the induction assembly. I don't look at the other students; I stand still and straight, waiting for the teachers to tell us to go inside.

My braids are so tight that my head hurts. My uniform is like stiff armour around my body, my brand-new shoes pinching my feet.

The teachers open the doors, and we file into the assembly hall. The floorboards shine underneath our feet, and the navy-blue seats face an enormous stage. Over it stands a carved arch covered with portraits that looks just like the iconostases in Russian cathedrals.

Mr Ambrose opens the assembly. He welcomes us to Spearcrest with a speech about academic excellence, about the importance of education and scholarly pursuits. He talks about knowledge being not only the food of the brain but the food of the soul.

When he speaks, I feel as though he's talking only to me.

After the assembly, we are given our campus maps and timetables. Outside, teachers help students, pointing them in the direction of different buildings and paths.

The sun is bright in the deep blue sky—it still feels like summer even though it's the start of autumn.

Students form little groups. I hear them talk.

"Oh, are you also in Miss Bailey's form? Let's go together."

"We're going to the main building, are you going the same way?"

"My form room is in the art building too, I'll go with you."

I look down at the papers in my hand. I'm in Professor Mecardo's form in the main building. I open my campus map, looking at the tiny illustrated buildings and paths. They all look so small on the map, but in reality, Spearcrest is enormous, almost a small city of its own.

"Hello, Theodora."

I look up, although I already recognise the voice that spoke to me. Not the voice, but the tone of the voice.

Well-spoken, intense, a little bleak.

Zachary's school uniform is impeccable, his face as serious as it was the last time I saw him. Instead of holding his timetable and map in his hands like the other students, he carries them in a smart brown folder.

"Would you like me to help you find your way around?" he asks.

I recoil from him as if I've been hit, taking two quick steps back. My stomach churns. My father left for Russia more than a week ago. There's no way he could be in Spearcrest—he's not even in England.

And yet I feel as if he's standing right behind me, watching me with his stormy face. Waiting to see what I'll do.

Waiting to see if I'm a whore.

Every part of me turns to ice. So does my voice when I answer Zachary.

"I don't need your help, thank you."

"Are you sure?" He tilts his head. "You look lost, and I was here in the summer, so I can—"

"I'm fine." My voice is firm and hard. Why couldn't it be that way when I was in the car with my father? "I know where I'm going."

"Alright." He gives a small, courteous smile. "Well, I hope you are settling in okay. Would you like me to walk you to your form?"

There's a panic inside me I can't describe. Terror and anger and anxiety and regret and a horrible, sickening fear.

"I would like you to leave me alone." I look straight into his eyes. "Thank you."

For a moment, we just watch each other. I'd forgotten how nice the colour of his eyes is: a deep, rich brown, several shades darker than the brown of his skin. His eyes are the warmest part of him, but there isn't enough warmth in them to melt the ice in my words.

To melt the ice I've filled myself with.

He straightens himself like a soldier regaining his composure.

"I'm sorry for bothering you." His tone is stiff and formal.

He turns around and walks away, and I hasten in the opposite direction. I still have no idea where I'm going, and I end up getting to form late.

I don't speak to Zachary for the rest of Year 7.

It's not an easy year. I struggle to make friends, and the work is harder now we're in secondary school. I spend a lot of time studying, trying to keep up, and making sure I do well enough to stay in the top classes for every subject.

Sometimes, I see Zachary in the corridors, in classes or during assembly. He always looks the same: his uniform impeccable, his curly hair short and tidy, his expression intense and earnest. When we cross paths, he looks at me but never speaks to me.

I always look away first.

At the end of Year 7, the summer exam results are displayed in the main corridor of the Old Manor, in great glass cases. I don't bother searching the lists; I just look at the top, where I know my name will be.

For every subject, the top line reads the same.

#1: Zachary Blackwood and Theodora Dorokhova.

CHAPTER 4

GLASS COFFIN

Zachary

THEODORA DOROKHOVA DOESN'T LET me anywhere near her.

She's like Snow White in the glass coffin; I can see her quite clearly but never reach her. Like Snow White with the bite of poisoned apple in her throat, Theodora seems to be suspended in some dormant state, waiting to wake up.

Maybe waiting for somebody else to wake her up.

I spend all of Year 7 watching her from afar. We both end up in the top sets for every subject, which means that, more often than not, we end up sharing classes. I see her in the corridors, in the lower school dining hall. Sometimes I even see the pale shape of her move like a phantom down a path on the grounds or crossing the green lawns.

Sometimes, our eyes meet. She says nothing. There's no hatred and dislike in her eyes—but that doesn't make it easier to guess why she's refusing to have me near her. It only makes it harder to figure her out, like a scientist trying to come up with a theory with too little evidence.

When our first term at Spearcrest is almost over, Mr Ambrose keeps me behind after the last assembly of term.

"You seem to be settling rather well into Spearcrest Academy, Zachary."

I nod. "I think so, Mr Ambrose. The teachers here have high expectations. I'm working my hardest to meet them."

Mr Ambrose smiles and lays a hand on my shoulder. "I know you are. You've made an excellent first impression on all your teachers, Zachary. I hear nothing but the best."

My chest swells with pride. I'm not surprised to hear this—I've worked very hard for this.

"And how about Theodora?" Mr Ambrose asks. "Have you kept an eye on her as we discussed? Is she settling in alright?"

I pause before I answer. This is something my father taught me: when answering a question, only open your mouth once you are certain of your answer. Opening your mouth before you know your answer is the surest way of rushing yourself into saying something foolish.

My father was right. Every day of my life at Spearcrest, I witness my peers open their mouths before they know their answers, only to rush themselves into saying something stupid.

So. The answer to Mr Ambrose's question.

Have I kept an eye on Theodora? Of course—it was my sacred duty, wasn't it? And how could I not keep an eye on her when my gaze is drawn to her like a moth to a flame?

The sense I had during that first meeting—that she was special—never went away. It only strengthened with time. Theodora is special, and Mr Ambrose asked me to keep an eye on her, and that also counts for something.

Whatever it is that sets the events of our universe in motion—call it God, or fate, or the cosmos—chose me for this task for a reason.

If Theodora wishes me not to approach her, that doesn't mean I have to give up my mission. I can give her what she wants and still not fail in my duty. I never have to speak a word to Theodora if that's what she wishes, but if anything were to happen to her in Spearcrest, I'd know. I'd be there if she needed me.

So is Theodora settling in alright? That's what Mr Ambrose wants to know. He seems concerned about her. I don't blame him.

"Theodora works extremely hard, Mr Ambrose," I say finally. "She's in all the top sets now."

Mr Ambrose smiles and gives a slow nod, as though deep in thought. "I had a feeling that would be the case." His gaze focuses on me once more, and he raises an eyebrow. "Is she giving you a run for your money?"

It's hard to tell. Theodora is quiet and reserved. In class, she keeps her answers to herself and never raises her hand. When the teachers pick her to answer a question or solve a problem or give her opinion on a topic, she gives short, thoughtful answers without elaborating.

"I'm not sure yet, Mr Ambrose. I guess we'll find out at the end of the year."

"Well, I wish you both luck. I think you two could really help drive each other."

I give Mr Ambrose a courteous smile. In theory, he's correct. Theodora and I could help drive each other—how many great achievements in history have been spurred by rivalries?

But Theodora seems to be an ivory tower of her own at the moment. An ivory tower within the ivory tower of Spearcrest Academy—an impressive achievement, actually.

Unfortunately for me, it's difficult to compete with someone who refuses to even acknowledge your existence.

I'm patient, though. Like two celestial bodies bound by the same gravity, Theodora and I can never quite escape one another.

Of that, I'm certain.

At the end of Year 7, I inspect the boards displaying the exam results for each class. I'm not surprised to find my name at the top of each board—but I'm more surprised than I should be to find Theodora's next to it.

Zachary Blackwood and Theodora Dorokhova.

I would have preferred my name to stand alone at the top—a confirmation of my intellectual superiority over my peers—but seeing my name next to Theodora's feels right, somehow.

Our names look good together.

Important. Significant. Powerful.

When I return home that summer, my parents ask me about the summer exams. They ask me at dinnertime on the first day of the holidays; they don't even bother to act like this isn't the most important question on their minds.

I tell them the truth—that I came first alongside another student. My mother raises her eyebrows.

"Oh?" Her voice is all affected surprise. "How odd. Your sister was first in all her classes—perhaps her school works out academic rankings differently?"

I look across the table at Zahara. She's two years younger than me, but that never stopped our parents from putting just as much pressure on her as they do on me.

If anything, they've engineered a clever system. In that system, I can never win, constantly blackmailed with the potential humiliation of my younger sister somehow outdoing me. And Zahara can never win either, always being made to compete with a brother two years her senior.

It's a system designed to keep us forever competing but never victorious. But it's not a system that's clever enough to work on us.

Because in the cold hostility of our home life, Zahara and I have an alliance forged in marble and gold.

I have her back, and she has mine. This is something I know will never change—not now that I'm away at Spearcrest, not when she goes away to a private girls' school in France, not when we'll both be at university and not when, one day, we are both living our own lives wherever we are across the globe.

"Congratulations, Zaro," I say. "That's an amazing achievement—makes me proud to be your big brother."

Zahara gives a little smile and looks down at her plate, which is what she always does when she's trying not to laugh.

My mother frowns at me. "That's not what I meant, Zachary."

"I know, Mother." I give her my most earnest look. "Don't worry. I promise I'll work harder next year. I'll see some tutors over the summer as well."

She nods, somewhat pacified, and glances at my father, a glance like the passing of a baton in a relay race.

"Don't forget, son"—his voice is deep and gravelly like I hope mine will be one day—"being great is good, but being the best is better."

"I won't forget," I say.

How could I? He's been telling me this since I was old enough to walk.

The phrase is as good as engraved into my consciousness.

IN YEAR 8, I do exactly what I told my parents I would do.

I study harder and longer. Every free moment I have is spent in the library or my room, poring over books. I read voraciously, on everything, even the things I'm not quite capable of wrapping my head around yet. My afternoons are spent on after-school clubs designed to develop my brain faster and broaden my range of skills, and my weekends are spent on extra homework.

During the holidays, I have my tutors on a rotation designed to imitate my school timetable, and I ask them all to set me homework.

During term time, I excel in all my classes.

Unfortunately, so does Theodora.

It's difficult to tell how she does it. She could be doing the exact same thing as me: spending every minute of her time studying, working and reading. Or she could be one of those prodigies born with extraordinary minds. But somehow, in every assignment, every project and every examination across all our subjects, Theodora is always fighting me for top of the class.

Sometimes, she wins out: she gets a higher result than me on a poetry unit in English class, and she beats me in the biology and religious studies exams. I beat her several times in maths, physics and geography. We both tie pretty consistently on history and languages.

All of this happens, and as it happens, so does something else.

Theodora changes.

At first, I can't quite tell how. Then, one day, all of a sudden, I realise it's her appearance.

One day, completely randomly, we are both lining up outside our English classroom, waiting for the teacher. I stand by the door, she stands by the window, her eyes glazed over, fixed on a point that seems to be both far beyond the window and yet not quite penetrating the glass.

And that's when I notice it.

Her hair is no longer in those two long braids she wore that day I first saw her outside Mr Ambrose's office—the same way she wore her hair all through Year 7. Instead, the top of it is bound by a white ribbon tied into a bow, and the rest falls down her back like a river of pale gold. Her eyes have some pink eyeshadow on the lids, and her lips are glossy and the colour of raspberries.

There are tiny silver stars in her ears, and her bag is designer. I didn't notice any of those things until today, and I don't know how. Theodora, at some point during the year, started looking different—and I didn't notice because the whole time, I was too busy trying to stop her from beating me in every subject.

I thought I'd been paying attention to her, but I was wrong.

I'd only been paying attention to what I needed to do to keep up with her.

I'd only been paying attention to *myself*.

Chapter 5

Necessary Beauty

Theodora

THE FIRST SUMMER BACK from Spearcrest, my mother and grandmother look at me, exchange a glance, and then my mother says, "Does your school not serve healthy food?"

I know immediately what she means and lower my head in shame.

"They do, Mummy."

"Perhaps you are eating a little more than you should," my mother observes in a light tone.

If my father is the owner of the object that is me—the doll that is Theodora Dorokhova—then my mother is the maker. She is the one who ensures that every time my father sees me, he is satisfied with what she is presenting. She's the one who ensures that I look small and endearing, that my hair is long and combed to a high shine, that my dresses are clean and pleasing to the eye.

Perhaps it's because my father blames her for giving him a girl, and now my mother must atone for this betrayal.

Or perhaps it's because, when she was growing up, her own mother would stop her from cutting her hair, and carefully measure out her portions, and admonish her when her posture was not straight.

"I'll be more careful," I tell her. "I promise."

"We'll have to come up with a little diet plan for you." My mother's tone is cheerful, and she gives my cheek a little squeeze. "Nothing too strict, of course. I don't want you to have an unhealthy relationship with food."

It is the magical sentence she always speaks, like a spell to ward off eating disorders. My mother is deathly afraid of me looking anything less than perfect, but she's also deathly afraid of being accused by some British tabloid of giving me an eating disorder.

So I nod and agree and do what she says. That summer, she takes me shopping, flitting from one designer store to the next so that I should have the perfect bags, the perfect shoes, the perfect clothes. She takes me to her aesthetician to have my eyelashes tinted because they are too light, to have the fine fuzz of pale hair removed from my upper lip, my arms, my legs.

In my mirror, my reflection changes day by day, becoming more smooth and shiny and pretty.

And more doll-like than ever.

In Year 8, I discover poetry.

I don't mean I study it for the first time. I learned about poems in primary school; we even wrote haikus in Year 5. We studied poems in Spearcrest in Year 7 too, a half-term spent looking at war poems from different times and cultures.

But I discover poetry when I'm in Year 8.

Poetry is like an object I'd seen before but never truly looked at. And one day, I just saw its true form, the vast and almost breathtaking beauty of it. I discovered poetry, and it filled my heart with an unspeakable feeling.

Waiting for my English lessons became torturous. I was too impatient. I wanted to read it all the time, to fill my brain with it. I would go into the Spearcrest library, my favourite place on campus. The poetry section there took up almost an entire floor of its own—which seemed fitting.

I discover John Keats near the end of Year 8, and one day, I open the first page of his *Endymion*. It's a poem long enough to be a book, and I know it's going to be special.

The first lines stop me in my tracks.

"*A thing of beauty is a joy for ever:*
Its loveliness increases; it will never
Pass into nothingness—"

I read those lines over and over again, my heart in my mouth.

Beautiful things do not pass into nothingness. This is a truth that hits me hard because it's a truth my mother has been trying to inculcate in me for a long time.

A truth the other girls in my year already understand. They know that beauty gives them importance, that it will stop them from being nothing. That's why they watch tutorials on their tablets and work for hours on end learning how to do their hair, their make-up, learning how to make their skin nice and clean and shiny.

I always believed my beauty should come from within me—from my character and my mind and my soul. But I was wrong. My fellow students knew it. My mother knew it. Even Keats, sensitive and erudite as he was, knew it.

That year, I start paying attention to my reflection in the mirror. Not letting my gaze slide off the doll-like thing standing there, but actually paying attention to it, scrutinising it. Every day, I ask myself: is this thing beautiful, or will it pass into nothingness?

So I stop wearing my hair in braids and start curling the ends, tying it into the satin ribbons my mother bought. I clean my skin and begin to develop a skincare routine, and I wear make-up to enhance my features, which are too plain to be beautiful. I watch my body closely and measure my food portions carefully, declining sweets and desserts.

The next summer, when I arrive home, my mother stops at the foot of the stairs to watch me as I descend towards her.

"Oh, Theodora! You look so beautiful!"

Her eyes, the same blue as mine, are wide, her rose-pink mouth rounded. She's being completely sincere. I know this because it would never occur to her to lie to me just to be nice. And because she's never before called me beautiful.

That moment cements two things in my mind.

One, that my work is bearing fruit. Depriving myself of desserts and sweets, carefully watching the mirror every night for any sign of imperfection that must be eradicated, spending hours trying on my new make-up to find the perfect balance of looking beautiful without appearing like I've tried to make myself beautiful. Wearing the designer clothes and accessories, shaping my hair into waves with the curling iron.

All that time and effort was not wasted.

Two—and most important—that Keats was right.

I was becoming beautiful, and as a result, I was finally becoming worth something in the eyes of my mother.

Not quite worthy of love, yet. But, for the first time, worth something.

And so in Year 9, everything becomes more difficult.

Being clever and being beautiful aren't things that just happen. They both require an enormous amount of work.

Eating enough to have energy but not enough to gain weight.

Getting up early enough to wash, do my make-up, do my hair, but also staying up late to keep up with after-school clubs, homework and reading.

Being sociable enough to form friendships and make myself popular, but always being focused enough to impress all my teachers.

My hard work pays off, though. In Year 9, for the first time, I have friends. Not real friends, of course. Real friendships—the types of friendships I read about in books and poems—real friendships are deep, genuine connections. True friendships come with loyalty, companionship, connection.

But those are not Spearcrest friendships.

My Spearcrest friendships are with the prettiest, most popular girls: Seraphina Rosenthal, Camille Alawi, Kayana Kilburn and Giselle Frossard. They are friendships of convenience, much like the friendships I watched my mother curate all my life. We become the girls everyone talks about, girls every other girl in the year wants to sit with.

I'm very aware of the implications of popularity. Just like beauty and intelligence, it's a double-edged sword. You gain a lot from it, but it's something that must be maintained.

Now, I have to work hard to be beautiful, work hard to be clever and work hard to be popular.

So I sleep less and work more. There's always more to be done. New ways of being popular, new books to read, more homework to do, more socialising.

There's always more to do, and the more I do, the less I seem to become. The more I become this perfect imaginary doll I'm expected to be, the less Theodora there is.

I don't have hobbies—I have extra-curricular activities and work and tasks.

I don't have dreams—I just try to stay on top of everything.

I barely have time for the things I love, only the things I must do.

I don't have anyone I talk to about anything real, even though I'm almost never alone.

I'm clever enough to understand this but not clever enough to know how to fix it.

So I just let it happen and watch with a mixture of surprise and fear as my sense of self flutters away like leaves falling from a tree in the autumn.

It doesn't upset me. This is something else I find out about myself: I don't get upset much anymore.

Sometimes, I wonder if I'm broken, if there's something wrong with me. Everyone around me is bursting with emotions: anger, frustration, joy, sadness, triumph, love, hatred.

I feel none of those things. Mostly, I feel tired and numb. Sometimes, if I'm reading poetry good enough to move me, I sense the emotions of it, but not directly, not fully. I sense them like ghosts. The emotions are real, but I can only feel their shadows.

Maybe that's because I've become a shadow too.

Then one day Mr Kiehn, my English teacher, changes his seating plan.

After a brisk announcement, he makes us all stand at the front of his classroom, and he points at each desk and calls out students' names.

When he's almost done, he points at the front desk by the window. "Theodora and Zachary."

My heart sinks. The emotion I feel is real, then—not a shadow. It takes me by surprise. I look across the room. Zachary meets my gaze but doesn't say anything.

I look away first and slink to the desk with my head down, sitting on the side closest to the window.

Zachary Blackwood's presence in Spearcrest is like the sun. It's bright and hard to ignore and can't be directly looked at. Zachary is everywhere on campus: he's in most of my classes and in my after-school clubs (we're both captains of our debate club teams).

Worst of all, his name is always printed next to mine whenever exam results are put up on the corridor walls of the Old Manor.

Ignoring him is hard work because Zachary is well-spoken and sharp and intelligent. He always gets involved in school discussions. In maths class, he always volunteers to go to the front and solve the equations on the teacher's board. He's always first to get involved in experiments in science class, and he's always first to arrive at chess club, and I know his debate team like him more than my team like me.

Every time we start a debate and have to shake hands as team captains, I barely sleep the night before because I'm so nervous.

Zachary's handshake is like him: solemn and just a little bit too intense.

Now, we sit next to each other. I've never sat next to him in class before. He smells good—he smells like an adult, like soap and a rich, sophisticated cologne. Unlike all the other boys in school, he doesn't carry his things in a backpack but in a satchel of leather that makes him look like a Victorian university student. He opens his notebook:

his handwriting is a clean, spidery cursive, and all his lines are drawn with a ruler.

His presence radiates heat. Our shoulders and arms don't quite touch, but the warmth of his body pushes against mine. I'm cold all the time, and I have the sudden urge to place my arm against his to get more of that tempting warmth.

What would it feel like to place my body right against his and let him wrap his arms around me?

The question startles me like sudden thunder. Guilt, shock and shame fill me as if I've just thought of something deep and dark and completely forbidden.

Chapter 6

Promethean Myth

Zachary

For almost three years, Theodora and I have been building a long line of teetering dominoes. Dominoes of silent tension made out of every moment when our paths crossed, but we said nothing.

Mr Kiehn changing the seating plan is the tiny puff of air that tips the first domino.

After that, they all topple.

The first time Theodora speaks to me is when she drops a highlighter on the floor in English class. We both look down: it lies in the narrow space between our two chairs. Theodora looks up. Our gazes meet.

Mascara darkens her eyelashes, a rose tint lends her cheeks a slight artificial blush, and her lips have a fine layer of raspberry-pink lip gloss. She's found ways of disguising her icy pallor, but I know it's still there. The cold inside her is as palpable as ever, it exudes from her like the wreaths of vapour that swirl from frozen things.

"Excuse me," she says. "Could I just—?"

She looks pointedly at the highlighter on the floor.

"Of course," I say, moving my chair away to widen the space between us. "Please, let me."

Before she can say anything, I swoop down and grab the highlighter. I hand it to her; she takes it with a dignified gesture. She clears her throat in a tiny noise.

"Thank you."

"You're welcome."

You're welcome, and you'll always be, I want to say. *I'll pick up every highlighter and pen you drop. I'll hold every door open and carry all your books. Just ask me, Theodora, and I'll do it.*

Mr Ambrose asked me to look after you—let me.

Of course, I say none of those things. We don't speak for the rest of the lesson. When the bell rings and Mr Kiehn dismisses us, she packs her things as she always does, with quick, clinical precision. She stands, hesitates, gives me a nod and leaves.

"Bye, Theodora," I answer.

During our final term in Year 9, everything ramps up. Once we've all decided on our GCSE options and we all know the grades we need to make it into our desired subjects, everyone feels the pressure coming down. Our teachers, intent on giving us a "taste" of what GCSEs will be like, suddenly crank up the difficulty in every subject.

Thanks to all the hard work I've been putting in since Year 8, I'm as prepared as I could wish to be. Both Theodora and I seem to be keeping afloat, but the teachers just take that as a personal challenge.

In English, Mr Kiehn decides to end the year strong with a unit on the study of the Modern Prometheus. I go into the topic feeling confident since I have good knowledge of Greek mythology.

Except Mr Kiehn isn't concerned with mythology. He's concerned with the Prometheus myth and what he calls "the Prometheus character". He wants us to question why the Prometheus myth resonates so much with mankind, specifically focusing on the Romantics. He pulls out Shelley's and Byron's poems and tells us our investigation of the topic will culminate in the reading and study of Mary Shelley's *Frankenstein*.

The escalation feels drastic, but at my side, Theodora is calm in her glass coffin. She's like a statue of ice when she sits, her back straight, reading Byron's "Prometheus". I steal sidelong glances at her. Prometheus's stolen fire could not have melted the ice Theodora is made of.

I tear my attention away from her and read through the poem, making notes on words I'm going to have to look up. I reach the final line of the poem and frown.

"*And making Death a Victory.*"

I stare at the line, then whisper it to myself. The words "Death" and "Victory" both make sense—separately. My eyes climb back up the lines like a ladder, trying to find the beginning of the sentence.

"*To which his Spirit may oppose
Itself—and equal to all woes,
And a firm will, and a deep sense,
Which even in torture can descry
Its own concenter'd recompense,
Triumphant where it dares defy,
And making Death a Victory.*"

I raise my hand, and Mr Kiehn smiles at me, eyebrows raised. "You're done reading it, Zachary?"

"I've just finished, sir. But I don't understand the ending. How can death be a victory?"

Mr Kiehn gives a sphinx smile. "That's what we'll be seeking to find out."

He gives us instructions to have another read of the poem and start our annotations while he writes some questions on the whiteboard. When he's facing away from the classroom, Theodora speaks without looking up from her poem.

"If you understood the Prometheus myth, you'd understand why death is a victory."

Her voice is quiet, barely above a murmur. I turn my head, taken by surprise.

"I do understand the Prometheus myth. I'm just not sure Byron understood it."

"You think you have a better understanding of the Prometheus myth than one of the most influential poets of the Romantic movement?"

"Just because someone is influential doesn't mean they were necessarily more perceptive or intelligent than everybody else. Look at our society right now. How many influencers do we have? Would you trust their opinions on the Prometheus myth?"

She looks up, finally meeting my gaze. Her eyes are cold, and there's a slight frown on her face, perceptible because of two tiny furrows between her eyebrows.

"You're really comparing Byron to an influencer?" she asks.

"That's essentially what he was. We only remember him the way we do because he was the equivalent of a rock star in his day and age.

Just because everybody wanted to sleep with him doesn't make him a savant."

"What makes *you* one, then?" Theodora says. "Since you know the Prometheus myth so well?"

"I never said I knew it well. I just don't necessarily agree with the interpretation that to Prometheus, death would have been a victory."

"That's because you're a fourteen-year-old boy. The idea of infinity doesn't register in your mind, let alone the idea of an infinity spent being tortured."

I sit back in my chair, narrowing my eyes at her. Part of me is amused by her austerity. Part of me is annoyed that she's reduced the complexity of my existence and personhood to merely being a "fourteen-year-old boy".

"The idea of eternity doesn't register in my mind because of my young age and lack of experience—how does it register in yours, then?" I smile at her and tilt my eyes. "What kind of creature are you, Theodora, that you look my age but have lived so much longer than I have?"

She stiffens in her chair, but her voice is carefully measured when she speaks.

"That's not what I'm saying. And the brain's ability to understand certain concepts doesn't necessarily have to do with age—that was just a simplification. What I was trying to say is that I think there is a stage of consciousness where one can conceive why death might be a victory and a stage of consciousness where one is not yet ready to see death as anything but punishment or tragedy."

"Ah—so what you are saying is that you are more evolved than I am, and, therefore, able to understand this poem in a way I cannot?" I let out a low laugh.

Theodora's face is set like stone, hard and unamused. The furrows between her eyebrows multiply as her frown deepens.

"Why are you laughing? I wasn't trying to say something funny—and you certainly didn't."

"No, no, you're right. I didn't say anything funny—and neither did you. What I find funny is how it only took you a couple of years spent in Spearcrest to become a snob."

"A snob?" Her voice goes high with surprise. "I'm not a snob at all. How am I a snob?"

"Well, for one, you've gone from advocating for the merits of children's books to passing judgement on my lack of perception and maturity due to the fact I'm nothing more than an insignificant fourteen-year-old."

"I never said you were insignificant," she says. Her tone is almost as stiff as her posture is. Her hand curls around her pen, knuckles white.

"You're correct about that—I'm not." I smile at her because I mean that sincerely. I'm not insignificant—I have never been nor will ever be. Especially not to her.

Theodora can pretend I am the shadows she treads on the ground, or she can pretend I'm the wall she passes by without seeing, but she cannot pretend I'm insignificant.

She glares at me as if I've just doused her with cold water. "All this just to get me to say something nice about you?"

"If that's you being nice, Theodora, I'd hate for you to insult me."

We stare at one another. Her eyes drop to the easy smile on my mouth. She's unsettled and annoyed, and I'm not, and that counts for something.

Especially since she just accused me of being intellectually incapable of comprehending the poem we're studying.

"If it only took me a couple of years to become a snob, then how long is it going to take you to learn how to have an intellectual debate without resorting to petty arguments?"

"I wasn't being petty, although I would like to point out you made the choice to begin our intellectual argument—as you call it—by asserting that I'm too young and immature to comprehend the concepts explored in the poem."

Her lips move, the lip gloss on them catching the light like the glimmering surface of a river, forming a tiny pout.

Then, as suddenly as an unexpected ray of sunshine falling through stormy rain clouds, her face smoothes itself out. The furrows between her eyebrows vanish—gone is the frown, the tiny pout. Like erasing the scribbles on a page, her face becomes a blank mask with an insincere pencil smile forming on her lips.

"I apologise," she says finally, "if I offended you."

"You didn't offend me," I reply with an affable smile. "You couldn't if you tried."

She watches me for a moment. Her face is still unreadable, but I can almost see her thoughts like swirling mist glimpsed beyond the glass windows of her gaze.

"I would never try to offend you, Zachary. Unlike you, I don't take casual conversations so personally."

Do I take things personally? Perhaps I do. I still remember the sting of her comment that *Animal Farm* was a short book that day we first met. And her supposition that I'm too young to understand Byron's "Prometheus" did sting—still does.

I'm mature and honest enough to acknowledge that, though. Whereas Theodora would never willingly admit she said those things intending to be offensive. That might make her appear as if she's more human than she wishes to appear.

Because Theodora Dorokhova doesn't wish to appear human. She wishes to appear like a being made of steel and marble and glass, smooth and polished and unstirred. There's a reason for that—a reason I can't yet understand. Nobody builds a wall unless they've got something to protect. Nobody wears armour unless they fear pain.

The mystery of Theodora is like a book—like a philosophical text in an ancient and cryptic language. I can look at the pages but I can't understand what they say.

I'm in Year 9, though. I'm young, and as she so hurtfully stated, I'm not yet clever and perceptive enough to understand certain things.

The book of Theodora sits in the middle of my heart. It's not going anywhere, and I'm very patient. I'm going to learn its language, and I'm going to decipher its code. I'm going to read every page until I know the text better than I know myself, until every word of it is inscribed on every part of me.

No matter how long it takes. No matter the obstacles Theodora sets in my way.

And I have a feeling she'll set many.

Chapter 7

Summer Ball

Theodora

THE END OF YEAR 9 is marked by the Summer Ball—a Spearcrest tradition seeking to denote the end of an era and the beginning of another. A rite of passage of sorts.

Unlike the glittery proms movies filled my imagination with—wristfuls of flowers, spinning disco balls filling blue darkness with coruscating lights, orange slices floating like wheels in blood-red spiked punch—the Summer Ball is a solemn affair. Black tie and ballgowns (though Spearcrest, surprisingly, allows boys and girls to wear whichever they prefer), a formal dinner, then a dance with a string quartet.

Although no student wishes to admit it, everyone is excited for the dance. The entire month leading up to it, it's all anybody can talk about. Students complain about the over-the-top formality of it, the old-fashioned dress code, the fact there's not going to be any "good music".

But above all, they complain about finding a date. They complain about having to ask someone, having to be asked, having to learn a dance. The girls loudly state there's not a single good-looking boy in the year and that they'd rather go with one of the Year 11 boys.

The boys ostentatiously question why girls are so difficult to approach when they all secretly want to be asked out. Everyone jokes about going to the dance with their same-sex best friend.

Everyone is lying, of course. The girls are desperate to be asked out by the boys, and the boys are both petrified of asking and petrified of not asking.

I feel nothing at all.

The thought of being at a formal dinner makes me ill. I rarely eat in front of people anymore. My relationship with food is too complex for that. Like an abusive marriage, it requires utter privacy.

As for the thought of being squeezed into a ballgown, of having to look more beautiful than ever when looking beautiful is already a daily effort, it is disheartening. And dancing with a boy when I'm not allowed to date just sounds like a complete waste of time.

In my group of friends, we all decide to pair up and go together as friends. I get Giselle Frossard, the pretty French girl who flirts with any boy that enters her field of vision. Once the boys find the courage to start asking girls, I can imagine she'll be one of the first bastions to fall, so I don't hold out much hope of making it to the Summer Ball with her.

I have other things to worry about anyway, like trying to make sure my name finally appears alone at the top of the exam results boards or trying to give myself as much of a head start for my GCSEs as possible since I know for a fact Zachary will be doing the same.

And worrying about a silly dance isn't going to give me the advantage I desperately want to get over him.

The Spearcrest library is mostly empty at this time of the year. Exam groups, like Year 11s and the upper school years, have all more or less finished their exams by now, leaving the library eerily deserted. The cold sunrays of early summer drop from the glass cupola crowning the building, tilted columns of light alive with the faint glimmer of dancing dust.

I'm sitting at one of the reading tables near the poetry section one afternoon, a volume of Keats open in front of me, my cheek resting on my palm. Keats is the poet I tend to gravitate towards in my more sedate moments, his lyricism soothing as a lullaby. My eyes open and close slowly as I read each line to myself, my lips moving but my voice shut.

The cushioned sound of footsteps draws me out of my torpor, and I know before I even look up who I'm about to see. Maybe it's because I can simply sense him, or maybe it's because I'm used to the smell of him by now, soap and a rich, alluring cologne.

"Theodora," he says, standing by my reading table.

His hair is longer now, and the curls of it, normally so neat and tight, become looser and softer the longer they are. The light catches them and outlines them in a warm halo. He's wearing the summer uniform without a blazer, his short sleeves revealing newborn muscles.

While I spent the entire year working so hard trying to become beautiful, Zachary simply blossomed into his beauty. A natural sort of beauty, warm and polished.

I remember the first time I saw him, the way his bleak intensity brought to my mind the icons of saints in their iconostases. That bleak intensity has morphed into something different. A burning intelligence in his gaze, an aura of conviction and self-faith.

Three years ago, Zachary was austere as a saint.

Now, he's as beautiful and intimidating as an angel.

"Zachary." I greet him in the same formal tone as he greeted me.

We watch each other like two wary animals. At first, I guessed he was here to study, but his leather satchel is nowhere to be seen, and he stands by my table, fixing on me the full beam of his attention.

"Can I help you with something?" I ask, tilting my head slightly.

He gestures at my book. "What are you reading?"

"Keats."

"Keats?" He raises his eyebrow, his lips curling in a sardonic smile. "I wouldn't expect you to enjoy such a sentimental poet."

"I happen to find him more emotional than sentimental, and there is a lot of beauty in how emotional he is."

"You know Byron hated his poetry, right?"

I raise a hand in an indifferent motion. "So? I don't like Byron?"

"You don't like Byron?" His tone is incredulous. "You seemed to like him well enough that time you defended him like he was paying you to do it in Mr Kiehn's class."

We've had many arguments since, but it's almost amusing he's still not over that particular one.

"I wasn't defending him," I point out. "I was just saying his interpretation of the Prometheus myth had more merit than yours."

"Ah, so what you're saying is that in the list of your esteem, Byron might rank low, but I rank lower?"

There's laughter in his eyes when he says this. His eyes are a rich, satisfying brown, but in the sunlight flooding down from the glass dome, they are limpid gold.

I lean back against my chair to transpierce him with a sharp gaze. Zachary is doing this thing he does where he thinks he has the upper hand because he's amused and I'm not. He's also doing something else, something he's quite adept at.

"You're normally much more subtle than this when you're fishing for compliments," I point out with a mocking smile. "Feeling a bit desperate?"

"I'm always desperate for a compliment from you, Theodora." His smile is easy and guileful. "They are the rarest of treasures. How could I not want to collect them?"

I can't help it. I laugh. "Fine. Your handwriting is incredibly tidy. There's your compliment—take it and go."

He takes out his phone and types a note.

"Excellent," he says, looking up. "So far this year, I've got 'not insignificant' and 'tidy handwriting'." He locks his phone and slides it back into his pocket. "You're really sweeping me off my feet, Theodora."

I roll my eyes, though there's still laughter tickling my throat. "Is that all?"

"No." The amusement fades from his eyes and the intensity I always associate with him returns. "I didn't actually come here to beg for compliments, believe it or not."

I frown. "What did you come here for, then?"

"I came here to ask you if you wanted to come to the dance with me."

My heart squeezes like a fist and drops in a sickening sensation. I stiffen in my chair, my entire body feeling both as if it's turned to ice and filled with flames at the same time.

"Are you being serious?"

"Deadly serious."

"You're asking me to the dance as—what, as a..." I hesitate and decide to proceed with caution. "As a friend?"

"No, not as a friend. As a date. As *my* date."

We look at each other. Of all the things I expected, this was the very last of them. Zachary, though, is full of fervent conviction, that disturbing self-confidence I envy so much. Unlike the other boys I've watched ask girls to the dance, he's not blushing or making excuses. There isn't a hint of anxiety or embarrassment to chink that impenetrable aura of determination and certainty.

For a moment, I fumble through my thoughts. Sirens wail in my head, warning me to be alert, to be sharp, to be cautious. Reminding me of my father's words, his warnings.

I give Zachary the safest answer I can think of—the truth.

"I'm not allowed to date."

His eyebrows raise. Faint surprise registers for a moment, then is immediately erased by a calm smile. "That's fine. Are you still allowed to go to the dance?"

"Yes."

"Are you allowed to go with a boy?"

"I suppose."

"Alright. Well, would you like to come to the dance with me as my date for the dance? We don't have to do anything else. It doesn't have to mean anything else."

I stare at him. His serenity and sincerity is nothing short of disturbing. His unshakeable calm is somehow making me feel more unnerved and nervous by the second.

"I..." Again, I make sure to be cautious. I don't want to be rude, or unkind, or insensitive. The honesty with which Zachary approached me deserves a courteous response. "Would you not rather ask someone else? A girl who's—well, allowed to date?"

He shakes his head. His eyes don't leave mine, not for a second, the golden-brown depths of his irises a glimmering pool for me to drown in.

"No. You're the only girl I intended to ask. There's nobody else I wish to go with, and therefore I won't ask anybody else."

My heart is so tight I'm convinced it's not even beating. I have the sinking feeling that something incredibly important and meaningful is happening. Zachary, with that unswerving intensity of his, has somehow taken me by the elbow and led me through a gateway of sorts, a point of no return.

I swallow. "But what if I say no?"

He waves a hand. "If you say no, then it's a no. I'll go alone." He tilts his head questioningly. "Are you saying no?"

Going to the Summer Ball with Zachary is the only thing that makes sense. Out of everybody in Spearcrest, he is my true peer, my true equal. My relationship with him, as strange and fraught as it is, is the only relationship I have in Spearcrest that is steeped in truth. His soul and my soul sit across the chessboard of life, and everything between us is the game, each move real and urgent. Nothing with him is a shadow of a thing. It's all real.

Going to the dance with him wouldn't be real, though. It would be a shadow. I can't be his date for the dance because I can't be his date. Whatever happens between Zachary and me, my father's voice will always stand between us, asking, *Are you a whore?*

Saying yes to Zachary wouldn't be truthful, and it wouldn't be fair.

"I'm saying no." I sigh. "I'm sorry, genuinely. But it wouldn't be right."

"That's fine," he says. "You don't have to apologise to me. Well, I should go." He tilts his head and one corner of his mouth lifts slightly. "At least I got a compliment out of it."

I swallow around the sudden lump in my throat. "You should ask someone else."

A serene smile blooms on his face. "I won't."

He walks off with a casual wave of his hand. The rays of sunlight fade as he leaves. I look up at the cupola with a frown. Clouds, dragged by the wind, have hidden the sun away, taking away its warmth.

I resume reading Keats, but his poetry, too, seems to have lost its warmth.

Chapter 8

Alone Together

Theodora

True to his word, Zachary goes to the Summer Ball alone. Even if he hadn't, he would still stand out amongst the other boys in our year. Not because he's better looking than all of them or because he is dressed better.

Zachary stands out like a beacon of light. His confidence, his intensity, the way he carries himself. In a place full of people our age, he stands out like someone older, like someone important. Like a young lord, not a schoolboy.

Everything I work so hard to project—beauty, elegance, intelligence—Zachary exudes innately without having to try.

The Summer Ball is a depressing ordeal without a date, but Zachary doesn't seem depressed. He stands amongst his friends, talking and laughing. When everybody ends up on the dance floor, he leans against a pillar, sipping his drink and watching thoughtfully.

Later, I even see him chatting with some of the teachers. He stands with one hand in his pocket and the other gesturing confidently as if spending his time with teachers instead of dancing with girls is the most natural thing in the world.

Although I, too, end up sitting out most of the dancing, I don't approach him. It's my fault I'm here alone—he asked me to come with him, and I refused. Commiserating would be sweet—doing so with full knowledge I caused this situation would be too bitter.

It's Zachary who ends up approaching me. He brings me a cup of punch and hands it to me. I take it and sip tentatively but wince at the sugary taste. He drinks his and lifts an eyebrow.

"Not to your taste?"

"It tastes like sugar and chemicals."

"I can imagine that's the recipe, yes." He hesitates, then asks, "Would you like me to bring you something to eat? I noticed you barely touched your food at dinner."

"I'm not hungry," I say automatically.

It's my go-to response anytime anyone mentions food, and the words unspool from my mouth with practised ease. Zachary nods slowly, his eyes on mine.

"Mm. Are you sure?"

His tone is feather light, almost playful. Part of me wants to stick to the safety of my go-to response, but part of me senses the strange, silent companionship that exists between us. I want to lean into it, let it pull me in, lull me.

Zachary doesn't press me for a response. He simply watches me, waiting for my silence to transform into words.

"I don't like eating in front of people," I say finally.

"Oh, right."

I wonder if he knows I'm only giving him a part of the truth, not all of it. The truth would be too difficult to explain because it would mean telling him I've been depriving myself of food for weeks to look good in this dress. The truth would mean telling him that I am always hungry.

"Well," Zachary says after a few seconds, "if you want, we could steal some snacks from one of those tables and sneak off to the grounds. They've opened some of the French windows to let in some cold air since the dancing was turning a little feral. We could sit on a bench—it's dark enough that nobody will see us." He grins. "We can even sit back to back if you like."

I give him an eye roll, but we end up doing what he says. Zachary fills an embossed paper plate with finger foods and covers it with another paper plate. He half-hides behind me—a ridiculous notion since he's now taller than me—as we make our way through the crowd of dancing bodies and past bored teachers to one of the windows.

Outside, the evening air is cool and crisp and full of the scent of trees and dewy grass and the sweet perfume of honeysuckle.

We make our way to one of the marble benches lining the path, picking one that's half-hidden in the shadows cast by the spiky branches of an enormous juniper tree. We don't sit back to back but shoulder to shoulder. Zachary's arm is warm against mine. He lifts the makeshift cover off the food and eats. He keeps the plate on his lap and doesn't make any attempt to offer me food or prompt me to eat.

We sit for a while, him eating and me preparing myself to eat. That involves a sort of inner ritual where I remind myself how all human beings need nutrients for survival and that eating is necessary and that it's okay for me to do it, right now.

When I finally reach for the food, Zachary doesn't look down. He just stares ahead, his eyes glazed over in thought.

Surprising myself, I'm the first one to break the silence.

"You should have asked someone else to come with you."

He turns. In the darkness of the night and the shadows of the junipers, I can barely make out his features.

"Why?" he asks.

"Because being at this stupid party alone is the most depressing thing that's happened so far in Spearcrest."

He lets out a low, soft laugh. "Mm, yes." He's quiet for a moment, and then he says, "You should have said yes, then."

There's no resentment or anger in his tone, only a wry sort of amusement that makes him sound far older than he is.

"It didn't feel like a fair thing to do."

"Making us both endure this party alone is unfair."

"I specifically advised you to ask someone else."

"And I specifically told you I only ever intended to ask you."

I give him an unimpressed look, which I'm sure he can see about as much as I can see his expression—hardly at all.

"Don't pretend like you don't have options. I know you and your friends are the most popular boys in our year."

"I didn't say I didn't have options. I didn't need options. I made a choice and that choice was you. That's all."

"Why me?"

He laughs again, this time soft and mischievous.

"Who's fishing for compliments now, Theodora?"

My cheeks flush with heat, and I'm thankful for the cover of darkness. "I don't place value in flattery."

"A compliment isn't the same as flattery."

"What if I told you there's no need for either if you just answer the truth?"

"I like the truth," he says. "It has this nice, clean, stark quality to it. But sometimes, speaking truthfully and speaking the truth don't mean the same thing."

"That's a nothing sentence—you love those."

He leans closer as if trying to peer into my eyes even through the darkness. I don't move back, refusing to retreat.

"A nothing sentence?" he repeats.

"A sentence where it sounds like you're saying something meaningful, but you're not actually saying anything at all."

"I've never spoken such a sentence in my life."

"You use them all the time when debating. It's your signature style. Every time your team loses, it's because you've used one, and I've pointed it out to my team."

There's a moment of silence that spins and glimmers like a cosmos between us. It's not uncomfortable or awkward. It's not even hostile. It's like intimacy but without affection.

"How's your team going to win next year?" he asks in a light tone. "Now you're about to lose your secret weapon."

"I'll just have to find a new weakness of yours to exploit."

"You'll struggle to find one." I can almost hear the arrogant smile on his mouth. "You might wish to consider beating me fair and square with strong arguments and clear logic."

"I'll do that too, don't worry."

He lets out a sigh that turns into a laugh, and I laugh too. The summer night air is cooler, and a plume of wind brushes against me, making me shiver. Zachary crumples the now-empty paper plates and stands to throw them into a nearby bin.

When he's done, he returns to the bench and stands in front of me, reaching his hand out to me.

"Shall we go back in?"

"Alright."

I give him my hand, and he helps me up, even though I don't need his help. For a moment, we just stand near each other, his hand still on mine, our fingers brushing in a delicate touch. His presence is bright and warm next to mine, the heat of it thawing the ice of me.

Zachary finally releases my hand, and we cross the pebbled path back to the French window we escaped through.

Right before we step through it, Zachary turns to me and says, "Since we're both stuck here alone and it's too early to leave, shall we dance together?"

Now that we're standing in the violet and silver lights of the ballroom, the darkness can no longer conceal the flush in my cheeks, so I answer quickly, giving him no time to search for an answer on my face.

"Yes."

He leads me inside to the dance floor. The string quartet has moved on from the more formal waltzes of earlier and is now playing scintillating renditions of modern songs.

Zachary wraps his arm around my waist. He holds me close but not close enough to press my body into his. My senses are full of him—his presence, his warmth, his intensity, his scent. We dance, and the moment is soft and unusual and special.

We dance, and although I would sooner have died than admit it to him, Zachary was right.

I should have said yes to him when he asked me to the dance.

Chapter 9

Ice Queen

Theodora

In Year 10, everybody is dating.

The fumbling awkwardness, the coy giggles, the furious embarrassment—all seem to be a problem of the past. Everyone seems older and bolder. Everyone wants attention and affection. Everyone, in short, is touch-starved and horny.

There are a few exceptions to the rules, like the most erudite students of our year—the students I can only assume are under immense pressure from their parents to excel academically—or the unwanted outcasts, like Sophie Sutton, whose parents work for Spearcrest, or a couple of scholarship boys.

The final exception is girls who are in the same boat as me. Girls whose parents are religious or strict or consider the future of their families and businesses. At first, I assume those girls are just like me, sticking safely away from boys and dating.

Then, one day, completely at random, I walk into an empty maths classroom to look for a workbook.

Two students are sitting at a desk: a boy I don't know and Camille Alawi—whom I know quite well. Like me, she's strictly forbidden from dating. Like me, she has strict and religious parents. She even wears a small golden cross at all times. She's been telling anyone who'll listen that she's not allowed to date and that there's not a single good-looking boy in Spearcrest anyway.

But when I enter the classroom, she stands up so fast her chair falls, clattering back. Her cheeks are bright red, half-hidden by the black curls framing her face. Eyes wide with panic, she looks from me to the boy and then runs out of the classroom.

The boy, as red-faced as she was, stands as soon as she leaves. Still frozen by the door, I watch him as he fixes himself and buttons up his trousers. The bulge underneath the fabric is obvious to anybody who might look, so I raise my eyes to the ceiling as he mumbles incoherent apologies and sidles past me.

The door clicks shut behind him.

This is when I realise that not everybody who's saying they're not dating is, in fact, not dating. It's of no comfort to me—if anything, I feel more isolated than ever.

My group of friends are the most popular, and therefore desirable, girls in the year. Giselle Frossard, the French flirt, flits from boy to boy with blithe indifference and becomes the first one of us to have sex. Kayana Kilburn, who's arguably the most beautiful person I've ever seen in my life, ends up in a long-term relationship with the Montcroix heir, one of Zachary's best friends. Camille Alawi, for all her claims of innocence, seems to have boys following her around like puppies.

Even Seraphina Rosenthal, who is the most immature of us all, is going on dates in private places and coming back full of giggly, naughty stories.

The stress of keeping up with them is a problem I never thought I would ever need to deal with. For a while, I consider taking a page out of Camille's book, except in reverse: telling everybody I'm dating while I'm really doing anything but.

But the fear of my father finding out—somehow—is too paralysing to allow me to pursue such a reckless plan. So I endure the endless questions and gentle mockery from my friends and eventually earn my title of ice queen.

THANKFULLY, IN YEAR 10, I make a new friend—a real one, this time.

During the summer, my father informed me in an imperious tone that my uncle would be sending his daughter, Inessa, to Spearcrest. When my father refers to someone as my uncle, I'm never quite sure what it means. Both relatives and friends, so long as they are close to him, are referred to as my uncles, and since I can't quite bring myself to speak to him, I never find out whether or not Inessa is my real cousin.

And then I meet her, and it doesn't matter at all. Because Inessa doesn't feel like a friend or a cousin.

She feels like a sister.

She's a pale, thoughtful girl, introverted and principled. Even though she's a year younger than me, she intimidates me a little with how serious she is. But, unlike my Spearcrest friends, Inessa likes to talk about real things.

As we grow closer, we talk about our parents, our homes, Russia. She tells me about her siblings, and I tell her about my grandparents.

Like me, Inessa is a hard worker and an avid reader, although she favours religious and historical texts, whereas I favour poetry and literature. Still, that makes our conversations more interesting. Soon, I find myself seeking her out, spending my precious free time sitting on her bed or strolling through the lawns, talking about our lives at Spearcrest, our plans for the future.

"I can't wait to go to university," I tell her one day. "I hope I get to study in Oxford—it's the most beautiful place I've ever seen."

"Would you not like to come to Russia?" Inessa asks, turning her big grey eyes up at me. "You could go to St Petersburg University—it is the oldest and greatest university in Russia, you know."

"I never thought of it," I said. "My Russian isn't great, I'm not fluent like you."

"I could teach you if you wanted."

I smile. "As if either of us has the time."

"I would make the time for you, Dora," Inessa said, squeezing my arm. "If it means I can still see you after we leave Spearcrest."

I squeeze her arm and say nothing, but there's a little ache that sets in my heart that day.

***

Worrying about the future of my friendship with Inessa is a luxury I soon can't afford anyway. There's simply no time.

Since I ended Year 9 tying with Zachary at the top of every class for the third year running, I'm determined to win outright this year. So I double my efforts with everything I possibly can, and I work harder than I ever have before.

But for every victory I painstakingly earn, Zachary sweeps by and effortlessly gets his own.

I come out on top of the class in chemistry in the winter exams, but Zachary gets invited to Doctor Zheng's Advanced Physics for upper school students. I become captain of my debate team, but Zachary becomes captain of his. I become a prefect, but Zachary wins at a national chess tournament. A teacher enters some of my creative writing pieces into a national competition, which I win, but Zachary writes an essay on the myth of Echo and Narcissus in Latin class that receives full marks and ends up in a display case outside Mr Ambrose's office.

I don't resent Zachary his successes—they drive mine, after all.

What I resent is the ease with which Zachary achieves those successes. He never seems tired, or overworked, or stressed. He looks as if every challenge is something he embraces, even relishes. Worst of all, he seems to be enjoying himself.

Spearcrest is a furnace, and the heat of it is forming Zachary into a diamond—strong and brilliant.

As for me—I'm just burning alive.

Chapter 10

Staghorn Fern

Zachary

THE FIRST TIME I have a panic attack, I'm sitting outside Mr Ambrose's office.

The meeting I'm about to have with him isn't serious—I just want to discuss early entry to the Latin exam so that I can start the Latin A-level early and give myself room to study other subjects when I'm in the upper school. My Latin teacher's already discussed it with him, but Mr Ambrose wants a more informal discussion before we make any decisions.

I sit in the same green chair I always sit in when I'm waiting outside his office. It faces his door, and the light from the window falls right on it. Even though Mr Ambrose is finishing a meeting with a teacher, I keep my posture straight while I wait for him, unwilling to let him catch me slumping in my chair.

My fingers are laced in front of me, my arms resting on my thighs. I look at my hands, at the watch around my wrist.

When it happens, it happens for no reason whatsoever.

I'm not thinking of anything particularly stressful. I'm not even having a particularly stressful day—especially compared to the days I've had recently.

Out of nowhere, my heart lurches. It's a sickening sensation, and I clutch my chest, startled. My heartbeat accelerates, and each beat is a tremor, a horrible shock inside my ribs. My fingers dig into my chest, and I realise, with stone-cold certainty, that I'm having a heart attack.

I fall forward out of my chair, hitting the ground on my knees and elbows. A dull groan leaks from me—a sound of absolute terror. My mind, at this moment, isn't a cacophony of thoughts—it's the opposite. It's calm and empty.

I watch myself as if from afar, and I know I'm going to die.

I'm too young to die, and I have so much left to do, to see, to learn. I've still not deciphered the mystery of Theodora. I can't die without knowing all her secrets, without having the shape of her heart and soul imprinted within me, without holding her close even once.

I collapse to my side and my mouth opens noiselessly. I want to scream and call for help, but I can't. I try to catch my breath—enough air for a scream, but I can't even scream.

I don't even notice Mr Ambrose's door opening.

Then, Mr Ambrose and another teacher are crouching on either side of me. The teacher holds my shoulder gently, rubbing my arm. Mr Ambrose looks down at me, his hazel eyes grave.

"Zachary, you're having a panic attack." His voice is calm and very gentle. "What you're feeling right now might feel incredibly scary, but it's not dangerous. You're alright. I need you to breathe with me, alright?"

He gives me a count and breathes with me, in through the nose, then out through his mouth. I imitate him as best I can, squeezing air into my too-tight chest. I try to tell him about my heart—about dying, but words don't come out.

I want to tell him to go get Theodora.

I want to see her. I need to see her.

I want to tell Mr Ambrose how worried I am—that I'll never be able to keep her, that she's too good and too strong. I want to admit the truth to him, that I failed the sacred duty he gave me, that I never really helped her at all when she first arrived in Spearcrest, that I've never truly been able to help her.

Mr Ambrose and the teacher help me up gently.

"Alright, Zachary, you're doing great. Now I'd like you to do something for me. Concentrate, alright? I want you to name three things you can see around you right now."

I swallow and look around. A task—I can do that. I'm good at tasks.

"Daylight," I croak. "Blue chair. Staghorn fern."

Mr Ambrose raises an eyebrow. "You're correct—well done, Zachary. As usual, you impress me. How do you know this is a staghorn fern?"

"My little sister," I croak. "Loves plants. I recognised the leaves."

Mr Ambrose nods. "Well done, Zachary. Alright. Now can you name three sounds you can hear?"

I nod. "Heartbeat. Clock. You."

"Excellent. You're doing great. Finally, can you name three parts of your body?"

I look down. My body feels strange, as though the relationship between myself and it has changed. I never expected it to betray me like this, to turn against me so suddenly and ruthlessly.

"Hands. Legs. Skull."

Mr Ambrose taps my shoulder. "That's great. How's your breathing?"

It's still laboured, but at least I *am* breathing. I'm not going to die—I know this now. I'd be embarrassed about my earlier panic if my chest wasn't still feeling like it's caved in on itself.

"It's alright, sir."

Mr Ambrose stands and pulls me to my feet.

"Let's reschedule our meeting for now, Zachary, alright? I want you to go to the infirmary and see the nurse, make sure you're alright. I'd like you to go there now, can you do that?"

"Yes, sir."

"Would you like me to go with you?"

I shake my head. "No, thank you, sir, that won't be necessary."

He gives me a solemn smile and a short nod. Grabbing my bag from the side of the chair I fell from, I turn and walk away, too embarrassed to look back.

THE NURSE ASKS ME some questions that are clearly designed to guide me towards some specific conclusion. She asks me about my sleep, my diet, my emotions, my health. She asks me if I've been having headaches, if I'm struggling with schoolwork, if I sometimes feel overwhelmed.

I know what she wants me to say.

That I'm struggling to cope with the workload, that this year has been difficult and that I'm suffering from stress. She wants to diagnose me, to give me a good reason why I randomly had a panic attack.

I don't resent her. She's only doing her job. If I was suffering from stress and anxiety, she would be asking me the right questions, and she'd certainly be the right person to help me. And if I needed her help, I'd take it.

But I don't need her help, and she's not asking the right questions.

The questions she *should* be asking are: are the sacrifices you are making necessary to your success? Is this temporary suffering worth the reward? Are you ready to sleep less, work harder, have more panic attacks if it all means that you get to win against Theodora Dorokhova?

If she asked me those questions, she would know the answers are all yes.

Yes, this is necessary.

Yes, it's worth the reward.

Yes, I will do anything it takes to win against Theodora.

Otherwise, what would be the point? Who else in Spearcrest—in this world, probably—would make me feel the way she makes me feel? The thrill of her expression when I solve a problem first in maths class? The slight pinch of her lips when my name gets called out before hers as our teacher hands us our marked essays back? The satisfaction of being invited to the sixth form lectures when she's not?

The sweetness of those moments is worth the bitterness of falling to the floor in front of Mr Ambrose, the tightness in my chest, the constant exhaustion—all of it.

It's worth *every* bitterness.

The nurse, getting nothing but short, formal answers from me, sighs and tells me to be careful. She tells me about burnout and about the importance of rest and recovery. She tells me to look after my mental health, that it's as important as my physical health. Then she reaches for some leaflets, hands them to me, and tells me she'll write me a note to excuse me from the rest of today's classes so I can go back to my room and rest.

"No. Thank you, Miss, but that won't be necessary."

She watches me for a moment. Her eyes are full of sympathy, but her sympathy is about as necessary as her note. I need neither. Neither is going to get me to the top of my classes, neither is going to buy me a victory against Theodora.

In the end, she sighs. "Alright, Zachary, that's fine. Feel free to come see me if you're ever worried about anything. And don't forget to read the booklet I gave you on panic attacks—it's better to be prepared for things like that, to have coping mechanisms."

On that, we can agree. "Of course, Miss, please don't worry. I'll have a read of all the booklets you've given me."

She nods, clearly not completely satisfied with the exchange, but since there's nothing I can say to soothe her, I thank her, excuse myself and leave the infirmary.

Outside the door, I sigh and rub my hand across my too-tight chest and the treacherous heart within it. Then I slide the leaflets into my bag and head straight for the next lesson.

Chapter 11

Sweet Dreams

Zachary

The following months, I catch myself watching Theodora for signs of weakness—for any indication that she's finding this year as difficult as I am.

But Theodora remains as impenetrable as ever.

She glides from class to class with the heavy cloak of her pale hair on her shoulders, her face set like stone, unreadable. Over the years, she's developed a look that's uniquely hers: raspberry lip gloss and natural make-up aside from her eyeshadow, which is always a delicate colour: mint-green, carnation-pink or periwinkle. She wears almost no jewellery apart from silver earrings, and she always uses the same bag to carry her things, a Kate Spade tote in a pale shade of pink. Her hair, she wears either down or half-up, tied with ribbons or pinned with silver clips.

In class, she carries herself with dignity and still keeps to herself most of the time. The only times she comes out of her shell is when I force her to, and it's easy enough to do that: all I have to do is be overly critical of something without good enough reason to be or else make a statement where I present my opinion as fact.

In those instances, Theodora will cast me a look of exasperation. Sometimes, she'll try to bite her tongue, but most of the time, she can't.

That's when she comes out of her shell, and that's when she truly shines. Theodora is an excellent speaker: she doesn't rush, she enunciates everything, she's thoughtful and eloquent. I like her voice too: it's quiet but clear, and it has this musical lilt to it. Her voice suits poetry and it particularly suits Shakespeare. When our English teacher picks her to read out loud, everybody listens like they're under a spell.

Watching Theodora, though, yields no result. It's almost impossible to tell what she's really feeling—ever—so working out whether or not she's struggling is impossible. She might very well be—she might feel as much panic and anxiety and exhaustion as I do.

She might be haunted by the same terror as me: the paralysing fear of slipping up, of falling behind and never being able to catch up.

But if she does fear this, she doesn't show it.

Then, one evening, I'm on my way out of the library when I see a figure at a table half-hidden by a row of bookshelves. I frown—I was under the impression I was the last person in the library—and draw closer. The figure is leaning against the divider that separates the desk into semi-cubicles. On the desk in front of her are books and an open laptop with a dark screen.

I recognise Theodora by the pallor of her hair, by the pale pink bag in the chair next to hers. I draw closer, keeping close to the bookshelf, hoping the shadows will keep the secret of my presence.

Theodora doesn't look up, not even when I finally reach her desk. I realise why as soon as I step next to her.

She's sitting tucked against the divider, her arm folded, her hand squished between the divider and her cheek. She's fast asleep, her face softened, her mouth a pink pout. Her hair is gathered into a bun from which wispy strands have escaped. One of those strands falls over her face, and it moves with each of her exhalations like a muslin curtain in a summer breeze.

I pull out the chair next to hers and sit on the edge so as not to crush her bag. My mouth has moved of its own volition, stretching into a smile. My chest feels strange, but not the way it did when I had that panic attack—the opposite. Instead of feeling too tight, it feels wide and expansive, like the open sky.

Theodora in sleep looks soft and delicate and sweet as a marshmallow. I could take a bite out of her—I have the incredibly childish urge to reach out and press my mouth to her cheek, just to see if she tastes as sweet as she looks.

Reaching out, I place a hand on her shoulder and squeeze. "Theodora."

Her eyes blink open slowly, and a sigh leaves her mouth. She smiles sleepily, and her eyelids close again as if she's sinking deeper into sleep. Then she sits bolt upright, startling both of us.

"I fell asleep!" she exclaims, tucking the loose strands of her hair behind her ears and wiping her eyes.

There's a panicked expression on her face like she's been caught in the middle of a crime, not a nap. I smile at her and scoot back, giving her space. "It would seem so, yes."

She shakes her head. "I didn't mean to."

"No, I can't imagine you did. You didn't exactly look comfortable."

She's fixing herself now, and I watch in real-time as sleepy Theodora retreats behind the façade of ice queen Theodora. She fixes her hair, straightens her tie, arranges the books in front of her into neat piles.

"I was just tired," she says. Her posture, which is always so straight and formal, is more rigid than ever.

"I don't blame you."

I stand. Theodora's mortification is obvious and painful to watch. Is she embarrassed because she feels like I've caught her in a moment of weakness?

She takes such great care to appear always perfect, always in control—maybe it's her way of keeping the balance of power between us always even. Maybe this has made her feel as though the balance of power has now tipped in my favour?

She's packing her things away, every motion rigid, but there's a faint smear of colour on her cheeks. If she feels as if the balance has been tipped, then what if I tip it the other way?

"To be honest, I'm tired too," I tell her with a shrug. "I'm exhausted, actually. I don't know about you, but I feel as if I haven't had a good night's sleep since the summer."

She looks up, and a corner of her mouth lifts ever so slightly.

"I didn't think you ever needed sleep."

I laugh out loud. "Like a vampire?"

Theodora looks up at me a little slyly. "More like a shark. Like you'll die if you stop."

I narrow my eyes, watching her closely. Her embarrassment from earlier seems to have eased—maybe I succeeded in redressing whatever imbalance was making her uncomfortable. Her playfulness is an added bonus—an unexpected boon.

Part of me wants to play too, to rake my claws against hers. But maybe I'm tired, or maybe I'm moved from her presence. Either way, I have the urge to be sincere instead of playful for once.

"Maybe you're right," I tell her, my gaze locked into hers. "Sometimes, it does feel like I'll die if I stop. But sometimes, it also feels like I'll die if I keep going, too." I tilt my head. "Know what I mean?"

She nods, her smile fading. "I know what you mean."

"Well..." I offer her my hand. "Shall we go back to the dorms?"

With a nod, she takes my hand, and I pull her to her feet. She shoulders her bag and reaches for the pile of books on the desk, but I stop her, placing my arm between her and the books.

"I mean to sleep—not to study."

She narrows her eyes at me. "Are you going straight to sleep?"

I smile and extend my hand out between us. "I will if you will."

She hesitates, looking down at my hand. I sense her exhaustion because it feels the same as mine. She takes my hand and shakes it. "Deal."

We part ways outside the library.

"Goodnight, Theodora."

"Goodnight, Zachary. Sweet dreams."

I cast her a look of surprise, taken aback by this gentle goodbye, but she's already turned away.

That night, I fall asleep fast, and my dreams, not daring to disobey her, are sweet indeed. I dream of Theodora half asleep and tender and dressed in nothing but moonlight, and I wake up hard and full of desperate longing.

Chapter 12

ELUSIVE ANGEL

Theodora

Year 11 is relentlessly horrible.

Endless studying, endless work, endless parties. I'm voted head girl, which also means more responsibilities, meetings with the other prefects, with teachers, with the school leadership team.

My father insists I perfect my Russian, so I'm taking my Russian GCSE as an independent candidate on top of all my other GCSEs, which means taking online classes with a tutor and practising with Inessa for hours. I'm forced to drop out of most clubs, aside from the debate team, since I'm still the captain of my team.

Everyone is stressed this year—and the coping mechanism of choice is sex. The days in Spearcrest are intense, especially in the top classes—and the parties match that intensity. Everyone is partying hard when they can, and I can't blame them. For them, it's an outlet.

I don't have an outlet.

I go to those parties and stick to my limit of three drinks. Any more and I risk being drunk—and being drunk at Spearcrest means being filmed by no less than a dozen people. Too many scandals have erupted after footage from a party was posted online, and I'm paralysed by the fear of my father ever finding such footage of me.

I wish I wasn't so scared. The idea of letting loose grows more tempting as the year goes on. Even a single night of freedom from the constant stress and anxiety would be a godsend at this point. Would the payoff be worth the risk?

I don't think so, and I'm not going to find out.

As depressing as it is to watch everyone have fun at the parties while I remain rigidly in control, it also comes with a gift of its own.

Just like I'm friends with the most popular girls in the year, Zachary is part of a small and elite group of boys, the Young Kings of Spearcrest. That group includes Séverin Montcroix, the heir to the aristocratic Montcroix family; Evan Knight, the star athlete of Spearcrest; Luca Fletcher-Lowe, the fencing champion and heir to the Novus group; and Iakov Kavinski, whose father is even more powerful in Russia than mine is.

Zachary has little in common with them—he outshines them all in intellect, manners, and pure quality of personhood.

The Young Kings represent everything you would associate with wealthy, privately educated boys: they are entitled, arrogant, horny and immature.

I imagine Zachary is friends with them in the way I'm friends with Giselle and the others—because social ties are a necessity like food and air here at Spearcrest. When I see him with his friends, it's obvious he's not like them—I often wonder if he feels as alienated as I do.

If he does, I can't tell. But one thing I can tell is that Zachary isn't as averse to partying as I am. Maybe he drinks because he, too, wants an escape from the stress of Year 11. Or maybe he's drinking to keep up with his friends—but he drinks and plays party games, and I never see him leave a party before I do.

This is unexpected, and at first, I'm a little disappointed in him—until I realise the position of advantage it puts me in.

For one, while Zachary is nursing hangovers at weekends, I get some extra studying time. Since all the Young Kings seem pretty determined to sleep their way through the year group, I'm certain Zachary must also be trying to keep up with that aspect of his social life, so that's even more time he won't be spending studying.

And last but certainly not least, there's delicious power in being sober while someone is drunk.

I DISCOVER THAT DELICIOUS power at the Year 11 unofficial Halloween party.

It's a wild party—everyone is dressed up, and the party is kickstarted by a big game of boys-versus-girls hide-and-seek in the woods at the edge of campus.

I skip out the game of hide-and-seek. I have no intention of running through the muddy woods in my pristine angel costume, getting chased around by drunk, horny boys.

So I turn up late enough to miss the game and head straight for the bonfire, hoping to have a couple of drinks in the company of my friends and get seen long enough that I can then go back to my room to prepare for the upcoming winter exams.

When I arrive, the firelight illuminates a wild scene.

Everyone is in costumes, each more lavish and elaborate than the last. The hide-and-seek games must have taken on a wild edge because some people are splashed with mud up to the thighs, and others have scratches and stains on their arms and cheeks. Some girls have torn clothing, some boys have bruises. Whatever happened in the woods, it seems like it was far from innocent fun.

I spot Camille and Seraphina, whose glassy eyes tell me they're already pretty drunk, swaying by the bonfire. Seraphina hands me a bottle of champagne, and when I drink, she tips the bottle, forcing me to keep drinking. I take a couple of extra gulps and then just pretend to drink until she finally lets me stop.

"Who won the game, then?" I ask.

Camille lets out a delighted cackle. "The girls did! Thanks to you!"

I frown. "How? I wasn't even there."

Seraphina and Camille look at each other and burst out laughing.

They are like reverse mirror images of each other: Camille with her raven-black curls, Seraphina with her Barbie-blonde tresses. Camille is dressed in a tiny sparkly dress and a satin prom-queen sash, fake blood smeared on her legs and chest, and Seraphina is dressed like a murderous cheerleader, her hair in long pigtails, a knife taped to her thigh.

"Exactly," Seraphina says, stifling her giggles behind a pompom. "We told the boys you were playing, and since nobody found you, the girls won."

I laugh, shaking my head. "Isn't that cheating?"

"So what?" Camille sneers. "Trust me, the boys cheated too. We said no phones but I'm pretty sure that sexy creep Luca had some sort of CIA-grade tracker to find us."

That sounds highly unlikely, but Camille is still almost definitely right about the boys cheating.

Both girls make me swear to never betray the girls' secret, and then Camille gets pulled away into the woods by a boy, so Seraphina and I dance together by the fireside. It's a challenge trying to keep Seraphina from falling headfirst into the bonfire; she's so drunk she can barely keep herself on her feet.

Eventually, she spots Evan Knight, the golden-haired star athlete, standing with some of his friends, and runs off after him, tossing me her bottle of champagne as she goes.

With a sigh of relief, I take the bottle and sit gingerly down on a dry part of a tree leg next to the fire. The bottle is almost empty, so I finish it. There's a gentle buzz in my head and body, but I'm not even tipsy. I sit, contemplating the pointlessness of being in a dark, soggy wood, dressed like an angel and huddling as close to the fire as I can so I don't get pneumonia.

When I decide I've been at the party long enough to have paid my dues, I abandon my empty bottle in the graveyard of empty bottles near the bonfire and make my way into the trees. I've not even made it three steps into the woods when an arm laces around my waist and I'm pulled back against a firm, warm chest.

I let out a cry and whirl around, pushing my captor away. He makes no effort to keep ahold of me, and I take a hasty step back to find myself face to face with Zachary.

I glare at him. "You scared me."

He shakes his head and raises his palms in a gesture of contrition. "I'm sorry, I didn't mean to. I didn't want you to run away." His eyes rake the length of my body, lingering on the white wings at my back. "Angel," he adds with a curl of his lips.

"I wasn't running away," I say.

"It looked like you were." He steps closer and tilts his head, fixing me with a thoughtful gaze. "You always run away."

"No, I don't. You of all people should know this."

"I mean from parties." His eyebrows knit together in a slight glare. "You always run away from parties, angel."

My eyes have adjusted to the light and I can see him more clearly now. He's wearing an elaborate costume: black velvet doublet and breeches in the style of the seventeenth century, with an ornate white collar and buttons that gleam faintly as they catch the distant light of the bonfire. His eyes are framed with thick lines of kohl, giving his face a wild edge.

"Who are you dressed as?" I ask lightly, pointing at him.

He raises his right arm, showing me the gleaming hook at the end of it. There's a slight grin on his face.

"Captain Hook? Thought you weren't a fan of children's literature."

He shrugs. "So? It's your favourite book, isn't it? I thought it might amuse you."

I purse my lips in thought and point at his head. "You're missing the long curls."

"'*Like black candles*'," Zachary quotes. "I know. I had a wig but took it off, it was too hot."

It's at this point that I realise Zachary is more than a little tipsy. It's funny and sweet because he's still enunciating perfectly, and his posture is still as rigid and formal as that of a royal guardsman. What gives him away is something else—something I can't quite explain. A sort of softness, I guess.

A feeling that his drawbridge has been lowered, the gateway to him hanging open, his armour laid aside for once. The softness of him, all exposed to me, makes me want to soften, too.

"It's a crying shame," I tell him, brushing my fingers down his velvet sleeve. "I would have loved to see you in the wig. You know, I've never told anyone this, but I used to have a crush on Captain Hook when I was a kid."

Zachary's eyes widen. "You did not."

I nod quite seriously. "I did."

"What was it that so fascinated you?" Zachary lifts his arm again. "Not the hook, surely?"

I shake my head. "No, not the hook. It was the handsome countenance, the excellent diction, the Oxford education. I was obsessed with his death scene, the way he went. His final words to Peter—bad form." I shiver. "So dignified."

Zachary stares at me for a moment.

"I've never read the book," he says in a thoughtful tone.

"No?" I sigh. "I doubt you'd like it anyway. It's very fanciful."

We stare at each other. Zachary speaks again, but this time, it's not about the book.

"Where were you hiding, angel? I looked for you everywhere."

My heart tightens without warning. "You did?"

"Everywhere." His tone is solemn. He reaches towards me and touches the feathered edges of my wings with his hook-free hand. "Maybe I should have gone to the chapel, in retrospect. Probably the wisest place to seek angels."

"Mm, or maybe you should have searched the heavens."

Zachary lets out a sigh of laughter. "Yes, I imagine you'd be right at home in the sky."

I shake my head. "I wasn't hiding in the sky or the chapel. You shouldn't have bothered to look for me—I wasn't even at the game."

He catches his breath in an audible gasp—his drunk self is more prone to melodrama than his sober self, it would seem. "You cheated?"

"I didn't cheat. I wasn't even there."

"Your friends all told me you were there. They swore it. I looked everywhere. I went all the way up to the lake." His tone is almost rueful.

It's hard not to be amused—or touched—by his disappointment.

"Well," I say, trying to speak in my most bracing tone, "did you at least manage to catch any other girls during your search?"

"No," he replies glumly. "I only cared about catching you."

Even tipsy, his intensity still unfurls from him like veils of heat from a furnace.

"Oh." My heart is beating a little faster than it should, my throat is a little tight. I wonder if I drank more than I realised, if I'm tipsy too and just don't know it. "Why?"

"Because catching anybody else wouldn't feel worth it." He smiles suddenly, a flash of white teeth. "My victories only ever taste like victories when they're won against you, Theodora."

He steps closer, standing inches away, and gazes down at me from the height of his stature, which is outgrowing mine at an alarming rate. His voice is low and thoughtful, his gaze is a dreamy caress as if he's seeing me for the first time.

"Theodora Dorokhova." He speaks my name solemnly, like a vow. His face is inches from mine. Is he going to kiss me? I dread a kiss—I long for one. My heartbeat is the flapping wings of a trapped butterfly. I hold my breath, suspended between hope and terror.

Zachary's words brush against my lips, more intimate than any kiss. "My beautiful nemesis. My formidable adversary. My dearest rival."

Kiss me, I want to tell him. *Kiss me open, Zachary Blackwood, and take all my darkness and cold and pain away.*

He doesn't, and in the end, I'm the one who whirls around in the darkness and runs fearfully away through the trees.

But when I revisit it that night in my dreams, he does kiss me. He kisses me deep and wet and tender and lays me open on the forest floor to fill me with him like Danaë's golden rain, and I wake up in a shock of loneliness, hot wetness between my thighs.

Chapter 13

LEFT HAND

Zachary

IN THE BRIEF SUMMER of freedom between the end of GCSEs and the start of A-levels, I read *Peter Pan*.

It's better than I imagined it would be, but reading it is nevertheless a joyless task. I annotate it obsessively, scrutinising every line for insights into Theodora's mind.

By the time I finish the book, the fore-edge is a dense forest of tabs.

Amongst the forest, the red tabs reign supreme—they are the tabs I used to denote passages regarding James Hook.

In the drunken mist of that evening in the woods—the search for Theodora amongst the trees, the heavy drinking afterwards, egged on by my friends, then glimpsing her gliding fey-like away from the bonfire in a flutter of feathers and skirts—one memory stands out among the rest.

Theodora's pretty smile emerging from the shadows to tell me she had a childhood crush on James Hook.

It was the first time Theodora ever told me something conversational, pointless—personal. Every time I speak with Theodora, it's to debate or argue or discuss. She never just tells me things about herself. I could teach an entire curriculum of Theodora's debating style, her oracy, the words, terms and arguments she favours, the philosophers and historical figures she draws inspiration from.

But if I were to sit down and write a list of facts about her, I wouldn't even get past the basics. I have no idea what month her birthday falls in, what her favourite colour might be, or if she likes animals. She might be a single child, or she might have many siblings—I would never know.

So this unexpected reveal about Hook isn't just a random fact. It's a precious nugget of knowledge, a treasure I never hoped to gain. And now I have one, I want more; I want a treasure chest full of glittering nuggets of information.

I re-read Hook's death scene several times over.

Irrational anger fills me with every quote. Quotes like *"That passionate breast no longer asked for life"* and *"Not wholly unheroic figure"* seem to taunt me. Tragedy and dignity, elegance and despair—this is my impression of the death scene. Is that what appeals to Theodora?

I re-read the chapter, angrily seeking signs of myself in Hook.

Zahara enters the library—which is more of a mixture of a home office and a lounge but gets its nickname because it's furnished floor to ceiling with bookshelves filled to the brim. She's home from Sainte-Agnès, the private girls' school she's attending in France, although she'll only be home for a few days before she goes off to some summer camp.

Every time I see her, she looks less like the little girl of my memories and more like a stranger.

She's taller now, graceful as a dancer, dressed in the preppy style of a private school girl. Her hair is long, well past her shoulders, a nimbus around her head, then looser curls down her back, the black streaked with warm shades of caramel and russet.

"I thought I'd find you here," she declares. "What are you reading now?"

I lift my book to show her the cover. Her eyebrows shoot up. "*Peter Pan*? Didn't think that would be your cup of tea."

"It's not," I tell her, snapping the book shut. "Do you think Hook is an attractive character?"

She smirks. "I suppose—dangerous man, tragic figure... that hook. Every girl loves a villain." She perches herself on the leather-top surface of the enormous desk and frowns down at me as I let my head roll back into the desk chair. "What is this about? Homework?"

"No, not homework. There's this girl in my year—it's her favourite book."

"Oh, Theodora?" Zahara gives me a pointed look and rolls her eyes. "You can just say her name, you know. It's not like you ever talk about anybody else."

"She's the girl who keeps tying with me for top of our classes."

"I know who she is." Zahara's tone is half-exasperated, half-amused. "I don't care what her favourite book is—what I want to know is when you two are finally going to get it on?"

I grimace. "Get it on? They teach you this sort of stuff at your convent?"

She laughs. "Oh no, not at all. There's no chance I'm going to learn anything inappropriate from a bunch of severely sexually frustrated teenage girls, right?"

When I asked my parents why they didn't send Zahara to Spearcrest with me, they told me they have no intention of sending their daughter to a co-ed boarding school where "anything could happen". Their implications were clear, and at the time I'd thought their fears unfounded.

Now, I know for a fact they're not. Everyone in Spearcrest is having sex, and anyone who isn't having sex is doing everything but. I'm the only exception, and I get my share of grief for it.

Grief—and, of course, my unimaginative nickname. Bishop Blackwood.

I sigh. "There is nothing for us to get on, as you put it. Theodora isn't allowed to date, and she seems to be taking that rule very seriously."

Zahara covers her mouth with her hands. "Ew, Zach, don't tell me I'm going to be losing my virginity before you."

I use my copy of *Peter Pan* to whack her forehead. "Virginity is a social construct, Zaro."

She kicks my arm and hops off the desk. "That's not what I've been learning at school."

"Then you need better teachers."

"Maybe." She gives me a sly look. "Is having no girlfriend a social construct, too, then?"

"I don't need a girlfriend," I tell her in my most dignified tone. "I have a beautiful rival instead."

"A beautiful rival—yeah." Zahara cackles. "And a left hand!"

She runs out of the room before I can reply, her laughter echoing behind her.

I would laugh, too, if she wasn't so tragically right.

IT's NOT LIKE I'M not used to this kind of discourse. Sharing my social time with the most popular boys in the year means constantly being surrounded by girls. I used to think Evan—the all-American star athlete—and Séverin—the French aristocrat playboy—would be enough to divert most of those girls' attention, but I learn that there is no accounting for taste.

Some girls prefer the strong and silent appeal of Iakov's monosyllabism and bruised knuckles, and some prefer the dark edge of Luca's borderline-sociopathic tendencies. And so of course, I have my own appeal and my own suitresses.

None of them have any appeal to me, though. At the end of Year 11, in a moment of drunken hubris, Luca and Evan made a bet that we, as a group, were going to sleep with every single girl in the year. It was a stupid idea and probably did more to repel girls than it did to attract them.

Unfortunately, it was also filmed on someone's phone and subsequently widely distributed.

After the summer, when we return for upper school, I half hope the bet is buried and long-forgotten, but I'm quickly disappointed.

Sev, who unwisely proposed to his girlfriend Kayana at the end of Year 11, is now single and mending a broken heart. Evan, still nursing his inexplicable obsession with wanting and hurting his former friend Sophie Sutton, is keen for a distraction. Iakov doesn't date much, but he always comes back from his summers home in a depressive mood and is probably just craving some friendly human contact.

And Luca, I'm beginning to suspect, is just a cold-blooded animal looking for a smaller creature to sadistically toy with.

In short, my friends begin Year 12 with their A-levels being last on their list of priorities.

"I'm going to put a dent in our numbers for the bet," Séverin states on our first day back after we've all gathered in the centre of the sixth form common room. "We only have two years left here and almost one-hundred-and-fifty girls to get through still."

"You're keeping count, are you?" I ask him, making no attempt to disguise the mockery in my voice.

He nods quite seriously. "I still have the list we made on my phone." He swipes open his phone and pulls up his note app, brandishing his screen in my direction. "See?"

"Let me have a look," Evan says, grabbing Sev's phone and peering at it.

Luca takes Sev's phone out of Evan's hand and smirks. "Don't worry, Ev, our little prefect isn't on there."

"What little prefect?" Evan asks, but his jaw is clenched, muscles twitching there.

Luca ignores him, scrolling through the list with a vicious smile on his pale face, his grey eyes sharp as knife blades. "So many names missing from our illustrious list. Are we calling dibs on anyone, gentlemen? Or is every girl game this year?"

Luca has one type: girls his friends want. It's the reason Evan would never in a million years admit he was checking for Sophie's name on the list, the reason why Sev and Iakov both shrug at Luca's question.

"Blackwood?" Luca asks, his playful tone hiding a dangerous edge. "I see Theodora's name is still missing from the list. Are you claiming her?"

"She's not an object or a territory, so no, I'm not claiming her."

"You're right." There's a glib smile on Luca's pale face. "It's not like she'd ever sleep with you anyway."

He's purposely misconstruing the meaning behind my words, but Luca likes nothing more than to provoke others. And I'm not so foolish as to fall for his artless manipulation.

"She's not sleeping with anyone," Iakov replies before I can. "Her father's got a bounty on the head of anyone who touches her."

I look up sharply, meeting Iakov's dark eyes. He's just spent the summer in Russia, where Theodora's father lives. Of course, Russia is a large country—the largest country in the world—but I wonder if the world of the ultra-wealthy is as small there as it is here in England. I want to quiz him on whatever he knows, but not now, not here.

Besides, knowing Iakov, he might just have been joking. It's almost impossible to tell with his deadpan tone and neutral expression.

I drop his gaze and find Séverin looking at me with narrowed eyes. Seizing his phone out of Luca's hand, Sev speaks with sudden authority.

"Theodora's off-bounds."

Luca raises his eyebrows. "Why?"

"If Zachary isn't sleeping with her, none of us are," Sev responds with a shrug. "I'm just being realistic."

"If she's off-bounds," Evan says, slapping me on the arm in a gesture of sportsmanly support, "maybe this year you can set your sights on someone you actually stand a chance of sleeping with."

I shake my hand and shrug his hand away with a grimace. "That's not happening."

Evan blinks—as if he, of all people, should be confused with the concept of having your heart irrevocably set on one person.

"What do you mean?" he asks.

"I'm not setting my sights on anyone. Theodora is the only one worthy of my desire. I couldn't set my sights on anybody else if I tried. She and I are fated somehow. Anything else would be doomed by principle."

My friends all stare at me without speaking as if I just spoke in a language completely foreign to them. Luca finally breaks the silence with a mocking snicker.

"If she's your fated soulmate then why aren't you two together yet?"

I shrug. "We're seventeen. Life is long."

"Fucking hell," Séverin blurts out. "You're already the only virgin left in the group and now you're telling us you're willing to wait until you're an old man because of fate—what the fuck even is fate anyway?"

If I cared at all what they all think of me, I would perhaps bother explaining myself. But when I look at their faces, I find myself overwhelmed with indifference. Sev's and Evan's mouths droop open in child-like confusion, Luca's is twisted in a derisive smirk.

Iakov alone, sitting a little away from us, seems utterly unconcerned.

"It's his dick," he says. "He can do what he likes with it."

His blunt words of wisdom seem to shake Evan and Sev out of their state of stupefaction. Sev sighs and turns back to me.

"And what if you can never have her?"

It's a good question—one I've thought of often, alone at night in my bed, hard and tense with frustration and desire and despair.

"Then life is going to hurt like a bitch."

CHAPTER 14

DEFUNCT PHILOSOPHER

Theodora

AT THE END OF the first academic day of Year 12, I finish my last class and head straight to the library.

Armed with a reading list a mile long for my new subjects, I climb the broad marble steps up to my usual desk nestled in a corner of the top floor. I lay down my things and hang my blazer on the back of my chair, and I almost jump out of my skin when a dark figure bursts from amongst the bookshelves.

"Why on earth are you not taking philosophy this year?"

Zachary looks different. Not just because I've not seen him since the summer and he's now taller, broader, more handsome—but because he's all out of sorts, and Zachary is never anything but calm and composed. His hair is longer and slightly ruffled, and his eyebrows are drawn into a thunderous frown.

"Pardon?" I say, not because I haven't heard him, but because I'm on the back foot and not sure what to say.

"You weren't in my philosophy class earlier, and when I asked Dr Duvigny why, he told me you weren't enrolled in the course."

I sigh and compose myself. Gathering my windswept hair, I smooth it and then twist it into a topknot. It's so long and heavy now it feels like a constant distraction—a distraction I don't need right now.

Zachary's eyes follow my movements, and I wonder if he's as distracted by my hair as I am.

"I didn't enrol in the philosophy class," I answer him. His eyes fall back to mine as soon as I speak. "I'm not sure why this surprises you. I never told you I would enrol."

"You never tell me anything," he says with a dismissive wave of his hand. "But I've spent every Wednesday afternoon for the past—I don't know, five years?—debating ethics and philosophy with you, so forgive me for assuming you might care about this topic."

He seems genuinely upset about this. Zachary never displays strong emotion, but he should. It suits him. He has an air of the Byronic hero about him.

Part of me wants to calm him down, to soothe and pacify him, but another part of me wants to stoke the flames of his emotions, watch them burn bright and gold.

The former wins out.

"I do care about philosophy, of course. But as you know, we can only choose three A-levels. Even if I'd argued for a fourth, it wouldn't have fit into my timetable."

"What made the cut if philosophy didn't?" His tone is cold and imperious, but when he steps closer, I'm enveloped in the heat of his presence.

"If you want to know what A-levels I chose, you could just ask."

"I am asking," he says.

"You're disguising your question," I tell him. "You ambush me with your anger and your demanding tone—" I change my voice, deepening it in a purposely paltry imitation of his voice. "*I command you,*

Theodora, for the sake of the love of philosophy—tell me what A-levels you chose." I go back to my normal voice. "When what you could have done is come to see me and ask me, quite normally and calmly, what A-levels I've chosen."

He watches me for a moment, his expression softening into something thoughtful and inquisitive. From this close, his cologne is rich and intoxicating, a smokey, woody scent that seems mature for someone his age. I hold my breath because smelling his cologne makes this moment feel intimate even though it's not.

And the last thing I need in my life is to think about intimacy with Zachary Blackwood.

"What are you going to do now we no longer have debate club?" he asks in a gentle, ponderous voice. He tilts his head. "All that carefully contained belligerence, Theodora. What are you going to do with it now you no longer have a formal outlet?"

The library is quiet at this time of day, especially this floor. The silence is thick and satiny, and the heavy sunlight of early autumn afternoon droops from the cupola and lies like a blanket over us. Zachary's hair and skin and eyes catch that luxuriant sunlight and he glows like a young god.

I answer in a clipped tone. "Luckily for me, we still have literature class together. I'll still get to prove you wrong all the time."

He laughs and shakes his head. "No, no, it's not the proving me wrong you like, Theodora. It's what comes before that—the weighing me up, the scratching at me with the tips of your barbed words, the seeking of weak points for you to pierce. That's the part you like—that's the outlet."

"Congratulations," I reply. "You're the first person to discover that the best part of a debate is the debate itself."

He steps forward again, but I retreat once more, and this time, the corner of the desk comes between us to stop his approach. Unfazed by it, Zachary rests his elbow on the corner of the polished wood partition that keeps the desk shielded from distractions.

"I'm not talking about debating," he says, never dropping my gaze. "I'm talking about you and I and that need we have to wage war." His lips curl into a sardonic half-smile. "If you cared about debating, you'd be in my philosophy class with me."

I sigh and look away, busying myself pulling my things out of my bag and finding my reading list.

"I couldn't take philosophy even if I wanted to, Zachary." I glance up at him, seeking the hurt that brought him here in his eyes. "I'm sorry. You are right, I do love waging war with you, and I do love philosophy. I would have loved to be in the class with you. I just didn't have a choice."

He nods and slowly bites down on his lip, dragging the pillowy flesh with his teeth. My honesty works on him like a soothing balm. The tension melts from his shoulders, and he sighs. "What did you take instead, then?"

"I'm taking English lit, history and Russian."

"Oh. I thought you already spoke Russian."

"I speak some. I need to be fluent—I should be fluent. That's why my father—" I interrupt myself. "That's why I need to take Russian this year."

"Ah, I see." His tone is calmer now, almost gentle. "Want me to ask Iakov to help you?"

"Iakov Kavinski?" I ask. "He knows about as much Russian as I do—we were in the same class last year."

Zachary, for the first time, looks genuinely surprised. "What? I thought Russian was his first language."

I shake my head. "No, it's Ukrainian."

"I didn't even know he'd been there."

"He grew up there." I lean towards Zachary slightly. "Aren't you two best friends? Shouldn't you know this?"

He sighs and drops his head onto his arm, which is still resting against the wooden partition on the desk. "Yes, I should. Iakov isn't very chatty, though. He keeps his cards close to his chest." He raises his head and gives me an accusatory glance. "Just like you."

"Cards, Zachary?" I give him a small smile. "You know I prefer chess."

"Chess pieces don't keep secrets—they have no mystery. You always know where they can go and where they'll end up." He smirks. "If only it was that easy with you."

"Don't be so dramatic." I wave a hand at him. "You found me here, didn't you?"

"Yes, I found you here, where I hoped to confront you and get you to change your mind and study philosophy with me. And yet here you are, being a wild card, and telling me you'll be studying Russian instead—a subject in which you know perfectly well I'm incapable of competing with you."

His tone is playful, so I keep mine playful too.

"Why do you need me there anyway? Can't you study philosophy alone—without competition? Or are you scared you'll become lazy and complacent if I'm not there?"

"Every sword needs a whetstone," he says.

I narrow my eyes. "And in this lovely little metaphor, the sword is…?"

He has the audacity to smile. "My intellect, of course. And yours is the whetstone I've been using to sharpen it."

"Is that so?" I sneer. "And what if you're wrong, Zachary? What if my intellect is also a sword, and all you've been doing these past few years is dulling your blade against mine?"

He tilts his head and gives me a slow, enticing smile.

"I suppose we'll find out at the end of the year."

"Not this time."

He raises a questioning eyebrow.

"This is the first year of A-levels—no formal examinations," I tell him. "That means no results list. For the first time, we won't have to see our names next to each other's at the top of the boards."

The lazy gold of the slow-setting sun glitters in Zachary's eyes, which are smiling even when his mouth isn't.

"What a shame," he murmurs. "It was a bittersweet sight, but I've always thought our names look good next to each other's."

Chapter 15

PERFECT PARALLELS

Theodora

Starting Year 12, I was both relieved and devastated to find I was only sharing a single class with Zachary.

Relieved because Zachary's presence is a distraction—a complication—which becomes harder to ignore with each passing year. Devastated because I would miss our conversations, our debates, and, yes, our rivalry. Mostly, though, I would miss him.

Zachary is unlike anybody else at Spearcrest—unlike anybody else I've ever met. And being around him is like being in the presence of some sort of ineffable being. Being around him gives me the same breath-catching sense of consecration one might get from entering a magnificent cathedral or an ancient shrine.

As it turns out, I never need have worried at all.

Now that we are in the upper school, students have a lot more freedom, especially those of us with powerful parents. My friend group is the female equivalent of Zachary's group—the hyperbolically titled Young Kings—and so instead of barely seeing each other, we end up seeing each other all the time.

Parties are a strange social obligation. They come with the crushing pressure of needing to look beautiful and having to socialise even when I'm not in the mood.

But now I know my own limits better, I can drink a little more, and alcohol gives me the fuel I need to make it through the long evenings in crowded places and dimly lit clubs. Alcohol gives me a reprieve from the pressure, the crushing loneliness, the numbness that makes me feel cold from the inside out.

Alcohol also allows the wall between Zachary and me to blur and transform, becoming glass-like—invisible but impenetrable. During those parties, with the burn of alcohol searing away our inhibitions, we meet each other carefully in the middle of the neutral no-man's-land.

"How are you getting on with the metaphysical poetry essay?" Zachary launches in one night at the Cyprian.

I'm sitting in one of the booths, nursing a glass of wine and waiting for my head to stop spinning after dancing a little too hard with a perfectly wasted Kayana.

I look up at the sound of Zachary's voice, which has become deeper and more melodic over time. He slides into the booth and sits down facing me, half collapsing into the dark leather of the curved seat.

He's more than a little tipsy: his eyes have a glaze like sugar, his eyelids droop heavily, and his mouth stretches in a frank, open smile, displaying those dazzling white teeth. In a room full of men in expensive clothes, he still manages to appear over-dressed, but the top three buttons of his shirt are undone, and his neck and collarbones gleam with sweat.

I take a sip of my wine and drag my gaze back up to his face.

"I've not started yet," I answer.

His eyes brighten.

"Oh? Struggling with it? The great Theodora Dorokhova, the patron saint of perfect grades, stumped?"

I am, but I could never admit it. It would only disappoint him if I did. "Never. I've just been putting it off."

"How come? You're the"—he waves his arm in a sweeping flourish—"*mistress of poetry*, are you not?"

I purse my mouth to hide a smile. "I'm not the mistress of poetry. More like poetry's secret admirer. I just lurk and admire it from afar. But metaphysical poetry just isn't setting my heart racing like I thought it would."

"I didn't know there was *anything* capable of setting your heart racing," Zachary says, a wicked edge to his widening grin. "I thought your heart was a thing of marble, not of flesh and blood."

This is Zachary's way of drawing me out into unknown, dangerous territory. I ignore it and veer safely away.

"Thank you, Zachary." I lift my glass and tip it towards him. "You always know how to compliment me."

He laughs. "You're exceedingly easy to compliment."

"Is that so?" I can't help but be tempted. "What makes me so easy to compliment, then?"

"Where to begin?" He speaks in a ponderous tone, his gaze bold and unashamed. "Your dazzling intelligence, of course. Your brilliant use of rhetorical devices in debates. Your exquisite beauty and the tantalising way your body looks in that green dress."

I tilt my head and give him a look of warning. "Your flirting is in excellent form tonight. You shouldn't waste it on me."

I'm giving him an easy way out: all he needs to do now is deny he was flirting with me.

But Zachary doesn't take the easy way out.

He never does.

"It's not wasted at all," he says instead, with that easy Blackwood confidence. "I could spend a fortune of flirtation on you, Theodora, and it would still not be a waste. I could lay treasures of compliments and tenderness at your feet like offerings to a cruel goddess, and you could ignore them all, and I would never once regret any of it."

He's definitely drunk—drunk and in a rather sensuous mood. There's a glowering desire inside him that he's not even bothering to hide.

It's hard not to be tempted by the heat of him, especially when I feel so cold.

If only I was free to do so.

I shake my head and fix him with a prim look as I stir the conversation back to safer ground. "You are a natural poet, Zachary. Maybe that's why you're enjoying all that metaphysical poetry and I'm not."

He leans forward, drawn in. "Why are you not enjoying it? What is it you dislike about it?"

"It's a little... overwrought. Laboured."

"And your soft boy Keats? Is his poetry not overwrought and laboured?"

"But his poetry comes from a place of genuine emotion and beliefs," I explain. "Overwrought or not, it rings true. And it's beautiful."

"If his poetry comes from a place of truth, then metaphysical poetry seeks the truth. Is that not beautiful in its own way?"

I finally allow myself to smile. "I didn't realise you were such a fan. You don't normally like poetry. Am I to assume your own essay is written and of the highest quality imaginable? Are you about to finally gain the upper hand on the battlefield of our literature class?"

Zachary leans forward, lacing his fingers together with adorable formality. He answers with perfect sincerity.

"I've actually not started either." He holds my gaze. "I'll be working on it tomorrow in the library. Join me, if you like."

"I don't need your help."

He nods. "Good—I wasn't offering it. I'm just being tactical. Keeping my enemies close and my rivals closest."

I laugh. "Don't you mean closer?"

"No, that's not what I mean." Reaching across the table, he takes my fingers in his and lifts my hand to brush a light kiss over my knuckles. "I know exactly where I ought to keep you."

Taking my hand back, I cast him another warning look. "Tread carefully, Blackwood."

"I always do, Dorokhova." He stands and gestures to the dance floor. "Dance with me?"

Reason tells me to say no.

Desire begs me to say yes.

I do my best to compromise.

"One song only."

"Perfect," he says and leads me to the dance floor.

We dance the next three songs together. I let him wrap his arm around my waist, and I let my head rest against his shoulder. The mingled scent of his cologne and sweat are a heady perfume, and my body feels hot all over against his.

Kiss me, I want to whisper in his ear. *Kiss me, Zachary Blackwood, and hold me tight and never let me go. Please.*

He doesn't kiss me, but I'm sure I feel his lips brush the top of my head one time. After the third song, I pull away from him, but he catches my hand, stopping me. I meet his gaze. His eyes are a dark glitter, a sensuous promise. I pull away with a breathless laugh, and he follows me off the dancefloor.

I send him to get me a cup of ice to press against my flushed throat, and after that, we spend the rest of the night arguing about everything and anything.

It's the only way to relieve the unbearable tension.

And it's barely a relief at all.

THE NEXT EVENING, WE sit side by side in the library, the green banker's lamp lit between us, our books and laptops open in front of us. We take turns reading stanzas from Andrew Marvell's "The Definition of Love", swapping annotations as we go.

When we finish, we swap poems to compare annotations. My poem is a spectrum of colour-coded pastel lines of highlighter, the annotations matching each colour; Zachary's poem is underlined and annotated with the same smooth black ink, every inch of the page covered with his fine, spidery handwriting. I'm taking notes of some of his observations on Post-its to add to mine when Zachary reads a line out loud.

"*As lines, so loves oblique may well themselves in every angle greet; but ours so truly parallel, though infinite, can never meet.*" His tone is low and ponderous. "That's just like us."

I stare at him. His chin rests in the palm of his hand; his eyes are still fixed on the page.

"How is it like us?" I ask.

He looks up and gestures elegantly towards the page as if I don't know he's talking about the poem. "Two perfect parallels that can never meet—that's us."

There's a sudden lump in my throat I struggle to swallow back. "He's talking about love."

"Obviously." Zach raises his eyebrow, a dark, amused arch. "Don't look so surprised. You're quite intelligent, and for all your angelic features and forget-me-not eyes, you're not naive either. You know perfectly well that I love you."

It's a Saturday afternoon in the middle of the school year. Outside, cold rain drizzles from the ashen sky. In the corners of the library, other students sit alone or in pairs, stooped over their books and laptops. The library is silent but for the white noise of raindrops hitting the glass cupola far above our heads.

It's an entirely ordinary day—or rather, it was an entirely ordinary day.

Now, it's anything but ordinary.

Now, tension swirls around us in a great glimmering whirlpool with us at the centre. Zachary, with his brown eyes and black curls and the silk sheen of his skin and the assured curl of his smile, which seems to exist only for me.

Only Zachary Blackwood could have uttered something so outrageously reckless with such serenity. Like an archer certain of his aim, he drew his bow strong and shot his arrow straight into my chest and watched it take my breath away with the most tender of smiles.

I look into his eyes and speak in a breathless murmur. "You don't love me."

His eyes soften in a way that's almost unbearable to watch. He sighs, his entire body melting with a longing so tangible it wraps around me like the folding of warm wings. He pierces me with the softness of his gaze, with the naked desire in his expression.

"Ah, of course I do. I love you atrociously." He smiles, the hue of desire in his expression shifting, darkening into a sort of yearning melancholy. "I love you with every atom of my being, and I love every atom of yours. I love you desperately, like a starving man. I love you to distraction. And I think maybe you love me too, Theodora Dorokhova. You just aren't quite ready to say it yet."

APOSTLES

Chapter 16

PORCELAIN DOLL

Theodora

My voice is locked inside my chest. After all these years, my father still holds the key. All I want is to get that key back.

The summer before my final year at Spearcrest, my father comes to stay at my mother's ancestral home, Breckenridge House in Surrey.

The stately home, normally so cavernous and hollow, becomes claustrophobic in his presence, which looms like an eclipse, filling the atmosphere of the house with a heavy, eerie silence.

We all feel the weight of his presence. The staff, who make themselves sparse as best they can, my mother, who drinks a little more wine than she normally would, and me, with the marble egg lodged inside my throat making it difficult to breathe and talk.

Just like he always did when I was a child, my father brings gifts with him when he arrives. Designer dresses in beautiful boxes, a watch encrusted with diamonds, jewellery in velvet caskets. I open each present under his watchful eyes, and my throat tightens when he commands me to try each one on.

I obey him, putting on the jewellery and the watch, leaving the room to change into one of the dresses. When I return in an ethereal

Valentin Yudashkin gown, the glittering skirts heavy around my legs, my father rakes me with a measuring look.

His eyes have the calculating aloofness of a businessman inspecting merchandise.

"You are very thin," he comments. "Does your school not feed you well?"

My entire being recoils at his words like a slug doused in salt, curled up and seething and agonised. I shake my head and try to speak.

"The food is good, Papa." My voice is a pathetic squeak.

"If the food was good, you'd be eating it," my father says, waving a hand. "And you wouldn't be looking so awful. A skeleton with skin."

I don't look like a skeleton with skin, I want to shout at him. *I look like all the other beautiful girls in my school. I look like the models and influencers society adores. I look exactly the way you and mother wanted me to look, and I've worked hard to look this way, I've made countless sacrifices.*

Of course, I can say none of this.

My father, so sure of himself, continues.

"I will speak to Ambrose—that headmaster of yours. He will see to it that something is done about the food."

"Please," I breathe. "Don't, Papa."

He frowns at me. "I'm not sending my daughter to one of the best schools in the world for her to be starved."

"I'll eat," I say. I don't even know if I can because, by now, my relationship with food is so comfortably dysfunctional that I wouldn't even know how to start mending it. But I'm desperate, and I make the promise out of desperation. "I'll eat, Papa. I swear."

He glares at me, then gives a curt nod. "Make sure you do. When you move to Russia next year, I won't have it said that my daughter looks weak and sickly."

A black panic blinds me for a second.

My heart becomes a dark void in my chest, and my skin crawls and puckers.

I give my father a look of pure incomprehension. He flicks his hand in a gesture of impatience.

"I've already spoken about it with your mother. Once your education is completed, you'll be moving to St Petersburg."

My education is far from complete, I want to tell him. *My education is only just beginning.*

But how can I say this when I can barely string a sentence together in his presence? How can I tell him about my dreams of going to Oxford, of completing a degree, then a master's, then starting a PhD? How can I explain to him that I've barely scratched the surface of everything I have to learn, that I want to spend my life in the pursuit of knowledge, that I want to read and write and absorb and create?

He wouldn't understand. He still sees me as the scared little girl he always sees when he looks at me.

The scared little girl I still am, deep inside.

My education, my skills, my growing confidence—my wealth of top marks and won debates—they fade to nothing when I'm around him. Everything I am shrivels and withers under his gaze, leaving nothing but a mumbling, pathetic creature.

It takes me every atom of courage I can scrape together to squeeze my voice out.

"I want to go to univer—"

He doesn't even let me finish the sentence.

"You don't need to. You'll never have to work a day in your life, Theodora, and you will serve a far more important purpose. You are educated, young and obedient—you will make a desirable bride, and right now, that makes you my most powerful asset."

A wave of nausea knocks through me. "I don't—"

He raises a hand. "I'm not a monster, Theodora. You don't have to marry straight away, and I won't force you to marry someone you despise. I will try to keep your happiness in mind—but you *will* marry. You must."

He speaks without cruelty and without empathy.

That, right here, is the true core of my painful, complicated feelings for my father.

My father doesn't hurt because of all the times he's grasped me or struck me in anger, but because he's never once held me or comforted me. I'm not hurt by his insults and orders and demands, but because he has never once told me he loved me or shown me he cared for me. His cruelty has never been as painful as his utter lack of kindness.

And so the fear I feel when I'm around him isn't the urgent, red fear of danger, it's not the flinching fear of an abused child.

My fear of him is kenophobia—the heart-pounding, choking fear of emptiness, of the void where something ought to exist.

The gaping nothingness exuding from my father seeps into my skin, is absorbed like a disease until it's filling every part of me, until I become that void. I stand in front of my father in the gifted gown, and the abyss inside of me yawns wide, swallowing everything inside of it until I become a listless, hollow doll.

My spirit, my hopes, my dreams. Everything is devoured, reduced to nothing.

My father watches it happen.

He must be able to see the emptiness in my eyes, the limpness in my body. He must understand what's happening to me because, for the first time in a long time, he gives me the rarest of all his gifts.

A smile of approval.

I spend the rest of the summer holiday in a sort of numb state of dissociation.

It's not depression or despair. It's not even sadness. It's less than all those things.

It's less than not feeling anything.

Like barely existing at all.

I walk through my mother's house, sit at the dinner table next to my father, attend my parents' social gatherings and dinner parties. I wear the beautiful clothing and jewellery. I eat when my father tells me to, forcing food inside myself, swallowing through the nausea. I dance with the young men my father introduces me to. My face shapes itself into the polite smile required of it. My mouth forms courteous, empty sentences.

And my soul—my mind—my consciousness, whatever it's made of—floats somewhere above, watching thoughtfully. My body is a chess piece gliding across a chessboard, but I'm not the player.

That summer, I don't read at all.

I don't touch a single school book, not a volume of poetry, I don't even re-read old favourites. My hands don't so much as brush longingly over a book cover. My notebooks and laptop remain untouched. I don't write a single word.

I become the Theodora my father always wanted. The obedient doll.

I'm surprised to find there's a sort of dull relief to be found in not quite existing.

When he finally leaves near the end of summer, the habitual rush of relief doesn't spread through me to warm my cold limbs. I watch his car pull away down the long drive to the gate and feel nothing at all.

That night, I sit at the dinner table and push my food around my plate, staring at nothing. I sleep dreamlessly and wake up already tired.

The following day, I pack my things in preparation for my return to Spearcrest. My final year of school. My final year of freedom. My final year battling it out with Zachary Blackwood.

I should be excited, nervous, elated, scared—but I'm not any of those things. The thought of Spearcrest leaves me untouched. The thought of Zachary doesn't even feel real. A dream. Less.

A shadow of a dream.

Did I imagine him?

Maybe.

I return to Spearcrest under the shadow of a great hourglass. My father's hand turned the hourglass, and the sand has already begun to pour and gather. It'll be pouring down with all my hopes and dreams until there are none left and I'm suffocating in sand.

If only there was somebody to save me.

But why would there be? I can't even save myself.

Chapter 17

BLACKWOOD TRIPTYCH

Zachary

THE SUMMER BEFORE MY final year at Spearcrest is a long series of unexpected events.

The first of those occurs on my first day back at home: my father summons me into his office as soon as I arrive. The solemn look on his face is disconcerting. As far as I'm concerned, I haven't done anything to draw his displeasure.

He asks me to sit down and then announces in the glummest of tones, "Your sister will be starting at Spearcrest Academy in the fall."

"Pardon?"

It was the last thing I expected him to say.

"She'll be starting in the upper school a year ahead of schedule."

"How can she possibly do that?" I'm honestly so stunned I can barely organise my thoughts. "She can't skip Year 11, she has her GCSEs to—"

"She sat them this summer with the Year 11 students at her school."

I stare at him.

Zaro and I haven't seen one another since last Christmas holidays. She was only home for a week, and she was a little more quiet than usual, but she never mentioned sitting her exams early. I think about our texts—I check in on her more or less every week—but again, she never made any mention of early exams, skipping a year, or coming to Spearcrest.

"I've had the transfer arranged, and I've already spoken to Mr Ambrose. She'll be starting in the upper school, and the reason for that is that I want you to keep an eye on her." My father sits back in his chair, flicking off his glasses and fixing me with a direct, insistent look. "I'm not asking you this lightly, and I'm not asking you to do this casually. I mean it. I want you to keep a close eye on her, do you understand?"

The implications of his words leave a distasteful flavour in my mouth. I narrow my eyes. "You want me to *spy* on her?"

His eyebrows lower into a glare. "Don't be so melodramatic. I want you to keep an eye on your sister and make sure she stays out of trouble. I need you to swear to me you will."

By this point, it's clear something's happened. But if my father thinks he can get me to swear to spy on my own sister without sharing whatever information he's withholding, he's gravely mistaken.

Settling myself into one of the seats facing his desk, I prop my elbows on the armrests and sit back, watching him closely.

"What happened?" My voice is firm; this isn't a question I'll allow him to ignore.

My father watches me for a moment, his mouth pinched in annoyance. He's always resented the shifting dynamics between us. If he could, he would continue to treat me as his inferior, but I'm not. The fault lies at his feet—he didn't raise me to be his inferior.

He lets out a loud sigh. "Look. Your sister was caught having an inappropriate relationship. I won't be telling you anything more, so don't bother asking. She won't be returning to Sainte-Agnès; that's all you need to know."

My stomach churns. An inappropriate relationship could mean anything according to my father. Zaro could be dating the most well-mannered boy, and if my father so much as suspected they'd done more than hold hands, he would probably deem it inappropriate.

For all the Blackwood family prides itself on being a "modern" aristocratic family, my father's views are positively Victorian when it comes to his daughter.

What's making my stomach churn with unease is that she's not returning to Sainte-Agnès. Leaving her school, skipping a year and transferring to Spearcrest—where my father has thus far been refusing to send her—would surely be an overreaction, even by his standards.

"Now give me your word," he snaps. "I won't ask you to spy on her—you don't even need to report back to me. I just want you to keep an eye on her and make sure she stays out of trouble. No wild parties, no... *inappropriate* behaviour. Nothing compromising."

This is going to be my final year at Spearcrest—my time to prepare for my exams, to work on my university applications, and my final year to best Theodora. I have a thousand things to do without adding to that the responsibility of looking after Zaro.

But she's my sister.

And Blackwoods always put family first.

"Very well." I stand. "I'll see to it."

"Make sure that you do." My father doesn't speak again until I reach the door. "And Zachary?" I turn back with a frown. "I want you to take this responsibility as seriously as any of your other responsibilities. If I have to find out through one of my contacts—or God forbid, via social media or the tabloids—that your sister has been getting into any sort of compromising situation or trouble—there'll be hell to pay. For both of you."

I nod. "Nothing's going to happen to her. I give you my word."

Zaro returns home the week after I do, preceded by a mountain of Louis Vuitton luggage.

She is summoned to my father's office, where she spends the afternoon. Dinner that night is a tense affair. I make some attempts at lightening the atmosphere, but my parents remain taciturn, and Zaro is doing everything in her power to avoid eye contact with me.

Later, when I'm certain my parents have gone to bed, I go to her room. She ignores my knocks, forcing me to sneak through the guest bedroom adjacent to hers and climb across the adjoining balconies.

But when I reach the guest room balcony, I stop. Wrapped in a silk robe, Zaro is standing on her balcony, arms on the balustrade and hair floating in the wind like a modern Juliet.

Juliet with long curls and a bottle of whisky in her hand.

"Really? You're drinking now?"

She turns her head sharply at the sound of my voice and immediately relaxes with a roll of her eyes.

"Ugh, Zach, I'm not in the mood. There's a reason I didn't answer your knocks. Can't you take a hint?"

I ignore her and climb over the railing that separates the two balconies. I stand next to her and take the bottle out of her hands. She glares at me but lets me take it. I glance down at the label and lift an eyebrow.

"*Whisky?* Really?"

She shrugs. "Men love girls who drink like men."

"Since when do you care what men love?"

With a roll of her eyes, she snatches the bottle back from me.

She's changed—not just from when she was a child, but since the last time I saw her. She's only fifteen, but she has the confidence and attitude of someone older. She reminds me of the scintillating party girls of Spearcrest, Kayana Kilburn, Seraphina Rosenthal, Camille Alawi—the way they carry themselves with that mixture of supreme confidence and desperate need.

Like the world belongs to them, but also like they belong to the world.

"I know Dad told you I'm transferring to Spearcrest," she snaps. "And you're obviously here to ask me what happened, so ask already."

"What happened?"

"I was dating a teacher. The school found out. That's all."

My eyes widen at her words, my mouth dropping open, but she continues in a sour tone. "Please don't bother. He lost his job, and I was forced to transfer schools, and now I get to spend the next year away from friends and being spied on. We've both been punished, so spare me the telling-off."

"I'm not our father," I tell her. "It's not my job to tell you off."

"Hah, right." She takes a swig of her bottle and hands it to me. I despise whisky, but I drink anyway. I hand her the bottle back, and she takes it slowly, glancing up at me. "Are you... disgusted with me?"

I shake my head. "No, not disgusted. I suppose I'm... disappointed."

I realise how it sounds as soon as I say it. Zaro's entire body grows stiff, but instead of the angry tirade I expect, she bursts out into icy laughter.

"*Of course* you're disappointed!" She throws her head back in a hollow cackle. "Just like Dad—just like always. You know what I loved about Jerome?" She's not laughing now. Her tone is hard and hurt. "He never made me feel like I was a disappointment."

I swallow. I want to say something comforting, but I can't help but say the truth instead. "That's because he was *grooming* you, Zaro."

She watches me for a long moment. When she finally replies, her voice is low and soft and sad.

"Want to know a little secret, Zach? I'm not some naive teenager. I know exactly what it was. I knew about the age gap between us—and, before you say anything, the power imbalance. I knew exactly what he was doing—but I also knew exactly what *I* was doing. And do you want to know the sad, ugly, pathetic truth? Grooming or not, Jerome is the first person who ever made me feel like I was enough." She pushes off the balcony and throws me a cold look. "So if you're going to judge me, go ahead. But judge me for the right reasons."

And then she walks away from me, slamming her window shut and shoving her curtains closed.

The final tableau in my triptych of summer misfortune comes several nights later, over dinner.

My parents, who are still icing Zaro out with a sort of courteous silent treatment, are recollecting their days in Cambridge, where they met.

My father is just finishing an anecdote when he laughs and says to me, "That's old Professor Wyle for you. I should get in touch with him—ask him to keep an eye on you and make sure you have a great supervisor. You know how it is—politics is all about who you know."

He says all this so casually I barely register it at first. When his words finally sink in, I pause with my fork inches from my mouth.

"I'm not going into politics."

My father laughs and waves a hand, the thick gold crest on his ring catching the light. "Of course you are. You're a Blackwood."

"Be that as it may, but I'm still not going into politics."

My father stiffens in his seat, and my mother's posture, too, becomes almost imperceptibly more rigid.

"Our position in society—our name—doesn't just come with privileges, Zachary," he says in a lofty tone. "It comes with responsibilities, too."

"I know that." I hold his gaze. "I have every intention of serving society. But I'll do it in my own way."

"Where could you serve our country better than in politics?" my father asks in a withering tone.

My mother lifts a hand and lays it on his forearm. She doesn't need to say a word for him to bite down and breathe in, nostrils flaring, as he pulls on the reins of his anger.

"You're doing a great disservice to many sectors by implying politicians serve this country best," I tell my father in a cool tone. "Sectors such as, oh, I don't know—medicine and healthcare? The justice system? Academia and education?"

"You think a *schoolteacher* has as much impact as a minister?" My father's voice quivers with cruel amusement.

I shrug. "In certain ways—more."

He opens his mouth, but my mother finally speaks up.

"Caleb, please." She doesn't look at my father when she says his name but smiles at me, a gentle smile that doesn't quite reach her eyes. "Zachary is free to choose his own future, of course." She squeezes my father's arm and tosses me a look. "All we ask, Zachary, is that you make your choices carefully."

"I always do," I assure her.

Her eyes widen slightly—the same fawn brown as Zaro's, framed by the same curly black lashes that give them both that doe-eyed look of innocence. She's unhappy with me, that much is easy to tell, but she's a politician through and through.

"Excellent," she says. "That's all we can ask." Then, with an airy laugh, she releases my father's arm and picks up her wineglass. "Besides, it's so early in the year. You still have plenty of time to decide."

I want to tell her I've already decided—that I've known all along—what I want to study when I leave Spearcrest. But I suppose I have some politician in me, too, because I answer her insincere smile with one of my own.

"Exactly."

Chapter 18

Spearcrest Wolf

Zachary

On the way back to Spearcrest, I brief Zaro thoroughly on everything she needs to know, from how to get around campus to the kind of expectations teachers have. I give her a thorough breakdown of the social hierarchy of the school, both the staff and students, and I tell her which students she should befriend and which she should stay away from.

I answer all her questions with complete honesty, even the ones that force me to paint my friends and myself in a negative light.

When she's finally out of questions, I take her hand and squeeze it in mine.

"I'm going to ask one thing of you, and that's it. One thing."

She sighs but nods. "What is it?"

"I want you to use our mother's maiden name while you're at Spearcrest. I'll speak to Mr Ambrose myself about it if you let me."

"You don't want everyone to know I'm your sister?" she asks.

"I don't want everyone to know I'm your brother," I correct.

"That means the same thing."

"Almost. Trust me, Zaro, please. Whatever you've done, whatever you do—I've told you before, I'm not our father. The only thing I care about is that you're safe and happy. You don't want people to know I'm your brother. Spearcrest is just like the real world, there'll be people there you can't trust. People that might wish to use you as a way to get to me or my friends, or worse, people that might wish to use you *against* us. I want you to have a blank slate when you get there—and trust me when I say people will be scouring the internet for any information they find about you. You don't want them to have anything over you. I'll be there for you regardless. But trust me on this, alright?"

She stares at me, and for the first time, I see a flicker of worry in her eyes. Her glossy sheen of confidence wavers and she swallows nervously.

"Alright," she says. "Alright. I'll do as you say."

I SPEND THE FIRST day back at Spearcrest, making sure Zaro's arrival goes as smoothly as possible. I visit Mr Ambrose and ask him to have Zaro's surname changed to our mother's maiden name—Auvray—on the school registers. When he asks me for my reasons, I give him nothing but the truth.

After everything is settled, I return to the sixth form boys' building. Instead of going to my room to unpack my things, I head straight for Iakov's room, knocking sharply on his door.

Silence answers me at first, but I wait patiently. Eventually, a grunt resounds from the other side of the door.

"Come in."

I enter the room and close the door behind me. Even though it's almost eleven in the morning, the curtains are still shut. An enormous body forms a mountain underneath the blankets.

The mountain shifts. A corner of the blanket is pulled down to reveal dark almond-shaped eyes blinking slowly.

"What," Iakov says, the inflection of his voice indicating an accusation rather than a question.

I fling his curtains open, flooding the room with daylight. A scene of chaos is illuminated: a black duffel bag slumped into the desk chair, a crumpled school uniform hanging on the wardrobe door, two empty beer bottles glistening next to the bed, a pile of cracked boxing gloves shoved into a corner.

"Get up," I say, yanking Iakov's blanket off him. "It's nearly eleven, for god's sake."

Iakov throws an arm across his face and then says his favourite word. "Fuck."

"Had a good holiday with Papa Kavinski, huh?" I ask.

"Don't call him that," Iakov grunts.

He rears up to sit at the edge of his bed. Grabbing a bottle of water from the floor, he drinks in long, loud gulps. He's wearing black boxers and nothing else. Stark daylight falls over him to reveal a map of bruises and cuts over his back, his ribs, his arms and legs. Some of them are old and fading, with yellow edges, while others are mottled, raised and red, betraying more recent injuries.

I resist the urge to avert my eyes. Sometimes, looking at Iakov is physically painful.

Iakov doesn't seem ashamed of the way he looks, and he has this way of never explaining his injuries which makes it impossible to question him about them. His bruises are like his tattoos, black boots and buzz cut: unapologetically a part of him.

Iakov downs the water and tosses the bottle onto his blanket. He stands with a groan and stretches, his bones cracking as he twists his torso around. He shoves open his en-suite bathroom door, stands in front of his toilet and unceremoniously starts pissing.

"What do you want, then?" he asks over his shoulder.

"I'm not having a conversation with you while you're urinating." With a grimace, I shove the duffel bag off his desk chair and take a seat. From the bathroom, I hear the sound of the toilet flushing then the water running. Iakov comes back out with his face and hair dripping with water, his toothbrush in his mouth.

"Go on, then," he says, leaning one shoulder against the wall and brushing his teeth with unnecessary aggression.

"I have a favour I need to ask you," I tell him.

"Yea?" He lets out a low, growling laugh. "It'll cost you."

"A favour for a favour—I know." I link my fingers together and lean back into the desk chair. "This one's a big one."

Iakov nods, then disappears back into the bathroom, where I hear him spit and rinse his mouth out. He returns and crouches by his duffel bag, rifling through it.

"Big favour, huh?" he asks without looking at me.

"Yes."

He looks up. "Need me to kill someone?"

It's impossible to tell whether he's being serious or not. His tone is solemn, but then Iakov is always solemn, even when he's being sarcastic. Equally, Iakov strikes me as the kind of person who is fully capable of taking a human life—I wouldn't even be surprised to find out he already has.

That's the reason I'm here, after all.

"No, I don't need you to kill anyone. I need to give you some information before I tell you the favour, but you have to swear you won't tell a soul." I raise an eyebrow. "I mean that, Iakov. Not a soul."

He nods. Grabbing a zipped black case out of his duffel bag, he tosses it on the bed and then sits down. Leaning forward, he props his elbows on his knees and looks directly at me.

"Right." His voice is low and solemn. His black eyes are fixed on mine. "I swear." He jabs his chin out. "Tell me."

There's only one person in Spearcrest whose word I could trust completely. That person is Iakov. I've never known him to betray a secret or break a promise. Iakov's head is Fort Knocks. Nothing ever leaves that dark place he has for a mind.

"I have a little sister—Zahara. She's sixteen. She used to go to a private school in France, but something... bad happened there and she had to leave."

"Right," Iakov says.

No expression crosses his face. If he has any questions about what happened to Zaro, he keeps them to himself. I suspect he has none—I've never known Iakov to be shocked by anything.

"Long story short—she's starting at Spearcrest in the fall. She'll be in the upper school like us. Her name on file is our mother's, so nobody's going to know she's my sister, apart from Mr Ambrose. I don't want anybody to know."

"But you're telling me," Iakov says. "Why?"

I swallow. "That's where the favour comes in."

"Mm." He reaches for his bedside and grabs a box of cigarettes. Taking a cigarette out, he taps it against the box, rolling it between his fingers. He's not allowed to smoke indoors, but Iakov always plays with cigarettes when he's thinking or concentrating or worried. It's a little tic that easily gives him away. "Alright. Spit it out."

"I need you to look after her." I'm more nervous than I thought I would be, asking him this. "Zaro is... Zaro's changed these past few years. I always assumed she was going to be alright. Foolishly so. I don't think she's alright at all. She's incredibly bright, and she's sharp—she'll draw blood if she can—but that makes me forget how young she is. And I want to look after her, but I'm going to be busy, and I don't want her to slip between the cracks just because I'm concentrating on other things. She's too important for me to leave what happens to her up to chance."

Iakov's eyes rest on my face, dark and neutral. He thinks his thoughts the way he always does, without feeling any need to express what he's thinking and without filler words to bide his time.

When he's ready to speak, he does. And when he does, he takes me completely by surprise.

"I had a little sister too," he says. "I know what you mean. I'll do it."

I didn't know Iakov had a little sister. I notice that he said it in the past tense—he "had" a sister. Iakov's sentences are often monosyllabic, but his grasp of English is perfect. This won't have been a mistake.

I give him time to elaborate but he doesn't. Instead, he grabs the black case from his bed and unzips it, laying out its contents next to him. Saline water, iodine, gauze.

This feral beast of a man has a whole med kit for his injuries.

He starts to tend some of his wounds and glances up at me. "Tell me what you need me to do. Be specific."

"I need you to keep an eye on her. Just casually, around campus, at parties. If she's staying out of trouble, if she seems safe and happy, then there's no need to interfere. The main thing I'm worried about is her being taken advantage of. And I don't want her going off campus."

"Why?" Iakov interrupts. "We do."

"She's *sixteen*. She's not going off campus. Anything could happen to her."

"Alright," Iakov says. "And if she tries?"

I sigh and rub my hand across my face, suddenly tired. "Fuck, I have no idea. Stop her. No, tell me. Maybe follow her discreetly, make sure she's alright, and tell me. I'll deal with it. It's probably better if she doesn't realise I've got you looking after her."

Iakov cleans a wound on his thigh with almost professional efficiency before dressing it. When he's done, he sets his things aside and looks straight at me. "Bad idea."

"Really?"

"If she's smart, she'll work it out."

Iakov, of course, is right. Zaro *is* smart, and Iakov isn't exactly the kind of person who can lurk behind corners unnoticed.

"So you think I should tell her?" I pinch the bridge of my nose, sensing a headache forming behind my eyes. "She'll think I'm having you spy on her."

"You are," Iakov says with merciless honesty.

"Not really—only for her own good." I think for a moment. "What if telling her only makes her *more* secretive?"

Iakov shrugs. "Maybe she'll be more secretive. But maybe she'll be more careful."

For a moment, we just sit in silence. Me in the chair with my nascent headache, Iakov sitting on his bed like a tattooed, bruised version of Rodin's *Thinker*.

"Alright." I stand up, full of grim resignation. "We'll just have to do the best we can. I'll call and tell her."

"No." Iakov stands and plucks the battered black denim jacket that hangs on the back of his door. He pulls his phone out of one pocket and hands it to me. "Put her number in there," he says. "I'll sort it out."

I take his phone and raise my eyebrows at him. "Are you sure? She's not going to take it lying down."

"What is she going to do?" Iakov asks. "Beat me up?"

I save Zaro's number in his phone and hand it back to him. "She's a Blackwood. She fights with her words, not with her fists."

"Hm," Iakov says, tossing his phone onto his desk, where it lands with a clatter. "Better if she can fight with both. Maybe I'll teach her."

I open my mouth to tell him that sounds like a terrible idea, but an image flashes into my mind. My little sister, Zaro with the long curls and doe eyes, being clumsily seduced by that disgusting creep at Sainte-Agnès. My stomach clenches with hatred so visceral it makes my skin crawl.

If I ever met that man, I know for a fact I would rather fight him with my fists than with my words.

And one day, Zaro will feel exactly the same way.

I smile at Iakov. "Maybe you should."

Chapter 19

Thrown Gauntlet

Zachary

With Zaro settled in and only one day left before my final school year begins with a vengeance, I have only one thing left on my mind.

I haven't seen Theodora since the end of last year—a party in the empty study room which devolved into chaos and from which Theodora disappeared all too fast—and we haven't spoken since then either.

Last year, in a rare moment of peace and camaraderie, Theodora and I exchanged phone numbers. She never texted me, and I fought long and hard with my pride over whether or not I should text her first.

I did, in the end.

Right in the middle of the holiday, tormented by loneliness and frustration. I tapped on her profile picture: a slightly blurry photograph of a swan in a sparkling lake.

The white feathers remind me of Theodora's angel wings that time in the forest, the sight of her white skirts floating through the trees as I chased her like a lascivious god chasing a gorgeous nymph.

The instinct that made me follow her into the trees then is the instinct that pushed me to tap on her profile picture in the middle of the holiday. What I truly craved, at that moment, was to see her face. To devour the sight of her like a delicacy: the pretty eyes, the graceful features, the lovely bones underneath the silk skin.

What I did, at that moment, was text her. A short, harmless, cautious text that did nothing to convey the turmoil of desire and longing lashing like ocean waves in a night storm.

It was a risky move, that text, and I held my breath as I sent it. I felt as though I had lain my head upon the wooden block, hoping that the beautiful executioner would lay down her axe and grant me a caress.

My beautiful executioner did nothing; I never received a reply.

So the day before school starts, I make my way to the library, right to the top floor. I approach Theodora's usual desk, and my heart sinks.

It's empty.

I sit for a while, thumbing through the pages of Descartes's *Meditations*, but I skim the lines without registering them. The thin pages of my paperback turn in my fingers, the whisper of paper like tiny sighs.

My gaze finds the line, *"Is there anything more intimate or more internal than pain?"*

Descartes seems to be mocking me with that sentence; I close the book with a sigh.

Stuffing the book back into my pocket, I stand and glare at the vacant space where Theodora should be. Why is she not here? Does she not have work she should be doing, books she should be reading? A volume of poetry to pore over or a literary villain to romanticise?

When the sun drops beyond the reach of the cupola, plunging the interior of the library into sudden dusk, I accept defeat and leave.

The next time I see Theodora, she's sitting outside of Mr Ambrose's office, and I'm struck with a powerful emotion I can't name.

The only way I can think of describing this emotion is as a sort of reversal of déjà vu, like everything is wrong, upside down, not as it should be.

For one, Theodora and I aren't alone outside Mr Ambrose's office. Several students from our year group—all of them familiar faces from the gifted and talented classes—sit or stand in the small waiting area, some conversing, some silent.

Theodora is sitting and silent.

This time, she's sitting in the blue felt chair I sat in the first time I saw her. The blade of sunlight falling from the window is dimmer today than it was back then, silver and not gold. It falls over her long legs, making her skin gleam like porcelain.

The thing that strikes me the most, the thing that makes my gut clench and my heart sink, is Theodora herself.

She's changed since the last time I saw her: she's slightly taller and much leaner. Her hair is so long now it's well past her waist. The heavy, almost white-blonde strands fall around her like a pale cloak. Her blue eyes are huge in her drawn face. She doesn't look emaciated, but she doesn't look healthy either. There's no colour in her cheeks, and the only colour on her lips is the artificial glaze of her raspberry-pink lip gloss.

I can't even describe the expression on her face.

Not quite sad, not anxious, not afraid, not pained, not angry.

It's just... vacant.

My throat feels tight, and for the first time, I don't quite know what to say to her. She doesn't seem to notice me. Her eyes have the haze of someone lost deep in thoughts, except that I know what Theodora's thoughtfulness looks like, and it looks nothing like this.

What's happened to her? That's what I want to ask, what I'm desperate to know. In reality, I have no idea what Theodora's life might look like when she's away from Spearcrest. Does she live in England? In Russia? Does she travel? Who does she stay with? Does she go out, date, live a normal life? Does she spend time with her family?

Theodora is one of the few students in Spearcrest who's perfected the art of maintaining a social media presence without compromising any of her privacy. She posts about books she's reading, quotes she loves, pretty shots of statues or landscapes, and she posts beautiful selfies of her outfits—but none of these things ever give away any information about where she is or what she's doing.

Something has happened to her during this holiday. Something bad. But what?

The door to Mr Ambrose's office opens, and he greets us all with a solemn nod before welcoming us into his office.

Everybody follows him inside in solemn silence. We all know exactly why we're here. I expect we've all dreamt of this moment.

Theodora is last to stand, but I wait to let her through the door and enter the office after her. She brushes past me with her gaze still lost somewhere far away. I reach to her and touch her elbow with two fingers.

She looks up. I raise my eyebrows at her, asking her with my eyes what I can't ask with my mouth. *Are you alright?* She lifts the corners of her mouth in a wan smile and nods.

It's not like I'm going to get any answers now, but I still choose to stand next to her seat, close enough that I can smell the sweet fragrance of her perfume, like roses and peaches.

Once we're all assembled in front of Mr Ambrose's desk, he sits down and looks us all over. I notice his eyebrow drawing into a shadow of a frown when his gaze sweeps over Theodora, but he doesn't linger on her or say anything.

Instead, he clears his throat.

"Thank you all for being here. Every single one of you here tonight has been personally selected by me, and you all represent the pinnacle of academic achievement. As such, I'm sure you can all guess why I've asked you all here."

There's a pause. I don't need to glance at the others to confirm the veracity of Mr Ambrose's words. He gives a small but sincere smile and continues.

"It is my honour to officially invite you all to participate in the Spearcrest Apostles programme. I have no doubt most of you are well aware of this programme—its reputation precedes it. Past Spearcrest Apostles represent the programme well and have contributed to its reputation as one of the most challenging academic enrichment programmes in the world. One day, you might very well do the same.

"You all excel in different academic areas—many of you excel at many. But the Spearcrest Apostles programme, above all, is one that seeks to elevate students' minds and souls. As such, this programme will have a heavy focus on philosophy. Not just the theories and history of philosophy but its ethics and applications. Should you be successful in it, this programme will not only enrich your mind and knowledge—but it will also enrich your spirit, your morality. It will make you a more thoughtful person with a powerful understanding of the world and those who live within it.

"Now—I know you all know the honour being bestowed upon you, but the decision of whether or not to enter should be fully and freely yours. I do not wish to ask anything of you that you are not willing to do. This programme is incredibly demanding: it will include weekly lectures and seminars as well as a variety of projects, challenges, assignments and essays. It is extra-curricular in its most real sense: you will be expected to follow it alongside your A-levels, not instead of them. You will still be expected to attend all your classes and submit all homework, essays and coursework on time.

"I could not possibly exaggerate how demanding this programme is. Every year, more than half of students drop out by the end of the winter term. Your year group is one of the strongest cohorts Spearcrest has seen in a long time. As a result, I predict a particularly high drop-out rate. Many of you will end up choosing to prioritise your grades and university applications—this is understandable and commendable.

"For those of you who wish to pick up the gauntlet, understand that you will need more than hard work to succeed. The Spearcrest Apostles programme carries with it a great and noble pedigree, but it comes without any formal certificate or qualification. However, at the end of the year, I will personally select the best student in the programme—this student will receive a scholarship to Oxford University and will be personally mentored by Lady Alessandra Ashton, Countess of Lyndham, the Vice-Chancellor."

When Mr Ambrose stops speaking, silence descends upon the room like a heavy mantle.

He was right about everything, of course: we've all heard of the Spearcrest Apostles. Nobody has ever managed to get any information about it, though. Past alumni seem to all have a pact to leave the air of mystery surrounding the programme untarnished.

Even my father, who sits on Spearcrest's board of governors, knows very little about the programme.

I expected it to be as challenging as Mr Ambrose describes it—but I could never have expected the prize he might offer for the best student in the programme.

By the sudden tension in the room—none of us had.

By the sudden tension in the room—I'm not the only one who realises the implication of such a prize.

Mr Ambrose nods solemnly.

"I would like to give you all one week to seriously consider whether or not you wish to accept my invitation. One week—a full week. I do not wish for any answers in the meantime. I ask you all to think about it—really think about it. What you want out of your final year in Spearcrest; if this programme is right for you, if it is something you desire or something you covet. If it will fulfil you or break you. If you decide to accept my invitation, return to my office at the same time next week, and you shall receive your programme schedule for the winter term."

He stands, thanks us warmly for coming, and then dismisses us from his office, leaving us all reeling.

Chapter 20

Broken Goddess

Theodora

Mr Ambrose's words wash over me like waves over the listless body of a beached sea creature. I roll and sway under their movement, longing for them to drag me away into their current.

When he dismisses us and everybody's leaving the room, his eyes find mine, and he gives me a slight frown with a question inside of it.

"Thank you, Mr Ambrose," I answer.

I stand and leave the room, melting into the line of students trickling out of the office.

Desperate for some fresh air and space, I make my way to the back of the building, which leads out to a small courtyard garden with four benches surrounding a small marble fountain. A hand brushes my arm, startling me.

"Hey—Theodora."

Zachary's warm voice is different, his stiff formality replaced with gentle worry.

I turn and look up. He's taller than he was the last time I saw him. I'm not sure when Zachary stopped looking like a boy and started looking like a man, but that's what he looks like now.

Brown eyes full of intelligence, framed by thick, curly eyelashes. Handsome, regal features, graceful cheekbones over carved cheeks. A tall stature, elegant posture. The emotive, romanticised masculinity of a Hellenistic statue.

My heart strains in my chest when I see him. I want to throw my arms around his neck and hang on his chest like a medallion.

My own heartbeat has felt so distant lately; would his make me feel alive again?

"Hello, Zachary."

He caught me just as I was leaving the building. I know better than to try to escape him anyway, and I'm too light-hearted to walk back to the girls' dormitory anyway.

So I put my arm through his with an affability that's designed to keep him close while keeping him at arm's length and lead him to a bench.

"Did you have a good summer?" I ask. My voice sounds faraway and mechanical. "Congratulations on being invited to Mr Ambrose's Apostles programme, by the way."

He watches me as I sit down but doesn't sit straight away. His eyes search my face, but no matter how clever Zachary is, he won't find anything in my expression.

There's nothing there because I feel nothing inside.

"My summer was fine," he answers finally. "Far from perfect, but adequate. Thank you for asking."

He draws closer and takes a seat on the bench next to me. Not facing the fountain, like I'm doing, but facing me, one leg folded in front of him, the other pointing towards me, his knee against my thigh.

"How was yours?" he asks.

"Fine." I smile. "Adequate."

"Did you manage to finish your lit homework?"

I shrug. "I've barely started it."

"That's not like you."

"You don't know what is or isn't like me."

He lets out a chuckle like a sigh. "You're proud of that, aren't you?"

"Of what?"

"Of how you always manage to keep me at arm's length. Of making sure I'm only ever one step removed from a stranger."

I shake my head. My chest feels tight and my head the opposite, like my skull is a wide, empty space full of swirling galaxies. I'm so light-headed I'm afraid I might keel over right into the fountain, into the aquamarine water aglow with the light of underwater bulbs.

"You're not a stranger," I tell Zachary. "You're my friend."

He's silent for a moment. Even through my torpor, I can tell he's surprised. He raises an arm and gently cups my cheek, turning my head so I'm facing him.

"If I was your friend, you'd tell me what's wrong."

"I feel light-headed."

His eyebrows rise in concern. "You do? Have you eaten dinner yet?"

I shake my head.

"You probably need to eat. What time did you have lunch?"

I shake my head again.

He sighs. "Did you not have lunch?"

"I forgot."

It's not quite a lie. I woke up too late for breakfast, rushed to my classes, and then was too tired to go pick up some food from the dining hall. I had two apples before going to Mr Ambrose's office because I didn't want to embarrass myself by swooning in front of him.

Zachary, to my surprise, doesn't roll his eyes or tell me off.

"No wonder you're light-headed, Theo. I'm impressed you're still able to walk." He brushes the hair back from my face and smiles.

"Would you like to come to the dining hall and do me the honour of dining together?"

I shake my head. "I don't want to go to the dining hall."

He watches me for a second. "Do you still prefer to eat in private?"

It's my turn to be surprised. I didn't expect him to remember this—I barely remember telling him.

"Alright," he says. "Come with me."

He gives me his hand, and I take it, letting him pull me to my feet. He guides me back into the Old Manor and into one of the empty classrooms. They are all locked at this time of day, but he has a key—I don't know why since he isn't a prefect and never was. The teachers probably love and trust him enough to let him have access to empty classrooms.

It's not until he leads me to one of the desks and pulls up a chair for me that I realise he's still holding my hand. His warmth trickles into me via our connected palms. When I sit down and he lets me go, the flow of warmth is immediately cut off.

Zachary looks down with a solemn expression. "I want you to stay here and wait for me, alright?"

I nod.

"Promise me, Theo."

"I promise."

He smiles and then darts out of the classroom, leaving his leather satchel in the seat next to mine. My head is still spinning, so I fold my arms on the desk and rest my forehead on them.

I close my eyes. Zachary called me Theo. He's never called me that before.

Theo.

It's short, boyish and affectionate. It doesn't suit me at all, but I like it.

I like it because of the way Zachary said it, without explanation, as if my name takes enough space in his world to necessitate a nickname.

As if the lie I told him before—that we are friends—is actually the truth.

Zachary returns, carrying a brown paper bag against his chest.

I watch him with a slight frown as he hurries back to our desk and sets the things out of his paper bag: some plates, glasses, cutlery. A bottle of wine, bread, and two containers of food still warm enough to steam up the lids.

Once his little picnic is assembled, Zachary dishes out some food on both plates and pours a little wine into both glasses.

"Where on earth did you get wine?" I ask, staring at his display.

"The kitchens, of course."

"The kitchen staff gave you wine?"

He smiles at me—a victor's smile, a hero's grin. "I asked nicely."

I raise an eyebrow. "I'm sure you won it with your charm and not just because your father is a generous financial patron of Spearcrest Academy."

He lets out a laugh. "How long have you been keeping that particular bullet loaded in the chamber of your mind?"

As he speaks, he pulls his plate towards him and picks up a fork and knife. He doesn't touch the second plate he made, doesn't push it in my direction, doesn't even point or look at it. He eats without prompting me to do the same as if it doesn't matter to him what I do with the food he's put on that plate.

"I wasn't taking a shot," I concede. "I don't know why I feel it's my responsibility to keep you humble." He half-rolls his eyes with an amused smirk, so I add, "Maybe I'm just scared your ego will inflate so much you'll explode one day."

"I'm as modest as a monk," Zachary replies.

"Does that make me the divinity that keeps your bald head bowed in devotion?"

"Always," he says, "my beloved goddess." His tone is no longer mocking but deep and sincere.

I glance down at the plate in front of me, my stomach squirming. Spoonfuls of a creamy vegetable bake and an array of greens. There's sliced-up steak in some of the containers, but he didn't place any on my plate. I've never told him I was vegetarian—but of course, Zachary would never presume to know my dietary habits.

When he calls me a goddess with such reverence, the plate he's placed on the table in front of me, with its accompanying cut of wine and slice of bread, appears to me in a new light.

Is this Zachary's worship? His offerings at the altar of my well-being?

I pull the plate to me and pick up my fork, staring at the food.

When I started following my mother's dietary plans all those years ago, I was so certain I would always remain in control. I wasn't naive, not even back then. Just like my mother, I was well aware of what an eating disorder was—I thought I was clever enough that I would never allow my relationship with food to become dysfunctional, to tilt into the territory of illness.

Maybe this is punishment for my hubris: this sickening sensation every time I look at a plate of food. The wave of panic, the desperation to ascertain control through small, manic gestures—cutting up my food into tiny pieces, breaking bread into a line of morsels.

Does Zachary know? Can he tell?

Does he think it's pathetic that I can't even fulfil one of the most basic human functions?

Would he treat me the same if he knew?

After all, who would worship a broken goddess?

"Who do you think will win the prize at the end of the programme?" Zachary asks, his voice piercing through my thoughts. "The Apostles programme?"

His question is arch, but it makes my heart sink in my chest. I drop my gaze, not daring to look at him.

Because I don't have the courage to tell him I've not yet decided whether to accept Mr Ambrose's invitation. Because I don't have the strength to tell him the path of my life has been redirected, rerouted, into a direction I never chose.

Because I don't have a way of explaining to Zachary—because I can't yet quite accept—that he and I won't always remain Marvell's perfect parallels.

Soon, I'll go spinning off at a sharp angle, drawing forever away from him, until his presence in my life becomes little more than a memory, a distant dream.

"*I* will," I answer him. "Obviously."

Chapter 21

FEAR & FATE

Theodora

I MANAGE TO EAT almost half of what's on my plate, and I finish the cup of wine, which makes me feel warm and drowsy.

When we're finished, Zachary clears everything away, and we walk together to the empty dining hall, where he returns the plates, cutlery and bottle of wine to the kitchens. Then Zachary offers me his arm to walk me back to the sixth form girls' building.

The sun has long set, and the campus is deserted. A cold wind chases the remnants of summer away, the fragrance of honeysuckle carried into the night air. The lamp light dots the azure darkness of early evening with spills of gold. The night is peaceful and still, a cocoon wrapping itself around Zachary and me.

"Did something happen during the summer holiday?" Zachary finally asks.

The question has been balanced on his tongue all evening. I watched him try to swallow it back, worry it with the tip of his tongue like poking a sore spot. I watched him debate whether to let it loose or swallow it back.

But Zachary has never been one to shy away from questions—no matter how difficult.

The philosopher in him would never allow him to.

I shake my head slowly. "No."

It's not quite a lie. Nothing happened over the holidays, not really. A conversation with my father doesn't count as something. Finding out that I won't be going to university and will be moving to Russia to live with him and be thrown like a rack of meat onto a stall at the marriage market—well, that counts, maybe, but how could I possibly tell Zachary?

Will I ever be able to tell him?

He's worried about me, and if our positions were reversed, I'd worry about him too.

I hesitate and add, "The atmosphere in my family home is... a little tense."

He squeezes his arm around mine in silent acknowledgement. "I can relate to that, trust me."

"Tense summer at Castle Blackwood?" I ask.

"Tense summer at the Blackwood *Manor*," he corrects me with a half-grin.

The relationship between Zachary and me has never permitted such sharing of information before. In the past, the boundaries between us were always clear. We could discuss any topic so long as it wasn't personal. We avoided anything that might tip our rivalry into the territory of friendship.

But all we managed to do, it seems, is bypass friendship and land straight into something else—something far murkier and complex.

"Tense in general or tense for you?" I ask.

"Both," he answers.

The wind follows his statement with a sudden gust that makes the leaves rustle like a sigh.

"I can't imagine how Lord and Lady Blackwood would ever be displeased with you," I say.

"If I'm honest, neither did I," he replies. "I would consider myself the perfect son, really."

I suppress a laugh, envious of his self-assurance.

"You would, would you?" I murmur. "The perfect son: clever, handsome, modest…"

"You think I'm handsome?"

"I said clever and modest."

"You said *handsome*," he says. He pulls his phone out of his pocket with his free hand and mutters, "I'm adding it to my collection of compliments."

"I don't think I've ever complimented you in my life."

He opens a note and points his phone screen at me. "Here. Written, dated evidence."

I peer at his screen. "I don't remember ever complimenting your handwriting."

"That's worrying," Zachary mutters as he types into his phone. "Maybe you've filled your memory with so many Keats stanzas that you've not left room for any core memories."

"I don't think telling you that you have nice handwriting counts as a core memory."

He shakes his head. "Well, you calling me handsome counts as one of *my* core memories—and now you can never deny it." He shows me his screen. "There—three compliments. Three compliments in almost seven years. That's how stingy you are with them."

"All of this, just so you don't have to tell me what you did to annoy your parents."

He laughs. "You didn't ask."

"I'm asking."

"I didn't do anything."

I roll my eyes even though he's not looking at me. "Of course not."

"They want me to pursue politics," he says after a short silence. "And I have no intention of doing so. Since they have no way of forcing me, a stalemate ensued, resulting in tension at the dinner table. There you go."

I didn't expect him to be so forthright, to deliver so much information. I don't know why since Zachary never shies away from asking or answering questions. Zachary, for all his wit and arrogance and sarcasm, lives grounded in truth.

And part of me knows he would never deny me anything I asked.

"How do you know?" I ask. My voice almost breaks. "How do you know they have no way of forcing you?"

He shrugs. "What are they going to do? Lock me up and fill out my university applications for me? Force me to sit my exams at gunpoint? Chain me to a bench in the House of Lords chamber?"

His answer is like him, full of airy arrogance and sarcasm. But it sends ripples through me.

I find myself asking myself the same question: how could my father force me to return to Russia? Take me to the airport at gunpoint? Lock me up in his house and chain me to whatever husband he chooses for me?

My blood runs cold. My father is infamous for being a man who's willing to do whatever it takes to get what he wants. I wouldn't put anything past him.

Zachary turns to fix me with a curious look. Maybe he felt the ice in my veins—sensed it somehow. He frowns. "So what happened with your family? Why was the atmosphere tense?"

I swallow, trying to keep my voice from giving away too much.

"Same as you," I say finally. "General disagreement about the future."

"Oh." He's silent for a moment, and I realise we've reached the sixth form girls' building. We stand at the foot of the stairs and watch each other. He lifts an eyebrow. "And?"

"And nothing." I smile. "The future is just the future. Is there really a point in worrying about something that cannot be changed and hasn't yet occurred?"

He frowns. "I'm not sure I agree with that."

"This isn't debate club, Zachary," I say. "It's just what I think. You don't get to argue with me."

He takes my hand in his and stares down at me with theatrical melancholy. "Too bad. I dearly love to argue with you."

"You dearly love the sound of your own voice," I correct him.

"I dearly love the sound of yours, too."

He kisses my knuckles, and warmth melts through me like molten sugar, sweet and comforting. I let out a small laugh and take my hand back. "You're shameless. You need to go."

But I reach up and kiss his cheek. His skin is smooth against my lips, the smell of him fills my senses, and I have to resist the urge to draw closer, to wrap myself in his presence, his arms, his warmth.

"Thank you for the food, Zach."

"Anytime." The amusement fades from his face, replaced with that solemn intensity of his. "I mean it. Anytime."

"I know. Goodnight."

"Night, Theo."

We part ways, but his warmth and perfume cling to my skin for the rest of the evening, chasing away the creeping numbness.

The following day, I sit down at my desk and methodically list out my reasons for accepting and declining Mr Ambrose's invitation to the Apostles programme.

Reasons I should decline:

The programme will be demanding, and I'm already struggling to maintain academic excellence in my subjects as well as balance my frankly precarious mental health and social responsibilities.

I also have my head girl duties to worry about.

If I join the programme and win—which I would do everything in my power to do—I would be taking the prize from someone who could actually use it, like Zachary.

Because if I win—which I would, I'd have no choice—I would be unable to collect the prize, no matter how badly I want it. I would have to admit to Mr Ambrose that I'm not going to university.

Reasons I should accept the invitation:

Win and have concrete evidence of my intellectual superiority over Zachary.

Winning against Zachary is something I've always wanted, a prize I've long coveted.

But is it enough?

I wish it was—I desperately want it to be. I desperately want a future where I finally prove to Zachary that I'm academically superior to him, sweep the prize from under him and then lord it over him when we both end up in Oxford.

This is the future I long for—but it's not my future.

Not anymore.

Even though the answer to my dilemma is clear, it takes me the rest of the week to accept it. I review the list every night, hoping I'll somehow figure out a solution, a way to get what I want.

I think about Zachary's words about his parents being unable to force him to follow the fate they've chosen for him. I think of my father, the impassive stone of his face, the crushing flood of fear it sends through me even though he's not here.

It's a fear I can't escape—a fear I don't think I'll ever escape. It lives inside me like a disease, keeping me forever its host and hostage.

The following week, I deliver a handwritten letter to Mr Ambrose's secretary, politely declining his invitation. Instead of going to the meeting in his office, I go for a long walk around the outer rims of the Spearcrest campus.

I want to cry, but, of course, I can't. I've not cried since I was a little girl.

No matter how often I've wanted to.

Luckily for me, it's raining. I let the raindrops roll down my cheeks, weeping the tears I don't get to weep.

Chapter 22

POETIC ANALOGIES

Zachary

Being invited to Mr Ambrose's Apostles is an honour I long coveted.

Year after year, watching the Year 13 students gather after school to attend the seminars in Mr Ambrose's office, I couldn't help but envy them. I imagined how I would feel if I wasn't invited—if Mr Ambrose hadn't deemed me one of the brightest minds of Spearcrest.

I imagined such a scenario only to shake my head with an inner smile. As if Mr Ambrose wouldn't choose me. Mr Ambrose is like me, an alumnus of Spearcrest. He attended Oxford, like I intend to do. He studied classics, a sister subject to my dream alma mater, philosophy. Like me, he is a son of politicians who chose the path of academia and education.

I knew Mr Ambrose wouldn't pick me because of those things.

In almost seven years at Spearcrest, I've never seen Mr Ambrose allow anything to influence his actions aside from his own mind and convictions. Flattery and threats slide off him like water over feathers.

Secure in the knowledge Mr Ambrose chose me because I'm worthy, how could I decline this invitation?

The challenge will be undeniable, of course, and I have no doubt Mr Ambrose didn't exaggerate the gruelling hard work ahead, but I'd face these challenges a hundred times for the sake of the prize at the end of the programme.

Not the Oxford scholarship or even the mentorship of Lady Ashton. Though worthy prizes, they pale in comparison to the triumph of finally, undeniably beating Theodora for academic achievements.

After so many years of seeing our names linked at the top of the results list, an eternal stalemate that kept proving to both of us that neither of us won—this competition will break the stalemate once and for all.

Theodora might not be in top form right now—whatever happened over the summer clearly impacted her—but she's not one to give up. If I was beaten and bleeding out, I would scrape myself off the floor if it meant competing against her, and I know she would too.

The tug of war between us, this battle that's been raging for so many years, is set too deep into our lives. She can't avoid it any more than I can.

The Apostles programme will be our final arena, our final battle. There's never a moment when I don't imagine meeting Theodora on the battlefield.

Until the week is over and I arrive at Mr Ambrose's office as per his instructions. Out of the twelve students he invited last week, eight came.

Eight students, including myself.

But not Theodora.

Could she be late?

Theodora is never late, but it would make more sense in my mind that Theodora would be late rather than absent. Mr Ambrose invites us all to sit and gives us a breakdown of what we'll be doing in September and October. He hands us schedules, reading lists, and booklets of material he wants us to read before the first lecture the following week. I listen to him restlessly, glancing at the door every few minutes.

I expect Theodora to show up the entire time, even when Mr Ambrose wraps up by congratulating and then thanking us for being part of the programme, even when he finally dismisses us.

My mind is a roar of questions as I fold my sheaf of papers into my satchel and stand. I let the others leave, looking at Mr Ambrose, who's leaning back against his desk, his arms folded. We both remain silent until we're alone.

"Where is she?" I ask. My voice comes out low and rough as if I'm unwell.

I feel unwell.

I feel as if a deep black pit has opened in my guts, and everything inside me is sinking.

"Theodora has chosen to decline my invitation." Mr Ambrose's face is as calm as usual, and it's difficult to work out whether the sadness and disappointment I hear in his voice are real or a projection of my own emotions.

"Why?" I want Mr Ambrose to think I'm like him—calm in the face of any situation, unshakeable as marble—but unlike him, I can't keep the emotion out of my voice. "I don't understand—she's perfect for this, we..." I don't even know what to say, so I stop myself and take a deep breath. "I was certain she would accept."

"She didn't give me a reason," Mr Ambrose says. "Neither does she owe me one."

"But you know, don't you?" I stare into Mr Ambrose's hazel eyes, set deep into his grave face, searching for any clue, any information I can draw out of him. "Something's wrong with her, isn't it? What is it?"

"Zachary"—Mr Ambrose's deep voice is solemn—"Theodora's life is her own. She is entitled to make her own decisions, just as she is entitled to her privacy. I suggest you go speak to her. You're her friend, she'll talk to you."

"Mr Ambrose"—I let out a frustrated laugh—"being Theodora's friend is like standing next to the mountain instead of far away. It doesn't matter how close you are, the mountain is still a mountain. You'll never get to its heart, to what's inside."

"Theodora isn't a mountain, Zachary. Not some mysterious creature from the heavens nor a tightly furled blossom nor any other metaphor your mind might conjure. She's a young person, just like you. Just like you, she has dreams and hopes and problems and a mind and a heart and a voice. If you're worried about her, then look after her. If you have questions about her, then ask her."

"What if she refuses to tell me anything?"

Mr Ambrose sighs.

"My dear boy, she doesn't owe you anything. Love is neither conditional nor transactional. If you truly love someone, you can't love them less because they don't give you what you want. And you certainly can't expect them to give you what you want just because you love them. That's simply not how love works."

Mr Ambrose and I watch each other in silence for a moment. It's not jarring to me that Mr Ambrose is speaking of love. He sees everything, and my love for Theodora is about as inconspicuous and discreet as a raging inferno.

I don't even bother to deny it.

I know he's right anyway. He's a fiercely intelligent man, and he's been alive for much longer than I have. His wisdom is something I trust implicitly.

With sincere thanks, I leave his office, determined to be the kind of man Mr Ambrose wants me to be: calm, collected, and mature. I decide to go talk to Theodora, to be composed and mindful, to avoid a confrontation at all costs and to keep my emotions under control.

My determination holds firm until I reach the top floor of the library.

And then I see Theodora.

And then every reasonable thought in my head is obliterated.

She's sitting at her usual desk. Her long hair is half gathered in a gold hair claw. She's wearing a sage-green sweater that looks impossibly soft, the sleeves long almost to her knuckles. When I approach her, she looks up from whatever she's writing, and her face is small and pretty as a pearl.

The beauty of her melts me completely. It melts the reasonable thoughts out of my head and the measured words out of my mouth.

I didn't want a confrontation, but my voice is a harsh accusation when I blurt out the question that's been burning my tongue.

"Why are you refusing to be an Apostle?"

Our gazes meet. The forget-me-not blue of her eyes is highlighted by the delicate pink of her eyeshadow. Her face is a porcelain mask, with no expression marring the fragile surface.

Her emotionless calm kindles my despair like gasoline thrown into a fire.

Laying down her pen, she folds her hands together on the desk, leaning forward slightly to give me a small, mocking smile.

"What is it, Zachary?" she asks. "Is this the blade and the whetstone again? Are you afraid your blade will grow dull without the whetstone of my mind?"

I immediately understand what she's doing. This is a sharp deflection disguised as a blow. She wants to appear as if she's striking when she's only really parrying.

"You know perfectly well that's not the case," I answer, narrowing my eyes at her. "Any whetstone can sharpen a blade. I don't need you in the programme to excel—I need you there so that I can win."

"Then win against the others."

"A victory is only worthy if it's against you."

"So you've said before. But I know you, Zachary—so proud, so competitive. You'd prefer your victories to be against me, but any victory will feed your appetite."

"No." My entire body thrums like the chord of a harp after it's been plucked. "No, Theodora. You can tell yourself this if it helps soothe whatever you feel about your decision, but you're wrong. I know that doesn't happen all that often to you—being wrong. But this time, you are. Because the truth is that I'm not competitive by nature and winning means nothing to me. It's *you*. I need to win against *you*. You're the only person in this world who's my perfect equal—the only person who is worthy of me. Two beings like us cannot exist without a battle—we've been fighting it all along, and we'll keep fighting it until there's a victor."

"God, do you hear yourself?" She sits back, her face set in a sneer. "You're so arrogant, you don't even realise how you come across right now."

"How do I come across right now?"

"Like you're better than everybody else in the world."

"I'm not better than everybody else in the world—*you* are. That's why it always has to be you, Theodora."

She lets out a laugh that's the coldest sound I've ever heard, so cold it almost burns.

"Whatever image you've created of me in your mind, Zachary, one day you'll wake up and realise it was just a dream. I'm not an angel or a goddess. I'm just a human being, and I'm certainly not better than everybody else. If I seem like it, it's only because I'm good at pretending. I'm not better than everybody else. I'm barely as good as everybody else. Just because we've tied grades over the years doesn't mean you and I are trapped in this great cosmic battle of higher wills. This is just a story you've told yourself—a story as fanciful as any children's book you might look down on."

Her words wash over me, and I let them do so, taking my time to reply. Theodora's talk of making up stories resonates with me—but not because I'm the one making them up.

"And what fanciful story have you made up to justify not following the programme when you know it's perfect for you, when you know there's a hunger deep inside you for knowledge and ideas and debate, when you know how much you want it? What image is it you've created to justify your actions, and how will you feel when you wake up?"

I don't want to be cruel to Theodora, and I don't want to fight with her. But this is like a debate. Not two sides debating one motion, but two sides debating two motions.

My house believes that Theodora should be a Spearcrest Apostle because there is no other way, because she wants to be there as much as I want her to be there, because neither of us can or should be doing this without the other.

Her house believes something else, something small and dark and ugly I can't quite get her to spit out. Something which makes her believe that she's not an angel and a goddess, that she's barely as good as everybody else around us.

A blatant lie—but the kind of insidious lie that grows deep underneath someone's skin, sprouts seedlings and grows into something uncontrollable and barbed.

"The truth isn't whatever you choose to believe, Zach," she tells me in the severe, almost patronising tone of a schoolteacher. "You don't get to state your opinion and will it into truth through sheer power of confidence."

"Fine, Theodora. Since you know the truth and I don't, why don't you tell me?"

She stiffens in her seat. At this angle, the glow of a light somewhere behind her catches the pale sheen of her hair and makes it gleam like a golden halo.

How ironic.

"Tell you what?" she asks, her tone as rigid as her posture.

"Why did you turn down Mr Ambrose's invitation?"

"Why is it so important for me to accept?"

I answer immediately. "Because I know you want to."

"If you don't bother telling me the truth, why should I?"

"What truth?" I draw closer, resisting the urge to pull her to her feet, to draw her into the circle of my arms, to force her to speak to me while we're heart to heart so that I can feel her emotions in the rise and fall of her chest.

"The truth, Zachary. Do you want me in the programme because you think I want to, because of the enrichment of my soul, or because of Andrew Marvell's perfect parallels?"

I didn't expect her to go there.

It's my turn to stiffen—not defensively, but proudly.

"Are you asking me if I want you there because I love you?"

Colour rises to her cheeks. Perhaps she expected me to tiptoe with my words just like she did, to speak in veiled allusions and poetic analogies. But not in this case, not about this.

"You don't love me," she hastens to say as if hoping to do some damage control—as if the idea of me loving her is damage that needs to be controlled.

"No," I answer without shame. The balance of calm and emotion has tipped now. I'm as calm as a sea after a storm; her eyes are wide with panic. "I absolutely, undeniably, inexorably love you."

Chapter 23

Adored Adversary

Zachary

For a moment, she's almost speechless. When she replies, it's in that stiff, formal, almost matronly voice she uses in debates when she needs to appear self-assured and authoritative.

"I've told you I'm not allowed—I can't date." There's a visible flutter in her throat as if her heartbeat is too powerful for the slim column of her neck. "We'll never be together."

All I hear is that she's not telling me she doesn't love me or that she doesn't want me to love her. When she gives me the reason I shouldn't love her, all I hear is that if it wasn't for that reason, then we would be together.

"I know," I tell her in a reassuring tone. "I don't expect us to be together, Theo, but that doesn't mean I can stop feeling the way I feel. Remember the poem? The parallel lines can never meet, but they can never stray from one another."

She watches me for a moment, an expression of incredulity on her face. And then she gets to her feet and stands in front of me. I can smell that delicate perfume of hers, roses and peaches. I gaze down at her, now almost a head shorter than me, to see her face turned up to mine like a flower.

Her expression is nothing like a flower, though.

"Is this enough, Zachary?" she hisses as if there's barely enough air in her lungs to speak. "Is it really enough to have me right here, at arm's reach, even though you can never have me?"

"Of course, it's not enough. It'll never be enough."

I smile at her and raise my hands, my palms brushing up her arms and shoulders on their way to her face. I cup her cheeks through the silk strands of her hair. Her face feels delicate as porcelain in my hands.

"I could have you in my arms and in my bed every day and every night, Theodora, and it would still never be enough. Having you this close and this far all the time is a constant torment. But my pain is soothed by the fact you'll be suffering too."

"Suffering? How?"

"Because while it burns me to have you so close when we can never be together, deep down, you're burning too."

"Burning?" She laughs coldly, but she doesn't move her face out of my hands. Our bodies are locked in each other's gravity fields, in the warmth and perfume of each other's bodies, in that trembling heat haze of tension between us. "Are you sure of that?"

"Certain beyond doubt."

"How?"

I sigh and tilt her face up, and she lets me, her pink lips gleaming as they part.

"Because I know you, Theodora. I know you better than I know my own soul. I know every expression on your face like they are the lines of my favourite poems. Everything you think you keep hidden from the world, you can never quite hide from me. The beautiful things—your determination, your strength, your gentle soul—but the ugly things, too. Your ambition, your pain, your fear. Your desire. They're naked to my eyes."

She says nothing for a long time. Her eyes are wide, thrown blue jewels in a blue ocean. Her lips tremble for a moment, forming the shape of words. The silence between us speaks a thousand words. Truthful words, painful words, words of denial, words of want.

Words she doesn't have the courage to say aloud.

With a defeated sigh, she steps away, freeing her face from the cradle of my hands, freeing her body from the heat of mine, freeing herself from the burden of truth.

"Fine." Her voice is low and defeated. "I'll tell Mr Ambrose I made a mistake. I'll join the programme—if it matters so much to you."

I smile. "Oh, it matters. And you'll find me to be generous in my gratitude. I'll even reward you with a gift."

She narrows her eyes in suspicion. "What gift?"

My gaze sinks into hers. I lower my voice. I speak low and tender, not like a secret, but like an intimate promise—a sacred vow.

"I'll give you something you've always wanted but never dared to ask for. Something you dream about at night, alone in the dark, alone in your bed."

She retreats in a hasty back step. I let her. Her fingers clutch the long hem of her soft green sleeves.

"What would that be?" she asks, her voice quivering but defiant.

I tilt my head. "Your first kiss."

She scoffs. "Or maybe I'll take yours."

I laugh. "Please do, Theodora. I'll offer it up freely. I'll even give you my second and my third, and all the ones after that—every kiss, if you want. I'd give you anything you'd ask for. If your love demanded my prostration, I'd get on my knees for you, I'd kiss the ground at your feet. I'd do everything you've ever thought about in those secret midnight moments and everything you've never even dared to imagine. I'd melt all that ice in your skin, Theodora Dorokhova, and replace it with flames. All you need do is ask."

"You don't know what you're saying," she hisses, eyes wide with panic, cheeks flooded with colour. "You need to stop."

"I know exactly what I'm saying, and I mean every word of it." I tilt my head. "Would you like me to prove it to you? Do you want to claim your gift right now?"

"I've not spoken to Mr Ambrose yet," she says, backing away in quick steps.

"Mm." I grin at her. "You're right. Better do that first and claim your prize second."

"I'll go speak to him now. As for your gift, you can keep it to yourself."

She gathers her stuff hastily, piling her laptop and books and throwing them into her bag. I watch her, leaning on the wooden desk separator, not bothering to hide the idle smirk of satisfaction on my face.

When she's all packed up, she shoulders her bag and throws me an imperious glare. "You know you've messed up, right?"

"How so?"

"Because you'll never get your victory now."

I laugh. "You're certain of that?"

It's her turn to smirk. "Certain beyond doubt."

MR AMBROSE WASN'T EXAGGERATING the nature of the programme. By the end of September, I find myself forever climbing a pile of work that only ever seems to grow however hard I work.

There is reading for my A-level classes, practice papers and essays and research assignments, and then there is the Apostles work. The first assignment Mr Ambrose gives us is a research project asking us to write a detailed explanation, history and comparison of Plato's Akademia and Aristotle's Lyceum, with our essays exploring a mix of both our opinions and references from notable scholars.

It's an enormous project which takes me upwards of fifteen overall hours to complete. The night before the deadline, I'm in the library—on the top floor, but not in Theodora's territory. I know she's there—I can almost sense her presence—but I don't want to be accused of trying to distract her for fear of sullying my eventual victory.

I'm proofreading my assignment, headphones on and reeling off my proofreading playlist, which consists mostly of Satie and Debussy, when a pale form appears from the shadowy corridor of an aisle. I look up with a slight start and immediately relax.

Theodora's hair is gathered in a twisted bun at the top of her head, loose strands framing her face, almost silvery in the low late-night lights of the library. She's out of her uniform and dressed plainly in high-waisted jeans and a white silk top. She looks more like an air-borne nymph than a student crumbling under the pressure of too many assignments.

She looks perfectly beautiful.

I take my headphones off and smile up at her.

"What an unexpected pleasure, Theo." I raise an eyebrow. "You've not come to claim your prize, have you?"

She rolls her eyes. "Believe it or not, it's not a priority right now."

She stops near me and peers at my laptop screen. Her perfume wraps around me as she leans on my shoulder, eyes across the document displayed on my laptop. I fight the urge to place a kiss on the ivory column of her neck.

My mind trails off after that thought, imagining all the places I would love to kiss and taste.

"You're working on the Plato-Aristotle project?" Theodora asks, bringing me back to reality.

"Mm-hm," I answer her, my eyes still on her throat. "I've just finished. I'm proofreading."

"Perfect—me too." She hesitates, pursing her lips a little. "How would you feel about proofreading each other's work? I'm so tired, and I've re-drafted and re-read mine so many times it feels like I'm trying to read a palimpsest."

"That's surprisingly trusting of you," I say, genuinely a little surprised. "You don't fear sabotage?"

"Not for a second."

"No?"

She shakes her head and lifts a corner of her mouth in a half-smirk. "If you sabotage me and win, then you'll know your victory wasn't truly earned. If you sabotage me and still lose, then you'll probably hate yourself for the rest of your life. So no, I'm not worried."

"You know me so well, huh?"

"Is that a yes or a no?"

"Have I ever said no to you, my revered nemesis?"

"I'm not your nemesis."

"Bring your essay over. My adored adversary."

"Just say Theodora."

"Yes, my sublime Theodora."

Although I never really expected her to, Theodora does claim her prize in the end.

There's a Young Kings party in the study hall—a small one, with champagne and pizza and games, where we've only invited an elite group of guests.

Theodora comes late, dragged in by Camille and Rose, who hold her arms tightly in theirs. She's wearing a short dress in blue satin and strappy white heels. Her hair is tied in a high ponytail, and she's got a faraway look in her eyes. If I had to guess, she would rather be in the library than at this party, and I can't blame her—so would I.

As I watch her from afar, a huge body throws itself against the side of mine, almost toppling us both into a nearby table. The study hall, a cavernous chamber underneath a vaulted ceiling, is dark, lit dimly by a few lamps and the green glow of the emergency signs.

In those hazy lights, Iakov's face appears. He curls one arm around my shoulders, and I wince as his thick biceps squeeze my neck. Iakov's eyes are glazed over, which tells me he's already inebriated. I wouldn't put it past him to choke me in a drunken underestimation of his own strength.

"Thorny thing, your Zaro," Iakov slurs in my ear.

"Yeah?" I laugh. "Are you rethinking your idea of teaching her how to fight?"

"No." He shakes his head. "I wanna teach her, but she doesn't wanna learn."

"Blackwoods aren't big fans of physical violence."

Iakov rasps out a dark cackle. "No, but big fans of verbal abuse."

"Not verbal abuse. More... fighting with the sharpness of one's wit."

"Like you do with your Theodora?" Iakov asks with an enthusiastic nod.

I'd been searching her face in the dark room, but Iakov's words bring my attention straight back to him.

"We don't fight. We debate, like fighting but without violence."

"You don't debate, you argue, like fucking but without touching."

"You're drunk, Kav." I grab the bottle out of his hand. "What're you drinking that's got you spouting such obscure shit?" I peer at the label and give Iakov an appreciative nod. "Cognac? Very classy of you."

He shrugs. "It's Sev's. I ran out of vodka."

"Of course you did."

I END UP TAKING more than one sip of Sev's expensive cognac while Iakov updates me on Zahara, and soon, the ground starts wavering under my feet.

Unlike Evan, who just had to run out of the room to throw up, I know my limits, so I pass Iakov his bottle back with a wince. Iakov doesn't know his limit, but only because he probably doesn't have one at all.

We're both startled when a slim body barges past Iakov to stand in front of me. I'm surprised to find Theodora glaring up at me. Her hair is impeccable in its ponytail, but her cheeks are flushed, and her eyes have the same glaze as Iakov's.

My heartbeat stutters in surprise. She's drunk.

Theodora never gets drunk.

But then again, I rarely do. Maybe the pressure of this year is crushing her just as much as it's crushing me, and she's seeking the same reprieve I came here to seek.

"Are you too lofty to say hello?" she asks in a withering tone.

The music is louder now. Earlier, everyone was still sober enough to worry about getting caught. Now, though, everyone is too far gone to care. If the party gets discovered and broken up, I don't even think I'd be terribly heartbroken. I'm so tired lately I could fall asleep standing.

Not too tired to respond, with verve, to Theodora's blatant attack on me.

"I've been standing here for the past hour," I say with a wave of my hand I hope comes across as nonchalant. "You could have come up at any point."

"You saw me come in. You could've come up to me."

"I've come here to let loose and relax after a rough week of deadlines, not to pay tribute to you like some sycophant in your royal court."

"So much for all that talk about getting on your knees if I asked you to," she says in a mocking tone.

"You weren't asking me about getting on my knees. I'll get on my knees for you anytime, Theo. I'll do it right now, if you like, right here in front of everybody."

She bristles. "I'm not asking you to. I'm asking you for some common courtesy."

"Common courtesy is not screaming at your friends at a party."

"I'm not screaming, and we're not friends."

"Don't lie." I step closer to her. "Where's all this anger coming from, Theodora?"

"I'm not angry."

"Then what's the problem? You wanted me to say hello, well, here. Hello, my lovely Theodora, how do you do?" I give a flourish. "There. Have I satisfactorily soothed your bruised ego, goddess of wrath?"

"I'm not your Theodora or a goddess of wrath, and rich of you to mention my ego, Lord Blackwood."

"Why are you starting an argument with me?" I ask, drawing closer to her.

As I speak, I'm suddenly reminded of Iakov's line about fucking without touching.

I turn my head and realise Iakov is long gone. Smart of him, I suppose. He probably didn't want to risk getting caught in the crossfire.

"Are you feeling worked up, Theo?" I ask, turning back to her and pressing closer to speak in her ear. "Are you feeling... *frustrated*? Like there's an itch deep inside you that you can't quite scratch, and maybe fighting me will soothe the itch?"

She flinches back. "What are you talking about?"

"I'm talking about the strange, irresistible urge you felt to find me and draw all my attention to you with the flimsiest excuse imaginable. Look deep inside yourself, Theodora, and you'll see what I mean. It can't be that hard—everyone except you can see it."

"I've no idea what you're talking about. You're just spewing off nonsense sentences, as usual. Don't worry, it's not your fault. I suppose it's how one ends up when one is raised by politicians."

"Oh, you love a good deflection, Theodora, don't you? You never have the guts to fight back, but you're too scared to take a hit, so all you ever do is deflect. That's why we always draw, that's why it's forever a stalemate with you."

"You're drunk," she says with an angry burst of laughter. "You're making no sense whatsoever."

"And you're drunk too."

"I'm not drunk," she lies. "I came here to claim my prize. Or have you already forgotten?"

She's *definitely* drunk.

A stone-cold sober Theodora would never claim a kiss from me. A stone-cold sober Theodora would never let me draw her into such a ridiculous argument. A stone-cold sober Theodora would never lose control like this and let me pluck the harp strings of her emotion to make such intoxicating music.

"I've not forgotten," I say, too elated to repress a grin of triumph. "Claim it."

Chapter 24

Green-Eyed Monster

Theodora

A MONTH OF NUMBNESS followed by a month of back-breaking intellectual labour results in the most overwhelming exhaustion I've ever felt. A feeling like both the adrenaline rush and the inevitable crash but happening simultaneously.

By October, I'm so profoundly tired my skin feels like a burning hot veil around my body and my head and eyes ache almost constantly. Every morning, I wake up like a corpse dragged from the darkness of death, consciousness forced upon me like a disease.

So when Rose and Camille drag me to a party I desperately don't want to go to, I don't even have the strength and energy to fight them.

Before the party, I lie the wrong way around on my bed, head almost dangling off the end, hydrogel eye patches covering the grey shadows under my eyes. I've almost fallen asleep when my bedroom door opens and my eyes fly open.

"Oh. Hey, Ness."

Inessa is still in her uniform, and there's a packet of sweets in her hands. Inessa is one of the true good girls of Spearcrest—the Sophie Sutton of her year group. She doesn't go to parties or make out with boys in the various hook-up spots around campus. She reads, goes to after-school clubs, and attends services in the chapel.

The ultimate good girl.

My father wishes I was like her. I know because he's told me so many times.

"Your friends are so annoying," Inessa says with a roll of her eyes, oblivious to my bleak train of thought.

Sitting next to me, she brushes her hands down the length of my hair, which dangles over the edge of the bed like a cascade.

"They're just giddy girls," I say cautiously.

I love Inessa. No matter how much my father tries to install her as a rival in my life, she'll always be the closest thing I have to the sister I've always wanted.

"They keep asking when you're coming down. Apparently, you guys have somewhere special to be."

I sigh and reluctantly sit up. "The Young Kings are having a... get-together."

"I thought you hated those guys? They're so arrogant and annoying."

"I've been invited. It would be rude not to go. And I don't mind them."

"Hm. I'm just saying. You're too good for any of them." Inessa gives me a little prim roll of her eyes and then breaks into a smile. "But since you're going... what are you going to wear?"

"I have no idea." I stand in front of my mirror to peel off my eyepatches and observe with consternation that the shadows under my eyes are just as dark as ever. "Maybe a shroud, given I look like a corpse dug up by a Victorian resurrectionist."

"You don't look like a corpse," Inessa says with a frown. "Not even a little bit. You're quite literally the most beautiful girl I've ever seen in my life. Look at your hair. I want it so bad. Like Zarya-Zarenitsa."

"More like Baba Yaga," I reply belligerently over my shoulder.

I'm not in the mood for compliments, or for partying, or for anything. The only thing I want is to be in bed and unconscious. But Inessa stands on her feet with a humph of determination and goes to throw open my wardrobe doors.

"Right, come on then, Baba Yaga. Let's get you dressed up."

"I DON'T KNOW ABOUT you girls," Camille says on our way to the study room, her arm squeezed tightly around mine, "but I've had the most outrageously, relentlessly shit week. I need—like, I need to be so drunk, and I need someone to make me come so hard."

Rose lets out a cackle. "You'd have better luck with Mr Gold than the boys at this party. Unless you get yourself a Young King."

Mr Gold—or Eric Victor Gold—is the name of Camille's bullet and the star feature of her many stories about the elaborate dates she has with it. Lingerie and caviar dates, mirror and a fifty-year-old bottle of Cabernet dates. Camille's dates with her vibrator are better than most dates girls in our years have been on.

Not that I would know since I've never been on one.

"I've already had them all," Camille says with a wave of her hand.

My blood runs suddenly cold, and I suppress a shudder. Rose almost stops in her tracks. "No, you haven't."

"Okay, so I've not *fucked* them all," Camille clarifies, "but I got pretty close. I slept with Psycho Luca and that hot French fuckboy, and I used to fool around with Evan back in Year 9 before he went all weird for Sophie Sutton. I made out with the future Lord Blackwood in the back of a limo, and I got super drunk at a club and bumped into Iakov in the back alley when I went for a cig, and he went down on me—I would highly recommend it, by the way, the guy really knows how to eat p—"

"You never kissed Zachary," Rose interrupts. "You're such a fucking liar, Camille."

"I did! We were both really drunk, but I still remember it."

Camille looks at me from under her impossibly long eyelashes. She's dark and voluptuous and passionate—she looks like a princess straight out of an Arabian Nights tale. How could any boy resist her?

It's not like Zachary is my boyfriend. I have no reason to expect him to be faithful to me. It's never something I expected from him. In fact, I've always encouraged him to pursue other girls.

So why does it hurt so much to hear Camille's story?

Maybe Camille senses my pain; there's a sadistic edge to her smile when she turns to look at me.

"Wanna know what it was like?"

I raise an eyebrow. "Why should I care?"

"You two are always at each other's throat," Camille says. "You've got to be wondering about him, at least a little bit."

"Wondering what, exactly?"

"You know. What he's like"—Camille blinks that slow, sexy blink that gets all the boys to fall for her—"in bed."

"You didn't go to bed with him," Rose points out tartly. "You made out a little bit at the back of a limo. Hardly the same thing."

"But I think Theodora would want to know what that's like," Camille says, addressing Rose even though her eyes are still on mine, "to make out a little bit with Zachary Blackwood at the back of a limo."

There's a deep, lush part of my mind that's reserved for poetry and literature, the part of my mind that transforms words into rich imagery. It's normally a sacred place, but its sanctum is suddenly violated by Camille's words.

A picture appears in my mind, vividly detailed.

Black leather seats, city lights blurring past, dark, cold glass. The smell of expensive leather and champagne mingled with a sophisticated cologne, sandalwood and blackcurrants. A warm lap, an arm around my waist, surprisingly strong, and a hand on my back, fingers fanning out, digging ever so slightly into my skin through the silk straps of my dress. Zachary's mouth opening against mine, molten heat and desire so strong it makes me undulate like a flame in his embrace.

I swallow and fix Camille with my iciest smile.

"My standards must be a little higher than yours. I can conjure more satisfying fantasies than fumbling kisses with my old debate team rival."

"Really?" Camille lets out a bark of incredulous laughter. "That's all he is to you, your old debate team rival?"

"What else would he be?"

I ENTER THE PARTY and sense Zachary's presence like a beacon. He sees me but doesn't say anything, doesn't even raise his hand in a wave.

That's fine, of course. Zachary doesn't owe me anything. As he said, he's only ever one step removed from a stranger, and after this year, he'll go back to being a complete stranger.

But I'm shaken—so much more shaken than I ought to be.

It's as if the blow Camille landed somehow left an opening big enough for every other blow to land. I feel it all, all at once.

The pain from the summer, the fear of my father, the loss of my dreams, the dread of the future. My longing for Zachary, the realisation I can never have him, that he'll go back to being nobody. The crushing pressure of Spearcrest, of killing myself getting the best grades when my qualifications will become little more than pretty paperwork. Being an Apostle, the desperation to beat Zachary even though I know I won't be able to accept the mentorship, lying to Mr Ambrose.

It all hits me like an avalanche.

Rose hands me a bottle of something strong, watching me with amused eyes as I take a sip. She holds her hand out, waiting for me to give her the bottle back after a sip, but I shake my head and drink in long, hard gulps.

The liquor leaves a burning trail down my throat, filling my belly with fire. Rose's eyes are wide with a mix of surprise and admiration.

"You're getting fucked tonight, Theodora?" she asks.

"Literally or metaphorically?"

She waggles her eyebrows. "Thoroughly."

Weak laughter rises in my throat, strong enough only for a single exhaled chuckle. I'm shaking all over, I feel feverish and stripped raw.

"I don't want to remember a single second of this night," I answer, the bottle trembling in my hand. "I want to be so drunk I don't even remember my own name. I want to find the kind of obliteration that will make me doubt my very existence."

"Jesus, girl," Rose says. "Doesn't sound like you're looking to have fun."

"Oh, I'll have fun." I take another gulp. "Why shouldn't I have fun?"

"You should," Rose says, "but—"

"I want to have fun," I assure her. "I want to stop feeling like this."

Rose is frowning at me now. "Like what?"

But I've already turned and plunged into the crowd.

ALCOHOL MAKES ME SWAY and burn and laugh.

Later, when the music becomes a loud, urgent beat and everyone gathers close together to dance, I join them. I dance with every girl I know and every boy who dares to approach me. I even let Luca Fletcher-Lowe, who has soulless eyes and laughs like the god-defying Satan of Milton's *Paradise Lost*, take me inside his arms and hold me a little too close, his fingers digging into my upper arm.

"Come outside with me," he murmurs in my ear during a lull in the music. "Come on, mysterious Theodora, lonely ice princess. Let me rough you up a little bit."

I lurch away from him in disgust, and he throws his head back with a feral laugh, melting back into the crowd of dancing bodies like a pale, nightmarish vision.

Fury fills me, but it's not aimed at Luca. It's aimed at Zachary. Because why isn't *he* the one pulling me into his arms, whispering dirty, dangerous things in my ear?

He's probably too busy finding a limousine in which to kiss Camille, that's why.

The jealousy inside me sears like poison, and I know it's making me sick. I'm well-read, logical and intelligent—I know jealousy, I know it's a green-eyed monster which only mocks the meat it feeds on. A parasite that only ever harms its host. I need to get away, sleep it off, let it run its course and be reabsorbed back into the general ache of being alive.

But I'm too drunk and tired. I'm dizzy with a sort of bright, coruscating pain. My skin feels so brittle it might shatter at a touch. I'm freezing inside, so cold I ache, but my skin burns like I'm in the grip of a mortal fever.

And then, somehow, I'm standing in front of Zachary, simmering with anger. He's drunk too, I can tell, and he smiles at me like he knows the real reason I sought him out.

We argue—I don't even know what I'm saying. I angrily tell him I came to claim the kiss he promised me—but I don't want it. I don't want it at all.

I wouldn't want to kiss Zachary Blackwood if I was cursed to die an endless, torturous death for a thousand years and the only way to break the curse was to kiss him.

"I've not forgotten," Zachary says, with a hateful smirk on his angelic face, oblivious to my fury. "Claim it."

Chapter 25

Glass Armour

Theodora

"You promised me a kiss, didn't you?" I ask. "My *first* kiss, right?"

Zachary nods. His eyes glitter with hunger. Desire ripples through him; I see it in the tightening of his fists, the slight shudder that runs up his spine, and the sinking of his teeth into his bottom lip.

"Yes," he murmurs. "Your first kiss."

"Well, you can't give me that," I tell him. "Someone beat you to it. But you can give me my second... no, my third... well—" I laugh. "You can give me a kiss, anyhow."

Pain and anger flash across Zachary's expression, too quick and raw for him to conceal.

"Busy summer, Dorokhova?" he asks, a sharp edge beneath his ostentatious amiability.

"My summer was awful, as you well know, Blackwood," I answer, matching his false courtesy, "but parties are always so rife with temptation, don't you agree?"

"I thought you were too strong to give in to temptation," Zachary sneers. "That armour of yours must be made of glass to shatter so easily."

"Plenty of ways to kiss with armour on," I say with a smile.

"And was it everything you could dream of?" he asks suddenly, almost interrupting me. "Was your chosen purveyor worthy of you?"

"I think so. Someone worthy of being your friend should be worthy of my kisses, no?"

He laughs, sharp and unamused. "My friends would never dream of kissing you. They'd never dare."

"Luca would," I say, thinking of Luca's feral laughter earlier, his repulsive offer.

Zachary's entire body goes stiff. "Luca kissed you?"

"I never said that," I answer.

Pinning my lie on Luca is a perfect solution. One, because whatever code of honour the Young Kings have between them, Luca doesn't seem to care. Two, because Luca would probably go along with my lie out of nothing but sadistic amusement. And finally, most importantly, because Zachary hurt me, and I want to hurt him back.

"So much for this prize, then," I say, filling the silence left by Zachary, who stands frozen and jaw clenched in front of me. "Maybe next time offer me something you can actually give me."

With the same satisfied smirk he gave me earlier, I turn and leave.

Outside the study hall, the silence is almost deafening. I'm far drunker than I've ever been before, and the darkened corridor sways around me as I walk. At the end of the corridor, a face appears in the gloom, startling me.

I draw closer and let out a breathy laugh of surprise.

A marble bust of Apollo on a plinth—the god of music, poetry and archery. I draw closer until I'm standing right in front of him. I stare into the empty eyes and trace with my fingertips the curls of his hair, the folds of the cloak he wears thrown over one shoulder.

He's handsome and beardless, with an earnest expression—almost a frown—and the slight pout of his pillowy lips is rendered in loving details by the sculptor.

I lean forward, close my eyes, and press my lips to Apollo's.

The marble is cold under my lips—a metaphor for the coldness inside my heart. I lied to Zachary for pride, and I hurt him for vengeance, but I feel no satisfaction, no triumph.

I don't feel anything at all.

MARCUS AURELIUS WROTE IN his *Meditations*, "*How much more grievous are the consequences of anger than the causes of it*". Easy to say when you lean towards the philosophy of Stoicism, which values logic over everything else.

Letting logic rule your actions is a noble goal, but how does it work when alcohol takes over and suddenly you're acting out of pure, petty impulse?

And does that mean that the natural impulse of humankind is towards emotion and that logic is, therefore, unnatural?

I don't know. I used to think there was an answer to everything, so long as I worked hard enough to find it. Now, I'm two months into my last year of college, two months into the Apostles programme, and all I know for certain is that I know nothing at all.

Well, no, I know something for certain.

That my actions during the study hall party have consequences. I realise this first in literature class, my first time seeing Zachary after the party.

We sit next to each other, of course, since every English teacher in Spearcrest seems to be under the impression that the only way for us to achieve top marks is if we are helping each other, not realising that the only thing driving us is competition, not cooperation.

Zachary is there first, already sitting down when I enter the classroom. I considered not turning up at all, but I've been doing exceptionally well in literature and can't bring myself to give Zachary a potential advantage over me by missing a class. I slink into the room, clutching my bag, and sit down quickly, taking out my books and letting my hair fall like a curtain between Zachary and me.

If we don't make eye contact and don't speak, and never interact with one another ever again, then everything will be okay. That's my lie of the day, and I hold on to it like an amulet against an angry god.

"Alright, folks, today is the moment we've all been dreading—act five scene two of *Othello*. When we first began the play at the start of September, I asked you all to read up to act five but no further. Can any of you guess why?"

A girl somewhere in the room raises her hand. "Because you wanted us to make predictions about how it would turn out?"

Professor Elmahed shakes her head. Another girl raises her hand. "Because you wanted to watch us suffer?"

Professor Elmahed laughs. "Am I so transparent? Now—my instructions were clear, and I asked nicely. So why do I know for a fact some of you defied my instructions and read this scene already? I suspect some of you have even finished the play already."

She's standing in the middle of the desks, a bit behind the desk I share with Zachary, but I can still feel the weight of her gaze on us.

"How do you answer my accusation, Theodora?" she asks.

I sigh. "I'm sorry, Professor."

"Zachary?" she asks.

Zachary turns to look at her, and I allow myself to sneak a look at his profile as he speaks. "I did read it, Professor, although I won't apologise. I had read it before the class—I'm sure you understand there's a limited pool of classical literature featuring central characters of colour."

"Mm." Professor Elmahed's lips quirk in amusement. "What an excellent answer, Zachary. A politician's answer. Still, since you both have read the scene before, you're best qualified to bring life to these characters. I know you'll both do the scene justice."

My heart sinks, and I cringe into my chair. Zachary loves reading aloud and is always one of the first volunteers, but I'm the opposite. Reading out loud in front of the class makes me almost shrivel with anxiety.

But I know better than to refuse Professor Elmahed. Even if I refused point blank to read, she's the kind of teacher who is perfectly comfortable sitting in excruciating silence, waiting for me to bend to her will.

Before either of us can say anything, Professor Elmahed flips open her copy of the play with a theatrical gesture.

"*Act five, scene two,*" she reads. "*A bedchamber in the castle: Desdemona in bed asleep. A light...*" Professor Elmahed pauses heavily. "*Is burning. Enter Othello.*"

"How would you like me to read Othello in this scene, Professor?" Zachary asks, looking up from the page. "Sad? Reluctant? Angry? Determined?"

"Why don't you tell me, Zachary? How would Othello feel?"

"Hurt," Zachary says immediately. "Like he's about to lose everything. Like he's already lost everything."

Professor Elmahed nods, and Zachary begins Othello's monologue.

"*It is the cause, it is the cause, my soul—*"

His voice is deep and almost shakes with emotion. He reads on, bringing a world of pain to Othello's voice as he considers the consequences of taking Desdemona's life, as he realises killing her will be a point of no return, something he can never take back or undo.

But Othello interrupts his monologue—he must wake the sleeping Desdemona up so that he can confront her. And even though he's about to kill her, he loves her still—he loves her desperately.

That's why he wakes her up with a kiss.

Zachary pauses at the end of his line to let Professor Elmahed read the stage directions. She does so in a hushed tone of reverence.

"*Kissing her*," she reads. She looks up and asks, "How do we think he kisses her?"

"Like a first kiss," Zachary answers immediately. "With all the tenderness and reverence and importance of a first kiss."

"It's their last kiss, actually," I say, my patience finally snapping. "And he's about to kill her. He kisses her with a liar's kiss, a traitor's kiss."

Zachary's jaw clenches, but his voice remains stony.

"She's the love of his life. Every single kiss between them is a first and last kiss, every single kiss is momentous. That's what love does. It heightens everything, it makes everything raw and intense and important. Every touch, every word, every strawberry-spotted handkerchief—and yes, every kiss." He gives me a sharp, sudden smile. "One day, Theodora, you'll kiss someone you actually love. Maybe then you'll understand."

My mouth drops open. I look up at Professor Elmahed, whose eyes have widened. I'm speechless, and heat floods my cheeks in a way that has me praying to every saint that I'm not blushing.

Professor Elmahed lets out an incredulous laugh. "When literature touches true emotions, it can often be easy for the line between fiction and reality to blur. Zachary, let me remind you that Othello is not a real person, and neither is Desdemona—neither is their kiss, for that matter. Theodora, on the other hand, *is* a real person, and you just spoke to her in a way you perhaps should not have. Consider apologising to her after class—privately. Now let's resume reading, please."

We finish reading the scene—Othello sounds hurt and desperate but never remorseful, and Desdemona is full of anger and sorrow. We let our emotions bleed right into the characters, and everyone watches us like we're a little insane.

Maybe we are.

Chapter 26

OLEANDER PROMISE

Zachary

AT THE END OF the class, Theodora packs her things and leaves the classroom like a hare that feels the hot breath of the hounds on the back of its legs.

Professor Elmahed is right; I owe Theodora an apology. My behaviour in class was rude, immature, and borderline childish. I behaved like a spurned lover who is caught in a barbed net of rejection and frustration and strikes out at the very object of his desire.

I've allowed myself to become the dissolute Roderigo, whose unrequited obsession with Desdemona would have him bring about her downfall rather than allow her to be happy with the man she loves.

Except that Theodora isn't Desdemona, and Luca is no Othello. She didn't kiss him because she fell in love with his story, his pain, his bravery. She didn't kiss him because of love, or even, I suspect, because she wanted to.

Why *did* she kiss him? Because he was there and because he was the only Young King who would go near Theodora? Luca would kiss Theodora not despite the fact she's mine but precisely because of it. Does Theodora know? Is that why she kissed him?

I've been turning the mystery of it in my head ever since I last saw her. My desire for Theodora is mirrored by hers for me—so why did she kiss him and not me?

The truth I seek is poetic and complex. That's the nature of the truth in poetry, in literature, in philosophy. The truth is romanticised into something grand and fulfilling, the catharsis of revelation.

In reality, the truth is common, obvious and underwhelming.

Theodora might have kissed Luca for the mere reason that she wanted to. That she could. That he was there.

She might have kissed him for no reason at all.

Theodora has lived trapped in the cage of my heart, where she exists as rival, friend, companion, angel, lover, prize, conqueror, saint and sage.

Except that this whole time, the real Theodora has been living in the real world. She's been living a real existence—a mysterious existence of unhappy summers, meals left untouched, kisses given to boys bold enough to take them. How can I blame her for this?

I can't.

Logically, I must let it go. I must release the pain. And I must absolutely apologise to her for my unacceptable behaviour in class.

Except I *can't* do any of those things. I can't let it go. I can't release the pain, which digs into me like thorns pinned into my flesh. And I definitely don't apologise to her.

And I don't act with maturity or honour or poise.

I do the complete opposite.

"Did you kiss Theodora?" I ask Luca that evening, interrupting him halfway through his dinner.

The dinner hall is loud around us, and Evan and Sev, who sit across from Luca, both look up in surprise.

"Who told you I did?" Luca asks without flinching.

His hair is slicked back with sweat, and his mouth is full of food, so I guess he's just come back from fencing or archery practice. But without his fencing blades or his bows and arrows, Luca is as lean and weak as a reed stalk, and right now, I want nothing more than to snap him in half.

"She did."

Luca shrugs and shoves another spoonful of food into his mouth. "So?"

"So, did you kiss her?"

"What do you want me to say? She's fucking hot, why shouldn't I kiss her? It's not like you've claimed her for yourself."

"Nobody gets to claim her. She's a person, not a *thing*."

"Exactly." Luca pushes back a strand of bone-pale hair from his forehead and gives me a shark's grin. "She can kiss me if she likes. She can do whatever she likes, and if she wanted to fu—"

I grip him by his collar before he can even finish his sentence, half pulling him out of his seat.

"Touch her again and I'll make sure the rest of your life is short and painful."

He stares at me, unsure for a moment, and then he laughs a raspy cackle.

"If you say so, Blackwood."

I release him and walk away under the bewildered stares of our friends.

But just in case Luca doesn't believe me, that night, I pay a visit to the Spearcrest greenhouse. There's an oleander tree there—it's no longer in bloom, but that doesn't matter. I only need a single leaf to slip Luca a small dose of oleandrin.

He's violently unwell for the following week, so unwell he has to leave campus for a while. If he draws a link between my threat and his sudden medical emergency, he never mentions it.

Afterwards, I don't feel any guilt whatsoever. If anything, I feel like he's quite lucky.

I only used the leaves of the oleander. If I'd used the bark, I could have poisoned Luca with rosagenin.

Which is almost as deadly as strychnine.

***

When I next see her Theodora, at our weekly Apostles lecture, we sit on opposite ends of the small lecture room in the Old Manor.

This month, we're learning about aesthetics and ethics (ironic, considering my poor ethical choices recently). Mr Ambrose ends his lecture by writing out a question on the blackboard.

What makes something beautiful and why?

He turns to face us with a grave smile.

"This time, I don't want you all to consider this question too theoretically. I don't want vague and rambling explorations of what might make something theoretical beautiful to some theoretical someone. I want *you* to tell me what makes something beautiful in your eyes. I want you to give me a specific example of something *you* find beautiful, and I want an exploration of that. What is that thing? Why is it beautiful? How do you define beauty, and how much value do you give it?"

My eyes seek Theodora of their own volition.

She's sitting with her chin in one palm, her eyes fixed on Mr Ambrose. But her eyelids are a little heavy. Her mouth is relaxed into a pout, slightly smushed by her palm. The heavy cloak of her hair falls over her shoulders like moonlight.

I tear my eyes away with a sigh.

In general, I've approached all of Mr Ambrose's assignments with honesty and vulnerability. But there's no chance I can possibly be truthful for this particular assessment.

Because if I was, I would need to admit that beauty for me is a quiet girl with a brilliant mind, a debate team captain with a calm voice and textbooks covered in colour-coded annotations. Beauty for me is a girl with cold skin and a faraway gaze, a girl who loves children's books but rarely laughs. Beauty for me is sage-green silk and soft white wool and forget-me-not eyes.

My definition of beauty starts and ends with Theodora.

And as for the value I give her, it's immeasurable. She is worth dying for, living for. Killing for, probably, or at least poisoning for. She is worth every academic failure, every restless night, all the suffering and yearning and hopelessness.

She isn't worth everything. She *is* everything.

So how could I possibly stay angry at her?

I'M ABOUT TO SET off to the library for my pilgrimage of redemption when my phone starts vibrating on my bedside table. I finish pulling on the thick woollen jumper I just fished out of my wardrobe and pick up my phone to see Zaro's name flashing up at me.

We've barely spoken since she arrived in Spearcrest. The most I've received from her have been curt half-texts that scream resentment and barely repressed anger.

I answer immediately.

"Zaro? Are you alright?"

"You need to call off your fucking dog." Her voice trembles with fury. "Right. *Now*."

I wince. "Don't call him that."

"Why not? Isn't that exactly what he is? You snap your fingers and your little guard dog comes running out to snap at my ankles and keep me in check?"

Her words smart, and guilt flares through me. Guilty for both of them: Iakov, for making him into a prison guard, and Zaro, for making her into a prisoner.

"I'm sorry, Zaro. It's not my intention to keep you in check or make you feel like I am. Why don't you tell me what's going on?"

"Nothing is going on! I can't fucking *sneeze* without this giant oaf acting like I'm in mortal danger!"

"Where are you?"

"It's none of your fucking business! You're not my fucking father, and neither is your stupid friend, and none of you can tell me what to do! Call him off—now!"

She hangs up before I can say anything.

"Shit," I mutter to myself.

I call Iakov. He answers at the first ring.

"Hey," he grunts.

"What's going on? Where are you two?"

"King Lane," Iakov says. "London."

I frown. King Lane is one of the most exclusive clubs in London. "King Lane? How did she get in?"

"She met a guy at another club."

"A guy? What guy?"

In the background, I can hear traffic and a female voice letting out a litany of insults. Zaro.

Iakov speaks on, unruffled and matter-of-fact.

"Says his name is Erik. Crypto-bro type." There's a moment of silence, Zaro speaks in the background, and then Iakov adds, "He's invited her back to his hotel. She wants to go. I don't think she should. Now you're caught up."

I've started pacing without realising, my stomach in knots, my heart rate twice what it was before Zaro called me. Before I can reply, I hear scrambling noises, and then Zaro's voice replaces Iakov's on the phone.

"None of that is any of your business. I'm not a fucking nun, Zach! If I want to go back to this guy's hotel, I should be able to!"

"Pass the phone back to Iakov."

"No! This conversation is about *me*! And you two are talking over my head like two parents discussing their child at the dinner table. Are you kidding me?"

"You're right, Zaro, you're not a child, so I'm not going to treat you like you're making the mistakes of a child." My voice is low, my throat tight with a mixture of fear and anger. "I'm going to treat you like you're making the mistake of a complete fucking *idiot* because that's what you're doing. You're mad at our parents, and I get that, and I actually empathise with you—but what you're doing is not only counter-productive, it's downright dangerous, and, frankly, embarrassing. So—"

The line goes dead. I look down at the phone. She hung up on me.

I press the call button. After a few seconds, Iakov answers.

"What do you want me to do?" he asks.

"Bring her back to Spearcrest."

Iakov grunts. In the background, I hear Zaro exclaim, "Come one step closer and I'll call the police!"

"She won't call the police," I say into the phone. "They'll call our parents the moment they find out who she is. Bring her home, Kav."

"*Tak tóčno,*" he says, hangs up.

I NEVER MAKE IT to the library and wait for Iakov's return in the sixth form boys' common room. It's mostly deserted, everyone either out partying, getting laid, or in their bedrooms.

I put the television on to distract me while I wait for Iakov, but the constant reports of kidnappings and murders on the news do nothing but escalate my already soaring heart rate.

Iakov returns an hour later, the plod of his heavy footsteps preceding him. He emerges into the lights of the common room, and I stifle a curse.

He looks rough as hell. His black bomber jacket and jeans are drenched with rain, there's a purple bruise nestled in his right eye-socket where he's soon going to have a new black eye, and a crimson hand mark imprinted on his cheek, so bright and raised it looks like it's just been tattooed on with red ink.

"What the fuck," I breathe out.

He shrugs and peels off his jacket, tossing it over the back of a leather armchair. Underneath it, he's wearing a plain black T-shirt which is also wet and sticks to his skin, but he ignores this. Grabbing a bottle of beer out of a half-torn carton on a side table, he sinks into one of the big chesterfields, propping his muddy combat boots on the table.

"Did you get her home?" I ask, sitting across from him.

He nods. "Yea. Dropped her off at her dorm. Made sure she didn't sneak back out."

"What happened to your face?"

He takes a sip of his beer. "The crypto-bro took a crack at me. Missed my jaw but got my eye. Not a bad punch for such a soft cunt."

"He *hit* you?" I say, covering my mouth. "That was brave of him. What did you do?"

"Just knocked him about a bit. Maybe cracked his skull with mine—not sure. He went down like a sack of bricks. I wanted to throw him in the Thames, but your Zaro begged me to spare him. Got shit taste in men, your sister has."

"I know." I sigh. "But she also probably didn't want you to go to jail either."

"Nah, she did." Iakov takes another sip, rolling his head back against the headrest of the chesterfield. "Called the cops on me."

"She fucking *what*?"

Iakov lets out a rough laugh. "Called them with my own phone." He sounds genuinely amused. "She's a real fucking handful, you know."

"Jesus, Kav." Unlike Iakov, I'm far from amused. If my parents find out what she's been up to, she's going to end up in an actual convent this time. "What did they say?"

Iakov waves a hand, and I notice his knuckles are caked with thick blood clots. "Nothing, man. As soon as they started asking her questions, she lost her cool. Said it was a prank and hung up. She apologised to them—good manners on her when she wants."

"Did she let you bring her home, then?" I ask.

Iakov laughs again. "Did she fuck. Slapped the living shit out of me." He points at his cheek—unnecessarily so since the handshape glows like a beacon on his face. "Had to throw her on my shoulder like a sack of potatoes and bundle her into the limo." He scrunches his face in a wince that looks painful just looking at it. "Bit grim. Made me feel like your fucking *shestyorka*."

I'm not sure what he's talking about, but his bruises and voice tell me everything I need to know. "I'm so sorry, Kav. You don't deserve this."

"Nah, it's alright." Iakov gives a dark chuckle, wholly devoid of amusement this time. "I do."

I have no idea what to say to that, but knowing Iakov, he doesn't need me to say anything. Grabbing a beer from the pack, I crack it open with a sigh and clink my bottle against his.

"Thanks, Kav."

His only response is a half-grin through his mask of bruises.

Chapter 27

Sibling Negotiation

Zachary

THE NEXT DAY IS a day of contrition.

I begin with Zaro.

It's not an easy meeting to set up. In Spearcrest, you can't exchange a glance with someone across a corridor between classes without the entire school somehow knowing about it. The walls have eyes around here, and if one person sees one thing, social media ensures that everybody else will know of it.

Fortunately for me, the Spearcrest campus is a sprawling place, and I have the key to places most students don't have access to. I text Zaro and ask her to meet me in a maths classroom on the top floor of the New Manor. The awkward angle of the door means that even if you stood right against the glass panel at its centre, you could only see a small corner of the classroom.

Of course, finding somewhere to meet is the easiest part. Given how furious Zaro has been with me since she found out I asked Iakov to keep an eye on her, and given I had her quasi-kidnapped the night before, I can't imagine she has much goodwill towards me.

But this is a day of contrition, so I'm willing to wait. Zaro has read my text, but she hasn't responded. She might come, she might not. There's no way of knowing.

So I sit in a corner of the classroom that's the furthest from the door and take out the paperback book that's tucked into my coat pocket—a collection of David Hume essays I'm going to reference in my aesthetics assignment for Mr Ambrose—and start reading.

She makes me wait almost two hours.

She turns up just before midday.

Seeing her is a bittersweet feeling, a strange mingling of melancholy and nostalgia. In her face, I see remnants of the little sister I remember so vividly: in the big, dark eyes with their forest of curly eyelashes, in the natural glow of her skin and the roundness of her cheeks, in the pout of her lips, which remind me of how her mouth would wobble every time she was about to cry as a little girl.

Those are the remnants of the old Zaro, but they are set like jewels in the shape of the new Zaro. A taller Zaro, with the grace and poise of a dancer, a Zaro with a direct, defiant gaze. A Zaro in Gucci tights and an oversized blazer, a belt around her waist, her long black curls half-up, the tips now honey-gold.

Zaro has always been a soft being, but whatever softness is left inside her is well hidden now. Even from me.

Maybe especially from me.

"Morning, Zaro," I greet her. "You didn't need to dress up on my account."

"I have somewhere to be after this," she snaps. "So it better not take long."

I want to tell her it would already be over if she'd come earlier, but I'm too grateful that she came at all to care. I nod. "It shouldn't take long. Where are you headed to anyway?"

"Why?" she asks in a sneer. "So you can sic your dog on me?"

I sigh. "Look, Zaro. I'm not going to beat about the bush with this. I am sorry for asking Iakov to keep an eye on you. Not sorry because I regret it or because I think it's a bad idea. I'm sorry because of how it makes you feel. I never wanted that. I never, ever want you to feel like I don't trust you or like I look down on you."

She lets out a burst of angry laughter. "Oh, you don't want me to feel that way, do you? You don't want me to feel like you see me like a little girl who can't look after herself and make her own decisions, so to show me that you really respect me, you don't get your hands dirty trying to control me, you just get your big scary friend to do it for you?"

"I'm not trying to control you," I say immediately. "I'm trying to protect you."

"Great. Great. I feel so blessed and fortunate to be surrounded by so many men who wish to protect me—by controlling me."

I clench my jaw, forcing myself to carefully consider my words. The last thing I want to do right now is to speak out of anger. I asked Zaro to meet me here because I want to sort things out with her, not deepen the trench between us.

"Look—I understand why you feel this way," I say slowly.

She interrupts me sharply. "Don't patronise me."

"Alright. Why don't you tell me how to fix this, then?"

She stares at me for a second as if she wasn't expecting me to say that. She recovers quickly and blurts out, "I want you to get your stupid friend to leave me alone."

I consider my response. I realise I'm playing with my book, tugging at the pages and flicking them back and forth. It's probably making me seem nervous, and I don't want Zaro to think I'm nervous. I close the book and set it aside.

"Alright. I'll ask Iakov to stop keeping an eye on you. What happens next?"

"What do you mean?" Her tone is short and irritated.

"I mean when you're on your own, staking your independence, without a safety net and without my interference. What happens next? You go to private clubs in London with tech execs and then what?"

Dull colour flushes into Zaro's cheeks. She crosses her legs and breathes out through her nose. Her fingers curl around the edge of the table, squeezing it.

"I'm not stupid, alright?" she says finally. "I wouldn't have stayed the night at his hotel room."

"What if he didn't give you a choice?"

She glares at me as if offended by the bluntness of my question.

"I would've called the police—as you well know."

"What if he took your phone?"

She rolls her eyes. "Don't be so paranoid."

"Don't be so naive." I take a deep breath. "Look, I'm not saying it *would* have happened, Zaro. I'm saying it *could* have happened. That's what I'm scared of—don't you get it? I'm not afraid that I can't trust you or that you'll mess up. You're allowed to mess up. I'm afraid of things going wrong, of someone hurting you." She rolls her eyes again, but this time, it's more half-hearted. "You have every right to want to live your life the way you want to—but try to imagine, for one split second, how I would feel if something happened to you and I hadn't done anything to stop it. Try to imagine that the other way around—if something happened to me."

She sighs, and her shoulders slump. The bravado melts from her posture.

"I know you worry about me, Zach. I know you want to keep me safe, but you can't keep me safe by keeping me in a *cage*."

"That's not how I wanted to make you feel." I raise my hands. "I'm trying my best, but I don't know how to look after you without making you feel shit about it, Zaro. I just don't."

She nods and slides off the edge of the desk, pulling out the chair next to mine and sitting at my side. We stare at each other for a second.

"Trust me a little more, that's all. If you're scared for me, I'll start carrying mace. I'll—I'll keep you updated on where I am. And if I'm in trouble, I'll call you. I promise."

I nod slowly. "Alright. I'm willing to meet you halfway too. I'll call Iakov off—but I have two conditions."

She stiffens a little bit, but there's a spark of hope in her eyes. "What conditions?"

"I want you to let Iakov teach you some self-defence."

"Ugh, no, please. I hate exercising, Zach, and he's so big—can't I just carry a knife on me or something?"

"A knife will be useful until someone knocks it out of your hand." I take her hand in mine. "I know it's not fair that you should have to learn how to fight. I know none of this is your fault. But there's no use pretending danger isn't real. And if you don't want me to have Iakov look after you, then you're going to have to learn how to look after yourself. For real—not just by sending me a pin of your location when there's nothing either of us could do if something went wrong."

She sighs and throws her hands up in petulant acceptance.

"Fine! I'll learn self-defence." She narrows her eyes. "What's the other condition?"

"You don't have to be a nun, Zaro, but for god's sake—please don't hang out with old guys. There's a reason these men aren't pursuing relationships with women their age. They're not the kind of men who are looking to treat you as an equal."

She drops her gaze and then mumbles, "I know this."

"Do you?"

She glares at me. "Yes, Zach, obviously I do." Biting down into her lip, she glances away guiltily and then adds, "I was only going back to that guy's hotel because I wanted to piss your friend off."

For a moment, I just look at her. I don't doubt for a second that there is truth in what she's telling me. It wouldn't surprise me if Zaro was just testing Iakov. But Iakov wasn't around when she was at Sainte-Agnès, where she was groomed by a member of staff.

I don't want to judge Zaro based on something she was a victim of. But the knowledge of what happened at Sainte-Agnès is like an injury inside my mind. Even if it heals, it'll always leave a scar, a scar that will forever affect every decision I make when it comes to her.

"Promise me you'll be careful," I say, giving her my hand.

She rolls her eyes but takes it. I squeeze her palm against mine. "I'll be careful."

"I love you, lil sis."

Her face softens. When anger and hurt and resentment aren't hardening her features, the Zaro of old—my little sister who loved plants and flowers and would sit at the foot of my bed playing farming games while I read books out loud—comes melting through, making my chest ache.

"I love you too, big bro."

Chapter 28

Anti-Ophelia

Zachary

Thomas Aquinas, the patron saint of academics, believed that penance relied on three conditions:

Contrition—sorrow for sin.

Amendment—confessing sins without omission.

And satisfaction by means of good work.

All of those things sound reasonable—maybe even noble.

Sorrow for sins is easy because my sin resulted in Theodora's hurt and anger and her avoiding me like a plague of blisters. And I'm not afraid to do good work. Work, good or otherwise, has never intimidated me.

But confessing my sins without omission is a Herculean mission—maybe even a Sisyphean task.

Because it would mean telling Theodora while I'm unhappy with her, why I lashed out at her, and why I couldn't read a scene of *Othello* without projecting us onto the characters. It would mean telling Theodora that I wanted to be the first person to kiss her even though she never promised me her first kiss, even though not a single thing in this world entitles me to her kisses except the fact I want them. I would need to admit that she hurt me, hurt both my pride and my feelings.

Being honest doesn't bother me—I could confess to just about any sin in front of just about any person. But of course, Theodora isn't just about any person.

Still, not doing the right thing because it's difficult or because it's embarrassing isn't a good enough reason.

IT'S A COLD SATURDAY, cold enough for the wind to have chased away the clouds and crystallised the beads of moisture on leaves and window panes. Normally, whenever I need to find Theodora, all I need to do is to hunt her down in her usual spot in the library, but she won't be there today.

Theodora's use of social media is tactful: aesthetically pleasing and frequent without ever revealing much about her at all. Her friends, on the other hand, use their social media accounts very much in the same way as the Victorians used journals and letters—a medium in which to pour all one's thoughts and emotions.

And Seraphina Rosenthal—the Rose of Spearcrest—posted a GRWM less than half an hour ago.

In it, she filmed herself doing her make-up and picking an outfit, and although my phone was on mute and I couldn't hear what she was saying, her caption read, *Get ready with me: tate britain girl trip edition.*

I consider asking Evan if he'd like to come to London with me since he's always good fun on a trip, but he's been taking English lit more seriously since Sophie Sutton started tutoring him, and I don't want to be the one to distract him. So I order a private cab and make my way to London with only David Hume's collected essays for company.

I'm more than a little nervous—far more nervous than I normally am in any given circumstance—but luckily for me, David Hume's stream-of-consciousness style of writing is dense enough to require all my attention, and I soon lose myself in his words.

By the time the cab pulls to a stop, I'm still on the same section I was on at the start of the journey, but I've highlighted one quote which stays with me.

"We speak not strictly and philosophically when we talk of the combat of passion and of reason. Reason is, and ought only to be the slave of the passions."

This sentiment flies in the face of what I've always believed: that the whole point of reason is that it's there to govern the baser aspect of our minds—our emotions. I'm not sure I agree with Hume's assertion that reason has no other purpose but to "*serve and obey*" our passions rather than the other way around, but it gives me plenty to think about as I thank the cab driver and make my way into the gallery.

Once I'm standing inside, I pause. Above me is the white cage of the glass dome, which separates the icy-blue sky into squares like pale sapphires set in a lattice of bones.

I gaze into the sky and breathe deeply, steeling myself. I'm tempted to open my phone and find out Theodora's location by checking the regular and numerous story updates Rose is doubtlessly posting, but I find that I don't need to. I make my way through the gallery, chamber by chamber, and gaze at the paintings, looking for Theodora in each of them.

Not Theodora herself—but Theodora's interest, her attention. What would capture her gaze?

Turner's moody, shimmering depictions of nature, vivid suns seen through clouds like torn veils. The long-haired, unsmiling women of Rossetti's paintings—a depiction of femininity not softened for male consumption. Draper's fallen Icarus, with his brown skin and the tragic fan of his wings.

I spot Theodora before I spot any painting in the room she's in.

My eyes fall on her as if she's the artwork. She's standing straight as an arrow, holding something against her chest. She's in a short cream dress and an enormous pearl-grey cardigan.

Completely alone, she stands face to face with Millais's *Ophelia*.

The moment I spot her, I'm acutely aware of the fact that I'm now watching her, making her the focus of all my attention. It somehow feels like an intrusion, and I know I have no choice but to make myself known.

I stand next to her, shoulder to shoulder, as close as I can get to her without making any contact between her body and mine.

"Hi, Theo."

She doesn't look at me, doesn't start. I detect perhaps the merest hint of a stiffening of her posture, a tightening of her arms around whatever she's holding to her chest—a textbook, a map of the gallery and her tablet in its café au lait-coloured case.

"Hi, Zach." She's silent for a moment, her eyes still fixed on Ophelia. Then she adds, "Why do they always have to die for the men?"

"Who? Shakespeare's women? They don't."

"Not all of them—but those who do. Ophelia. Desdemona. Juliet. Why must they die? Why must the men wear their dead women as accessories to their own tragedies?"

"Maybe they're not accessories. Maybe they're the real tragedy—a reflection of the innocents who get sucked into the vortex of angry, flawed people and get hurt in the process."

"Maybe." Theodora lets out a sigh. "I guess after studying literature all these years, I feel a bit burnt out on female victims and female suicides and suffocated wives and hysteria and erotomania."

I'm silent for a moment, taking in what she's saying. Part of it, I take at face value. Women have it hard in literature—art imitating life and perhaps a little bit of vice versa at play. Making your way through the canon of classical literature as we have for the past few years has meant an almost constant parade of suffering or mistreated women, interrupted now and then by a Jane Eyre or a Lizzie Bennet, but even then, not without their share of pain.

But I don't think Theodora is just talking about literature.

There's a sadness inside Theodora, a sadness that was there the first time I saw her, sitting stiffly in her blue felt seat, a sadness that seems to cling around her like a heavy mantle, trailing behind her wherever she goes.

A sadness I wish I could tear off her—if only it was tangible to me.

I'm not sure what to say, and I'm not sure if there's anything Theodora wants me to say. I hesitate and then ask, "How are you, Theodora?"

She finally looks at me, a wry smile on her face. There's a brittleness to her, like porcelain so frail it's almost translucent. She looks as if a mere caress might send a crack running through her. Her eyes are cold, not cold like a distant glacier, but cold like fragile frost.

"I'm tired," she answers. "I'm so tired. And I have no idea what I'm going to write for Mr Ambrose's beauty assignment."

I frown. Theodora has excelled so far in the programme. She's not missed a single assignment, and Mr Ambrose has been raining praise on every piece of work she's submitted.

In literature class, she's finally managed to pull a little ahead of me, her essays always getting higher marks than mine. As far as I'm concerned, she's thriving—academically.

Hearing that she's stumped doesn't fill me with satisfaction, like I'm seeing my rival stumble in the race. It makes me feel devastated, like finding out the enemy you were looking forward to duelling has fallen ill.

"Maybe you're overthinking it," I say suddenly, remembering the reading I've been doing, all of it to find a way of avoiding writing an essay that will make Mr Ambrose realise how desperately I love Theodora. "Mr Ambrose specifically said he wants to hear about our interpretations of beauty—maybe that's all you have to write about."

"What if you're not sure what is or isn't beautiful? What if you are in an abusive relationship with beauty?" She's no longer looking at me, her eyes having drifted back to Ophelia's face. "What if I'm Ophelia and beauty is Hamlet, making me feel so awful I want to die?"

A pit opens at the bottom of my stomach—a dark pit of pure terror.

"Do you want to die?" I ask, keeping my voice as calm as I can when asking such a question and being so afraid of the answer.

Theodora sighs. "No. I don't want to die—I want to live. I want it quite desperately. Maybe I'm not like Ophelia after all." She finally turns away from the painting. "You've caught me at a bad time, Zach." She smiles at me, a smile that feels like she's just put a mask back on. "I'm sure you weren't expecting such despondency after taking the time to find me here."

"I came because I wanted to apologise to you," I blurt out. "I know it's an overdue sort of apology, which is why I didn't want to wait any longer than I already have."

She raises an eyebrow. "You don't need to apologise."

"I do. I shouldn't have been so rude to you in lit class the other day. I shouldn't have been so moody and immature. And I shouldn't—I didn't want to fight, that night at the party, but I felt so angry and aggrieved, I felt like you hurt me, and I wanted to hurt you back. But—"

I remember Aquinas's rules for penance. Confessing sins without omission. How could I possibly tell Theodora I wanted her first kiss—that I want all her kisses?

Telling her would feel both humiliating and manipulative.

"I regret our fight, Theo. And I miss our friendship, even if you keep saying we're not friends."

She watches me for the longest moment. I watch her back, my gaze stuck against the forget-me-not blue of her eyes, unable to penetrate the emotions beyond it. We're standing at arm's length from one another, and the gallery around us might as well not exist.

Existence right now is Theodora's blue gaze, her delicate skin, her long hair, the stormy ocean of restrained emotions I long to plunge into, the heat of every kiss and caress I want to bestow upon her.

I shiver, my skin burning with the want of hers.

"I forgive you," she says finally, voice surprisingly soft. "And I'm sorry for saying we aren't friends. We are. Well..." She lets out a little laugh. "We're not—are we? But we're something."

Something like love and hatred and desire, something like the inky depth of an abyss and the soaring breath of a zephyr. Something painful and exhilarating, the golden palaces of heaven and the dark wastelands of hell. Something like soulmates and lovers and enemies.

Something imperfect and sublime.

"Yes, Theo." I extend my hand between us. "Let's be somethings again. Let's not let anything get in the way of our somethingship."

She takes my hand and smiles, finally. "Best somethings forever."

Chapter 29

Open Wound

Theodora

Zachary and I go almost a month without arguments.

It's the last month of the term, and so we spend a significant amount of that time preparing for exams, but it's still a win for us. Our delicate alliance has seen the merging of our territories in the library, Zach and I sitting side by side to read and write in silence for hours on end.

During the Apostles seminars, our discussions are civil even when we disagree, and Zach no longer seems to be choosing his point of view based on a blatant desire to start an argument—his speciality since we were team captains in debate club.

But not arguing with Zachary comes with its own challenges.

Sitting next to him, with the warmth of his shoulder radiating against me, is stressful in a completely different way. The brush of his arm against mine as he turns a page in his book, his thigh brushing alongside mine when he shifts in his seat after an hour of sitting in the same position, become small, lingering acts of torture. Reminders of what could be between us—of what I'm not allowed to have.

The unnamable, unbearable tension between us, without the vessel of arguments to dispel it, has nowhere to go. So it stays right there, coiling itself tightly, making the air between us dark and hot and suffocating.

Like a serpent preparing to strike, it bides its time.

***

THE NIGHT BEFORE THE final lit mock exam, I'm at my usual desk, carefully writing out revision cards for key quotes, when Zachary arrives.

His philosophy teacher has him help out with debate club on some Thursday nights, so I expected him to be late. I'm not annoyed, but I am stressed. Tomorrow's exam is closed book, and I've not been getting enough sleep, and the Christmas break is coming up soon, which makes my skin crawl with unspeakable anxiety.

It's a sickening potion of emotions that boils and bubbles inside me while I do everything I can to stop it from spilling out.

Zach shrugs off his coat, folds it and drapes it on the back of his seat. Every one of his movements drips with elegance and grace. The deep azure of his sweater emphasises the creamy brown of his skin, and the gold armature of his glasses catches the light. He looks older than his years, poised with a deep inner confidence I could never have, his clever eyes focused on some inward thought.

His gaze meets mine, and he flashes me a smile.

I look away quickly as he sits down next to me, as he usually does, taking out his books and laptop from his leather satchel. He settles himself, his arm brushing against mine as he does.

I close my eyes. It's warm in the library, but I'm cold—I'm always cold lately. When he stops moving, his chin propped on the knuckles of one closed hand, I shift in my seat, tilting myself away from him with my arm right against his.

Zachary's warmth isn't like the normal heat that exudes from flames or skin. It's a delicious, molten heat, suffused with the scent of his cologne, his presence. I almost melt against it. He doesn't move, letting my arm rest against him.

We sit like this, the warmth of him an elixir of comfort.

When my revision cards are finally finished, I have no choice but to move, gathering my cards into a neat stack. Zachary looks up from his book.

"Want me to test you?"

I hand him the stack. "Go ahead."

He takes the stack and moves, turning his chair so it's facing mine. I mirror him, and we sit facing one another. He's relaxed in his chair, one arm casually thrown over an armrest, the other propped up, holding a card up to his face. I sit with my legs crossed, laced fingers holding one knee, watching him. Our chairs are so close that my shin rests against the front of his seat, between his legs.

"Alright." Zach sounds quite relaxed. He glances up at me and gives me a lazy smile. "Time to test that *Othello* knowledge. Why don't you tell me your best reputation quotes?"

I reel off my quotes one by one. Zach nods at each of them, lays down the card when I'm done, picks up the next.

"Three quotes about deception and betrayal."

I recite them. Zach's eyes flick up to mine. "You're good."

"Thank you."

"Let's lift the mood a little," Zach smirks. "Your best quotes on prejudice and racism."

I suppress a smile and recite them. Zach nods. "Cheerful stuff, huh? Alright. How about masculinity and honour?"

"My favourite." I give him a dry smile and recite my quotes.

"Love," he says next.

I recite my quotes. He cycles through the cards, testing me on each theme and character. After he tests me on the final card—Iago as a villain—he half-tosses it down on the rest of the pile.

"That was perfect. Word for word on every single one of those quotes."

He suddenly sits up in his chair. Because he was relaxed back in his seat, I could sit close to his chair without being close to him, but now that he's sat up, I find myself face to face with him.

He gives me a half-grin, showing off those straight white teeth, the gleam of his smiling cheek, the two dimples carved deep by the sharp structure of his face. My breath catches.

"Tell me the truth," he says in a lowered voice. I swallow, suddenly nervous. "Are you actually a machine?"

His lips are inches from mine. I know he expects me to be the one to back down; I'm *always* the one to back down. But the tension between us is heavy and electric as a storm—I can't pull away from it, and I refuse to.

"Do I look like a machine?" I ask. "Do I feel like a machine?"

"Hm." He hums in an overdramatisation of thought. "Certainly, you look like you could have been made in a lab, yes." He brushes his fingers over the knuckles of my hands, which are still propped on my knee. "Your skin is cold to the touch." He lifts his hand to my neck, pressing two fingers right underneath my jaw, his thumb resting in the dip between my collarbones. "There is a pulse," he murmurs, "but that could just be excellent engineering for the sake of verisimilitude."

He doesn't move his hand away, and a shiver courses through me. He responds to it with a thoughtful tilt of his head.

"Are you cold, Theo?"

"Always."

I look at his mouth. I know he wants to kiss me.

"Maybe that's why you're always cold," Zach says in a hushed tone. "Because you're not a real person."

"I'm a real person," I answer tightly. "I'm as real as you. I have skin and bones and a mind and a heart and blood running through my veins—just like you."

"Then how are you so perfect?"

The mocking edge has vanished from Zach's voice.

"I'm far from perfect. I'm cold and tired and stressed and angry and sad."

It's a more honest response than I intended to give him. Maybe part of me wants him to know how broken I am.

Maybe I don't want him to be in awe of me anymore. Maybe I don't want to be his equal, his rival, his nemesis. Maybe part of me wants him to see me for what I really am and pity me. Maybe I want him to want to fix me, to protect me, to take care of me.

It feels like a taboo thought to have. I'm strong and intelligent, a feminist in a society that is still profoundly, harrowingly patriarchal—I know that I should be the one to fix myself, to protect myself, to take care of myself.

But I'm so very tired, and I'm so bad at it.

Zach's eyes search mine like he's looking for the perfect reply. I don't want a reply. I just want to be saved.

I want *him* to save me.

"My beautiful nemesis," he whispers in a sigh. "What's making you angry? What's making you sad?"

There's a lump in my throat and a burning in my eyes. I'm not worried about crying in front of Zach. My tears don't fall when I'm alone, why would they fall when I'm not?

"Everything," I answer.

"Even me?"

My eyes flick to his mouth, to the kisses he refuses to give me, the pleasure that glimmers there, unspent and selfishly withheld.

"Even you," I tell him. "*Especially* you."

"I'm sorry," Zach says. His hand moves up my cheek to gently cradle my jaw. "I'm sorry, Theo. Don't hate me. Don't hate me. Please. Love me."

"How?"

"Love me like I love you," he says. "In every way possible. With your mind and your heart and your soul."

I know then I'm going to kiss him. It's inevitable, isn't it?

A shadow crosses the corner of my vision, and I look up with a start. A student emerges from one of the reading nooks on the top floor, making their way wearily to the staircase. I can't tell who it is, and we're sitting far enough into the shadows that I doubt the student saw us, but I'm startled back to reality as if I've been thrown into ice-cold water. I push my chair back and stand, feeling suddenly stupid, vulnerable, as raw and exposed as an open wound.

"We should get some sleep before the exam," I mumble. I don't dare look at Zach, so I stuff my things haphazardly into my bag.

"Theodora."

I grab my revision cards, my laptop, my pens, throwing them pell-mell amongst books and notepads. "Goodnight, Zach."

"Theodora."

Slinging my bag on one shoulder, I wave a hand. "I'm sorry I made tonight so weird—we barely got any revision done and..." He stands, startling me. I take several steps back, eyes wide, babbling on, "Please ignore what I said. I wasn't even really being serious, I—"

He reaches for me, and I cringe back, but his hand closes around the handle of my bag, which he slides off my shoulder. I pull away from him with a frown as he carefully sets my bag down on a chair before stepping closer to me.

I retreat once more, backing away from him and into the shadowy corridor of an aisle. The soft green carpet swallows the sound of my footsteps. Zach follows me, plunging into the darkness of the enormous Victorian bookshelves with me.

"I wish that—I wish I had..." I mumble without really knowing what I'm saying.

With slow, calm movements, Zach takes off his glasses and folds them, sliding them into his pocket. Then he reaches for me, and this time, it's *me* he's reaching for.

His hand catches the back of my neck, holding it through my hair. His touch is impossibly gentle, but he's firm as he pulls me to him by my neck and presses his mouth to mine.

My words melt on my tongue like snowflakes, becoming liquid and inconsequential. Zach's kiss is as gentle as his fingers as they glide down my neck.

It's a chaste, tender kiss, lingering yet pure. He pulls away first, and I retreat deeper into the shadows, my heartbeat an uncontrollable gallop, my cheeks smouldering like burning embers.

"Zach..." I breathe.

"Theodora," he replies, his voice low and firm.

He follows me until my back bumps the end of the aisle. Zachary lays his hands on the bookshelves at the sides of my head, trapping me between his arms. My senses are filled with the smell of old wood and old books, with the rich scent of sandalwood and blackcurrants. I'm dizzy and disoriented and terrified and elated.

He kisses me as if he aches, long and slow and deep. His mouth opens against mine, and I reach up, taking his collar in my hands to pull him closer, to anchor myself to him. His tongue brushes past my open lips, teasing me, tasting me. I meet it shyly with mine, not sure what I'm doing.

One kiss melts into the next, into another. Hot, burning, insistent kisses, full of anguished desire. His arm curls around my waist, pulling me flush against him. His body is solid and warm and strong, so much stronger than I expected for a scholar like him.

With his free hand, he cradles my head, tipping it up to his like a flower to the sun. His thumb caresses my cheek and tugs at my bottom lip.

And just like that, our kisses change, become something hotter, hungrier, *dirtier*.

Zachary lifts me into his arms, and I grip his shoulders, steadying myself, squeezing his waist with my thighs. His mouth moves wetly from my lips to my cheek, to the corner of my jaw, to my neck. I'm warm and tight and aching between my legs, I arch against him without even meaning to, and my head rolls back against the books behind me.

"Theodora," Zachary murmurs against my throat. His voice is rougher than I've ever heard it before, rough as if he's been screaming for hours, rough as if he can barely speak. "My beautiful nemesis. My delicious, darling adversary. My Theodora."

His mouth closes on the hollow of my throat, and he sucks on it until I let out a whimper. He presses me closer by my waist, his other hand propped against the bookshelf, and he traces a path of lingering kisses up my neck.

"I adore you," he breathes in my ear, his lips against my hair. "I adore everything about you, and I want you, I want you laughing and victorious and happy, I want you kiss-drunk and wet and breathless with pleasure. I want you so much I could die from the hunger of it."

His words send shivers through me that make my teeth chatter. My fingers are clenched so hard into his shoulders I'm sure I must have pierced through his jumper. I roll my hips into him, seeking the pleasure he's promising.

In the darkness of the aisle, sheltered by the thick mahogany and the silent tomes, I feel free and feral, as if the shackles of being myself have fallen away.

Zachary shifts me against him and then sets me slowly to my feet. I stare up at him, and his face in the shadows is solemn, his eyes a dark glitter, a burning intensity rising from him like black flames.

"What—what are you doing?" I ask.

With infinite tenderness, he brushes my hair back, fixes my clothes and then his.

"I thought perhaps you wanted me to kiss you," he says quite calmly. "And in any case, I desperately wanted to kiss you. I've desperately wanted to kiss you for a very long time. But I won't pressure you into doing anything els—"

"You're not pressuring me," I say quickly.

"—and we *do* have an exam first thing tomorrow morning."

Zachary pulls me out of the aisle and back into the golden lights. I half-expected the desire coursing through me like liquid lightning to melt away once we left the shadows, but it doesn't. If anything, the sight of Zach, with his smooth skin and his dark hair and his intense gaze and that tender, confident smile, sends a fresh wave of desire through me.

"Don't be cross at me," Zachary says. "There are a thousand things I would love to do to you, my Theodora, and I would do anything you ask. If you'd like me to pleasure you in the Spearcrest library, right against the works of the philosophers and poets we love, I will. I'll kiss every part of you and make you feel so good your cries will make Keats shiver in his grave. I'll do anything you desire, everything you've ever craved. You need only ask."

"You know I won't ask," I snap at him, grabbing my bag as he gathers his things with unhurried movements.

"No," he says, glancing up at me over his shoulder as he neatly tucks his things into his satchel. "I think you will."

APOSTATES

Chapter 30

Lucky Mouth

Theodora

For the final Apostles session of the year, Mr Ambrose greets us in his office with a small feast and some presents.

The usually austere office is decorated with green garlands tied with red velvet bows, and there's even a Christmas tree near the window, fully adorned in baubles and fairy lights.

There are only six of us remaining at this point. At first, we all stand in shock, exchanging confused glances. Mr Ambrose greets us with a smile.

"I've worked you all very hard indeed this term. I've been exigent, relentless, and at times, I'm sure, rather cantankerous. But we are one week away from Christmas, and God forbid I should ever be accused of Scroogery. So, please help yourselves to some mulled wine and food. I especially recommend the Christmas cookies—at least, I recommend you try them before they all inevitably make their way inside my belly."

It's odd seeing Mr Ambrose so jovial, and we're all a bit awkward at first, swapping looks of uncertainty. The table, with its gleaming pastries and colourful cookies, makes my stomach squirm uncomfortably. My eating is never the best around exams, but combine exams with the orgiastic displays of food that seem to be the defining factor of Christmas, and it's enough to make me want to crawl back inside my skin.

A shoulder presses against mine, and I find Zachary standing next to me with two small cups in hand. He hands me one with a little smile. "Will you at least have a few sips of mulled wine with me? Enough for a toast or two?"

I take the cup with a little smile. "Thank you. What shall we toast to?"

"Mm," he taps his chin. "I suppose to Mr Ambrose, the master of the feast. To you, my adored rival. And... well, to kisses?"

"You're ridiculous," I tell him, but I tap my cup to his, and we both drink.

He gives me an unrepentant shrug and a crooked grin which sends a flutter through my chest.

We sit side by side near Mr Ambrose's desk, and once everyone is settled, Mr Ambrose gives a brief speech about how impressed he is with us so far, how convinced he is that we are one of the best cohorts he's had in years, and how happy he is to see so many of us still in the programme.

He toasts each one of us individually, and we toast him in return.

Zachary speaks up, confident as ever. "Does your magnanimous spirit mean no assignment over the holidays, sir?"

Mr Ambrose gives a booming laugh. "It certainly does not, I'm afraid. Without an assignment to keep you all sharp while you're away, you might all return in the new year with your brains turned to mush. No—I must find a way of compelling you all to crack a book at least once or twice over the holidays."

"Boo, sir," Sai Mahal calls out. A prodigy in physics and maths, he is also the only boy, with Zachary, who is still in the programme.

"Easy, Sai," Mr Ambrose says, leaning back against his desk and crossing his arms. "I'm not a tyrant—and as I promised, not a Scrooge. This assignment will be a unique one among your Apostles assignments. You see, I was particularly impressed by your aesthetics essays, and the key to how successful you all were in that assignment, I think, lies in the fact I asked you all to veer away from research and references and dissections. I asked you all to look inwards, to write about your own emotions and opinions, and this resulted in a collection of essays I was not only impressed by but more importantly, intrigued by. And trust me, after a quarter of a century teaching, finding an essay interesting is a whole challenge in itself."

He pauses, and his face breaks into a beam.

"So, for your next assignment, I would like to present you all with a new challenge: happiness."

Silence follows his announcement. His beam doesn't break.

"Happiness, sir?" asks one of the girls in an incredulous tone.

"Yes. Happiness. Christmas is an interesting time: a festival that ostentatiously celebrates happiness, and yet doctors and mental health professionals report higher rates of depression and mental health issues during that period. What does that tell us? That the expectation of happiness is counter-productive to happiness itself? So what is happiness, and where does it stem from? Do you create your own happiness, or do you draw it from something? From Plato to Frankl, Al-Ghazali to Nietzsche, philosophers from every era, country and culture have tried to explore the meaning of happiness. From ataraxia and eudaemonia to utilitarianism to nihilism, from cynicism to hedonism—most philosophical schools concern themselves, either to a smaller or greater extent, with the question of happiness.

"So, for this assignment, I wish you all to do the same. Concern yourselves with happiness—that is all. You may do so in whatever way you wish. You may read and research the idea, you may explore it via the medium of poetry, fiction, art"—he gestures to Sai with a respectful nod—"or even through formulas and algorithms. You might try the simplest—and perhaps the most difficult—approach and set out to find happiness itself, then record your findings. You can do so in the form of journal entries, scientific notes and graphs, it's completely up to you. There will be no set word count, you are not expected to submit a bibliography unless you wish to. I will mark your assignment on the sole criteria of whether or not I glean within it a true exploration of happiness."

He claps his hands together, startling a few of us. "And that's it! That's your assignment—nothing more, nothing less. I hope you all learn something from it. The submission deadline will be the first Monday back. If you have any questions—I beseech you—do not email me during the holidays."

Mr Ambrose spends the next hour answering questions and discussing possible ideas with students, in groups or one at a time. Zachary has already whipped out a notebook from his bag and religiously notes down everything Mr Ambrose says, even when it's not addressed to him.

Finally, once it's time to leave, Mr Ambrose wishes us all good luck and an excellent holiday. We all bid each other goodbye and trickle out of the room one by one. Zachary is last to leave—I suspect he must have waited to ambush Mr Ambrose with a dozen final questions—but he catches up with me in the staircase.

"Theodora." He's slightly out of breath as if he's been running all the way from Mr Ambrose's office.

I look up and lean against the glossy black balustrade, watching him as he catches up with me. He goes down a couple of steps past me, turning around to face me, and standing, for the first time since we were kids, perfectly face to face.

"Here." Zachary pulls a white parcel out of his pocket and hands it to me. I open it: two of Mr Ambrose's Christmas cookies, one shaped and decorated like a bell and the other like a present, tucked neatly away in a snow-white handkerchief.

Zachary looks up at me with a little smile. "Thought you might want to try them alone, later. Or not—whatever you like."

I fold the cookies back up in the handkerchief and slip them carefully into my blazer pocket. "I actually wanted to try them," I tell him. "So thank you."

"Yeah, I noticed you glancing at them a couple of times. Caressing them with your gaze."

I roll my eyes. "I caressed nothing with my gaze."

"Ah—my apologies, maybe I was mistaken. If you do wish to caress something with your gaze, you know I am forever your servant in all things."

"You're in quite the ridiculous mood this evening, Zach," I point out. "What gives?"

"I'm having one of those days I can't explain. You know, one of those days where it feels like luck is on your side, like being dealt a hand and knowing your cards are going to be good before you look at them. That kind of day."

"I can't say I've ever had such a day," I tell him.

But Zachary's cheer is strangely contagious. I have the odd feeling that whatever luck Zachary might be having, it would spread from him and straight through me if I was standing close enough to him.

Following that impulse, I lean forward and kiss his smiling mouth.

When I pull away, he raises his eyebrows slightly as if in question. I tap my lips with a finger. "Hopefully, I'll catch some luck off you now."

"Mm, that kiss wasn't very lucky, I could tell. Here." He presses a kiss to my mouth, a kiss that tastes soft and warm and sweet as sugar cookies. "Now you'll definitely catch my luck." Taking my hands in his, he kisses both of them. "Lucky hands, too." He reaches up and kisses my eyelids. "Lucky eyes."

I laugh and push him away. "Alright, alright, enough. You'll have no luck left for yourself if you continue."

He tilts his head. "You can give me some of it back if you wish."

"No, Romeo, you're not getting anything back." I push myself away from the bannister and resume walking down the stairs, but Zachary stops me with a gentle hand on my arm.

"Theo."

"Yes?"

"Come spend the holiday with me."

My heart falters and stutters to a stop like a failing engine. My mind malfunctions: I stare at him with my mouth in an O, incapable of formulating a reply.

"Pardon?" I say finally, more to buy myself time than because I want him to repeat himself.

"Come spend the holiday at my house. My parents always have family and guests over and host those outrageous Christmas parties, so you wouldn't be the only guest—and I think my parents would enjoy meeting you—even if they can be, well, excessive at times. And you can meet my little sister."

"I—I wouldn't want to impose," I say, stealing the sentence straight out of my mother's diplomatic phrase book.

"You could never impose," Zachary says. "And in any case, I intend to take Mr Ambrose's assignment very seriously, and for research purposes, it would be best if I didn't have to be parted from you for the entirety of the holiday."

"I'd have to ask my parents..." I say in a murmur.

The thought of it fills me with dread.

My father would probably rather hang me himself than let me spend the holiday at a boy's house. On the other hand, Zachary isn't my boyfriend, and his family is old, powerful and influential—the kind of family my father married into.

And if there's one thing I know about my father, it's that he never underestimates the importance of making friends in high places.

The reality is that the moment I stand in front of him to ask him, my words will crystallise like a marble egg in my throat, and I'll choke on it before I can ever speak.

"What if we send an official invitation?" Zachary says. "From my parents, in their letterhead, to your house? Your parents might say no to you, but they might think twice before declining a Blackwood invitation." He raises an eyebrow. "We could invite them too if you wish."

"No."

"No?"

I hesitate and then give him the most tactful version of the truth. "I need to work on Mr Ambrose's assignment too, and... I could do it around you, but not around them."

His expression changes almost imperceptibly.

A flash of something appears in his eyes—something that almost looks like pain—and disappears just as quickly. He watches me in silence for a while, searching my face with those clever eyes of his.

Finally, he nods. "I understand."

It's the simplest of replies, but it makes my throat so tight I can barely breathe. I feel like I just handed Zachary a tiny, delicate morsel of myself, a morsel I've never shared with anyone else before, never so much as revealed.

And Zachary just took the morsel and folded it away, in his careful, calm manner, and tucked it, safely and softly, right inside his heart.

Chapter 31

BLACK DOBERMAN

Zachary

ON THE FIRST DAY of the holidays, my parents send out their formal invitation to Theodora's house.

They don't question me about it—which is surprising—but it's clear they are more than a little intrigued about meeting the mysterious girl who's been stopping me from being top of all my classes throughout my entire academic career.

On the third day of the holidays, Iakov comes to stay. When he turns up at the door, dressed all in black with snowflakes sparkling on the black spikes of his buzz cut and melting on the shoulders of his leather jacket, I stare at him like he's a ghost.

"What are you doing here?"

He shrugs. "Your thorny sister."

"*Zaro* invited you?" I stand aside, and he walks in with his black duffel bag. "I thought she hated you."

"She does."

"Ah, Iakov!" A voice exclaims from behind me. I turn to see Zaro come down the stairs, looking radiant in an excessively flouncy dress and beaming at Iakov as if he's her oldest, closest friend. "Did you remember my macarons?"

With a grunt of acquiescence, Iakov pulls out a pink and gold Ladurée box from the pocket of his leather jacket. Zaro takes it with a wince.

"Really? You thought of no better way to carry it than your pocket?"

He shrugs. "Rode the bike here."

"I hate that thing," she replies. "I would've sent the limo out if you needed."

"I'm good."

"Since when are you two friends?" I interrupt them.

"We're not," Iakov says immediately.

"We're not friends," Zaro says at almost the same time. "But my actual friends and I are doing New Year in Paris, so we need him to come along."

"To Paris? For New Year? Why do you need him? I thought you wanted me to—" I pull a face and gesture. "Call off my dog." I nod at Iakov. "Sorry, Kav."

"No, yes, I did ask that, of course." Zaro doesn't exhibit so much as an ounce of shame as she shrugs and opens her box of macaroons. "But it turns out your dog made my friends feel safer when we go out clubbing, so we decided to keep him around."

"He's not an actual dog, Zaro." I stare at her in complete disbelief. "And he's not your bloody bodyguard either. He was just looking out for you as a favour to me."

"And now he's looking out for my friends as a favour to me—he doesn't mind, do you, Fido?" With the giggle of a mischievous tyrant, Zaro reaches on the tip of her toes to pat his head.

Iakov's expression the entire time is completely blank as if he couldn't care less regardless of the situation. When she pats his head, he lets her, and when he does, he does remind me of a dog. A black Doberman Pinscher, muscular and intimidating and almost regal.

The kind of dog that might guard the gates of hell—or rude aristocratic brats, in this case.

LATER, I SPEAK TO both of them separately. Since we are both too old for me to climb onto her balcony, I catch Zaro in the pavilion, where it's her habit to hide while she smokes.

The pavilion is hidden from view from the rest of the house by the semi-circle of oaks and willows which surround our lake, and it has a small firepit in the middle to keep her warm.

"You can't speak to Iakov that way," I tell Zaro as soon as she looks up at me.

She rolls her eyes and exhales. I wince, avoiding the poisonous wreath of smoke to stand with one shoulder against a pillar.

"He doesn't mind," she says with a careless wave of her hand. "It's not like he gets offended."

"That doesn't matter, Zaro. He's still a human being, and he deserves to be treated with the same respect and courtesy we should treat everyone with—not just the people we deem worthy of our respect."

"You're making this into a bigger deal than it is."

"As I should. Especially since Iakov's only sin was to do me a favour and look after my ungrateful brat of a sister."

"Ungrateful brat?" She raises an eyebrow. "Sorry for not kissing the floor at your feet because you decided to get your friend to spy on me." Before I can reply to remind her we've already had this argument, she adds, "Anyway, I'm pretty sure your Iakov would rather spend

Christmas in our nice house and the Ritz in Paris than live in that horrible shithole in St Petersburg waiting for his dad to smash his face in."

A horrible lurching feeling sinks through me, like suddenly falling into a sludge of ice-cold mud. It's not a feeling I've felt often, but it's exactly the same feeling I got when Theodora told me she couldn't be happy around her parents. For a second, I can do nothing but stare at Zaro. She frowns at me, and then her eyes widen, and then her face drops.

For the first time in a very long time, a look of true devastation and regret darkens her features.

"Oh. You don't know?"

I don't even know what to say.

The sad, appalling truth is that I don't even know what I don't know. When it comes to the Young Kings, our friendship is a thing with its own set of rules. We party together, we hang out. We're closer to each other than to anybody else in Spearcrest.

But our friendship is like a ghost tethered to a house. Once we leave Spearcrest, our friendship becomes ephemeral. At most, I'll text Evan and Sev. Iakov is too busy, and I dare not even imagine what Luca gets up to when he's not limited by the restraints of being on school grounds.

Those of us who want to talk about our personal lives, our family lives, or our holidays, do. Those of us who wish to keep our privacy, do. We don't push one another for intimate details—we don't have that kind of friendship.

If anything, some of us go out of our way to keep secrets, like Evan falling in love with his prefect or the way Sev quietly obsesses over the fiancée he claims to hate.

Or me hiding Zaro from everyone.

So why shouldn't Iakov have secrets of his own?

Except that my secrets are harmless. Iakov's bruises and scars are as much part of him as his tattoos and black combat boots—but I never really questioned them before. I've seen Iakov on nights out, I know how bloodthirsty he can get once the night gets dark and there's more vodka than blood running through his veins.

But who am I kidding? Assuming that Iakov brought those injuries on himself was the easy assumption, the safe assumption. The assumption that holds me the least accountable for not giving a shit about my friend.

"He told you about this?" I ask Zaro.

She seems genuinely crestfallen about accidentally revealing what she thought I already knew about Iakov, and that makes me feel so much worse.

"No." She shakes her head. "No, but it—well, it was so obvious. He'd disappear for a weekend to go see his dad or do a job for him and then come home looking like meat. I asked him about it one time, half-joking, half-wishing he'd deny it, but he didn't. He just shrugged and said his dad was angry at him. God, what an arsehole. Makes you think how nice we have it with ours, right?"

I stare at her. The cold, muddy feeling inside me spreads. I'm almost nauseous with it.

"I never knew," I say. "I never thought to ask."

"Don't say anything," she says quickly. She squishes the rest of her cigarette against the marble bench she's sitting on, tosses it inside the bush of rhododendrons behind her and sprays herself with a bottle of Miss Dior. Then she stands and rushes to me, grabbing my hand. "Please, Zach. Don't say anything to him. I don't want him to think—" She shakes her head and waves her hand impatiently. "Just don't say anything, alright?"

"No, Zaro, I'm not going to ambush my friend and ask him all about his abusive father," I say drily. "You don't need to worry about that."

She narrows her eyes at me. "You don't need to snap at me. It's not my fault you don't communicate with your friends."

I glare at her, even though I can't deny that she may have a point.

"If this is going to be a respite from his shit family," I tell Zaro as we leave the pavilion, "can you at least be a little more polite towards him? I'm being deadly serious, Z. Make an effort."

"Ugh. I told you, he doesn't mind! But fine. In the spirit of Christmas... I'll stop calling him dog names."

"You call him dog names? On a regular basis?"

"It's an inside joke," Zaro says unconvincingly.

"You're the worst."

She rolls her eyes and scampers away from me.

My conversation with Iakov, much later that night, also sees me enduring the stench of cigarettes.

After dinner, Iakov asked where he could smoke without bothering anyone, and I offered to show him the grounds. Armed against the darkness and the cold with an old storm lantern and our coats, we make our way to the lake. Once we get there, Iakov crouches to sit on the shore, his boots right where the edge of the lake laps at the shingle. He lights a cigarette while I remain standing to the side.

"I'm sorry my sister is such a pain in the arse," I say suddenly.

I can't think of a more elegant way of starting this apology, but I doubt Iakov cares much for elegance. He just cares for saying what he's trying to say in as few words as possible, a skill which flies in the face of everything I stand for.

He shrugs and waves a hand, the butt of his cigarette a red glow. "Nah, it's alright."

"She told me she calls you dog names."

"Inside joke," he says.

Even though Zaro said the same thing, it sounded like a lie when she said it. From Iakov's mouth, it sounds like the truth.

Either that or bone-dry sarcasm. It's almost impossible to tell with him.

I press a little. "Are you sure you wouldn't rather spend the holiday with your family than looking after Zaro and her friends?"

"Definitely not."

"You sure, Kav?"

"Yea, trust me." He lets out a sudden bark of laughter. "My dad's a cunt."

He doesn't offer any elaboration, and I don't prompt him for some.

Iakov will tell me more if he wishes to tell me more, and I might ask him for more information someday, but this is not the moment to do that. I need some time first, time to process what Zahara told me, time to get used to this sudden change in the status quo of my life.

The change from a world where Iakov is a rough, silent giant with a proclivity for violence to a world where Iakov is a rough, silent giant with a proclivity for violence and an abusive father.

The following day, Theodora arrives.

She's welcomed into the house by the butler, who ushers her into the Blue Parlour—our cosiest living room—where I'm sitting in an armchair reading while Iakov slumps on the couch playing a video game.

We both look up when the door opens. Theodora stands a little behind Arthur, who introduces her before excusing himself. She thanks him and watches him leave, then she turns to look at me, then Iakov.

"Hey," he says, glancing up briefly from his game.

She tilts her head. "Hi, Iakov." She turns to me and gives me a stiff smile. "Did you invite everyone from Spearcrest?"

"Don't be ridiculous." I point at Iakov with my copy of Spinoza's *Ethics*. "He wasn't invited."

"Liar," Iakov says without any emotion whatsoever.

"Well, he was invited but not by me."

"Oh."

Theodora stands looking at me. She's wearing a cream coat in the palest wool, her hair gathered back and caught in the grip of a gold hair claw. Her posture is rigid, her shoulders a little hunched, and her arms are crossed over the lapels of her coat.

And yet she looks so soft I have to make a conscious effort not to wrap myself around her.

"Want me to leave you two alone?" Iakov asks suddenly, lowering his controller to glance from me to Theodora.

"To do what?" I ask, the sharpness of my tone perfectly matched to the sharpness with which Theodora turns to throw him a glare.

He shrugs. "Fight. Flirt. Fuck. Whatever you two do."

"Iakov," Theodora says in a tone of warning.

"We don't do any of that," I add.

"Is that a yes or a no?" he asks. "I can't pause this game." He points at the screen, where a man in ridiculous armour crouches behind a wall while hawks with knives attached to their talons fly threateningly around. "Decide."

"It's a no." I roll my eyes, set my book aside and stand. "You stay and do"—I point at the screen—"whatever it is you're doing. I'll show Theodora to her room."

He grunts and resumes his game. When I reach Theodora, I stretch out my hand between us, palm up. She glances back at Iakov, who's staring at the screen, where his character is now getting brutally assaulted by the beknived hawks, and then back to me.

A tiny smile appears on her face, and her entire posture softens as if the ice that was keeping her encased suddenly melted.

She places her hand in mine, and I lead her out of the room.

Chapter 32

FIRST EDITION

Theodora

Seeing Zachary in his own home is simultaneously a complete surprise while making perfect sense. His family home—his family estate, more accurately—is a perfect representation of what one imagines when one thinks of the British aristocracy. A beautiful stately home, well-kept and comfortable, yet with a certain old-world glamour to it.

I don't meet his parents straight away, but he wastes no time introducing me to his sister.

She looks exactly like him. Tall, elegant, her skin the same smooth, creamy brown, a sharp intelligence in her brown eyes. Her hair is long, almost to her waist, an explosion of curls black at the roots then threaded through with warm gold strands.

Where Zachary's style is old-fashioned and scholarly, her style seems to be a more elevated, feminine version of his. When I meet her, she's wearing a knitted top in a pale shade of brown, a dark plaid skirt and thigh-high black socks.

"Theodora, this is my little sister, Zahara." He gestures from me to her.

"Oh, it's Zahara all of a sudden, not ungrateful brat?" she asks, but her tone is more teasing than accusatory.

He rolls his eyes and continues as if no interruption had occurred. "Zahara, this is—"

"Don't be such an idiot—I know exactly who this is!" She fixes me with a look of utter delight. "The famous, the revered, the one and only Theodora Dorokhova." Without waiting for me to say anything, she launches into me with a hug. "I could not possibly be more excited to meet you at last!"

"It's a pleasure to meet you too," I answer, my voice muffled by the faceful of fragrant curls I get when she hugs me.

"Can I show her the library?" Zahara asks her brother as she frees me from her hug. "Please, Zach? You can show her the rest of the house, and I already know for a fact you're going to hoard her for yourself, not to mention how Mum and Dad are probably going to be obsessed with her the moment they get back home—and it's not like I'll be here all holiday anyway, so you'll get to—"

"You can show her the library," Zach says, removing his glasses to pinch the bridge of his nose. "Jesus, Zaro. It's not like she's your girlfriend."

"I'm sorry—is she *yours*?" his sister replies with the speed of a striking eagle. Then her eyes widen, and she turns to look at me. "Oh—you're not, are you?"

I shake my head, but my eyes meet Zach's, and there's a defiant expression in his eyes.

"I'm... not," I answer cautiously, tearing my gaze from his.

"The word 'girlfriend' could never accurately describe what she is to me," Zachary says in a tone of such complete earnestness that his sister and I can do nothing but stare at him, taken aback.

"If you say so." Zahara shrugs, and then she takes my elbow and leads me away.

The Blackwood library is exactly as I would have expected from Zachary's childhood library. A long, rectangular chamber, glossy floorboards, and floor-to-ceiling bookshelves filled with leather-bound collections. No pulp fiction or colourful covers are to be found in the Blackwood collection.

As I slowly walk along the shelves, tracing the gold-engraved spines, my fingertips brush over encyclopaedias, classics of English and French literature, volumes of poetry and an impressive collection of non-fiction books ranging from philosophy and politics to astrophysics and theoretical mathematics.

If the Blackwoods ever partake in thrillers or the occasional Regency romance, they must keep those particular books in a different part of their estate.

At the head of the room, a set of three French windows cast thick columns of light over an enormous pedestal desk that looks straight out of Victorian England. A leather seat stands like a throne by the desk, which is tidy apart from a closed laptop and a small pile of books.

"It's not the Spearcrest library, of course," Zach's sister is saying, hopping onto a corner of the pedestal desk and crossing her legs. "But it's not too shabby."

I turn to give her a surprised smile. "The Spearcrest library? But you don't go to Spearcrest..." I try to remember if I ever saw Zahara in Spearcrest. I'm certain I would know if Zach's sister attended the same school as us. I realise he never really mentioned it. "Do you?"

She lets out a little sigh. "It's a complicated story. I just started this year."

"Oh. I didn't know."

"Nobody does. Aside from Zach and his weird friend."

Zach, of course, might have a multitude of reasons for not telling anyone his sister is in Spearcrest. Being a Young King, I suspect, comes with drawbacks as well as privileges—something that's bound to happen when you're a ground of young people acting like a crime syndicate or a city-state. So it doesn't surprise me that Zach might wish to keep Zahara's presence in Spearcrest under wraps.

What doesn't make sense is him telling Iakov Kavinski. Why would Zach tell one of his fellow Kings and not the others? No, if Iakov knows, then the rest of the Young Kings must know.

Just like they'll know about me staying at Zachary's house over the holidays.

Several days ago, when I arrived home from Spearcrest, my mother greeted me with two pieces of news: that a formal invitation had arrived for me to holiday at the Blackwood estate and that my father would not be coming to visit during the holidays as he does most years.

"Some business problems are keeping him away," my mother explained, "and besides, you'll be spending next Christmas with him anyway."

The reminder that I would be moving in with my father after the end of Year 13 makes my gut churn as if I was about to be sick. My mother and I never speak about me moving to Russia—if it's bothering her, if it worries her or makes her sad, she doesn't show it.

Then again, it might not bother her the way it bothers me. She was only twenty when she herself was shipped off to Russia to marry my father, and it wasn't until she was in her forties that she moved back to the UK for my education and to spend time with her ailing father.

In all my life, I never heard my mother complain about any of it, not even once.

Maybe she doesn't mind. Maybe it's just her stiff upper lip.

When she told me I should go spend the holiday with the Blackwoods, I was pleased but not surprised. My mother is well-versed in the art of cultivating her place in British high society, and it doesn't get much higher than the Blackwoods.

"Will Papa not mind if I spend the holiday away?" I asked her.

"Of course not. Why should he? Your papa would be pleased to know you are nurturing such powerful connections. And he trusts you—we both do. You're such a good girl, Theodora."

When I was younger, being praised by my parents meant the world. If they called me clever or obedient or good, I thought it meant that I was loved.

I know better now.

So I accepted the Blackwood invitation and came. I came because, for once, I didn't want to be good, obedient Theodora, Theodora the doll, the puppet. I came because I wanted something for myself, I wanted to be selfish and unwise and maybe even a little wild.

I came because of that night in the Spearcrest library, because Zachary told me to ask him if I wanted his kisses, and I do want them. I came so that I could ask him, just as he told me to do, just as I assured him I never would do.

A lifetime spent doing the right thing—why should I not, for once, just one time before I go to Russia, do what I want?

Except that I arrived here to find myself face to face with Iakov Kavinski. A Young King, and more than that, a Russian. If Iakov knows I'm here, his father might know too. His father and my father are two sides of the same coin: two powerful, dark-hearted men, one turned towards the side of law and society, the other turned towards the side of crime and corruption. But the world of the ultra-rich in Russia is a small one.

I'm here now, and it's too late to go back.

But I haven't done anything reckless yet. I haven't done anything to draw my father's ire. All I've done is make it more difficult for myself to remain the perfect, obedient daughter. But that's what I must remain while I'm here. What choice do I have?

"Hey, are you alright?"

A gentle hand suddenly cradles my arm, and I turn, blinking slowly. Zahara is standing by my side, a frown of concern on her face. I smile.

"Yes, I'm so sorry, I was deep in my thoughts." I shake my head. "That was so rude of me, and I didn't hear what you said. I'm so sorry, Zahara."

"Oh, don't apologise. I was honestly just having a rant." She squeezes my arm. "Are you sure you're alright, Theodora? You look pale, and you're shaking a bit."

"I'm just cold," I say, moving away from her. "I'm completely fine, I promise. I'm always cold."

I look around, desperate for a way out of the conversation, a distraction. My eyes fall on the small pile of books on the magnificent desk, the embossed title gleaming in the cool daylight.

"Oh! Your copy of *Peter Pan* is beautiful."

Zahara laughs and saunters over to the desk to pick it up. "That's not mine. It's Zach's."

"I thought he hated children's books."

"He does. But he's obsessed with *this* one." She hands me the book. "You should see his annotations. They're like the scrawlings of a madman."

I take the book and turn it in my hands.

It's a first edition copy, with the olive-green clothbound cover and the gilded illustrated frames around the title. The pages are soft with time as I flick through them, Bedford's painstakingly rendered illustrations bringing the story to life with a wealth of details.

If I owned a first edition of *Peter Pan*, I would have never dared to write so much as my name on the inside cover. The book is too beautiful, and at over one hundred years old, too old to be sullied by my penmanship. Zachary, though, seems to have felt no such compunction. His sister wasn't far off when she described his annotations as the scrawlings of a madman, although that might be partly due to Zachary's slanted, spidery handwriting.

Flicking through the pages, I find the places where his annotations are most dense. His notes hint at a rather dark interpretation of the whimsical story: he seems to fixate on Neverland, Peter Pan's shadow, and, more than anything else, James Hook.

Chapter five, and the passage of Hook's first on-page appearance, is so heavily annotated that his words cover every margin, and some notes are even squeezed tightly between the lines. My eyes slide over the underlined parts: *In person, he was cadaverous and blackavised; his handsome countenance; his eyes were of the blue of the forget-me-not and of a profound melancholy; he was a raconteur of repute; the elegance of his diction; a man of indomitable courage.*

Zach's notes read: *Dark, handsome, sad, brave and well-spoken. A villain—but a melancholy villain. A complex character, not just a pirate. He's missing something, a part of him—his hand a metaphor? Missing his old life/the real world?*

At the bottom of the page, he's written in small letters, *Does she see me in him?* This is crossed out and replaced with, *Does she see herself in him?*

I remember, all of a sudden, Zachary at the Halloween party in the trees, drunk and dressed like Hook. He called me 'angel' that night, and he was drunk enough to be acting a little reckless. He told me he dressed as Hook to amuse me.

I told him I used to have a crush on Hook.

Laughter bursts from my chest like a bird from a cage, startling me as much as Zahara.

"You're right," I answer her questioning look. "The scrawlings of a madman, truly."

CHAPTER 33

DAUNTLESS DREAMS

Theodora

I MEET ZACHARY'S PARENTS a day later, and the day after that, we all have dinner together.

By this point, any nerves or anxiety I might have felt about staying at the Blackwood estate over the holidays has vanished. The house, with two days left until Christmas, is full of guests: a mixture of distant relatives and close family friends, and even a few people I know through my mother.

It's easy to blend in amongst the guests, and nobody seems to find it particularly odd that I'm there, which takes much of my unease away.

Dinner with the Blackwoods is illuminating—and a strange experience. We sit at a long table in a dining room fit for aristocrats: polished floor, high-backed velvet seats, antique chandeliers and candelabras bearing real candles, silverware and cloth napkins embroidered with the Blackwood crest.

I sit at the end of the table closest to the Blackwood family. To my left is Zachary, to my right is his mother, Lady Blackwood, and facing us from the head of the table, his father, Lord Blackwood.

Zachary and Zahara both look like a perfect mixture of their parents: they have their mother's doe eyes and long, curled eyelashes, their father's sharp, graceful bone structure—the prominent cheekbones, the proud chin, the aquiline nose. The Blackwood parents, like their children, are highly articulate, inquisitive and earnest, and prone to sarcasm.

"It's an honour to meet you, my darling," Lady Blackwood tells me when Zach introduces me to her. "Your name is spoken in awe around here—you have become as good as a mythical figure in this household."

She wears a gown in a rich shade of purple, gold bracelets on her arms, and her curly hair, black streaked with silver, is tied in a scarf of ochre silk. Her style could not be more different to my mother's: Lady Blackwood wears very little make-up, and if she's had any work done, it was subtle. There are lines around her eyes, but the rest of her face is smooth and polished, like Zachary's.

Even her smile, the mix of warmth and arrogance, is exactly like his.

"She means a mythical figure like Saint George who slew the dragon," Zachary tells me, tossing his mother a look. "With you, the sword-wielding saintess, and I, the slain beast."

"That's not at all what I meant," his mother says with a raised eyebrow.

"It's certainly how you made it sound—year after year. Have you finally defeated Theodora Dorokhova? Knocked her from the top of the results lists? Brought back her head to display at the top of our ramparts?"

"Everyone needs something to work towards," his mother says with a shrug.

Appetisers have just been served, and the room is filled with the silvery tinkling of cutlery. Although I attended many dinner parties and other events with my mother, I never saw her do anything other than sip on flutes of champagne.

But the Blackwoods, having served food at their house and hosting a dinner party, are actually eating the food. Even Zahara eats her appetisers with obvious relish.

I glance down at my plate: tiny white circles of bread, crème fraîche, caviar like tiny black pearls. The portion is small—it's only an appetiser, but I can't help the wave of panic that rises in my chest.

"It's not as though your son was ever defeated," I say quickly before Zachary or his mother can notice my discomfort. "We only ever tied." I smile ruefully. "Somehow, that was just worse."

"I disagree," Zach says, turning to look at me. "Our names at the top of those boards every year might have been a contentious subject in the Blackwood household, but I grew rather fond of the sight."

"Or perhaps you grew complacent," Lord Blackwood interjects.

He's been listening in silence so far. When he finally speaks, his tone is playful, not accusatory, and yet there's a look of challenge in his eyes.

Zach tilts his head, watching his father for a moment, and then turns back to me with an easy smile.

"Forgive my father—he's used to politics, where one's rivals must always be treated with the utmost disdain."

Lord Blackwood, to my surprise, responds exactly like his son, turning to me with an easy smile.

"Forgive my son—in the spirit of youthful rebellion, he must despise politics as best he can. One day, he'll come to his senses and realise a country cannot run on intellectual debate alone."

"Caleb," Lady Blackwood says in a tone of warning, "I thought we agreed to not bring up politics at the dinner table."

"We agreed, my darling, and I held up my end. Zachary was the one to bring it up."

"And you can be the one to let it go," Lady Blackwood says.

"A country cannot be run on intellectual debate alone," Zachary answers his father's statement as if no interruption had occurred, "but education is where every civilisation starts. Without education, there would be no civilization—no country to rule, and no politicians to rule it."

Lord Blackwood leans back into his chair, narrowing his eyes. "The baker bakes the bread; the hungry man eats it. Take away the bread, and the hungry man cannot feed himself on the presence of the baker alone."

"Take away the baker, and there would be no bread." Zach lets out a laugh. "Even by the logic of your analogy, Father, the baker still holds the most importance."

"You purposely misconstrued my analogy, Zachary." His father remains calm. "My point is that the baker is necessary to make the bread, yes, but the bread itself is what satisfies the hunger of the man and keeps him alive. The point of my analogy is that the baker and the bread both fulfil different functions—and that the function of the bread, ultimately, is more important than the function of the person who creates it. The politician might be taught by the teacher, but it is the politician who looks after the country and its people."

"Except that the way the government currently is, the baker is making fine, delicate cakes, cakes which might please the palate of the man who has already eaten without ever touching the lips of the hungry man."

"Hah!" Lord Blackwood lets out a booming laugh. "The bakers at your school must not know how to make those fine cakes you speak of, Zachary. I send my son to a private school and he comes home a socialist!"

Zachary grins at his father. "Ah, yes, socialism—the dirtiest word in your vocabulary, Father."

Lord Blackwood suddenly turns to me. "Please, forgive me, Theodora. My son and I have reached the point every father and son must eventually reach. I wish him to follow in my footsteps and use his voice, his intellect and his privilege to enter a political world that sorely needs young men like him. He, on the other hand, wishes to sacrifice his intellect at the altar of academia and education." He takes a sip from his drink. His tone is still somewhat playful but only thinly veils his displeasure. "What about you, Theodora? Your father is involved in politics, is he not? Are you thinking of following in his path?"

The question makes my stomach twist. I glance uneasily at Zach, reminded once again of the secret I'm keeping from him, the crucial information I'm withholding.

Looking back at Lord Blackwood, I give him the perfect mixture of truth and lie.

"I dream of being a writer, actually."

The truth—because it is my dream to study and read and write.

A lie—because unlike Zachary, who so bravely and openly defies his father's wishes for his future, I'll be following in my father's path. Exactly as Lord Blackwood said, except not as my father's equal, as Lord Blackwood sees Zachary. I'll be following in his path with a golden collar at my throat and a leash in his hand, a tool rather than a colleague.

"A writer?" Lady Blackwood asks with kindness in her voice. "What would you write?"

"I'm not sure yet." I turn to give Zach a slight smile. "Maybe children's books."

The conversation moves to other topics after that, and I try to take small bites of food whenever nobody's looking at me. When the main course gets brought in, my heart sinks, but soon after, I feel a warm touch on the low of my back.

Zachary leans into me, his fingers gently rubbing into my back.

"Are you alright?"

I nod. At first, I don't realise why he's suddenly asking me this.

Then, he says, "You don't have to force yourself to eat if you don't want to. I can take you to the kitchen later if you like."

It falls so easily from his lips that it takes my breath away for a moment. Of course, Zachary would have noticed my unease. Of course, Zachary would wish to comfort me when I'm distressed. Observant, sharp, lovely Zachary.

"Don't worry," I murmur back. "I'm alright." I give him a smile. "The food is lovely."

"Then eat as much as you like, Theo." His thumb traces my spine through the fine wool of my jumper, and I resist the urge to close my eyes with a sigh of contentment. "Nobody will notice—not when my father is so intent on monopolising as much attention as possible."

He gives his father a wry look.

Lord Blackwood is in the middle of an impassioned story about an argument he had in the House of Lords. He has the same diction and elegance of speech as Zachary, but his voice is deep and booming, carrying like the rumble of thunder down the length of the table.

"Your father seems to be a very... passionate man," I say cautiously.

Zachary raises an eyebrow. "Mm. My father is like a preacher whose own sermons whip him up into a frenzy. His passion stems from within. I'm afraid he finds it very difficult to accept any thought or idea that was not born in his own mind." His gaze softens as he looks at me. "I always promised myself I would never be like him, that I would always seek to enrich my mind with new notions, that I would seek knowledge from others rather than conviction from within myself."

"You really have no intention of going into politics?" I ask in a hushed tone.

He shakes his head. "Never."

His hand is still on my lower back. He's not moved it, and I find that I don't want him to. His touch is warming, comforting, and so natural it makes me wonder why we don't always sit like this.

"Your father seems like he really wants you to follow in his footsteps, though." I glance back at Lord Blackwood, his features set into a grim expression underneath the black and grey of his beard. "Are you not afraid he'll be…" *Angry*, I want to say. "Upset?"

"He is upset," Zachary says. "Don't let his playful tone and whimsical analogies fool you. He's more than upset, in fact. I suspect he's probably furious at me."

As he speaks, I can't help thinking of my father, the mere idea of his fury freezing the blood in my veins and sending a shudder through me.

"Does that not make you… I don't know, hesitant? Nervous?" Afraid?

Zachary shakes his head again. "Why should it? My life is mine, I may do with it what I may. By that same respect, my father's emotions are his, he may be as angry as he wishes. He cannot compel me to change my university applications or my dreams any more than I can compel him to stop deriding me."

I think of my father, his cold, dark eyes, his hand gripping my arm, his icy commands.

My father's word has always been law in my life, and he has always spoken and behaved as though it could be no other way. Objectively, I see the truth in Zachary's words—my life is mine, and my father's emotions are his, and he cannot compel me any more than I can compel him.

Except that I cannot picture Lord Blackwood compelling Zachary to do anything at all against his will.

But my father?

My father could easily compel me, with his fingers around my arm and his armed men flanking us and his privately chartered jets and the connections he has all over the world. My father could easily compel me to bend to his wishes. I doubt I would be the first person he would have forced into doing something they did not wish to do.

"I admire you," I murmur, turning into Zachary, smiling to mask the dark torrent of despair that seems to be drowning me. "Your bravery, your resolve, your dauntlessness."

"My dauntlessness?" Zachary lets out a soft laugh. "You're the most dauntless person I know." His fingers, in stroking my back, find the hem of my jumper and slip underneath it to brush against my skin in an ephemeral caress. Then his hand moves and his touch is gone.

"I wish I existed in this world as the version of me that exists in your mind," I tell him.

"You would," he says, voice full of tenderness, "if only you saw yourself as I see you."

Chapter 34

PIRATE LOVER

Zachary

THE NEXT FEW DAYS are long and full of exhausting social events.

First, there's the Christmas Eve party, where all the guests wear couture and dance awkwardly to Christmas music, and everyone drinks too much champagne.

There's always a tipping point at some point in the evening, usually a little after midnight, where the mood shifts from jovial to feral, a sudden edge hanging in the air like an invisible guillotine.

This is usually the moment I make a discreet exit, and this year is no exception.

Catching Theodora's waist with one arm and Zaro's shoulders with the other, I usher us out of the ballroom. Theodora has a little flush in her cheeks but seems mostly sober; she goes with me without protest. Zaro's eyes are glassy, and she complains the whole way.

"The Duke of Bridehall was inviting me to spend a weekend on his yacht," she whines at me as I drag her down the corridor. "I didn't even have the time to say yes."

"You're not spending *any* weekend on Bridehall's yacht," I say, not missing the little frown Theodora gives Zaro.

"Isn't the Duke of Bridehall in his fifties?" Theodora asks.

"Yeah." Zaro giggles. "Hot, right?"

Theodora laughs, sounding more surprised than amused. "I wouldn't say hot, no."

"Nor would I." I glare at Zaro. "I would even go as far as to say that's repulsive."

"It's a little sinister," Theodora says with more kindness. "Zahara, you're young, smart, extraordinarily beautiful. Don't you know how much better you can do?"

"If I could do better," Zaro mumbles, "don't you think I would already have?"

I frown at her. "You're sixteen, Zaro—what's the rush? You've all the time in the world."

She sighs and slumps against me with her head on my shoulder, almost knocking me into Theodora. "But I'm lonely *now*."

Theodora and I exchange a look, neither of us knowing what to say.

It never occurred to me that Zaro might be lonely. Social media tells me she has a small army of friends she spends her time with—even in Spearcrest, despite having been there for only a term. And Zaro's never struggled to make friends.

Not that friendships are a guaranteed shield against loneliness.

We walk Zaro to her bedroom, and I watch from the doorway as Theodora helps her into bed. Taking off her heels, opening her blankets for her, even wiping the make-up off her face before letting her head rest on the pillows.

Once Zaro is tucked into bed, Theodora kisses her cheek and straightens herself, but before she can walk away, Zaro grabs her wrist.

"Don't go," she mumbles. "Stay. Read me a story."

Theodora looks at me, eyes wide in a silent plea for help as Zaro pulls her down, and I cover my mouth to stifle my laughter.

Theodora narrows her eyes and then says to Zaro, "Don't worry, we'll stay. *Zach* is going to read us both a story."

She gives me a look like slapping a glove in my face. Since Theodora has never offered me a challenge I've not declined or embraced, I push off the doorway where I've been leaning and close the door behind me. Zaro's got a small set of bookshelves near her desk, so I take a quick look at her books, pushing aside the delicate garlands of her string of hearts plants.

"My god, Zaro." I wince at her books, searching for a single title that doesn't sound outrageous. "You have the literary palate of a horny spinster."

"Stop judging people for what they read," Theodora interjects immediately from where she's settled herself at the foot of Zaro's bed.

Her head is propped on one of Zaro's decorative cushions, the strands of hair escaping from her elegant updo glittering like pale gold in the soft lights of Zaro's pink lamps. Her legs are draped over Zaro's legs. Her silver heels lie abandoned on the floor by the bed; her toenails are painted the same dusty blue shade as her fingernails.

It's a rare occurrence to see Theodora so off her guard and relaxed, and I can't find it within myself to be annoyed with her.

"Fine," I tell her, "how about you help me choose, Theo, since you're so open-minded? Would you prefer"—I pull out one of the books on Zaro's shelves—"*The Pirate Lord's Captive Bride* or"—I pull out a second book at random—"*One Night with the Ruthless Sultan*?"

"*The Pirate Lord's Captive Bride*," Theodora says without a second of hesitation.

"That's a good one as well," Zaro mumbles approvingly from her pillow.

I glare at Theodora then down at the cover of the book, which depicts a woman with long blonde hair and scarlet cheeks melting in the muscular embrace of a mostly shirtless pirate.

Too late, I remember Theodora's proclivity for villainous pirates.

"Let's go with the ruthless sultan," I say quickly.

"No!" Zaro cries out.

"Absolutely not," Theo adds.

With the hopeless sigh of a doomed man, I slump down into the chair at Zaro's bedside, open *The Pirate Lord's Captive Bride*, and do my best to ignore Theodora's dreamy sighs as I read.

The next event is Christmas Day itself.

This time, the tone is subdued, the pace slower. There is a morning service at the local chapel, which is attended by almost all my parents' guests, presumably to atone for the fact that they missed midnight mass to get shit-faced and make advances on teenagers.

Having no religious inclination myself and little to atone for aside from the sin of reading poorly written pirate romance to my sister and the love of my life, I skip the service in favour of having breakfast with Theodora. She wears a pair of soft, faded jeans and a sweater top in pale violet. Her hair is tied in a simple ponytail, and she wears no ornament aside from silver-shaped earrings. The sweetheart neckline of her top exposes the creamy expanse of her throat, where I long to scatter a necklace of kisses.

Although the kitchen is already bustling with chefs and catering staff, Theo and I sit tucked in the little breakfast nook my mother had built, an alcove circled by windows that overlook the herb garden and the belt of trees leading to the lake. The morning is cold and frosty, leaves and grass ghostly apparitions underneath their icy shrouds.

Theo sits with a large mug of green tea, and we share a pile of banana pancakes and fresh fruit.

"Is Zaro still asleep?" Theo asks when I sit down next to her with a cup of black coffee.

I nod. "Given the state she was in last night, she's going to wake up with a killer headache and the hangover to end all hangovers."

Theo winces. "I imagine she will, yes." She hesitates. "Is she... alright?"

"That's a complicated question." I gaze out of the window at the pale blue of the distant sky. "In perfect sincerity, I'm not quite sure."

"She wasn't joking about the duke's yacht, was she? At first, I thought she might be, but..." Theodora's gaze follows mine out the window. "But you seemed genuinely concerned, and I've noticed some... I suppose *coldness* between her and your parents. At first, I thought I'd imagined it, but I'm not so sure now."

"You didn't imagine it." I sigh and turn back to her. "They're not very happy with her as of late. Although I suppose you could say that, strictly speaking, they've never really been happy with either of us, ever. But more recently, well, Zaro was at a private girls' school in France, and she was caught getting involved with a teacher." I curl my fingers around my cup, squeezing the hot ceramic with a grimace. "That's the reason she was taken out of her school and sent to Spearcrest—you know, under my *supervision*. And that's the reason for the 'coldness' you sensed. I don't think my parents have quite forgiven her for what happened."

"Forgiven her?" Theo's tone is appalled. "Forgiven her for what, getting groomed by a member of staff at her school?" She shakes her head. "That man should be in jail. I really hope your parents pressed charges."

"Pressing charges would make everything too public. I honestly believe my parents would rather die than have it plastered all over the news that their daughter was involved in such a scandal." I sigh and shake my head. "And honestly, in that respect, I agree with my parents, though not for the same reasons. Zahara's life would be over if what happened was made public. Victim or nymphet—regardless of how the media chose to portray her—her life would be as good as theirs. She'd be eaten alive, chewed up and spat out by magazines, newspapers and websites, torn apart by every tabloid reader and gossip blogger, crushed under scrutiny for years to come, probably decades. She'd never be allowed to forget what happened, never get to move on from it. It would kill me if that happened to her."

"I'm so sorry this happened, Zach." Theo places her hand on mine. Her fingers, normally so cold, are warm from cradling her mug of tea.

I turn my hand under hers so we are palm to palm and lace my fingers through hers. "I'm sorry too. I wish I could have protected Zahara better. I still wish I could do more to protect her. I even tried to get Iakov to keep an eye on her, but that just made her angry at me."

Theodora picks up her mug with her free hand, leaving the other in my hold. "She might have felt as if you were spying on her, or worse, trying to control her."

"That's exactly what she felt, she told me herself. She's quite frank when it comes to giving her opinion—as I'm sure you've noticed." I sip my coffee and then shake my head. "She can't have been that angry at Iakov spying on her, though, since she decided to go ahead and invite him to spend Christmas over."

"She did?"

"Yes. I think she and her friends use him as a bodyguard when they go clubbing."

"I can see that." Theo laughs from behind her tea. "I can imagine Iakov is the perfect guy to have around if you want other guys to leave you alone."

"Oh?" I lean into Theodora and cock an eyebrow. "Maybe you and Zaro need to start some sort of Iakov fan club."

"No need," Theodora answers in the sweetest of tones. "He already has one."

I pull back. "He does?"

"Of course. It's called the female population of Spearcrest. Wait, no." Theodora interrupts herself. "Who am I kidding? It's not just the girls. Let's just call it most of the population of Spearcrest."

"Are we talking about the same Iakov? Big, burly—barely speaks full sentences?"

"Tall, strong, silent?" Theodora shrugs. "What's not to like?"

I reel with a sudden surge of betrayal. Not from Theodora, but from Iakov, who has spent all these years passing for my vodka-drinking, fist-fighting friend and is suddenly revealing himself to be so much more complex, layered, and, clearly, admired.

"He's going to Paris with Zahara in two days," I tell Theodora, narrowing my eyes at her. "So don't get any ideas, and stick to your dark, well-spoken pirates."

I finally release her hand to pick up my knife and fork and take a bite of banana pancake. Theodora watches me with a sly smile.

"Seems you've also developed quite a fondness for James Hook yourself," she says in a tone of innocence. "Based on your interesting annotations of the book."

"My—"

I stop and narrow my eyes. Theodora's pretty blue eyes shine with amusement—a rare expression on her earnest face. Her pink lips quirk as she tries to keep her smile innocent.

"The desk in the library," I say in realisation. "You saw my book?"

She nods. "I took it."

I stare at her. She shrugs and adds, "It was a first edition of my favourite book, annotated by my favourite academic. How could I not?"

"Little *thief*." As we talk, I cut small morsels of banana pancakes and strawberries and feed them to Theo, who bites them obediently off the tip of my fork. "Give it back."

"Let me keep it. Please. It can be my Christmas present."

"If that was your Christmas present, what would mine be?"

"What's your favourite book? Something pretentious and onerous, no doubt—Tolstoy or Proust, or, no—Joyce. *Finnegans Wake*. I'll find you a first edition *Finnegans Wake* and annotate it."

"I don't want *Finnegans Wake*—I don't even like James Joyce. I'm hurt, Theo. I would have thought you would at least know that about me."

She shrugs. "It was natural of me to assume you would since you don't enjoy happy, whimsical books."

"I never said I didn't."

"Alright." Wrapping both her hands around her mug of tea, now almost empty, Theodora leans forward across the table. It's a small, round table, and we're not quite across from each other, so now we are face to face, almost nose to nose. "What's your favourite book, then?"

"I don't want a copy of my favourite book for my Christmas present."

"What do you want?" She glances down at my lips and looks back up to glare into my eyes. "Don't say a kiss."

"Because I can get one for free?"

"Because one can't wrap a kiss and put a pretty bow on it."

"I didn't wrap my stolen copy of *Peter Pan*, nor put a bow on it."

"I'll do it myself."

"I don't want a kiss anyway. I want something you can wrap."

She covers her mouth with her hand in an expression of shock. "You don't want a kiss?"

"I want to kiss you, of course—how could I not want to kiss those raspberry lips of yours when they look so delectably kissable?—but not for my Christmas present."

"Fine." There's a slight flush in her cheeks now, but she doesn't move away from me. "What is it?"

"I want your first book."

She frowns. "What do you mean?"

"You said you dream of being a writer, no?"

"Yes—I said *dream*, not that I was one. I've not written any books."

"That's fine—whenever you write it, then I want that book."

"I can't give you a Christmas present that doesn't yet exist."

"I'm happy to wait."

"Fine—what do you mean, you want the book? You mean a copy of the book? First edition, like *Peter Pan*?"

"No. I want the book. I don't want a copy of it, I want *the* copy of it. I want to own it."

"You want to steal my intellectual property?"

"I want you to gift me your intellectual property, yes."

"And what if my first book is just a single page that reads 'Zachary Blackwood is a thief' over and over again?"

"Then I'll be its proud owner."

She finally moves away, sitting back into the cushioned window seat. "I wouldn't do that—it would feed your ego too much to have a whole book written about you—even if it was only a page long."

"By all means, then write something else."

She purses her lips thoughtfully. "Maybe I'll write a book just like *The Pirate Lord's Captive Bride*. Something like... *The Buccaneer Captain's Stolen Fiancée*."

"You're too mature and sophisticated to be so obsessed with pirates."

"You're too mature and sophisticated to be so jealous of a fictional character."

"Jealousy? The green-eyed monster that mocks the meat it feeds on? Not I, no."

"Very well. You are far more mature and sophisticated than I gave you credit for." Theodora stops for a second to eat the forkful of pancake and blueberry I point at her mouth, then carries on. "Then it's decided. Your Christmas present shall be my first book, *The Buccaneer Captain's Stolen Fiancée*." She taps her fingertip on her lips thoughtfully. "Maybe the stolen bride will have blue eyes and long hair, and maybe the Buccaneer Captain will be tall and sullen with shorn hair and tattoos."

"I cannot wait to read it," I lie in my most courteous tone.

Later, when Theodora goes for a walk with Zahara and I sit in the Blue Parlour with Iakov while he silently chugs eggnog and plays video games, I spend the whole time fighting the childish urge to hit him on the back of his head.

Chapter 35

PRISON CELL

Zachary

Two days after Christmas, the guests leave, and soon after, my parents set off to Edinburgh for Hogmanay, which they religiously attend every year, and Zahara sets off with Iakov to meet her friends in Paris.

The house, once they're all gone, is eerily empty. Normally, I, too, would be leaving at this point, sometimes heading to the south of France to celebrate New Year's Eve with Sev, other times to meet Evan in New York. This year, though, Evan has invited his former friend, mortal enemy and reluctant tutor, Sophie Sutton, to stay with him at his home in the UK.

I'm surprised she agreed to do so since the two of them never miss an opportunity to drag each other's name through the mud—but I know better than to get in their way.

I'd only end up getting caught in the crosshairs of their eternal conflict.

Besides, I have my own guest to think about.

"What would you like to do for New Year's Eve?" I asked Theodora the evening after everyone left.

We were eating pizza out of a box in the Blue Lounge, Christmas movies on the TV. Theodora would pick a slice and tear it in two, and then tear those slices again, and then take tiny bites. I was just happy to see her eat.

"I'm not sure," she answered, delicately wiping the corner of her mouth with the tip of her ring finger. "What about you?"

"I just want to make you happy," I told her in complete honesty. "Anything you want to do, anywhere in the world—I'll take you."

She thought for a moment. "I'm happy here."

It made my heart ache to hear it. I might have thought she was lying if I couldn't see the difference in her. The slight flush in her cheeks, the ease with which she relaxes into chairs and cushions, the glitter in her eyes and the way I've never seen her smile as often as she has in the past few days.

"Alright, then. Let's do New Year's Eve here. Just the two of us? No parties?"

She shook her head quickly. "Oh, no. I'm all burnt out on parties."

"Yes, I suppose my parents' social calendar is overzealous, to say the least."

"Not just this holiday," Theodora replied. "Just in general."

I frowned at her. "Really?"

She nodded. "Yes, really."

"If you haven't been enjoying the Spearcrest parties, why go?"

"If I only went out of enjoyment, I'd never go at all."

We stared at each other, the lights from the TV plunging us in blue then orange, then blue again.

"Theodora, darling—not a party girl at heart? Who would have thought," I said, more gentle than mocking.

She laughed, dispelling the emotion that had suddenly settled upon the conversation.

Over the nothing days between Christmas and New Year, we settle into a comfortable routine: meeting for breakfast, going on long walks around the grounds, then spending the dark afternoons and evenings working on our various assignments. Later, we have dinner, something easy and wholesome, and then, sometimes, we sit and do nothing, playing cards or chess or just watching television together.

"If you don't like parties, why do you go to all the Spearcrest parties?" I ask her one evening out of the blue because it's been playing on my mind.

"Because it's what's expected of me," she answers.

I turn to her with a frown. "Since when do you do what's expected of you?"

She's lying draped on her stomach on the sofa in blue satin pyjamas, her hair a long fishtail plait dangling off the side. She props her chin up on her hands to throw me an incredulous look.

"What are you talking about?" she asks in a haughty tone. "Since when do I do *anything but* what is expected of me?"

I stare at her, waiting for her to elaborate, but she doesn't.

"How so?" I prompt her.

She gives a laugh bereft of any amusement or warmth.

"Oh, where to begin? I behave as expected, I go to Spearcrest as expected, I look as I'm expected to look, I say the things I'm expected to say. At home, I behave just as my father expects, and at Spearcrest, I behave as everybody expects me to behave. I spend time with girls I have nothing in common with, I go to parties when I barely even drink, I dance to music I don't even like. All because it's expected of me."

I'm seized with the same disorienting sensation I experienced when finding out about Iakov's personal life from Zaro. A feeling like realising someone who's been standing right at your side was mortally wounded the entire time.

"Why do you do it?" I ask. "If you don't want to do those things, why not just—stop?"

She shakes her head with a sigh. "Because it's not as simple as that, Zach. Failing my parents' expectations is not something I can just do—it's not something I could get away with, should I try. And as for Spearcrest, you and I both know the hierarchy exists whether or not we wish to acknowledge it. I cannot simply refuse the hierarchy—I cannot exist without a role. If I am not lofty, then I must be low. If I am not a queen, I must be a peasant. You know this just as well as I do."

"I don't… I just can't accept… I just don't understand how you can live this existence of—what? Duty?"

"What choice do I have?"

I sit up, leaning forward, elbows on my knees, suddenly wishing I could grab Theodora, shake her, make her see what I see, make her know what I know.

"You *do* have a choice, Theo. You're a human being with an independent mind. You have a choice."

She sits up and watches me with narrowed eyes, the same way she would watch me back in our debate team days, back when I could sense her scorn for my ideas like frost and the passion of her ideas like flames.

"I'm a human being with an independent mind," she says, voice clear and hard, "who is still bound by the rules and expectations of the world and people around me. Yes, my mind is free, but a prisoner in a jail cell, too, can think whatever they like—it still doesn't make them free."

"But you're not in a prison cell."

"It's an allegory."

"I know what an allegory is. But a prisoner cannot escape their cell because it's locked from the outside, because there are concrete walls and gates and locks and guards, because they are being physically stopped from leaving. What's stopping you?"

For a second, she just stares at me, her mouth moving soundlessly.

Is she speechless because I have a point? Or is she simply stunned by what she perceives as my stupidity?

I can't tell, and in the end, she doesn't say anything.

The conversation ends without any resolution; it ends like a heavy, uncomfortable cliffhanger where we both dangle over the edge of unsaid things, a yawning chasm below us waiting to swallow us.

THE YAWNING CHASM LEFT by our incomplete conversation puts me on edge, making it difficult to concentrate the next day when we sit in the study to work on our Apostles assignment.

Theodora sits in the big leather chair, writing notes out into a notebook with that frown of concentration she wears whenever she's working hard on something. I sit across from her on the other side of the desk, my laptop open between us. The word processor cursor blinks as it waits for me to type something incisive and poignant.

But even though I have some notes ready and an essay plan, I still can't write. I keep sneaking glances at Theodora, drawn by the beauty of her face, those delicate features, that raspberry mouth. My desire for Theodora deepens with every passing moment between us, each time gaining new dimensions.

My desire for Theodora used to be little more than intellectual curiosity—the hunger for knowledge. I wanted to understand her, to penetrate the armour she wears around herself, to *know* her. I remember thinking of her as a book in a cryptic language—wanting to break the code and avail myself of the words.

I never did that in the end.

Then, of course, I grew older, and my desire became something more alive and physical. A conqueror's desire: wanting to touch and hold and possess. Theodora is exquisitely beautiful in every way—even her flaws make her more beautiful.

How could I not want to caress that porcelain skin, to kiss those sweet lips, to lay her bare and wet and wanting in my bed?

And now, a new desire emerges, catching all the other desires in its wake.

It's this horrible, sickening, burning urge to *love* Theodora. Not just love her from afar, like a knight in a story. But love her from up close, love her like one loves a real human being. Cherish her in every way, and most importantly of all—keep her safe.

I want to hold Theodora and make sure nothing bad ever happens to her.

It never occurred to me to want to save Theodora because I never imagined for one moment she might need saving.

Now, I'm not so sure.

My eyes fall on the last words in my essay plan.

The necessity of happiness.

I look up.

"Are you happy, Theodora?"

Her eyes flash up to mine. She doesn't move at all at first, but her pen stops moving. "In what sense?"

"In the general sense. In your life—your existence. Are you happy?"

She gives a soft exhalation of laughter. "What a question. Is anyone?"

"That's not what I'm asking."

With a sigh, she places her pen down and crosses her arms on the desk, leaning forward and lowering her voice. "Are you sure you want an honest answer?"

"Why would I want anything else?"

"Because the truth, as we both know, can often be quite ugly."

I shake my head. "No, Theo, I don't believe that."

She tilts her head, fixing me with a measuring look.

"No, Zach," she says finally. "I'm not happy."

Her words are like a knife to my chest. The pain is so sharp it feels like she's inflicted a real wound. But she lets out a wistful laugh and says, "Do you think that means I've failed Mr Ambrose's assignment?"

"I don't think Mr Ambrose can penalise you for being sad," I say, my throat a little too tight. "I don't think he would."

"Let's hope so," she says, straightening herself up and picking up her pen. "Are *you* happy, Zach?"

"Right now, no. In general—yes. I believe I am."

"Well"—her lips quirk in a sad little half-smile—"we've finally found something you're better at than me. Maybe you can teach me."

I want to tell her that I would do anything to make her happy, that if I could scoop out every speck of happiness from my soul and pour it inside hers, I would. I want to tell her that her happiness might be the most important thing in my life because *she*'s the most important thing in my life.

"I'll do my best," I say instead, giving her my most charming smile. "I hope you find me a worthy teacher."

"I hope you find me a worthy student."

Chapter 36

Sage Lace

Theodora

For New Year's Eve, Zach tells me to dress warm, and he drives us twenty minutes down dark, winding country roads. We park in the frosty mud at the side of a road, and Zach takes my hand to lead me down a poorly lit hiking path, then through a shadowy copse of evergreens, using a torch to light the way.

"Why does this look like the place people go to get murdered?" I ask in a hushed voice, pulling myself closer to Zach's arm, which I'm holding in the crook of mine.

He turns his head and replies with his lips brushing my hair. "As if I would ever let anything happen to you on my watch."

When we finally emerge from the trees, we find ourselves on the edge of what seems to be a sort of precipice. Below us, the lights of a city glow like a dense constellation of yellow stars. A sweeping, breathtaking sight.

We settle on the bench, our shoulders pressed together for warmth. Zach pulls out a bottle of champagne and two glasses. Drinks in hand, we sit back and watch the shining city stretching at our feet. Now and again, fireworks shoot up and explode into the sky with a sudden burst of light.

"I didn't want you to miss out on the fireworks," Zach says. "But I thought you might prefer to watch them in peace and quiet."

My heart clenches in my chest. Part of me regrets having told him so much throughout this holiday—the part of me that feels exposed and vulnerable and afraid. But another part of me knows I couldn't have trusted anyone better with all this precious, sad knowledge—the part of me that knows, deep down, that Zach loves me more and better than anybody else in the world.

I rest my head on his shoulder.

"Likely story, Blackwood. You just wanted to make sure we're as far as possible from the rest of civilization when the countdown ends so nobody could steal my first kiss of the year."

"I'm a reasonable man," Zach says. "I would prefer it to be me, but if you wish to give your first kiss of the year to somebody else, by all means, Theodora darling, do. But you know your destiny for the year will be tied to whomever you choose, so choose carefully."

"If I kiss you, then will it mean I'm stuck with you for the rest of the year?"

"Would you rather be stuck with anybody else?"

No, I want to say. *I want to be stuck with you for the rest of the year—for the rest of my life. Because being around you is like standing in sunlight and because I don't believe any harm could ever come to me when I'm by your side. Because parting ways with you is going to feel like having the heart torn out of my chest, and every rending heart-string is going to be a death of its own.*

"I suppose not," I breathe.

We drink in silence for a moment, watching fireworks coruscating in the air beneath the canopy of white stars. The alcohol warms me up from the inside, strong enough to give my mind a pleasant buzzing sensation but not strong enough to make my head spin.

"Are you going to make resolutions for next year?" Zach asks.

"Only one. To win the prize at the end of the Apostles programme and finally prove my intellectual superiority over you."

"You're already doing better in literature than I am."

"That's not a guarantee of anything. You're going to manage to catch up somehow."

"I appreciate your confidence in me, my darling nemesis." He presses his lips to the top of my head in a fleeting touch, almost as if he didn't realise what he was doing. "What if my New Year's resolution is also to win the Apostles prize and assert my intellectual superiority over you?"

"Then I suppose we'll do what we've always done: pitch our wills against one another and let fate decide on the victor."

"Yes, I suppose so." His voice is low and thoughtful. "What an honour it has been, Theodora Dorokhova, to be your adversary. If I had made you myself in a laboratory, I couldn't have created a more perfect opponent."

The earnestness of this sudden declaration reminds me of the first time I saw him, the way he reminded me of the icons of saints in Smolny Cathedral.

Maybe it's this association that makes me suddenly blurt out, "I lied to you. I never kissed Luca."

He turns so suddenly that my head almost falls off his shoulder. In the distant glow of fireworks, I see his eyebrows shoot up.

"You never kissed Luca?"

"No. I lied. I was being... alright, I was being petty."

He's silent for a moment, slowly shaking his head. "Did you ask him to lie about it?"

"No—of course not. I don't trust him. I don't like him at all, in fact."

"He corroborated your lie, though."

"That doesn't surprise me. I thought he might."

"It doesn't surprise me either." A smirk dawns on Zach's mouth, slow and with an edge of wickedness like the glint of the knife's blade. "Oh well, he still deserves what he got."

"What did he get?"

"What was coming to him." Suddenly, Zach sets his glass down and turns to face me completely. He takes my cheeks in his hands, pulling me to him and peering into my eyes. "Does that mean that was your first kiss—that time in the library?"

"Yes," I breathe, my heartbeat quickening.

"And did you like it?"

"I loved it."

His hands slide down my cheeks to my neck. His palms are surprisingly warm given how cold the night is. "Did you want me? Back when I kissed you?"

"I always want you. I just can't have you."

"Why?" His mouth hovers close to mine, the warm mist of our breaths mingling. "What walls or locks or guards are keeping you prisoner right now? Who would even know?"

"I would know," I whisper.

"Theodora. If you can look into my eyes and tell me you don't want me, that you would rather I never touch you again, then say it. Say it, and I'll respect your decision. The only thing I care about is what you want."

I open my mouth to speak, but nothing comes out. My mind, shattered in fragments, is a confusion of clashing thoughts and memories.

My father's hard face as he asks me, *Do you know what a whore is, Theodora?*

Camille, in Year 10, rushing out of the classroom where I caught her with a boy, shameful and unrepentant all at once.

Zachary, the night of the Halloween party, telling me he loved me before ever telling me he loved me.

Every night I've ever spent in my bed with my eyes closed and Zachary in my mind and my fingers moving between my legs, the sudden flood of pleasure and shame.

Zachary's fingers on my pulse as he asked me if I was a robot in the library, and his mouth hot and hungry on mine.

The constant aching in my chest, the crushing loneliness, the black despair that settles on me whenever I think about leaving Spearcrest and moving to Russia.

For the first time in a long time, tears burn in my eyes, startling me back to reality. Real tears, rare as black opals. I close the sliver of distance between Zachary and press my lips to his.

WE MISS THE COUNTDOWN to the new year, and by the time the sky explodes with fireworks, we're already kissing anyway. Deep, hungry, aching kisses, like we might die if we stop—like we might die if we keep going.

Zach pulls me onto his lap, and I lace my arms around his neck, and I kiss him from above, like a goddess and her mortal. His mouth is unbearably soft, and a ragged sigh escapes from his throat when I give in to the temptation of biting into the cushion of his lower lip.

His hands slip under my layers of clothing, his fingers finding and gripping my waist, thumbs brushing over the ridges of my ribcage. I arch into him, rolling my hips against the hardness of him, exulting in the proof of his desire, the proof that he wants me as much as I want him.

He might have bid me to take all my clothes off, and I might have done it. I might have let him take me right there and then, underneath the fireworks and indifferent stars.

Except that it starts snowing. Negligible snowflakes at first, fluttering hesitantly to melt against our skin, then more insistently, until we are forced to part with sighs of frustration.

We drive back through a thick downpour of heavy snowflakes and run into Zach's house, laughing and breathless.

We stomp our boots to free them of snow and kick them off, leaving them right there on the atrium floor. Zach pulls my coat off my shoulders and lets it drop on the floor, pulling me away when I try to pick it up. He catches my mouth in a kiss as he wrestles his own coat off, and then we run up the central staircase, my hand in his.

He doesn't lead me to my room. Instead, he leads me down another corridor, our steps swallowed by the antique carpet below our feet until we reach a door, which Zach wrenches open and pulls me through.

I don't even have time to take a look at his bedroom before he slams his door shut and hauls me up into his arms. I meet him kiss for hungry kiss, wondering why I've deprived myself for so long.

Zach sets me down on his bed, and we finally pull apart as he props himself up on his elbows to gaze down at me. His eyelids are heavy, his brown eyes dark with desire. He's not smiling—his face has that expression I know so well.

Earnest. Ardent. Devoted.

Like a saint before a god.

"Don't look at me like that," I whisper, struck by the intensity of his gaze.

"How could I not?" he breathes. "How could I not, Theodora? When my every dream has been of this? Of you? Of having my beautiful nemesis right here in my bed?"

He catches my lips in a kiss, then kisses his way across my cheek to my ear.

"Do you know the dreams I've had in this very bed, Theodora?" His voice is a husky murmur. "Dreams of the things I longed to do with you—*to* you? Dreams of your mouth and your body and the thousand different ways I might bring you pleasure?"

I squirm underneath him. "Zach—stop."

His mouth moves from my ear to my throat. He covers my neck with wet, lingering kisses and stops against the hollow of my throat. He looks up, a feverish look in his eyes.

"Did you dream of me too?" His voice is a murmur.

I lick my lips and nod.

He takes the hem of my sweater, and I sit up to let him take it off. We sit facing each other, forehead to forehead. His fingers find the tiny pearl buttons of my silk blouse, pulling them loose. He slips the delicate garment down my shoulders, and I let it fall away.

I lie back and unbutton my trousers, raising my hips to let Zachary pull them off. My underwear is a simple green set, but Zachary gazes down at me as if I'm beautiful enough to take his breath away.

And in his gaze, I *feel* beautiful.

I always try so hard to *be* beautiful, but I've never really felt it, not the way I do as Zachary's brown eyes travel the length of my body.

I brush my fingertips over my chest, giving Zachary a soft smile.

"Do you like my bra?" I ask him, half mockingly, half to break the intensity of the moment.

"Sage green," he murmurs. "It's the colour I think of when I think of you." He leans down, kisses one bra strap, then the other. "Now, it's forever going to be the colour of my pleasure."

I laugh, but my laughter dies in my throat when Zachary's mouth drifts down the line of pale flesh between my breasts.

"It's a beautiful bra," he adds in answer to my earlier question, "but it's going to have to come off."

He takes it off me, and when I try to cover myself with my arms, he kisses my mouth, my cheek, my temple. "You're safe with me," he murmurs. "My beautiful Theodora. Let me look at you."

I always expected sex would make me nervous, but that's not it. It's the pure intimacy of the moment that shakes me to my core, that makes every nerve in my body tense up, that makes my heart pound uncontrollably in my chest.

Letting Zachary look at me means seeing the adoration in his eyes, the way his gaze softens, the way his eyes are dark with desire. When he kisses me, it's not hard and hungry—it's unhurried and tender.

He kisses my breasts like sunlight touching the petals of a rose. Wetness trickles through me as if my entire body is melting, the ache between my legs throbbing like a pulse. Zachary takes one nipple into his mouth, then the other, sucking on them both until they tighten under his tongue and my hips buck, rising of their own volition off the bed.

I want to tell him that I'm ready—that I'm ready *now*—but Zach isn't in a hurry.

He licks my nipples and traces a line of kisses down my chest, across my belly. He caresses my ribcage, my waist, my hips. He kisses the skin over my hipbones, and he kisses me through my panties so delicately I'm forced to arch into him, seeking the friction I desperately need to find my release.

When Zach finally tugs on the waistband of my panties, rolling them down my legs, I let out a sigh of relief. *Now*, I want to say. *Now*.

I've been waiting for this for so long—I had no idea how much I wanted this until now. I had no idea how much I need Zach's kisses, his mouth on my breasts, on my body—how much I need to feel him inside me.

Zach, though, doesn't answer my urgency. He lifts my legs to kiss the crook of my knees, to kiss his way up my thighs, small, gentle, slow kisses, first one leg then the other. Each kiss is an electric shock of desire, a reminder of the release I so desperately need.

"Hurry," I mutter, and frustration sends me rushing up against Zachary, mouth open on a demand, but he catches my face in his hands and kisses my open mouth.

"Do you know how long I've waited for this, how long I've *yearned* for this?" He pulls away, his eyes boring into mine, daring me to look away. "I have no intention of hurrying—quite the opposite. You've tortured me with waiting, and now I'm going to take my sweet time. I'm going to admire and kiss every part of that gorgeous body of yours; I'm going to taste all those secret places you've never let anyone touch. I'm going to get on my knees and worship you, Theodora, with my hands and my mouth and every part of my body." He pushes me back onto his bed and looks down at me with liquid fire in his eyes. "Now open your legs for me, my cruel goddess."

Chapter 37

COMPLETE COMBUSTION

Zachary

Theodora's body is a pale map, and I place kisses on it like markers. The soft peaks of breasts, the pink glaciers of nipples, the creamy plains of belly and thighs and the ridges of ribs.

I mark them all with kisses like an explorer claiming new land.

I take my time, just like I told her I would, but it's torture for me, too. I'm so hard I ache, and my need is devouring.

Part of me—a feral, primal part—wants nothing more than to pin her down and bury myself in her, to watch her squirm and tremble with the force of my thrusts, to watch her eyes roll to the back of her head as her mouth opens in a wild scream.

I know better than to listen to that part of me.

Theodora doesn't need to be broken—she needs to be seduced. The ice queen in my bed might shatter under too much force, but a slow heat might melt her.

When my mouth finally settles between her legs, I glance up to watch her lips part on a silent cry. Her fingers curl into my bed, her entire body quivering. Her hair is a golden veil draped across my bed, and a bright flush clouds her cheeks and chest.

Seeing Theodora like this is a sight both divine and obscene, like having a naked angel under my mouth.

But Theodora is no angel, no matter how much she looks like one. Her pussy throbs under my tongue, and she's so wet her thighs soon become slick with it. She's exquisitely wet—and exquisitely responsive. With every sweep and delve of my tongue, her muscles twitch, her hips arch, a symphony of moans rises from her mouth.

When I slip my fingers inside her, she clenches around me. She's slippery and so hot I have to ignore the sensation of my cock straining against my boxers.

But she's not ready yet. This is her first time, and I'm large—larger, I'm sure, than she can imagine.

So I work her open, loosening her, relaxing her, teasing her until she's moaning incoherent commands at me, mingled with pleas and insults.

"Who would have thought you had such a dirty mouth, my Theodora?" I tell her, straightening myself to look down at her. "Who would have thought that icy exterior would hide such delicious *heat*?" Bringing my fingers to my lips, I place them into my mouth, holding her gaze as I taste her. "You've a bitter tongue, my darling nemesis, but you taste—oh, *so* sweet."

She sits up suddenly, pushing me away and forcing me to stand. Sitting on the edge of the bed, she grabs at my belt, yanking it open.

"Stop talking and take your clothes off," she commands.

I smirk. "I am your servant in all things, always."

I pull off my sweater and T-shirt, then kick off my trousers, which Theodora has so helpfully opened for me. I watch her as I undress, and when I'm in nothing but my boxers, I watch with satisfaction as her eyes widen. She licks her lips in a nervous gesture.

Placing two fingers under her chin, I lift her face to look at me. Her gaze isn't nervous when it meets mine.

It's the burning blue of complete combustion.

"Take it off," she says.

I obey her. My cock springs free, and Theodora's throat shudders as she swallows.

"Oh," she says.

"Would you like to touch it?"

My question is more a dare than a request, but of course, Theodora never backs down from a challenge. She wraps both hands around the length of me. My jaw tightens as I stifle a groan deep in my chest. My cock twitches in her fingers.

How many times have I fantasised about this very scenario?

The reality is far more perfect than any fantasy I could conjure.

Her touch is firm but inexperienced. She strokes me, watching with wide eyes as I harden under her touch. She looks up at me, almost hesitant, and I nod at her, every muscle in my body tensed.

Because somehow, her lack of experience is such a fucking turn-on. Not because I'm her first, but because of her. Because of her alluring curiosity, her boldness in the face of this new situation, and something I could never have predicted about her.

Her natural sensuality.

It's the greatest irony of all.

That this cold, repressed young woman, this saintess who lives unkissed and untouched, should have such a natural affinity for pleasure. It's apparent in her gaze, in her movements. In how fast she learns to read the language of my pleasure, the way she adapts each movement to my reactions and moves in a way that feels so fucking good. In the way she lowers her mouth on me, opening her raspberry lips to suck on the tip of my cock, eyes flicking up to gauge my reaction.

"You like that?" she asks, smiling with her lips against my twitching cock, and for a moment, I'm genuinely terrified I might come right there and then against that beautiful mouth of hers.

"I like it a little too much, you delectable fucking seductress."

It takes me two seconds to grab a condom out of my bedside table, tear it free of its wrapping and roll it on. Then I grab her around her waist and haul her into the middle of my bed, propping myself up on one elbow and settling my hips between hers.

Angling myself against her, I coat myself with the hot wetness between her legs. I push against her entrance, and she stiffens underneath me, grabbing my arms, nails digging into my biceps.

I pause and breathe, "Alright?"

She nods, but her eyes are wide, and her body is trembling underneath mine.

I cradle her cheek in my hand, stroking it with my thumb. "We can stop if you want."

"No." She shakes her head. "I'm ready. Please."

She raises her legs, squeezing my hips with her thighs. My cock is straining, twitching against her. I want her so bad, and she's so fucking wet, it would be so easy to thrust into her, bury myself into the delicious heat of her.

But I hold back. I lower myself against her, lying heart to heart with her, kissing her mouth, then murmuring in her ear, "Relax, Theo." Slipping my free hand between us, I caress the wet length of her pussy, the tiny bud of her clit. "Breathe for me, my darling, and relax." I push against her slowly. "I'm not going to hurt you. I'm never going to hurt you, I'm never going to let anything bad happen to you." She relaxes against me, and I thrust in deeper. She's so tight I can hardly bear it. My voice grows hoarse, almost breaking. "Ah, you're taking me so well, darling. Theo. My darling fucking adversary, I— " Words fall out of my mouth, a litany of pleasure and want as I push deeper into her. "You feel so good, I want you so much, I fucking *adore* you, I—"

My hips meet hers, and then all I can feel is the hot wetness of her around my cock, her twitching thighs around me. I look down at her: her cheeks are crimson, her blue eyes a drowning ocean of want.

"God, you're so fucking beautiful." I speak in a ragged, reverent sigh.

I begin to move, then, slowly, giving her time to adjust. She squirms underneath me, her throat shuddering with each nervous breath. Her arms slide from my biceps to my forearms, caressing them, then grabbing them. I slow my thrusts, and she glares up at me.

"Fuck—" She gasps. "God, Zach, more. I n-need more. Please."

It's all she needs to say.

My self-control, already holding on by a thread, snaps.

I fuck her then—I fuck her with all the despair of not having her for myself, all the pent-up years of being held at arm's length by her, of wanting her like I've never wanted anything else in my life. I fuck her with the desire of all the dreams I've had of her, of every time I've touched myself thinking of her. I fuck her until she's screaming and clawing at my arms and chest with her nails. Until she throws her head back and her body arches off the bed and her thighs are shuddering uncontrollably around my hips.

Her pleasure is the cue to mine—I come with a sudden cry, burying myself deep inside her.

The rush of pleasure is overwhelming—it slams into me with terrifying force, and for a moment, I can do nothing but buck desperately into Theodora. My face is buried in her neck, and I kiss and bite down on the fragrant flesh in the animalistic urge to mark her.

When the waves of my orgasm recede, I slip out of her and discard my condom as she watches me. She props herself up on her elbows as if she's about to stand, but I push her back with a rasping laugh.

"Oh no, my lustful angel. I'm not done with you yet."

Her eyes widen as I kneel by the bed and grab her hips, pulling her effortlessly to me. Propping her legs on my shoulders, I kiss the creamy skin of her inner thighs, taking a sharp bite that makes her gasp. Then I lower my mouth on her, working her with slow, long laps of my tongue.

At first, she squirms and moans, and then her hips grow deadly still. I smirk up at her.

"Yes," I hiss. "Yes, darling. Come for me, my Theodora."

I caress her with my tongue on her and lick her until she's throbbing against me, until her thighs suddenly clench around my head, until she's thrusting against me like she's trying to fuck my mouth, until her voice breaks into a long, pleading cry.

I hold her hips still, forcing her to fight against me as her orgasm washes through her, until she's wrenching me away from her by a fistful of my hair. Then I laugh, harsh and wild, and I finally let go, grabbing her around her waist and rolling us both into the middle of the bed with her on top of me.

We lie entangled for a long time, catching our breaths. I stroke my hand up and down her back, relishing the sensation of her thighs still trembling uncontrollably.

I kiss the top of her head, then her shoulder, marvelling at the wonder of it, the wonder of kissing Theodora.

"Why did you lie about your first kiss?" I ask her through a sleepy yawn.

"Mm?" She lifts her head from my shoulder to give me a quizzical look.

"Why did you lie, that time, about kissing Luca?"

She laughs and takes my jaw in her hand. "Really? That's what you're worried about *right now*?"

Her hips are straddling my waist, the wetness between her legs smearing on my belly—a sensation that sends blood rushing back straight down to my cock.

"I'm not worried," I tell her. "I'm curious. You know I have an inquisitive mind."

She gazes down at me, her eyes searching mine. "I lied to you because Camille told me she kissed you in the back of a limo, and I wanted revenge."

"Camille Alawi?" I ask with a frown.

"I thought that if you should have my first kiss, then it's only fair I ought to have yours."

With a lazy smile, I roll us over in my bed, pinning her underneath my body, my hardening cock pressing against her thigh.

"You *did* get my first kiss, Theo. I never kissed Camille in the back of a limo, or anyone else for that matter. But I'd kiss *you* in the back of a limo."

"I got your first kiss?" she asks, a glimmer in her eyes.

"Mm-hm. All my firsts are yours, Theo. My first crush, my first fantasy. My first kiss. My first love. My first time."

"Your first time?" she asks. "Are you sure?"

"I think I ought to know."

"Must be beginner's luck, then," she mutters.

I smirk. "Or I'm just a quick learner."

"Definitely luck."

"Only one way to disprove your theory beyond doubt. Data-based research via practical experiment."

"Such dirty talk," she sighs. With a wicked smile, she arches up, her nipples sliding against my chest, sending blood rushing to my cock. "Who would have thought you were such a slut, Zachary Blackwood?"

"I'm not a slut." I laugh. "I'm *your* slut."

"You're mine?" she asks, wrapping her arms around my neck, tenderness blossoming in her forget-me-not eyes.

"Yes, my darling adversary. I'm yours. For now and forever."

"Promise?"

"I swear it."

Chapter 38

SUNSHINE SCANDAL

Theodora

I FEEL LIKE A different person when I go back to Spearcrest.

Not because I've lost my virginity—I don't really believe sex changes a person—or because I feel like I've suddenly aged. I've always felt older than my years, sex was never going to change that.

I feel different because, for the first time, I don't feel cold or numb or empty.

The last few days of the holiday, spending time in the warmth of Zachary's presence, or gossiping and playing games with Zahara, even the cosy evenings of sharing snacks while watching Iakov doggedly play his video game even though he kept dying—those were the best days of my life.

Never before had I realised the difference it makes to spend time around loving people. Like going from a cold, sunless winter to a summer flooded with sunshine.

The sunshine of Zahara's affection, the way she would ask me for advice, or go on walks with me, or sit and braid my hair while I continued our reading of *The Pirate Lord's Captive Bride*. The sunshine of the Blackwoods' admiration for me, the way they kept engaging me in discussions on a spectrum of subjects as if they were genuinely interested in what I had to say. The way they shamelessly expressed their approval of me as if Zachary had brought me home for a bride and they were happy to welcome me into the family—even though Zachary and I never gave away the changed nature of our relationship.

Love radiated from Zachary, richer and warmer than sunshine, when he would kiss my neck when we sat in his study working on our assignments or when he would sneak into my bedroom at night to lie between my legs and lick me until I was stifling moans and cries into my pillows.

By the end of the holidays, I even developed the closest thing I could achieve to a friendship with Iakov, given he barely ever spoke and that Zachary acted like a spinster chaperone whenever he was around.

Our return to Spearcrest was bittersweet.

The night before we returned, Zachary and I made love like we both never wanted it to end, slowly, achingly, holding on to each other desperately, kissing as if each kiss might be the last. Afterwards, we lay entangled in my bed, my head on his shoulder and his mouth pressed to my forehead.

"Please," I told him, my heart in my mouth, "don't tell anyone about us."

"Have more faith in me," he said then. "I would sooner die than betray your trust."

BUT OF COURSE, I didn't take into consideration how much happiness changes a person. I returned to Spearcrest feeling different—because the crushing loneliness was gone, because the bleak darkness of despair had ebbed away—but I assumed that change within me was only internal.

I was wrong.

I find this out on the first evening back while I'm in my bedroom unpacking my things. A knocking sound is immediately followed by the door opening, and there's only one person who enters my room without waiting.

"Happy New Year, Ness," I say over my shoulder.

"Happy New Year, Dora." Inessa loops an arm around my neck and kisses my cheek. "How was your holiday?"

I turn to answer her, but she narrows her eyes and steps away from me, looking at me from head to toe.

"What is it?" I ask, glancing down at myself.

I'm wearing faded blue jeans, a white woollen jumper and white trainers—nothing out of the ordinary.

"You look different," Inessa says, peering at me with a suspicious expression. "You look—I don't know." She waves a hand around while she tries to think of what she wants to say. "You look, well—happy."

I laugh. "Are you saying I looked miserable before?"

"Obviously not. Not miserable. But not like *that*."

"Like what?" I sit down at the edge of my bed, crossing my legs and lacing my fingers around one knee. "Use your words, Ness. Describe what you mean."

She stands in front of me, tapping her lips. "Hm. All pink in the face and soft and—I don't know. *Creamy.*"

"Creamy?" I laugh again. "What does that even mean?"

"Did you get yourself a boyfriend during the holidays?" Inessa asks, narrowing her eyes at me. "And you didn't tell me? We texted every day!"

"There are some things one cannot share by text," I say with a little shrug.

"You little whore!" Inessa cries. The word makes my guts clench uncomfortably, and for a second, my blood runs cold. "You know I live vicariously through you! I want to know every detail!"

I hesitate. The word "whore" is an unpleasant reminder of all the things I avoided worrying about when I was with Zachary: like my father and the promise he forced me to make—that I would never let anybody touch me before marriage, that I would never be a whore.

And what he said to me after I made that promise, those words that are indelibly burned into me.

Break this promise, Theodora, and I will punish you for it for the rest of your life.

"What is it?" Inessa asks, frowning. "I didn't mean to pressure you, Dora, I'm so sorry." She sits next to me and takes my hands. "You don't have to tell me anything you don't want to. I'm just happy you're happy."

"No, no," I say, lacing my fingers through hers and squeezing. "You're my best friend, Ness, of course, I want to tell you. I'm just nervous, that's all. I need you to swear to me you'll never tell anyone."

She pushes back her long hair and pulls out the tiny golden cross she wears around her neck. "I swear it," she says, holding the cross and kissing it.

Even though it's been a long time since I've stopped believing in saints and crosses, Inessa believes faithfully, and so I'm immediately soothed by the solemnity of her vow.

"Alright," she says, tucking her cross back into her top and holding my hands like she was doing before, "tell me everything, you scandalous woman!"

I laugh. "How do you know it's going to be scandalous?"

"Because you deserve to be scandalous for once."

BY THE TIME I finish telling her everything, Inessa and I are both lying on our stomachs on my bed, Inessa's chin propped in her hands and my head buried in a velvet cushion.

"It's always the quiet ones!" Inessa says, kicking into my leg. "You sneaky little devil!"

"I wasn't being sneaky! I didn't know it would happen."

"Liar—why else would you go to his house? To sit and talk and do homework?"

"We actually did a lot of that, too," I point out, peering over the cushion.

"Yeah, yeah—in between all the kissing and licking and fucking."

"Ness!" I cry, smacking her with the cushion.

She yanks the cushion out of my hand and tosses it away. "Oh, so you can do it but I can't say it?"

"I know you're younger than me, but can you try to be mature about this?"

"Alright, I'll be mature." She straightens her features into a solemn expression, lacing her fingers to rest her chin on them. "How many times did he make you come?"

I melt into embarrassed laughter, and this time, it's my turn to kick into her leg. "How is that being mature?"

Inessa purses her lips and shoves her face into mine. "Answer the question, young lady."

"I don't know, alright! Several times—every time we did it."

"Every time?" She jerks back. "How many times did you do it, you filthy girl?"

"I don't remember—I didn't count."

"No, I bet! You must have lost count."

I laugh and roll my eyes. "You're so ridiculous. Anyway, I told you everything like you asked, so it's your turn to tell me all about your holiday now."

"Are you crazy? You barely even gave me any details!"

"I gave you far more than you deserved." I half shove her off my bed. "You're not getting any more details, so go already."

"Alright, alright." She sits, and then she sighs, and her expression becomes more serious. "Alright, but genuinely. Were you, you know. Careful? Safe?"

"Of course." I hide my face in my hands. "Do we really need to have this conversation, Ness?"

"Yes, we do. I doubt you told anyone else, and that puts me in a position of responsibility."

"Calm down"—I laugh, poking her arm—"you're not my mother."

"No, more like your rich, hot, single aunt." She catches me in one arm and squeezes me. "You know I love you, Dora. I just want what's best for you. I'm glad you were careful." She looks at me, her grey eyes boring into mine. "And are you happy?"

My heart skips a beat and colour rises to my cheeks. I answer her truthfully. "I think I might be, Ness."

"Then that's all I care about." She grins and kisses my cheek. "You deserve happiness more than anyone in this world, you know that?"

"Stop it," I say, but my chest feels unbearably warm, and my eyes sting even though I can't cry.

"I mean it," Inessa says. "I love you, Dora."

"I love you, too."

Chapter 39

BISHOP BLACKWOOD

Zachary

THE ATMOSPHERE IS STRANGELY tense amongst the Young Kings when we all gather in the common room the day before classes resume. Luca Fletcher-Lowe, clearly recovered from his poisoning and with all the grace of a crashing meteor, passes around a bottle of ludicrously old whisky and brings up his favourite subject.

The bet.

"Fuck the bet," Evan says. His normally sunny countenance is all but gone. There are shadows under his eyes, and his face is one big frown. "It was stupid to begin with."

"Nobody's put your Sophie on the list yet if that's what's getting your knickers in a twist," Luca sneers.

"Sophie's too good for your shit list."

"You mean she's too good to sleep with you."

"Fuck off, Luca."

Luca laughs; Evan's misery clearly brings him nothing but joy. The bastard is practically glowing when he turns to Sev. "And you, Sev? Any holiday conquests while you've been living it up in the south of France?"

"I'm engaged," Sev says with great dignity.

Unlike Evan, he seems in a great mood, but that doesn't seem to be making him any more responsive to Luca's blatant attempts at creating chaos and drama.

"Anyway, get off my fucking case," he adds after taking a sip of whisky. "I've put the work in over the years. Half the names on this list are there because of me. I'm allowed to take a break."

"Why would you need a break, though?" Luca asks, tilting a pale eyebrow. "Your fiancée got you by the leash?"

"I fucking wish," Sev says.

I laugh out loud in pure admiration of his no-fucks-given honesty.

"Pathetic," Luca scoffs, shaking his head.

"And what contributions have you made to the bet lately, Luca?" I ask with a smirk. "What about your conquests?"

It's a well-known fact that he gets girls into bed because he's a Young King, but he's incapable of keeping them there more than a night. Whatever he's doing to them has them running for the hills.

He doesn't seem bothered by this. He turns to me, settling himself back into his armchair, the dark leather behind him contrasting with the dull pallor of his white-blond hair.

"At least I *have* contributed to the bet, Bishop Blackwood." He answers my smirk with one of his—and Luca's smirks are like the cold glint of steel. "You still a virgin?"

"You still a cold-blooded snake?"

He gives a laugh that's more of a harsh cackle. "Last time I checked."

I roll my eyes and sip my whisky. My leg bounces up and down impatiently, and I realise how much I'm missing Theodora.

Living with her is something I could easily have gotten used to. Feeding her banana pancakes for breakfast, kissing her neck while she bent over to write into her notebooks, even just reclining near her in the Blue Parlour, listening to her read that stupid pirate book while Zahara threaded the gold of her hair into plaits.

I grew used to that life much too fast—and now that it's over, I miss it like one might miss a limb, its absence a constant reminder of what I no longer have.

My eyes meet Iakov's. He's sitting in an armchair with his legs draped over the armrest, looking at his phone. He looks up when my eyes fall on him, and our gazes meet briefly.

He sits up, shoving his phone into his pocket. "Going for a cig," he grunts as he sits up. He twists his big body, cracking the bones in his spine. "Sev, wanna come with?"

Sev shakes his head and bats a hand, his rings catching the light. "No, man, I'm trying to quit. It's a filthy habit."

"Says who?" Iakov asks.

"My wife," Sev says.

"Romantic fucker," Iakov says affectionately.

Iakov displays about as much emotion as a brick wall, but he's always had a soft spot when it comes to Sev. My theory is that Iakov is chivalrous at heart, and Sev's long eyelashes and jewellery have somehow tricked Iakov's brain into treating him like a damsel of sorts.

"I'll go with you," I say.

"You don't even smoke," Luca points out.

I ignore him and follow Iakov to the door.

"Theodora!" Luca calls after me, and I pause in the doorway. "Am I adding her to the list, then?"

"Why would you?"

"I'm just asking."

"Her name doesn't belong on your stupid, pointless list," I snap. "And nobody cares except you. Stop embarrassing yourself."

"I'll add her just in case," Luca says with a slicing smile. "Since you two are bound to fuck at some point."

It's obvious he wants a reaction from me, just like he wanted one from Evan. But I won't give him the satisfaction. He doesn't deserve it.

I flip him off and leave the room, wondering whether I should pay the oleander tree in the greenhouse another visit.

"WHY ARE WE FRIENDS with Luca again?" I ask.

Iakov is leaning against the trunk of a willow, and I'm standing on the edge of one of the old abandoned fountains, the marble half-hidden underneath a tangle of moss and brambles.

We didn't need to go this far into the grounds for Iakov to find a place to smoke; he generally smokes wherever he feels like anyway.

Still, the fresh air and greenness of our surroundings are refreshing after the week of snow we've just had.

"Dunno." Iakov shoves a cigarette between his lips and lights it. "He's rich as fuck?"

"We're all rich as fuck."

"*You're* all rich as fuck." Iakov gives a growling laugh. "My home is a shitty flat in Chertanovo—you live in a fucking palace."

I pause in the middle of the circuit I've been carefully walking around the fountain rim and glance at Iakov. He meets my gaze with a level look.

I hold it.

"What did Zahara tell you?" I ask.

He exhales a wreath of smoke. "Told me she told you shit she shouldn't have."

"She didn't mean to."

He gives a half-grin that makes him look like a grimacing wolf. "It wasn't a secret. You two. So fucking British. Who cares where I live?"

"Why did you never say anything, then?"

He shrugs. "You never asked."

"And Zaro did?"

"Hah. No. Borrowed my phone and snooped. Little fucking spy. Would make a good FSB agent, though."

Although I'm appalled at Zaro's actions, I'm not surprised either. It's a wonder Iakov hasn't killed her yet. I might have if I were him, but maybe he's more patient when it comes to dealing with the antics of spoilt rich girls.

"How was Paris?" I ask.

He waves a hand. "Noisy. Hotel was nice, though. Food was fucking great."

I laugh. "You're a lover of French cuisine, Iakov? I never knew."

"Yea." He gives a dry, rough laugh. "I fucking love a petit four."

"A petit what?"

He holds out his hand with his thumb and index finger a few centimetres apart to indicate something small. "You know. Tiny cakes."

I stare at him, completely taken aback. "Really?"

"Mm."

I try to picture all six foot five of Iakov, with his tattoos and bruises and stapled cuts and big black boots, holding a tiny, delicate strawberry tartlet, and I shake my head at the ridiculous image.

"Thanks for looking after Zaro," I say instead. "I worry about her."

"No big deal," Iakov says. He jabs his chin at me. "How did it go with your woman?"

Oh, how I wish she was.

"She's not my woman," I say without resentment. Since I can't help the smile forming on my lips, I resume tracing a circle around the fountain rim, stepping carefully over strings of thorns and patches of wet lichen. "It went well." I point at him. "She said everyone in Spearcrest fancies you."

Iakov barks out a laugh. "Hah." He throws his head back and fixes me with his eyes narrowed into black slits. "But not her, though." He sucks on his cigarette and exhales around it. "The way you two were looking at each other, doubt I'm competition."

His implication is clear—but so is the promise I made Theodora.

"I think her family's religious," I say, straying on the side of cautious truth. "No matter how much I love her—no matter how much she loves me—I don't know if we'll ever be together."

It's a lie disguised behind a bitter truth.

Theodora and I never spoke about what our relationship would be like now we're back in Spearcrest. No matter what, I know I'll never be more than a secret. And I can accept that. I can accept it, trusting that the future will be different, that fate won't always keep us apart—that Theodora, one day, might be free to choose for herself.

"Yea." Iakov nods grimly. "Her father's a cunt." He finishes his cigarette and stomps on the butt. "Shame, man. You two have a cute thing going on."

"*Cute?*" I raise my eyebrows, taken aback by hearing that soft word in his wolfish mouth.

He frowns at me.

"Do you mean cute like your little French cakes?" I ask, stepping off the fountain edge.

"Miserable fucker." He grins and throws his arm around my shoulder. "Let's drink our sorrows away together."

"We have class tomorrow," I point out.

"So?" He shrugs, dragging me away. "Tomorrow's problems for tomorrow."

Chapter 40

TRUE SAINT

Theodora

THE FOLLOWING MONTH IS a barrage of work. There is coursework to complete, endless essays, and of course, university application deadlines looming.

I complete mine perfunctorily and submit them early. It's a bittersweet feeling: applying for courses and universities I would love to attend for the sole purpose of hiding the fact I won't be going. Being one of the highest achieving students in the school is a double-edged sword, with Mr Shawcross, our head of year, personally overseeing my applications. If I were to not apply, questions would be asked, and Mr Ambrose himself might get involved. This isn't something I can let happen.

The time I spent at the Blackwood estate taught me something important.

Happiness, the thing I thought would always be unattainable to me, is within reach.

It's just not something I can keep forever.

But if I can hold on to it, just for a while, just for now, then I will.

I'll cling on with all my might.

And that's exactly what I decide to do with what's left of my time at Spearcrest.

Happiness means allowing myself to sink into my studies, to enjoy my learning. It means sitting in the library with Zach in our spare time and letting him coax food past my lips. It means allowing myself to lean into him while we both work side by side or letting him drape his blazer, still warm from his body, around my shoulders when I'm cold. It means letting him draw me into the shadows beneath a tree when he's walking me back to the sixth form girls' building and kissing him breathlessly in the cold night air.

To the rest of the world, we're exactly the same as we always were. During our literature classes, our discussions are as heated and argumentative as ever. In the Apostles meetings, we debate like warring politicians in the House of Lords, tearing at each other's ideas with verbal talons.

Worst of all are the parties. The tantalising proximity, combined with low lighting and loud music and the burn of alcohol in our veins, makes for a deadly cocktail of risk and temptation. The safest approach is to stay away from each other, but that's almost impossible.

Inevitably, we always find our way back to one another.

Then the air between us becomes electricity, zapping at our skin, a slow, relentless torture. Our bodies want to touch, our mouths want to meet, but we can't.

So we do what we do best. We argue and debate and fight.

Any topic will do—and even when we end up on a subject we agree on, Zach will take on the role of the devil's advocate. Anything to keep our conversation going, anything to justify standing so close.

Anything to help us hold on to whatever shreds of self-control we have left.

The half-term following the holiday is short and feels even shorter, the last month blurring into an endless trail of gruelling exams. By that point in the year, there are only four of us left in the Apostles programme. Everyone, including myself, is exhausted and burnt out.

So, of course, the Young Kings throw a party. They always throw parties right after exams—probably to offer some sort of release for everyone's pent-up stress. Post-exam parties usually start off slow and sluggish, then derail into violence or debauchery—or both.

And maybe that's why I let Camille Alawi pick my outfit for me.

Normally, I stick to my collection of pale dresses and keep my make-up natural and conservative. My presence at these parties is a formality, and I keep my appearance as such. But this time, it's different.

This time, I go to the party for the release.

The stress of exams and the Apostles programme, the end of my time at Spearcrest looming ever closer, and the pent-up tension of always being so close to Zachary without being able to do anything—they're all getting to me.

Making me feel like my skin is burning and I need to find a way to douse the flames if I don't want to crumble into a pile of ashes.

"This one," Camille says, pulling a dress from out of her closet. It's crammed so full she has to physically shove herself against her clothes to extricate the dress. "I've been dying to see you in this one, Theo."

I look up from the bed where I'm sitting while Rose tongues loose waves into the ends of my hair.

"Red isn't my colour," I say, looking at the dress Camille is triumphantly holding out.

"But it *could* be," she says. "Trust me on this." She waves an arm. "I've seen it in a vision."

I give her a dubious frown. "A vision?"

"Trust me," she repeats.

My hair done, I stand up, and Camille wastes no time in pulling my silk dressing gown off me. She glances at my underwear, a simple pale blue set, and shakes her head.

"You're going to have to lose the underwear for this dress."

"I'm not going out without underwear."

"Panty lines are a fashion faux pas," Rose points out from the bed where she's now lounging.

"Put the dress on," Camille says pacifyingly, "then decide."

She helps me into the dress, cool satin sliding like water against my skin. I turn to the mirror, but she stops me with an arm.

"Hold on," she says. She pours three messy shots and hands them out. "Alright, girls. Shots for good luck on three. One, two, three."

I drink my shot, more to soothe my nerves than anything, and wince at the burn of alcohol and the taste of tequila. I *hate* tequila.

"Alright, you can look."

I turn to the mirror. The dress is a simple A-line shape, but the laced back is low, almost to my hips, and the skirt is so short it stops right at the top of my thighs.

"See?" Camille says, propping her chin on my shoulder. "I told you red could be your colour."

Camille can be a liar sometimes, but not this time.

The colour of the dress—the deep, lush red of garnets—perfectly offsets my skin. The laces make the dress hug my waist and hips, the short skirt lengthening my legs.

I turn, admiring myself, marvelling at how different I look. My first thought is of Zachary's reaction, and I almost jump when Camille laughs and says, "I can't wait to see Zachary Blackwood's face when he sees you."

Rose gives a wicked giggle. "It's going to be the face crack of the century."

Camille nods eagerly. "Bishop Blackwood is finally going to break." She wiggles her eyebrows at me. "Come on, Theo, lose the undies, girl. Don't you want to drive him a little bit crazy?"

"You two are so immature," I say.

But when we set off for the party later, I'm not wearing my underwear.

When he finally sees me, Zachary doesn't give me the satisfaction of a face crack, let alone the face crack of the century. He simply lifts an eyebrow and tilts his head as if in a silent question.

I raise my glass to him across the crowd. This time, the party is in the chapel—one of the Young Kings must have coughed up a substantial bribe to get their hands on the key.

It feels a little sacrilegious to be getting drunk and dancing to loud, pulsing music under the blank eyes of the candlelit statues of saints, but that doesn't seem to be stopping anyone.

Camille pulls me along with her, and I lose sight of Zachary.

"Forget him!" she yells in my ear over the music. "He's got a stick shoved up his arse anyway. Let's find some cute boys to dance with."

I follow her reluctantly and take my opportunity to escape when I spot the drinks piled on the altar. There, I bump into a hulking shape and look up into a pair of narrow dark eyes.

"Hey," Iakov Kavinski says.

"Hi, Iakov." I glance down. "What are you having?"

"Vodka," he says. He hands me the bottle. "Want some?"

"What are you mixing it with?"

He laughs but doesn't answer as if I've just told a joke.

"Ugh, you're just chugging it?"

He shrugs. "You don't want some?"

"Give me the bottle."

He gives it to me, and I drink, then hand him the bottle back with a grimace. "God, that's disgusting."

"Yea." He grins.

Behind him, I spot Camille, who's frowning as she looks around—probably searching for me and the drinks I promised to bring back. Ducking behind Iakov, I use him as a barrier.

"Who're you avoiding?" he asks.

"My friend Camille, she's... she wants to dance."

"You don't feel like dancing?"

"Not really. Do you?"

Iakov shrugs. "Most of the time, I just feel like smashing my own skull open against a rock."

That's when I realise he's drunk.

"Then who would be Zaro's bodyguard?" I say, hoping to lighten the tone.

"She'll find some other stupid fucker to follow her around like a dog."

"You're not a stupid fucker, Iakov."

"Yea." He gives a growling laugh and a swig of his vodka.

I grab his arm and start pulling him towards the dancing crowd. "Come on, Iakov, cheer up. Life gets better."

"Sometimes it gets worse."

I freeze and turn back to look at him. He grins a joyless grin that sends a shiver down my spine.

"We're in the same boat, Dorokhova, headed to the same hell." He suddenly slings his arm around my neck, almost sending me crashing into the floor. "C'mon. Let's dance like the doomed fuckers we are."

This time, when he hands me his vodka bottle, I take deep, long swigs.

Iakov Kavinski dances like a crazy person to a soundtrack only he can hear, which I'm certain must be music consisting only of heavy metal and the screams of the damned.

At first, it's a little scary—and then, it's just fun. I imitate him, flinging my arms around and shaking like I'm mad. He laughs, throwing his head back, and I laugh too.

Then a dark shadow appears between us.

"Having fun, you two?"

Zachary is dressed all in black, with the top button of his shirt undone. His hair is impeccable, and his handsome face is set in an austere expression.

"Bishop Blackwood, welcome." I curl an arm around his neck and press the length of my body against his. "You should dance with us."

"Oh, is that what you two are doing? *Dancing?*" Zachary's tone is acerbic, but he rests his hand on the low of my back, tangling his fingers with the laces. "Because you two look like you're out there fighting demons."

"I'm dancing," Iakov shouts hoarsely over the music. "Don't fight my demons—they've already won."

Zachary casts a look at the bottle of vodka in Iakov's hand. "Clearly."

"Do you like my dress?" I ask in his ear.

"He likes your dress," Iakov answers. "Trust me."

"You're drunk," Zachary sighs. He looks from Iakov to me. "You're *both* drunk."

"I'm a little tipsy," I admit.

"I'm stone-cold sober," Iakov says. "Tell your woman you like her dress, Blackwood, for fuck's sake."

"I'm not his woman," I say hastily, pulling away from Zachary.

"I like your dress," Zachary says. He crooks a finger and tugs on one of my shoulder straps. "I adore it, in fact."

I cast Iakov a worried look, struck by the sudden fear he knows more than he should, but he grabs both mine and Zachary's heads in his big hands, leans forward, and says very gravely, "You two should really fuck someday."

And then, with a roaring laugh, he stomps off into the crowd.

"You've not told him," I say to Zachary with some surprise.

"Of course not. I haven't told a soul."

"You really are a good man, Zachary Blackwood." I sigh, drawing closer to him. "A true saint."

He clenches his jaw. "Oh, if you knew the nature of my thoughts right now, my Theodora, you'd know I'm far from a saint."

I turn slowly, moving into the music, and flick at the hem of my skirt with my fingers. "And what is the nature of those thoughts?"

Zach takes me by my hips, pushing into me from behind, the hard bulge pressing against me, making clear the nature of his thoughts.

"You're playing a dangerous game," he murmurs in my ear. "I'm not a saint, Theodora, believe me when I say that."

Then he pushes me away and turns me to face him. His eyes have a feverish glow to them as he bends to speak quietly to me.

"One of us needs to leave right now."

"Why?"

"Because my self-control is holding on by the merest of threads, and I suspect you might be naked underneath that pretty little dress of yours." He straightens his clothes, the muscles in his jaw twitching. "So unless you wish for me to fuck you right here in the middle of this party for all to see, then I suggest one of us leaves now."

Chapter 41

INEXPLICABLE DREAD

Zachary

I MANAGE TO GIVE Theodora a fifteen-minute head start before following her out.

The cold night air does little to cool the burning heat in my skin, and I break into a run. I catch up with her on the main path, the one lined with birch trees, and I grab her by the waist, drawing a gasp from her as I bury my face in her fragrant hair.

"Come on," I groan, taking her by the hand.

We make it as far as the first classroom we find in the Old Manor. My keys shake in my grasp as I unlock the door, and I slam it shut behind us. As soon as I do, Theodora is on me, her arms wrapping about my shoulders, her mouth on mine.

She tastes like vodka and raspberries.

An addictive taste, and I know I'll never be able to drink vodka again without thinking of kissing her.

I haul her against me, ravishing her mouth with ravenous kisses as I carry her towards the teacher's desk, propping her on the edge. When I pull away, she looks up at me, her mouth open and wet and pink.

"Lift your skirt," I command her.

She bites into her lower lip and slowly lifts her skirt. The crimson fabric makes her look paler still—in the darkness of the unlit room, she almost glows.

"No underwear, Theodora?"

"It didn't go with the dress," she explains, laughter in her voice. "A fashion faux pas."

"And what was the purpose of the dress, aside from driving me to the brink of madness?"

"To get you on your knees," she answers. "Of course."

So I do. I get on my knees and bury my head between Theodora's legs, feasting on her, tasting the sweet nectar between her thighs, the intoxicating proof of her desire for me. She's incredibly responsive, every lap of my tongue drawing shivers and husky cries from her.

It's the most addictive sensation I've ever felt—the sensation of giving Theodora pleasure.

It's a sort of power, the only power I could ever hope to hold over her. It's a power I hold in my tongue, in my fingers, a power I use to dangle her right over the edge of a cliff. When she grows still, her breath caught in her throat, her fingers gripping the edge of the desk, the sensation is almost overwhelming. She comes against my mouth with a cry of shock and pleasure, and I don't quite let her ride out her orgasm, desperate to feel it with her.

Surging to my feet, I flip her around so she's facing the desk. She flattens herself down of her own volition, fingers splayed out, and tilts her hips to meet me in a silent invitation. I roll on a condom and guide myself inside her. She's dripping wet, and I let out a groan as I slide in with one thrust, forcing myself to pause, to let her adjust.

It's hard, desperate fucking at first, taking something I've been craving for so long, taking what I need more than air. And then, I lower myself against her, lacing my fingers through hers against the table.

Her head rises, settling into the crook between my shoulder and neck, filling my senses with the fragrance of her hair.

"Feels so good," she rasps, arching into me. "Oh god, Zachary, please... feels so good."

I come in a shudder of surprise, a broken cry escaping my throat. My thrusts grow frantic at first, then finally stop. We lie against the desk for a long moment as I soften inside her, and when I make to stand up, Theodora's fingers grip mine.

"No," she whispers. "One more minute. Please."

With a rasping chuckle, I settle against her, kissing her head through her hair.

"This would be more comfortable if we were in a bed," I point out.

"We don't have a bed," she replies.

"No. But we will, one day. We'll have an apartment and a bedroom and a bed where we can have sex for as long as we like and then cuddle twice as long."

Theodora's body stiffens underneath me, and I frown, wondering if she's about to push me away. But she doesn't.

We linger for a long time, and then we fix ourselves, and I walk her back to the girls' building. We bid each other goodnight and part ways, but for the rest of the night, a strange weight of inexplicable dread settles on my chest.

THE NEXT TIME I see Theodora, in our usual place in the library, she greets me with a quick little smile that immediately puts me at ease.

"Have you started Mr Ambrose's Hegel assignment yet?" She shakes her head and rubs her forehead. "It has to be the worst Apostles assignment yet."

"Not a fan of Hegel, then?" I ask in a light tone, settling myself down at her side.

She points at the pile of books on the desk next to her laptop. It's tall enough to reach higher than her head. "It's all the reading. And it's so dense. I genuinely don't know how I'm going to find the time."

"Would you like to collaborate?"

"Collaborate with you?" She narrows her eyes. "I don't know if I trust you." I open my mouth in a scandalised gasp, and she hurries to add, "Academically, that is. I don't know if I can trust you *academically*."

"I'm good enough to take to your bed but not good enough to help with your assignment?"

She looks around in concern, and when she's reassured there's nobody around to hear us, she leans towards me and says in a lowered voice, "That's because I trust you to make me come, but I don't trust what you're willing to do to win against me."

I let out a burst of frank laughter, flattered and amused by her honesty.

"The competition *is* stiff now there are only four of us," I admit, pulling my laptop open.

"Exactly."

"Well, if I can't help you with the reading, then would you at least like to have a look at my notes?"

She hesitates, glancing at my laptop screen. I open the document and show her my compiled notes. She frowns and gives me a dismayed look.

"What—when on earth did you manage to do all this?"

"At the weekend—probably while you were recovering from what I can only assume must have been one spectacular hangover."

She glares at me and then sighs. "It was the worst I ever felt."

"It's what you get for drinking Iakov's vodka."

"Jealous?" she asks with a smirk.

"You might've drank his vodka, but it's *my* tongue you came on." I smile, relishing the sudden flush of colour in her cheeks. "So no, Theo. I'm not jealous."

For a second, she's speechless, and then she collects herself, smoothing her sleeves and tucking her hair behind her ears.

"Maybe I need to sleep with somebody else," she says primly. "To keep you humble."

"You might do so, but I might poison whoever you choose for that purpose."

She gasps. "You wouldn't."

"Not to death, of course. Only just enough to make them spend a few very uncomfortable weeks. Luca's still alive, isn't he?"

"You *wouldn't*." This time, her voice is barely above a whisper. "You *didn't*."

I laugh and point at my laptop once more. "How about I give you five minutes—and only five minutes—to look at my notes? After that, you're on your own."

She hesitates, but as soon as I set the timer on my phone, she scrambles to grab my laptop and reads so fast her eyes fly across the screen like she's gone mad.

After that, we settle into our work.

Theodora wasn't exaggerating the difficulty of Mr Ambrose's latest assignment. Even my head start doesn't give me much of an advantage when the subject matter is so dense. The complexity of the ideas we are forced to absorb and synthesise requires complete silence, and neither of us speaks for the next few hours.

Now and again, though, Theodora's head rests against my shoulder as she concentrates on one of her books, or I find myself resting my hand on the low of her back, caressing it with a thumb while I re-read through whatever paragraph I've just written.

When we finish our essays, I make a trip down to the coffee machine to get us both drinks—a black coffee for me, a tea for Theodora.

I get back upstairs to find her resting her head against her pile of books, and she looks up with a sleepy smile when I hand her the cup of tea. I sit down next to her, and before either of us can take a sip of our drinks, I lean down to press a kiss to the soft flower of her lips.

"What was that for?" she asks.

"Because you've a mouth made for kissing."

She presses her fingers to her lips. "I do?"

"Mm." I brush the hair back from her shoulders with one hand. "And a body made for pleasuring and a mind made for admiring and a soul made for worshipping. You're a creature of love, Theodora, and I want nothing more than to give you that love forever, for as long as we live."

"You love me?" she says in a tone of surprise. "You've never mentioned it before."

I shake my head in a forlorn gesture. "It takes a cruel goddess to mock her worshippers."

She grabs me by my tie and yanks me to her imperiously.

"I love you too," she murmurs against my mouth, and then she kisses me in a long, hungry kiss, a kiss that luxuriates and lingers and fills the golden silence of the library with soft wet sounds.

That night, something strange happens. I wake up in the middle of a deep and dreamless sleep, my heart pounding in my chest. I sit up and turn on the lamp on my bedside table, half-expecting to see a dark shadow looming at the foot of my bed.

There's nothing there.

I look around the tidy room with a frown. What woke me up? I wasn't having a nightmare—I barely ever dream at all. I wait, but there's no noise, no movement. I'm alone in my room. I check my phone. It's almost four in the morning.

I lie back down, my heart still hammering, and turn on my side. It's been a couple of years now since I've had a panic attack, and I've never had one in my sleep. I don't know if that's even possible.

Forcing myself to take deep, long breaths, I remind myself that everything is alright. Eventually, I go back to sleep, and when I wake up, I'm completely fine.

That very same day, I'm sitting in literature class, shoulder to shoulder with Theodora as we are both bent over our notebooks, practically transcribing Professor Elmahed's lecture. A knock at the door startles everyone in the room, including Professor Elmahed, who looks up with a frown.

"Come in," she calls.

The door opens, and Mr Clarke, Mr Ambrose's personal assistant, apologises for interrupting her lesson. "Do you have Theodora Dorokhova?"

Everyone turns to look at Theodora, whose entire body goes stiff at my side. She raises her hand. "I'm here."

"I'm so sorry for interrupting your lesson, Theodora, but Mr Ambrose would like to see you in his office."

"Now?" Her voice is like I've never heard it before, small and frail, so frail it almost breaks.

It reminds me of her voice the first time I met her outside Mr Ambrose's office when she was so slight and so delicate looking.

"Yes, Theodora, I'm sorry," Mr Clarke says.

Theodora packs away her things. I watch her, clenching my fists on my lap to stop myself from taking her hand in mine, wrapping her in my arms. The expression on her face is one I've never seen before, confusion and a horrible fear that blanches the colour from her lips. She walks away, and I whisper, "See you later, Theo."

She turns briefly to cast me a look full of surprise as if she's forgotten I'm there, as if we're strangers and she's wondering how I know her name.

And then she crosses the classroom, and the door closes behind her, and she's gone.

Chapter 42

Last Assignment

Theodora

My father's anger is a creeping, gaping darkness that fills the space around him.

Mr Ambrose's office, a place where I've spent so much time, a place where I've sat and learned and grown, a place I've always felt so safe in—is completely transformed by my father's presence, by his palpable ire.

When I enter the room, Mr Ambrose stands, and his eyes and voice are warm as he greets me.

"Ah, good morning, Theodora—take a seat, please."

My father doesn't look at me. His eyes are fixed on Mr Ambrose. He's angry at him, too, I can tell.

But I also know that my father is a calculated man who never aims a bullet of anger into a target he cannot hit.

Mr Ambrose might as well be wrapped in Kevlar, and me, a doe with broken legs lying at my father's feet.

I'm so afraid my knees can barely hold the weight of my trembling body. I half-collapse into the seat at my father's side, not daring to look at him.

"Thank you for joining us, Theodora," Mr Ambrose says, settling himself into his seat. "Your father has come to discuss some..." He hesitates for a fraction of a second, his gaze moving from my face to my father's. "Some concerns. Some of those are of a private nature and nothing I can do anything about; however, I was hoping we could discuss our options in the light of—"

"No options," my father snaps. "Theodora is coming home. *Today*."

My heart stutters in my chest, and my stomach churns in a wave of nausea that almost sends the food in my stomach crawling up my throat. I normally skip breakfast, but Zachary gave me half his clementine earlier and a triangle of toast.

I wish I hadn't eaten them.

"I've explained to your father that A-level exams are coming up," Mr Ambrose says in a reassuring voice. "But—"

"She won't do the exams," my father interrupts. "I'm removing her from Spearcrest Academy."

"Mr Dorokhov," Mr Ambrose says, "I urge you to reconsider this decision. Removing Theodora from Spearcrest Academy will have serious consequences for her future, and I cannot understate how strongly I would advise you against making this decision."

I stare at Mr Ambrose: this tall, strong, intelligent man who's always been a figure of undeniable authority during my time in Spearcrest. He doesn't realise it yet, but this is a debate Mr Ambrose won't be winning.

In a room with anybody else, Mr Ambrose would hold seniority. Seniority of age, of experience, of education.

In a room with my father, Mr Ambrose is little more than staff.

Still, he tries. "You might not be aware of this, but Theodora is currently attending the Spearcrest Apostles programme, which selects only the very best student in the year group. The work she has submitted for the programme has been of outstanding quality—some of her writing is good enough for publication, even. And I shouldn't be saying this at this juncture, but if it should encourage you to reconsider your position, Mr Dorokhov, then it is worth saying. Theodora is a front-runner of the programme and likely to be the candidate who will receive a full scholarship to Oxford University to study under the tutelage of—"

"Theodora is not going to Oxford University," my father cuts in, deadly ice in his voice. "She's not going to university at all. She is moving to Russia to live with me."

Mr Ambrose is silent for a moment.

His eyes move from my father to me, his gaze settling on mine. His silence is a confirmation of my fate—I know right there and then that there's nothing he can do to help me. All the power Mr Ambrose wields means nothing in the face of my father's will.

"Mr Dorokhov," Mr Ambrose says carefully, "I understand your wish to have Theodora close—she is your daughter, and after being educated in the UK for all these years, I understand your wishes to be reunited with her. But Theodora is one of the most academically gifted students I've ever had the honour to teach, and I know that pursuing higher education is something she dearly wishes to—"

"You're not going to university," my father says, finally turning to me. "You know this."

I nod. I'm an eleven-year-old little girl again, my voice a hard egg in my throat, choking on it while I swallow down tears. I don't dare say a word, I don't dare even move. I sit still as a puppet, my hands clasped in my lap.

My entire existence is one big black blot of terror.

My father interprets my silence however he wishes. Most of the time, he takes it for obedience. Today, he takes it for rebellion.

"Or did you not tell your school? Did you lie to them, Theodora, like you lied to me?"

I never lied to you, I want to say. *I never lied to them. I hid the truth to protect myself, to protect your plans.*

"Theodora was encouraged by the school to apply to university, Mr Dorokhov," Mr Ambrose interjects. "We encourage all our students to apply, even those who are unsure, as oftentimes students' circumstances or goals may change after results' day."

"You encouraged her to apply to university?" My father sneers, looking straight at me. My eyes are trained on my feet because I don't dare look into the chasm of his eyes, but I feel his weight like a grip around my throat, making it difficult to breathe. "Did you encourage her to be a whore, also?"

I go numb all over, my mind a screaming blank.

He knows. But how does he know?

How could he *possibly* know?

Because someone must have told him.

The only person I told was Inessa—and Inessa swore on her cross she would never tell anyone.

Zachary, too, swore he would never tell anyone. But Zachary didn't swear an oath—he didn't need to, I trusted him too well. Zachary didn't swear an oath, but would he ever betray me?

And then I remember the Young King's stupid bet, that repulsive list they keep of girls in the year group they've slept with. If I check that list, will my name be on it?

And if it is, then what does that mean?

Does it matter?

My betrayal could only have come at Zachary's hands—whether accidental or not. Does that matter?

Does *any* of it matter anymore?

Mr Ambrose is speaking, his voice harder than usual. He's asking my father to remain respectful and refrain from using such language. My father doesn't care. I don't care either. I want to tell Mr Ambrose to give up, to let it go, that this is nothing compared to what my father will do once we leave Spearcrest.

Nothing compared to the lifetime of punishment my father has in store for me.

"Theodora," Mr Ambrose says to me. "Are you alright?"

I look at him and smile. "Thank you for everything, Mr Ambrose."

He frowns in confusion, but my father stands before he can say anything else.

"I'll have my people pick up her things," he says coldly. "We're leaving now." He throws me a look full of hatred and disgust. "Come."

He ignores Mr Ambrose's handshake and strides out of the office.

"Theodora," Mr Ambrose says, so quietly I barely hear him, "you're not alone."

I give him a surprised look but hurry after my father, who's already striding down the hall.

We leave Spearcrest in silence.

As I walk through the corridors, I see the faces of the students, the same pictures I admired the first time I came here. My head girl portrait stares back at me, a stranger's face because I'm not her, not really.

How is it possible that I came here a little girl of eleven, scared and voiceless, and that I'm leaving now, a young woman of eighteen, just as scared and voiceless?

Because I have no choice. Because I'm trapped, and I'll never be free from my father, from the fear that blots my heart when he's around.

We descend the steps out of the Old Manor, and I halt to a stop, blinking in shock.

The sky is cloudless, a deep blue—*siniy* blue. The rays of the sun are not hot yet, but they are warm and bright. Dapples of light glimmer through the burgeoning leaves of the trees lining the paths. It's springtime, and the air smells of rain and sunlight and grass.

A prisoner cannot escape her cell because there are walls and gates and locks and guards. Zachary's voice is gentle in my mind, his arrogant laughter ringing in his words. *What's stopping you, Theodora Dorokhova?*

I never answered his question, but I give myself the task of answering it. Of searching deep inside myself, of gathering the information I hold and synthesising it into a fresh new set of ideas. A thesis or a solution.

What's stopping you, Theodora Dorokhova?

I set it to myself like an essay question—the last assignment in my academic career.

Chapter 43

GONE

Zachary

THEODORA DOESN'T COME BACK from Mr Ambrose's office.

I wait for her outside her other classes, but she doesn't attend any of them. That evening, I go to the library, to our spot on the top floor, in the golden lights where our love waxed and waned like the moon. She's not there.

The next day, I catch all her friends and question them all. Rose, Camille, Kayana, Giselle. None of them have seen her. I hunt down Inessa, Theodora's cousin and her one true friend in Spearcrest, but Inessa frowns at me and tells me the same thing as the others, that she hasn't seen Theodora. The concern on her face mirrors my own, making my stomach squirm with dread.

My mind cycles through possibilities. A medical appointment. A family emergency. An accident.

The end of the week comes, and I walk into the Apostles meeting holding the tiniest spark of hope in my chest. The spark is extinguished when Mr Ambrose drearily announces that the programme is now down to two candidates. I glance at Sai Mahal, who sits next to me, and we exchange a shocked look.

After the meeting, I wait for Sai Mahal to leave and turn to Mr Ambrose. I don't need to ask him anything. He sighs and laces his fingers together.

"I'm sorry, Zachary. I'm truly, deeply sorry."

"Why did she drop out, sir? Where is she?"

"Her father came to collect her on Monday. He has decided to remove her from Spearcrest."

"What?"

Mr Ambrose tilts his head. I've never seen such a pitying expression on his face. "He told me she won't be going to university because she is moving to Russia to live with him."

"No—no, but she's going to university, she's going to Oxford—we *both* are."

"I don't think so, Zachary. I'm so very sorry."

My chest becomes suddenly tight, my heart hammering against the sudden constriction of my ribcage. I pull on my collar, stammering.

"She can't go to Russia, she can't—maybe, maybe he didn't tell her, and—"

"She knew, Zachary." Mr Ambrose sinks back into his chair, rubbing his hands across his face. He looks, for the first time in all the years I've known him, completely exhausted. "I suspect she didn't tell you for the very same reason she didn't tell me, the same reason she applied. Because she didn't want us to know the truth she wished to deny."

What was it Theodora had said to me?

Yes, my mind is free, but a prisoner in a jail cell, too, can think whatever they like—it still doesn't make them free.

"She can't go." My chest is too tight, my throat is too tight. My words come out in a gasp.

"She's gone, Zachary."

My heart lurches, and my throat closes up. I clutch my chest, widening my eyes at Mr Ambrose. Realisation floods his face; he's up in an instant. He's at my side when I drop to my knees. My face contorts as I try to breathe, my heartbeat too fast, my mind a howling scream.

Theodora. Theodora. Theodora.

"Zachary, my dear boy, you have to breathe. You have to breathe, alright? You're not dying, I promise you, even if it feels like you are. You just need to breathe."

He squeezes my shoulder while I gasp and hiss. I *know* I'm having a panic attack, I *know* I'm not actually dying, so why does it feel like I am?

I fall back, writhing on the floor of Mr Ambrose's office. Each breath is an overwhelming struggle, like trying to filter an ocean through a hole the size of a pinprick. I should be used to it, but I'm not.

I don't want to die. I want Theodora. I *need* her.

When I regain my breathing, after what feels like an eternity on the brink of suffocation, I rear up. Mr Ambrose sits back, watching me.

"Zachary, maybe you should go to the infirmary."

"No, sir," I gasp. I climb unsteadily to my feet, almost fall, catch myself against the edge of his desk. "I—I refuse. I refuse to accept it. I refuse to let her go. She can't go. I won't let her leave."

I stand. A tear rolls down my cheek, surprising me. I wipe it away with the back of my hand.

"Zachary—" Mr Ambrose says, standing up, but I've already turned, wrenched open the door and lurched out of his office.

When I get back to my room, I text Theodora with trembling hands.

Zachary: Are you alright?

Zachary: Where are you?

Zachary: Please tell me you're alright, that you're safe. Please tell me you're not gone.

Zachary: Wherever you are, whatever's happening, I'm here for you. I'll come get you, I'll help you however I can. I'll do anything. Come back. Please.

Zachary: Please. Theodora. I'm begging you. Please come back.

Zachary: I just want to know you're alright.

Zachary: I love you.

Zachary: I love you. I don't know how to exist without you.

I fall asleep that night with my phone clutched in my hand. The next morning, I wake up to find all my texts unread. I try to call her, but the polite robot voice informs me that the number has been disconnected.

She's gone.

She's actually gone.

My Theodora.

Angel, rival, beloved.

Beautiful, broken Theodora, whose existence is more precious to me than my own.

She's gone.

FALLEN ANGELS

Chapter 44

BRUTALIST PATRIARCH

Zachary

Everywhere I go, Theodora's absence haunts me with memories.

Her ghost sits at my side in literature class, her golden head catching the light of early spring, her fingers tickling the edges of the next page as she reads. Her ghost drifts in the corridors and down the tree-lined paths of Spearcrest. Her ghost lingers on the top floor of the library, typing quietly away on her laptop or stooping over her notebook or stretching her slim arms over her head like a nymph tempting a god.

I had decided to stay in Spearcrest over half-term to concentrate on my studies, but two days in, I change my mind and go home.

If I hoped home would be easier, less haunted, I was woefully wrong. Memories of Theodora linger there too, each more heartrending than the last.

Memories of Theodora sitting in my mother's breakfast nook, her hands wrapped around a mug of tea. Memories of Theodora on the couch in the Blue Lounge, her head on the armrest, Zaro's pirate book resting on her belly as she read. Memories of Theodora walking through the gardens with Zaro at her side, their arms linked together, the pretty contrast of Zaro's tumbling black curls and Theodora's silken gold tresses.

Memories of Theodora in my arms and in my bed, stifling cries of pleasure into my pillows, her body spread under mine, her starlit skin, the sensuous wetness of her.

Each memory is more torturous than the last. Most nights, I end up giving up on sleep and going downstairs to sit at the dinner table with a cup of coffee, distracting myself with research and essays and work, always more work.

Every day, I pull out my phone and call Theodora, to no avail.

Wherever she is, whatever's happened, she's turned off her phone or changed her number. Maybe she doesn't have a phone at all. She might not wish to talk to anybody—or the choice to do so might have been taken from her.

The not knowing is the worst thing.

Zaro comes downstairs one night, wrapped in a bathrobe and slippers, blinking sleepily in the light of the single lamp I've turned on. She pulls out the chair next to me and sits down, hugging a leg to her body.

"Hey, are you alright? Has something happened? You don't seem your usual self."

I had intended not to say anything, to keep my suffering to myself. But being home reminded me of the time Zaro and Theodora spent together, the easy friendship between them, the sisterly bonding, as though they were already sisters-in-law.

"Theodora's gone."

Zaro frowns, her whole face scrunching into her frown. "What do you mean she's gone? Gone where?"

"I have no idea. Russia, maybe. Her father came to get her right before the end of half-term. Removed her from the school."

"*What?*" Zaro's dismay is soothing in the way it gives voice to mine. "What do you mean, *removed* her? Maybe they're just having a family emergency and—"

"No, removed her, as in, from the school. Out of education. He told Mr Ambrose she's not going to university, that she's moving to Russia to live with him."

"What? Can he do that? But it's not even the end of the school year yet—what about the A-level exams?"

"I don't think he cares. And yes, he can do that. He can do whatever he pleases, it sounds like."

Zaro is silent for a moment, and then she voices the thought on her mind in a whisper, "Kind of like our father?"

I cast my mind back to the first time I met Theodora, the tall, dark man she was accompanied with, how little he resembled her, the way he commanded her to follow him without casting her so much as a glance.

"No, not like our father at all." I shake my head with a sigh. "Our father might be harsh, it's true, and he's not always kind—especially not to you. But he would never take your education away from you, he would never choose your future for you."

"Not for lack of trying."

"Father wants what's best for us, in his own rigid way. He might not approve of our choices, but he would never rob us of them."

"Maybe Theodora's father wants what's best for her too," Zaro says, and the sadness in her voice tells me she believes this about as much as I do.

"Or maybe he just wants what's best for *himself*."

Zaro leans forward to wrap a hand around my shoulder, pulling me towards her in a half-hug.

"Zach. It's normal to fear the worst. But if you keep telling yourself she's unhappy, you're going to drive yourself mad."

"I *know* she's unhappy, Zaro."

"How could you possibly know?"

"Because she told me herself." I bury my face in my hands. "I think she was trying to tell me all along, in that secret, subtle, silent way of hers, that something was wrong. I just never picked up the clues she was leaving me. I think I'm so clever, Zaro, I think I'm so fucking clever but this whole time, I've been blind, and now, I'm more blind than ever. Everything is ruined, she's gone, and there's nothing I can do to find her, to help her—to save her. What if I was supposed to save her, Zaro?"

"Maybe Theodora needs to save herself," Zaro says. "Maybe sometimes broken people have to fix themselves."

"But they don't have to do it alone. She doesn't have to do it alone."

"She knows this," Zaro says, grabbing my hand. "She knows this, Zach. She's smart—she's the smartest person I've ever met—far smarter than you, in fact. If anybody can figure it out, it's going to be her. You just have to trust her."

"It's not her I don't trust." I fix Zaro with a grim look. "It's that father of hers."

"He's her father," Zaro says. "He won't hurt her."

"Fathers hurt their daughters all the time." I squeeze her fingers, which are still wrapped around mine. "Whether or not they mean to. I think you know this."

She stares at me but says nothing.

There's nothing to say.

THE VERY NEXT DAY, I'm on my way to the study when a commotion somewhere in the house stops me in my tracks. I freeze to listen. Voices, running footsteps, and then one voice, loud and hard and booming, rising above the rest.

I hasten down to the corridor and towards the main staircase, in the direction of the commotion, which seems to be happening in the atrium. The voices become clearer when I reach the staircase, a chaotic jumble.

"Sir—please, follow me to—"

"Damien, you need to go get Lord Blackwood, hurry."

"Sir, you need to—"

And above all, the hard, harsh voice.

"Where is my daughter? I know she's here. Bring her to me. Bring her to me *now*."

I descend the steps, a spike of adrenaline making my skin bristle with invisible thorns, raising every hair on my body.

A man stands in the middle of the atrium. Tall, imposing, with the unpleasant, ugly strength of a Brutalist factory. He's dressed all in black, and there's grey streaking his dark hair, but he looks exactly as I remember him.

"*You.*" His eyes turn to me, two dark bullets boring into me with deadly intent. "The filthy dog who defiled my daughter."

Everything falls into place then.

Theodora, in Year 9, declining my invitation to the Summer Ball and telling me she wasn't allowed to date.

Iakov, in Year 12, mentioning in his deadpan tone that Theodora's father had a bounty on anyone who touched her. At the time, I had assumed he was just joking, maybe as a way to keep the idea of Theodora being off-bounds when it came to the bet.

Theodora, after we slept together, making me vow I would never tell a soul. Theodora, telling me she was as free to make her own choices as a prisoner. Theodora, always so pale and sad and broken, and that terrible fear in her face when Mr Clarke came to take her to Mr Ambrose's office.

"Is this it?" I ask, meeting Mr Dorokhov's gaze head-on, refusing to look away. "You would sacrifice Theodora's education—why? Because she didn't obey some archaic, misogynistic rule you set her?"

Mr Dorokhov steps forward sharply, and I notice the staff that surround him suddenly step back, fear flashing on their faces. Blackwood staff, in the heart of the Blackwood house, should have nothing to fear from this man—and yet they do.

I remember telling Theodora that she couldn't be a prisoner because there were no walls, or locks, or guards keeping her imprisoned. Shame bubbles through me, thick like tar. How cold and insensitive I must have sounded to her.

How despicably little I understood what she was trying to tell me.

"My daughter," Mr Dorokhov hisses, "is mine to do with as I please. And you, boy, have made her into little more than a whore."

I descend the rest of the steps in a surge of anger like I've never felt before. I stand in front of Mr Dorokhov, and I push back the wave of my fury. I turn myself to ice, just as Theodora was forced to do all these years.

"You will not speak of her like this in front of me again," I say, my voice low and deathly calm.

"I'll speak of her however I please," Mr Dorokhov hisses. "I am her father. Who do you think you are?"

"I'm the man who loves her. The man who's going to spend his life making sure she's safe from harm—safe from you. And one day, Mr Dorokhov, I'll be the man who marries her."

He lets out an ugly laugh. "I'll be cold in my grave before I let that happen."

"That can be arranged," I reply.

He raises his hand to me, but violence is stupid and predictable. I catch his arm, stopping his blow, and look him in the eyes.

"Theodora deserves better than to have *you* for a father."

Mr Dorokhov snatches his arm from me, letting out a vile string of curses.

A booming, steady voice interrupts him.

"There is no need for such language in my house." I turn to see my father appearing from a doorway. He's slowly lowering his rolled-up sleeves and buttoning them up. "Good morning. Mr Dorokhov, is it?"

Mr Dorokhov turns to my father and spits out, "You know exactly who I am."

"Then let *me* introduce myself. I am Lord Blackwood, and you, sir, stand in my house. You will show respect to me, my family and my staff, or else be escorted off the premises."

"*Respect?* What respect do I owe the people who have stolen my daughter from me? What respect do I owe the boy who debauched her?" Mr Dorokhov turns back to me. "What respect did you show my daughter when you used her like a whore?"

"Mr Dorokhov, that's enough." My father's voice is the deep, calm rumble of distant thunder. It brokers no denial. "I have expressed my expectations to you—you are incapable of meeting them. I will now ask you to remove yourself from my house."

"I'm not leaving without my daughter!" Mr Dorokhov bellows.

My father and I exchange a split-second glance. Mr Dorokhov thinks Theodora is here. My father doesn't know whether or not she's here—she could be. But I know she's not here. And she's not with her father either.

So where is she?

Mr Dorokhov shouts in the direction of the stairs. "Theodora! I know you're here!" He turns back to my father, pointing an accusing finger. "I know she's here, and you have no right to keep her from me. Bring her to me now, Blackwood, or I will—"

My father raises a hand, effortlessly interrupting Mr Dorokhov. My guts clench with terror. Is he going to tell Mr Dorokhov the truth?

"You will do nothing at all, Mr Dorokhov. You will turn around and leave this house. Outside my door, you will find several private security agents who will escort you from the premises and to whatever private airport you arrived from. You will leave the United Kingdom immediately, and ensure you do not return. Threatening a lord in his own home was most unwise, and I assure you that your return to this country would be considered a matter of national security." My father steps forward, and Mr Dorokhov steps back. "And now, Mr Dorokhov, on a more personal note. Should you go anywhere near myself or one of mine—be it my own children or my future daughter-in-law—I will personally see to it that your presence is permanently removed from our lives." A sudden smile brightens my father's face. "Is that understood?"

For a moment, Mr Dorokhov says nothing. A black rage seethes from him, and his hand twitches near the lapel of his coat. I'm strangely calm, given how obvious it is that Mr Dorokhov carries a weapon on him.

Behind him, the door opens. My father's private security agents wait outside the door, silent black shadows.

Mr Dorokhov turns brusquely and stomps to the door. Once he reaches the doorway, he stops, turns, and tells my father.

"Set foot in Russia, Blackwood, and you'll be dead before you can blink."

My father tilts his head. His smile broadens. "I see we understand one another. Goodbye, Mr Dorokhov."

Chapter 45

UGLY TRUTH

Zachary

"That was by far the craziest thing I've ever witnessed."

Zaro's voice behind me startles me. I hadn't even realised she was standing right there, my attention wholly absorbed by the black hole of Mr Dorokhov's presence.

Our father has already turned around and is walking away back to the small lounge where he takes meetings or sits with our mother in their free time. I follow him, and Zaro follows me, hot on my steps.

"Did you mean it?" she asks our father. "You can't actually get someone killed, can you?"

He stands in the doorway of his lounge and holds the door open, letting us through and closing the door after us. Our mother is out visiting friends, so it's just the three of us in the room. The calm atmosphere is in stark contrast to the adrenaline still pounding through me.

Casting Zaro a disapproving look, my father says, "I didn't say I would have him killed, Zahara. Simply removed."

"You can do that?" Zahara's voice is hushed as she drops herself down into one of the couches. "Just have someone removed?"

My father tilts his head and gives her a strange smile—mingled rue and satisfaction. "Of course. Why do you think I didn't press charges on that predator at your school?"

Zahara's mouth falls open. My father, calm as ever, stands at the small, glossy cabinet of his bar and pours three cognacs and hands us one each.

"You had Mr Perrin *killed*?" Zahara explains, taking her glass absent-mindedly, her attention completely fixed on our father.

"*Removed*." He shrugs and settles himself next to her on the couch. "He hurt my daughter, and I will never allow anybody to harm a hair on my children's heads. He received precisely what he deserved, Zahara. He was not a good man."

She stares at him, but he turns his attention to me. "Is Theodora here?"

I'm still standing in the middle of the room, the glass of cognac in my hands. The amber liquid splashes in the glass, and that's when I realise my hands are shaking slightly.

"She's not here." I sit at the edge of an armchair.

"Where is she?" my father asks.

I ignore his question. "Why did you let Mr Dorokhov believe she was here?"

"So he would stop looking for her, naturally." My father takes a sip of his drink. "Where is she, Zachary?"

"I don't know. *I don't know.*" I stare into my glass, the troubled surface of the alcohol as my hands shake uncontrollably. "I don't know."

"We need to find her. Do you have any idea where she might have gone?"

"She lives with her mother when she's not in school—somewhere in Surrey—but that's the first place her father would have looked. And she's not in Spearcrest—he removed her from the school. She might be with one of her friends, I don't know. Her phone—I've tried texting and calling her, but her phone isn't working."

"No doubt it's in her father's possession," my father says in a thoughtful mutter. "Hm. Very well. I'm going to need you to give me her friends' names—anybody you think she might have gone to for help. I'll make some calls." He stands, drains his glass and sets it down. "We're going to find her, Zachary."

After spending most of the following day on calls, my father joins the rest of us for dinner the following night and sits down with a heavy sigh.

"Any news?" my mother asks. Her voice is calm, but she can't quite hide the flash of fear and sadness on her face.

My father shakes his head.

"No. Nothing." He glances at me. "Were those all the names you could think of?"

I nod.

When I handed him the list, I didn't have the heart to tell him I doubted she would go to any of them. Because if Theodora needed help, if she needed a safe place to go to, she wouldn't have gone to Rose or Camille or Giselle or even Kayana, who lives in the UK, too. She wouldn't have gone to Inessa, her best friend.

She would have come *here*. She would have come to *me*.

"What are we going to do?" Zahara asks, swallowing thickly. "How are we going to find her?"

"There are people I can hire to try and track her down, but if she doesn't have her phone with her, it won't be easy."

"Where on earth could she have gone?" My mother sighs, shaking her head. "That poor girl. I would never have imagined this could happen to her. Such a bright, lovely girl. She deserves better than this."

My chest constricts. It's felt tight all day—it's felt tight ever since Theodora disappeared. But it continues to constrict, and a sudden terror seizes me. I grip my chest, realising I'm about to have another panic attack.

Zahara is first to realise. She scrambles up from her chair, crying out, "Zach! Zach, are you alright?"

I stand up, and my chair goes flying back behind me, crashing to the floor. My mother jumps, and my father's face drops. I back away, not wanting them to see me like this, but stumble over my fallen chair. I fall hard.

Then I'm curled up on the floor, trying desperately to squeeze some air into my lungs. My pulse is a deafening drumbeat, going too fast, too fast.

It's just a panic attack, I try to remember.

It's just a panic attack.

I know it for a fact, but knowledge, as I've learned, is just not enough sometimes. I know what I'm supposed to do. Stay still, remind myself it will pass, try to breathe as slowly as possible, the three three three rule. I know all these things, but that knowledge is like a book in the hands of a person who can't read. Completely useless.

Zahara drops onto her knees at my side and grabs my head to prop it on her lap. She bends over me and rubs my shoulder.

"It's alright, Zach, you're alright. I promise you you're alright, okay? You're alright." Her hand is gentle on my shoulder as I gasp and wheeze. "You're alright, Zach, you just have to breathe. Breathe for me, alright? I never ask you for favours, do I? So you have to do this for me. Breathe. Nice and slow. There, there."

She remains patient the entire time, murmuring encouragements and little jokes. When my heartbeat finally settles, the pinprick-hole through which I'm breathing finally widens, and the air starts to flow back into my lungs, she smiles at me.

"I'm pretty sure I just saved your life, you know."

I let out a strangled laugh. "Idiot."

"Drama queen."

I look up to see our parents standing above us. My father, as always, remains calm, but he's holding my mother in his arms, and she looks distraught. I've never seen her look like this.

I sit up, and my mother rushes out of my father's arms to sink to her knees, gathering Zaro and me into her arms and hugging us so hard she almost smashes our skulls together.

"I'm alright, Mum," I whisper.

She kisses Zaro's forehead, then mine. "We're going to find her," she whispers against my temple. "We're going to find your beautiful Theodora, Zach. I promise."

But we don't find her, and soon, half-term is over, and Zaro and I return to Spearcrest.

Everything seems to go back to normal: lessons, coursework deadlines, Apostles lectures. Our formal exam timetables are published, and we begin the final push of our studies.

But nothing is normal. Theodora's ghost still lives at my side wherever I go, and her absence weighs heavy on my shoulders, sometimes so heavy it crushes the air from my lungs. Every day, I still open my phone to dial her number. Every night, I wake up with the same shock of panic that awoke me the night before she left.

The first week back at Spearcrest goes by impossibly fast, torturously slow, the noose of hopelessness I carry around my neck progressively getting tighter.

Then, Monday morning, I emerge from the sixth form boys' building on my way to my classes and almost trip on something. I look down to see a blonde girl hastily stand up.

Inessa. Her lips are pale, and her eyes are red and bloodshot.

"Do you know where she is?" she asks without preamble.

I shake my head. "She's gone."

"But *where*?" Inessa's eyes fill with tears. "I didn't think she would leave—I didn't know this would happen."

My blood runs cold, immediately followed by a red-hot rush of adrenaline. "What did you do?"

She shakes her head, her mouth opening and closing as if she's trying to speak. She explodes into sobs, burying her face in her sleeves, her shoulders bouncing. I watch her, every part of my body turned to ice, bereft of any sympathy.

Because I know *exactly* what she's done.

"You told her father." There's no doubt in my mind, and the sentence comes out of my mouth as a statement, not a question. "She told *you*, and *you* told her father." I stare at her, a cold disgust making my skin crawl. "You're the person she trusts the most in Spearcrest. You're her best fucking friend. She loves you. I thought you loved her."

"I do love her, of course, I love her!" Inessa glares at me through her tears. "But her father—he wants what's best for her, and Theodora will never find a good husband if she's—if she's not a virgin, and—"

"Theodora deserves a husband that will value her for more than whatever price he puts on the idea of purity. The *myth* of purity, Inessa—because it's not a real fucking thing and it certainly doesn't dictate Theodora's worth as a human being."

"It's easy for *you* to say!" Inessa cries out, wiping her tears with her sleeves. "Nobody cares what boys do, nobody will judge *you* for sleeping around. But it's not the same for Theodora! She has a future to think of, she'll have to get married, and then—"

"Do you really think that's what she wants? All this time you've spent with her—you're her best fucking friend, and you *still* think that's what she wants for her future? To be some fucking trophy for her father to pass to some other man who'll also treat her like property?"

"And what about you?" Inessa sneers at me. "You think you're any better? You also used her like some object, just another girl for you to fuck!"

My fists clench at my side. Blackwoods may not believe in physical violence, but I have the cold, deadly urge to have her buried alive just for saying that.

"Theodora isn't another girl," I grit out through clenched teeth. "She's *the* girl. She's my match, my equal, my partner in fucking greatness. And if she let me, I would marry her, not for her name or her father's power or the worth of her body. I would marry her because her mind and soul are worth more than all the money in the world, all the stars in the fucking sky. I would marry her if she had sex with another man, and if she had sex with a hundred other men—it wouldn't matter. I would marry her because there's nobody else in this world I love more than her and because she deserves that love more than anybody else."

Inessa's cheeks are bright red, and she doesn't have the audacity to question my sincerity. I laugh in her face, a cold, ugly laugh. "And to think Theodora wasted her love on you." I sweep her with a look of disgust.

Inessa's eyes fill with tears again, but there are no sobs this time.

"Please. Don't tell her."

"I don't know where she is, and I won't give up on finding her. But when I do, I can swear to you I won't say a word about what you did. Do you know why?"

She doesn't answer. She doesn't need to; it was a rhetorical question.

"Because she loves you—even though you don't deserve it, even though she'd be better off loving a poisonous snake. And it would break her fucking heart to know you were the one who betrayed her trust. And unlike you, I love her. I love her with all my heart and soul—something you clearly don't know how to do. And the only thing I want for her is happiness and safety, even if it means protecting her from the ugly truth of what you've done."

Inessa's lips and chin tremble uncontrollably. I shake my head and clench my jaw, untouched by her sadness. Then I turn and walk away, the sound of Inessa's quiet sobs vanishing in the wind.

CHAPTER 46

PRIMROSE COTTAGE

Zachary

ANOTHER HOLLOW, EXHAUSTING WEEK passes. I try to call Theodora every single day, to no avail. It almost becomes a ritual of sorts, a way of acknowledging the ghost of her. Before I go to sleep, I find myself reading Keats, murmuring lines out loud as though they were incantations to summon her.

Friday night, I try to go to the library but quickly give up, unable to concentrate on any of my work. I'm on my way back to my room when I almost bump into Iakov, who's walking away from my door.

"What's up with your Zaro?" he asks without bothering to greet me.

"What do you mean?"

"Dunno. I've left her alone, like you asked. But she's been sneaking off campus."

"*What?*"

My heart sinks. In my worry for Theodora, it completely escaped my mind to worry about Zaro. Somehow, I thought things were better, that she was a little wiser. Then I remember her behaviour the night of the Christmas Eve party, the Duke of Bridehall's invitation to his yacht.

But Zaro was only joking about that—right?

Or am I simply refusing to learn from my mistakes? Refusing to see the damage in the people I love, the hurt plaguing them? Whatever's broken inside Zaro isn't something that's just going to fix itself, and I've been stupid to assume otherwise.

And Zaro knows how distracted I am at the moment.

"Do you know where she's been going?" I ask, opening my bedroom door and letting Iakov precede me inside.

He shakes his head. "Want me to find out?"

"How would you do that?"

He lets out a grunt of laughter. "Easy. By following her."

I hesitate. On one hand, it would be so easy to let Iakov do just that, follow Zaro and find out what she's up to and deal with the problem in his own way. But Zaro's not *his* little sister, and she's made clear to me her distaste for being assigned a guard dog.

No. Zaro is my little sister. I'm the one who ought to be protecting her, not my best friend. I'm the one who should be looking after her and protecting her. I failed to do so for Theodora.

I won't fail Zaro.

Iakov and I stake out the narrow country road every night of the week, waiting for Zaro to appear from the crack in the old fence everybody knows about.

Over the course of our stake-outs, we see an endless parade of runaways: Year 12 girls in tiny dresses sneaking out for a night of partying, boys holding girls by the hand—I even see Seraphina Rosenthal, the rose of Spearcrest, decked out in a vintage trench coat and Louboutin heels, sneak off, no doubt to meet her secret townie boyfriend everybody knows about.

My heart pits through my chest on Thursday night when a slim figure with an explosion of curly hair appears through the crack in the fence. A black cab is already awaiting her, and Zaro runs along the length of the fence and climbs into the taxi. Iakov starts his engine without a word, and we follow the taxi from as far as possible.

To my surprise, it doesn't head into London, where everyone tends to go for parties and hook-ups. Instead, the taxi takes the narrow, windy road straight into Fernwell, the local town.

Nobody from Spearcrest ever goes there since it's a small, sleepy hamlet with nothing more to it than a church, a supermarket, and a collection of small artisanal shops. But that's right where Zaro's taxi takes her, and Iakov and I exchange a bemused glance when it parks in front of a cosy-looking cottage standing all on its own a few minutes from the village.

Zaro gets out, hugs her coat around her, and enters the cottage. A sign above the bright green door reads Primrose Cottage B&B.

"What the fuck." Iakov's face, normally as expressive as stone, is crumpled into an expression of bewilderment that would be funny if the situation wasn't so strange.

"Maybe it's not what we think?" I ask, equally bewildered.

"What else could it be?" he asks.

We stare at each other.

Sudden realisation crystallises in my mind.

And then I'm yanking my seatbelt free and running out of the car, up the little pebbled path to the green door, which I wrench open. A woman in her forties, her brown hair in pigtails, is sitting at the counter, a big hardback book propped open in front of her.

"Can I help you?" she asks, looking up.

"The girl that came in here—where did she go?"

She frowns. "Who are you?"

The hallway is cosily furnished but small, and it's easy to glance down the adjoining corridor. There, I spot the Chanel umbrella I gifted Zaro at Christmas, propped next to a door.

"I'm so sorry, excuse me, I'll be right back!" I call out to the woman at the desk and set off running down the hall.

Once I reach the door, I go to open it, but it's locked. I slam both fists on the door, my head a frenzy of thoughts in a blizzard of hope and fear. "Zaro, open up! It's me!"

The door opens, and I stand face to face with Zaro, who stands with a hand on her hip and a disapproving look on her face. "I knew you were following me! You're such a—"

I push past her and into the room. It's small and provincially pretty: a bed with a patchwork eiderdown, a small blue rug on rustic wooden floorboards, a little stand with a coffee machine, tea cups and ceramic pots of sugar and tea bags next to a narrow armoire, plants and vases of wildflowers. At the other end of the room is a small window seat upholstered in blue felt.

On that seat, hugging her legs to her, is Theodora.

"Shall I ask him to leave?" Zaro asks in a tone of concern, turning to look at Theodora.

Theodora shakes her head, and I let out a burst of laughter. A sound of mingled shock, relief, and amusement—amusement at the mere idea that Zaro could make me leave when no force on earth could make me leave right now.

"Zahara." Iakov's voice is calm and grave behind me. I don't turn to look at him. "Come."

"I'm... I'm going to go now." Zaro goes to Theodora and squeezes her hand. "I'm going to wait outside with that big goon." She casts a glare over my shoulder, where Iakov must be standing. "Is that alright?"

Theodora nods.

Zaro casts a worried look from Theodora to me, but our gazes remain on each other. She sidles past me with a little awkward grimace, and then the door closes, leaving Theodora and me alone to face one another in raw, painful silence.

She looks exactly as I remember, and yet completely different.

Exactly as I remember because her forget-me-not eyes still have that odd quality to them, a gentle dreaminess undercut by a sharp intelligence. Her features are the same, those ethereally beautiful features, that raspberry mouth where all my kisses wish to live and die, that creamy skin. She's wearing loose, high-waisted jeans and a white satin camisole under a soft blue cardigan with enormous sleeves.

Different because, despite the melancholy set deep into her eyes and features, she looks the healthiest I've seen her in a long time—the healthiest I've *ever* seen her.

She's gained a little weight, which has settled beautifully into her body, cushioning the protruding bones of her chest and softening her delicate features. There's a faint flush in her cheeks, a rose tint within her skin that makes it look warm and kissable.

Different because of her hair: those long, heavy tresses of pale gold are gone. Her hair is cut right below her chin, and it hangs down in slight waves, as if freed of its weight, her hair has gained a new lightness to it.

My throat becomes tight at the sight of it, and I'm gripped with the sudden, horrible urge to weep. As if feeling the weight of my glance, Theodora raises a hand self-consciously to her hair, brushing the strands with her fingertips.

"How does it look?"

Her voice is an arrow straight to my heart. I almost crumple from it. I step forward. "Why did you cut it?"

"Because I've always wanted to cut it." She tilts her head and gives me a strange smile, full of rue and tenderness. "And I realised nothing was stopping me from doing so. No walls, or locks, or guards."

She stands and does a full turn, slowly and gracefully as a music-box ballerina, before stepping closer to me.

"I cut it myself. How does it look?"

"It's your hair, Theodora. How could it be anything but beautiful?" My too-hoarse voice fades in my throat.

And then I do what saints do when they see their angels. I fall to my knees at her feet and weep.

Chapter 47

Arm's Length

Theodora

STANDING UP TO MY father and running away from him was the most frightened I've ever been—but seeing Zachary Blackwood fall to his knees with tears streaming down his face is the saddest I've ever felt.

I've had plenty of time, the past weeks, to comb through my feelings for him.

Desire, affection, admiration, love, resentment, betrayal, hatred. The full spectrum of love and hate and all the emotions in between. It was my hatred that allowed me to stay away from him, to refrain from running to him for help and comfort when it was all I wanted to do.

And yet, now, watching the pain etched into his beautiful face, made more beautiful still by the wretched despair twisting it, my hatred drains from me like a poison being sucked out of my bloodstream.

Taking his chin in my hand, I raise his face to me. He looks up, a silent plea in his eyes. Tears stream down the smooth brown plains of his gorgeously chiselled cheeks. I wipe them away with my fingers.

"Why are you crying?" I ask him.

"Because." His voice is thick and raw. "Because I was so—so fucking scared. And because I missed you, and because I thought you were gone, and because—because I'm so angry at you."

"Angry? At me? *You?*"

"Me—yes, *me*. Angry at you, yes. You, Theodora Dorokhova, cruel goddess that you are. Do you know the fucking pain you've put me through?"

I grab his jaw in my hand. "And what about the pain you put me through?"

"I'd cut my own hand off before I ever used it to hurt you."

"And what about your tongue?"

I glare down at him. Tears still shimmer in his eyes as he frowns up at me. Then, the searching look in his eyes is replaced with sudden realisation.

"You think it was my fault. You think *I* told your father about us."

"No, I don't." My fingers tighten around his jaw. He's so beautiful, and I adore him so much, but part of me wants to hurt him. "I think you told someone who took that information back to my father, whether directly or indirectly. I don't think so—I *know* so."

He gazes up at me, and I feel the shudder of his throat as he swallows hard and the tensing muscles of his jaw as he clenches his teeth.

"Who do you think I told?"

"Isn't it obvious?" I sneer. "There was only one of your friends who stayed at your house at the same time I did, and it's not a coincidence he lives in the same country as my father."

"You think *Iakov* betrayed you?"

"No. I never put my trust in Iakov. I put my trust in *you*."

"And you really think I would ever betray your trust? What reason could I possibly have for doing that?"

A memory flashes through my mind: opening my phone to frantically search for that accursed list the Young Kings keep of their conquests. Scrolling through the names hoping with every fibre of my being not to find what I was looking for, and then the sharp fangs of despair biting down on my heart when I reached the end of the list.

My name never looked so much like a stranger's name as it did then.

I finally let go of Zachary's jaw. "I suppose I can't blame you. You had to wait a long time to get rid of that nickname of yours, and your contribution to that stupid bet must have been a great one indeed: you're the man who conquered the virgin of Spearcrest, after all."

He climbs to his feet and gathers himself to his full height. I realise at that moment how much he's changed since the last time I saw him, even though it was only a few weeks ago. He's taller, for one, and there's a hardness in him that wasn't there before—a palpable inner strength that makes me take a step back.

"You're an intelligent woman, Theodora." The wet track of his tears still gleams on his cheeks, but his voice is hard and cool as marble. "Far too intelligent to believe what you're saying."

"My father didn't *guess* what happened. He *knew*. How could he have known?"

"If someone found out about what happened from me, they could only have guessed, or I might have let it slip by accident without realising. I can swear to you that I never purposely told anyone."

The conviction in his tone, burning with that same intensity he was always full of when he was younger, makes me almost waver.

"Swear it on what?" I ask, shaking my head. "You don't believe in anything."

"You're wrong. I believe in *you*—I swear it on *you*, Theodora. On you and your soul, which I love more than my own. If I ever let slip our secret, it was by accident."

"And the bet?" I ask, my voice cracking even though I've been so strong so far. "Why was my name on that disgusting list?"

"Your name was on the list?" His eyes widen, and then his fists clench at his sides. "Luca," he bites out. "That fucking sociopath." He shakes his head at me. "He joked about putting your name on there—but he jokes about it all the time. It's his way of reminding me I can never have you. He just likes getting under people's skin."

He looks at me, and his gaze softens. He reaches for me, but I step out of his reach.

"You can be angry at me if you wish." His voice is full of a gentle fervour. "You can hate me for as long as you like. I'll wait for your forgiveness as long as you need me to, and if you never forgive me, I'll live a servant to your hatred. You can punish me every day of my life, Theodora, if you wish to. But you don't get to hate me from afar. You don't get to"—he gestures at the room, the cottage—"hide from me. You don't believe me, and you're hurt—and you're allowed to feel those things. But you don't get to push me away because I know I've done nothing wrong. My love is as valid as your hatred. You get to land a thousand blows on me, and I get to return each blow with a caress. So don't hate me from afar, Theo. Hate me from up close."

I let out an incredulous laugh. "You and your arrogance. You're not the centre of the world, Zachary. I'm not here because I'm hiding from you—I'm here because I'm hiding from my father."

"Your father won't be coming back to this country. I can guarantee it. So you don't need to hide from him."

My breath catches. When I finally got hold of Zahara, she told me what happened at her house. Hearing it from Zach's mouth makes it more real, but the fear inside me won't let me fully believe that my father is really gone.

I suspect the fear won't ever fully go away.

Zach steps closer to me. His presence, full of authority and that intense strength of his, seems to fill the small space of the bedroom.

"If you were hiding from your father, why did you tell Zaro not to tell me you were here?"

I lick my lips and pull on the sleeves of my cardigan. "I didn't ask her to keep it a secret from you."

"Liar."

"I'm not lying. She asked me if she should tell anyone. I told her I needed more time. That's all." I laugh, shaking my head. "Do you really think she would have let you follow her here if she was trying to keep me a secret? She practically *led* you here."

He frowns at me. "She didn't lead me here. It was Iakov who realised she was sneaking off campus."

"And Zahara definitely doesn't know that Iakov keeps an eye on her—at your behest?"

"She asked me to tell him to stop, and I did." Zachary crosses his arms. "Even I didn't know Iakov was still keeping an eye on her."

"And you really think Zahara didn't know?"

"If she wanted to lead me here," Zachary demands, "why would she not just tell me you were here straight away?"

"Because she's only known for a few days. I'm guessing she expected to be caught earlier." I smirk. "Iakov must be slacking in his duties."

We stare at each other across the room. Zachary steps forward again, but this time, the backs of my legs hit the edge of the window seat. There's nowhere left for me to retreat.

A grim determination settles in the rich brown depths of Zachary's eyes. He begins his cross-examination.

"When did you get here?"

"A few days ago."

"Where have you been?"

"Travelling from Surrey."

"On foot?"

"And trains and buses."

"Why haven't you been answering your phone?"

"My father took it away when he brought me home."

Zachary swallows visibly. Now that there is barely any space between us, caught in the heat haze of his complete attention and focus, my skin begins to tingle all over.

"What happened between you and your father?"

"I finally spoke to him." I give Zachary a small smile. "I remembered what you said about the prisoner and his cell. I suppose I realised I didn't have to be a prisoner after all. And I remembered the way you spoke to your father—something I never thought I could do. Well, I did."

There's a softness in his gaze—the glowering softness of molten lava. "Were you afraid?" His voice comes out hoarse and rough as if he's unwell.

"Yes. More afraid than I've ever been."

"Did he hurt you?"

"Only a little."

His fists clench at his sides, and he takes a deep breath, his chest rising and falling brusquely. "Why didn't you call me?"

"I didn't have my phone."

"Would you have called me if you did?"

My breath leaves my lungs, and my eyes sting. The truth drops from my mouth like the roses and diamonds dropping from the girl's mouth in that French fairy tale.

"I might have, even if I hated you then. I might have because there's a part of me that's always wanted you to save me."

My voice trembles—I remember how afraid I used to be of crying, my father's wrath at the sound of my sobs, and the way Zachary dropped to his knees to weep, unashamed, at my feet.

"I wanted you to save me for so long, Zachary Blackwood. Sometimes, my heart cried so loudly for you to save me, I couldn't understand how you couldn't hear it. I know princes and knights aren't real and that damsels ought to save themselves. But I thought you were something else, a saint, or an angel, to keep me safe when I couldn't do so myself."

A tear blossoms in Zachary's eyes and falls in a straight line down his cheek.

"I would have," he rasps in a broken voice. "I would have if only you'd let me. I would have saved you and protected you and never let any harm come to you. If only you hadn't always insisted on keeping me at arm's length."

"*One step removed from a stranger*," I say. "I know. I was scared. I've been scared for a very long time."

"And now?"

"Now? I don't know. I'm not so scared anymore, though I suspect there'll always be a little tumour of fear living in my heart. Now, mostly, I feel lost."

"You're not lost." He steps forward one more time, almost closing the space between us, and takes my hands in his. For the first time, it's his fingers which are cold and mine warm. "You're not lost, Theodora. I've found you. I've finally found you. And I'll never lose you again."

Chapter 48

Debt Incurred

Theodora

It's easy enough to let Zachary wrap his arms around me, to soften in the confines of his embrace. His touch is as warm and comforting as it's always been, but it's tainted somewhat, irreversibly damaged.

Damaged by all the fear and betrayal I've gone through, the shock of pain when I realised Zachary must have betrayed my secret, the memory of seeing my name at the bottom of that list.

Damaged, too, by my father's shouts, his bruising grip on my arm as he threw me into the back of his limo and called me a string of filthy names. The word "whore" is indelibly carved into my bones, somewhere nobody but me will ever know about.

All this damage is still too fresh, the wounds still bleeding bright.

Maybe Zachary senses it; he releases me with a sigh and takes my face gently in his hands. "Come back to Spearcrest with me."

I shake my head, pulling myself loose and sitting on the edge of the bed to create distance between us. "I can't."

"It's not too late to catch up on what you've missed, and Mr Ambrose will understand, he—"

"No, you don't understand, Zach. I can't. My father paid for my education—he paid for everything. Even if I somehow got in touch with my mother, I suspect most of her finances are tied to his. I can't go back to Spearcrest—I simply can't afford to."

He frowns and looks around the room. "How are you paying for this?"

"I took some cash with me when I ran away. It was enough to pay for my journey here, and it's enough for the room. It'll be enough to live on while I figure out what to do." I give him a wry smile. "But certainly not enough to pay for Spearcrest tuition fees."

"Mr Ambrose won't care—I'm sure of it, he'll—"

"Spearcrest Academy isn't a charity, Zach. You're not naive. Mr Ambrose might well wish to be generous, to let me back into Spearcrest, but he's not free to do whatever he likes. He has governors to answer to."

Zachary watches me, and then he sits down in the window seat with a sigh, leaning down to rest his elbows on his thighs.

He looks at me and speaks brusquely. "I know you won't want me to say it, but—"

"Then don't say it," I interrupt.

"I have to. We're both thinking it anyway."

"No, we're not. I don't want anything from you."

"I'm not offering you anything. But my parents—my father didn't go through the trouble of threatening legal and political action against your father out of pure altruism, Theodora. My parents like you—they seem to think you..." He meets my gaze and shakes his head as if he's deciding to not finish his sentences. "My parents would help you in a heartbeat."

"I don't want their help either."

"Then let me lend you the money, for god's sake."

"You'd never let me pay you back."

He doesn't deny this. He widens his eyes at me in frustration.

"You're really going to give up, to let all your hard work go to waste—because of your pride?"

"My *pride*?" I laugh out loud. "If you hope to provoke me into doing what you want, Zach, you'll have to try harder than that."

"You're not the poor little matchstick girl dying in the cold, Theodora." His voice is hard. "This isn't a fairy tale, and you're not the helpless, tragic victim. The help you need is being offered to you—if you refuse it, then you're the one victimising yourself."

"I never claimed to be a helpless, tragic victim," I retort. "I'm not sitting out in the cold waiting to die. I'm going to get a job, apply as an external candidate to a local college, sit my exams—and go to university, just like I always wanted to do. You're the only one who sees me as a victim in all this."

He stands up suddenly, his hands curled into fists at his side.

"And what about the Apostles programme?"

"That's the only thing you care about, isn't it?" I say. "The Apostles programme and winning. That victory you've always coveted, that trophy you want to hold up so that everybody will know you've bested me."

"Yes, you're right. I'm not too proud to admit the truth." The muscles in his jaw jump as he clenches his teeth. He straightens his clothes, fixing his shirt and tie the way he would always do when he stood up in debate club to present his closing arguments. "Don't come back to Spearcrest for me, don't come back because you want to, don't come back for charity or because I love you. Come back as a business exchange—I give you something you need, you give me something I want."

"What do you want?"

"I want my fucking victory. I've worked too hard and too long for it. You don't want to take my money—then trade me. I'll pay for your final term in Spearcrest, and in exchange, you come back, catch up with the assignments you've missed, and we see this through. And when I'm finally holding that figurative trophy you speak of, when I finally get to shout from the rooftops that I've bested you at last, then you'll know the debt is paid, and you never need to do anything for me ever again." He stands in front of me and sticks his hand out imperiously. "Do you accept?"

I look into his eyes, the blazing intensity there, the bleak, joyless conviction. Taking his hand in mine, I shake it in a formal motion.

"I accept."

Returning to Spearcrest is like returning to a place from a dream, except that this time, I'm awake.

Spring has finally arrived: the deciduous trees have all sprouted fresh new leaves and blankets of croci, bluebells and daffodils spread over the hills and fields of the campus. The turrets and spires pierce a sky blue as a robin's egg, and the windows catch the sunlight like the facets of diamonds. It's a beautiful sight, straight out of a fairy tale.

Except that it's real, and it feels real.

I never realised, all these years, how much life felt like a waking dream. How I floated from class to class, never fully aware.

But I'm awake now, and everything strikes me anew. The beauty of the campus, the fragrance of grass and flowers and fresh earth in the air, the majesty of the halls and corridors and pillars of Spearcrest.

Even my friends, the girls I'd spent so much time with without ever letting them close, seem different in my new awakened state. I notice, for the first time, how happy Rose seems. She's dating a boy from

Fernwell, apparently, and there's a new ease to her. Camille, whom I'd never seen as anything more than an outrageous flirt, spends most of her time studying. I never noticed before how hard she works. And Kayana, the carefree, glittering party girl, has an edge of sadness to her that was invisible to me until now.

Are all these things new, or am I only noticing them now that the veil of my misery has been lifted? It's hard to tell, and in any case, there isn't much time for introspection.

As soon as I'm settled back into my room, I'm summoned into a meeting with Mr Ambrose. I arrive to find all my teachers gathered in the room. The warmth with which they welcome me almost brings me to tears, but I manage to hold on to a semblance of dignity as they eagerly discuss how I'm going to get back on track.

My literature teacher explains that I need not worry too much about literature since my last mock exams all received full marks, and I've already learned most of the exam content. But I have fallen behind in my history and Russian classes, so the teachers come up with a timetable amongst themselves of extra sessions and one-on-one tutoring to get me caught up.

Once that's sorted, Mr Ambrose gives me the two assignments I've missed for the Apostles programme. He doesn't bother to ask me if I still wish to continue—and I'm glad for it. I had been bracing myself to plead with him to let me back in.

"One of these assignments has already been and gone, and the second is the assignment we're currently on. There's only you, Zachary and Sai left in the programme now—so work hard, Theodora." Mr Ambrose's face is one broad smile, beaming with kindness and pleasure. "You have some fierce competitors there, but you were the front-runner when you left. Time to reclaim your throne, my dear girl."

I thank him before leaving, and just as I open his door, he says, "I could not be happier to have you back, Theodora."

I pause in his doorway. "I could not be happier to be back, Mr Ambrose."

"I know."

THE WEEKEND OF MY return, my friends throw a little welcoming party in the girls' common room.

It's a far cry from the excess of Spearcrest parties or the debauchery of nights out in London. But it's perfect for me, and I suspect that was part of the design.

There are some drinks and bite-sized snacks, which I cautiously sample, pushing back the instinctive wave of nausea. Camille tries to quiz me on what happened to me while I was away, but I remain vague with my answers, sticking to my story of being away for a family emergency.

"Never mind me and my boring family affairs," I say, relaxing into one of the plush velvet couches in the common room. "I want to hear about Rose's townie boyfriend."

Rose's face drops a little, and she exchanges a glance with Camille. At my side, Giselle stiffens but says nothing.

"He's the loveliest man I've ever met," Rose sighs in the tone of a lovelorn princess leaning at her window. "And he makes me feel so loved and safe."

"And, apparently, he's a beast in the sack," Camille adds. "Better even than Mr Gold, by the sounds of it."

"If we're comparing men to vibrators, then the bar is getting too low," Giselle points out.

There's some invisible tension there, though I'm not sure why. Camille gives Giselle a smirk. "For the vibrators, you mean."

We laugh, and I turn my attention back to Rose. "I think you did the smart thing, dating someone outside of Spearcrest."

"Oh, right?" Rose says, sitting up enthusiastically and throwing her golden curls from her shoulder. "Spearcrest boys are so spoilt and immature. They have no idea what they want."

"They just want whatever they can't have," Giselle points out. "That's why they don't want us. I can't wait to go to university and finally date real men."

Talk quickly turns to university, and soon, Rose has hijacked the conversation with a happy rant about going to fashion school in London and working on her first collection and launching her own couture line.

I listen happily enough to her pleasant patter, searching the room with my eyes.

Out of everyone who welcomed me back to Spearcrest, Inessa is the only person I've yet to talk to properly. I saw her briefly the first day I got back, but she just gave me a little shy wave before hastening away. At the time, I thought it was because I was surrounded by the most popular girls in Year 13, and I know she's never liked them much.

But she's not spoken to me since, and when I've tried to knock at her bedroom door, she's always been out.

At first, I tell myself she's probably busy studying for summer assessments. It's not until the following week, when I spot her on her way to a lesson, that I finally realise what's going on.

Our eyes meet across the sunlit corridor on the second floor of the Old Manor—I'm just coming out of my Russian class, she's headed to hers. I wave a hand and smile. Her face falls when her eyes meet mine. She stops mid-step, turns, and then runs back the way she came from, leaving me standing, frozen in shock, in the middle of the corridor.

Inessa hasn't been shy or busy.

She's just been avoiding me.

Chapter 49

FRIENDLY FIRE

Theodora

That night, no matter how much I try, I can't fall asleep.

Why would Inessa be avoiding me? At first, there's no reason I can think of. Inessa's been my closest, truest friend ever since she transferred to Spearcrest. I did my best to keep her safe from other girls, and she's the only person I've ever fully let in, fully trusted.

But then, the more I think about it, the more reasons I begin to find for her avoiding me.

She might not know my father confiscated my phone and is angry I didn't message her for so long. She might be upset that I spent more time with my Year 13 friends instead of her when she knows I prefer her company to theirs. She might resent me for not having told her where I was, for being gone so long.

She might even be upset about what happened with my father since the more I think about it, the more certain I am she will know about it through her own father. Inessa returns home to Russia for every single holiday—while she was home and I was gone, her family might have said anything to her.

Does she think that turning my back on my father, my family, means turning my back on her? If she would only speak to me, she would know that's not the case. I would never turn my back on Inessa, no matter what.

I make the decision that night to confront her the following day, but when I wake up in the morning after a few hours of poor sleep, I change my mind. Inessa probably needs time and space, she doesn't need to be cornered and questioned.

I remember what Zachary said to me in that little room in Primrose Cottage.

Don't hate me from afar. Hate me from up close.

For the first time, I understand how he feels. Even if Inessa is angry at me—furious at me—even if she hates me with every fibre of her being—I would still rather she hate me right to my face, hate me from up close, just so I could still be near her.

I DEBATE WHAT TO do for the next two days, even though I should be concentrating on my studies and assignments. When I sit next to Zachary in literature class, his silent, steady presence is a wall of light next to me.

I'm desperately tempted to turn and ask him for advice. I know that no matter what, he would give me good advice. Well thought-out and balanced and kind and reasonable advice.

I sneak him a glance, and he catches me looking. He smiles at me, that beautiful Blackwood smile, bright teeth in that handsome brown face, dimples carving those sharp cheeks. A smile glowing with easy arrogance and shameless adoration. It makes my heart ache, and I drop my gaze quickly.

In the end, since I can't possibly bring myself to ask him for advice, I turn to the next best thing and go looking for Zahara.

A FEW DAYS AFTER I returned to Spearcrest, a package arrived for me, containing a school uniform in my size, brand-new clothing and pyjamas in shades of cream and white and blue and sage, toiletries, a brand-new bottle of my perfume, and a new phone still in its pristine white box.

There was no sender and no note, but when I started up the phone, two numbers were saved on the brand-new account.

Zachary's and Zahara's.

Although I never used Zachary's, Zahara and I texted almost every day since. So when I messaged her telling her I needed her advice, she replied almost immediately.

Zahara: Come to the creepy fountain by the old greenhouse. I'll be there.

When I get there, the sun is high in the sky, and dapples of soft sunlight fall on the moss-devoured marble of the fountain. I find Zahara there, sitting on the rim of the fountain in her summer uniform, her hair half-caught in a gold claw, the curls cascading around her slim shoulders. She's smoking a cigarette and seems to be talking to someone.

I draw closer to the fountain and spot a dark shadow towering amongst the trees.

"Oh. It's you."

"Hey."

Iakov in his uniform is always a jarring sight, but it barely looks like a uniform on him anyway. His shirt is untucked, the top buttons undone, and the tattoos covering his arms and chest make him look like a criminal, not a student.

I let my eyes fall scornfully away from him, turning to Zahara.

"Shall I come back later?"

"No, no." She pats a dry patch of moss next to her on the fountain rim. "We're just borrowing Fido's smoking spot for a bit."

"I can come back later," I say stiffly. "Once you're alone."

She frowns and then looks from me to Iakov. "You don't want him here?"

"I don't want whatever I tell you to go straight back to my father, no." I turn a cold smile to Iakov. "I think enough of my private business has been making its way back to Russia, no?"

"Wouldn't know." He shrugs. "Not been back there since October."

"He's not going to tell your father anything," Zahara says. "He would never do that."

"He spied on you for Zach, didn't he? What makes you think he wouldn't spy on me?"

"That's different," Zahara says. The frown on her face is both surprised and saddened. "I don't get it. What are you saying?"

"Ask him," I say.

Iakov blinks at me slowly. His narrow black eyes give nothing away. His expression remains perfectly neutral. He sucks on his cigarettes and exhales in a thick curl of smoke.

When he finally speaks, his deep voice is calm. "You think I snitched to your papa?"

"What do you mean?" Zahara's head turns from Iakov to me, lost. "Snitched about what?"

"You know what," I tell Iakov.

His stare remains blank.

"Zachary and I," I spit out. "What we did. Your stupid, disgusting, misogynist bet."

"Ah," Iakov says. "You two fucked, huh?"

"What?" Zahara's voice is a scandalised squeak. "You two had *sex*? *When*? I mean, thank god, because it was getting exhausting to watch, and—oh, I'm so happy to hear it, not in a creepy way, but because you two are so perfect, but—" She turns back to Iakov. "What bet is she talking about?"

"Don't pretend you didn't know," I tell Iakov.

"I didn't." He gives an indifferent shrug as if he doesn't care whether I believe him or not. "Zach told me you two hadn't done anything." He lets out a growling laugh. "Lying fucker."

"I would love to believe you, Iakov." My voice breaks with the truth, with how desperately I do want to believe him. "But if you didn't know, then how did my name end up on your list?"

His neutral countenance finally breaks. "What list?"

"Your stupid list for your stupid bet!"

"What bet?" Zahara exclaims.

"Him—his friends—the so-called *Young Kings*. They made this horrible bet at the end of Year 11 to sleep with every girl in our year group. And they put my name on that list after I had—after I slept with Zach."

Iakov pushes himself off the tree against which he's been leaning and pulls his cigarette from his lips to speak.

"Nobody gives a fuck about that bet. *Nobody*. Evan spends every minute obsessing over that prefect of his. Sev is lovesick over his pretty fiancée, can't talk of anything else. Luca has to leave campus to get laid because every girl here is scared of him. I certainly don't give a flying fuck about a fucking *bet*. And Zachary—hah!" He gives a bark of laughter. "He's only ever loved *you*—he's only ever wanted *you*. He didn't fuck you for a bet. He fucked you because he worships the ground you walk on. And when he did, he lied about it to me and didn't say a word to the others. If your name is on that list, it was because Luca is a sadistic piece of shit with a morbid sense of humour, and he was probably just hoping it would fuck with you two." He crushes the tip of his cigarette, extinguishing it, and sticks it behind his ear. "Sad to see it worked." He shoves his hands into his pockets and straightens himself. "Zachary fucked you and kept it a secret because he would rather die than ever hurt you. If your cunt of a father found out, it wasn't because of him. He didn't tell a soul. Can you say the same?"

And with a rough, harsh laugh, he shakes his head and strides away, disappearing beyond the drooping branches of the willow trees. I stare after him, my heart pounding, my mind a blank.

A gentle touch brings me back into the moment, and I look down to see Zahara's graceful hand on mine.

"Are you alright?" She's stubbed out her cigarette too and is biting down into her bottom lip anxiously. "Iakov wouldn't lie, Theo, and he's right. Zach would never do anything to hurt you. He's loved you for so ridiculously long."

I stare at her, at her lips forming words, her sincere brown eyes, the same rich shade as her brother's, almost gold. I'm hearing what she's saying but not registering it.

My mind is too hard at work, my thoughts organising themselves. For the first time in a long while, I have clarity. I work through what I know methodically, without emotion.

"Sit down, Theo, please." Zahara's tone is pleading and worried. "You had something you wanted to ask me about—you wanted my advice on something. Why don't you tell me?"

"It's alright." I squeeze her hand and lean down to kiss her cheek. "I know what I have to do." I pull away from her. "I'm sorry for leaving like this, but this is something I have to deal with now. I'll talk to you later, alright?"

She nods, and I sense the weight of her concerned stare as I walk away.

Away from the abandoned fountain and back to the sixth form girls' building to see the one person who's been avoiding me since I came back.

The one person I trusted enough to tell my secret to.

Chapter 50

Beautiful Nemesis

Theodora

This time, when I knock at Inessa's bedroom door, I don't let her ignore me, and I don't go away after a few knocks. I stay until she has no choice but to open the door and look me in the eyes.

She looks thinner since I've last seen her, the shine of her hair a little dulled, her eyes rimmed with pink. Her eyes meet mine, and all the air seeps out of her.

"I'm *so* sorry, Dora. *I'm so sorry.*"

I push past her into her room and let her close the door behind me. Her bedroom, where we spent so much time sitting on her bed and chatting, where we shared her desk while I helped her with her essays, now seems cold and unfamiliar.

I feel the opposite of cold.

At first, in the moment of realisation, I felt icy all over, frozen in the shock of understanding. But now, there's no ice to keep me numb. Emotions burn inside me, anger and hurt and resentment, a searing pain in my chest.

"I don't understand." In the end, my voice isn't strong and determined—it's weak and wavering. "You told him? Why would you tell him?"

"My father works for yours, and he offered to pay for my education, for everything—but Dora, he told me he only wanted me to make sure you were alright, that you wouldn't be in any trouble, and—"

"You've been..." I brush my hand over my face, suddenly exhausted. "You've been *spying* on me? For my father? All these years?"

"Not spying, just—just making sure you were alright, that nothing bad would happen to you—Dora, you are like my sister here, and your father has such great plans for you, I only wanted to do the right thing and help."

"This whole time." All the anger drains from me. I feel so weak I could fall. I step back, gripping the door handle for support. "You've been *spying* on me. You've been—" My eyes fill with tears, so fast that Inessa's image becomes a distorted blur. "And you told him about Zachary and me. You're the reason he came."

"I only told him because I was worried." Inessa steps forward, holding up her hands. "And I never thought in a million years he would be so angry, I never thought any of this would ever happen, I swear it to you, Dora, I swear it on my life, in front of God."

I watch her through my tears and say nothing at all.

I *feel* nothing at all.

The truth is that I believe her. Inessa loves me—she loves me too much, too openly, too completely for it to be a lie. And my father and hers probably had much time to fill her head with lies, to convince her whatever she was doing was for my own good.

My logical, sensible mind can understand all of those things. My logical, sensible eyes can see Inessa, the state she's in, how devastated she is.

But my heart, which I protected so well all these years, which I trusted her with above everybody else—my heart feels nothing but pain.

Deep, dark, ugly pain.

A pain I don't know I can ever heal from.

"He promised me he wouldn't tell you," she sniffles. "He promised you wouldn't find out."

I wipe the tears from my eyes and straighten myself. "My father isn't a good person, Inessa."

"Not him—your Zachary. He told me he wouldn't tell you."

"He didn't."

"Then how do you know?" Her voice breaks into a wail.

"You were the only person who knew. The only person I told. The only person I trusted."

And then, since there is nothing more I have to say to her, I turn my back and leave her bedroom.

CONFRONTING INESSA WAS NEVER part of my plan, but in the end, it was the closure I needed. I cry myself to sleep that night, but the next morning, I wake up feeling strangely new. Refreshed. Reborn.

I look at myself in the mirror: my short hair, so light now, catching the early morning sunlight in golden gleams, the slight flush in my cheeks, my eyes, which seem so much less empty.

I don't just look different, I *feel* different. Lighter, freer, but older too.

For the first time, I feel wholly, completely *myself*.

The real Theodora.

And, as it turns out, the real Theodora is strong and resilient and smart and hard-working.

I catch up on the Apostles assignments and the missed content from my classes. In my exams, my mind is crystal clear, all the knowledge within me appearing to me with perfect clarity.

Most classes have broken up now exams have started, and the Apostles seminars have been suspended. The last week of exams also comes with the deadline for the final Apostles assignment.

"There is only one good, knowledge, and only one evil, ignorance"—Socrates. Discuss.

Mr Ambrose gives us no word limit for this particular essay. I think it's his way of testing us, of seeing how much we've learned and how capable we are now of expressing ourselves. I draft a six-page essay on the subject; I've had a lot of time to think on the nature of good and evil, knowledge and ignorance.

But I've also not spoken to Zachary yet. I don't know why. I keep telling myself it's because I'm too busy with exams—we both are. That's part of the truth, but not all of it.

The truth is that I don't know what to say to him. I don't know how to undo everything that's been done or fix everything that's been broken.

I don't know how to make everything alright, but I do know the one thing Zachary wants above all things. I know he deserves it, too.

So on the day of the final Apostles assignment deadline, I make my submission.

But it's not my six-page essay.

It's, in its own way, my apology to Zachary—and a love declaration.

I COME OUT OF the final literature exam buoyed by a strange sense of serenity.

Having retrieved my bag from the little hallway outside the exam hall, I emerge into the warm sunlight and take a deep breath, filling my lungs with the fragrance of fresh-cut grass and honeysuckle.

Although I amble away from the building, I linger amongst the trees, careful not to crush the bluebells at my feet. Students come drifting one by one or in pairs from the dark portal of the exam hall entrance, and I wait until I spot Zachary.

He steps outside and stops.

His satchel is strung across his chest, which is now the broad chest of a young man. His dark curls gleam in the sunlight, and he turns his face up towards the sky, taking a deep breath the way I did.

A smile blossoms from my mouth, unbidden, and I brace myself to take a step in his direction.

And then Evan Knight, beaming and golden and as excited as a puppy, comes bounding out of the hall and throws himself at Zachary, wrapping his arms around Zachary's neck and squeezing tight.

I almost laugh when Zachary shoves him off with a wince and straightens his uniform with the dignity of a monk. They talk for a moment, and then Evan's head whips around to stare at Sophie Sutton, who's just emerged from the exam hall.

The three of them stand and talk for a little while. Sophie and Zachary are their usual selves, both standing prim and straight and proper, but there's a smile on Evan's face that could rival the glow of the sun as he stares at Sophie.

It's something I'll never understand—the love between them and the way it lives in the black castle of hatred they've built for themselves over the years. But Evan's love for Sophie is unmistakable.

It makes my heart hurt to watch—not because I want what they have, but because I could have had it—all along.

Eventually, the group breaks up, Sophie walking away first, then Evan and Zachary ambling off in the opposite direction. I watch them leave with a sigh, seized with sudden melancholy.

Whatever sense of relief I was hoping to feel now the exams are over is yet to come, and I know I won't get it until I speak to Zachary.

Since I have, for the first time since I arrived in Spearcrest, no work to do, and since I'm not in the mood for being around others, I end up making my way aimlessly around campus, bidding a private, secret goodbye to the place I've called home for so long.

I go past the peace garden, with its flowers now in full bloom and the gazebo standing in the middle like a marble crown. I pass the arboretum, with its evergreens and carpet of pine needles, and past the old botanical garden, with its curtain of ivy and long, dusty windows. Then I make my way around the back of the campus, past the staff car park, the cobblestone path up to the clock tower, then back to the main campus.

Finally, I head into the library. It's quiet this time of year, almost completely deserted.

Sunlight falls in thick, heavy ribbons through the glass cupola, dust sparkling like magic powder as it spins in slow motion. I make my way up floor by floor, hand gliding up the smooth surface of the bronze railings, past the reading nooks with their big chesterfields, past the monsteras and the book trolley, past the polished bookshelves with their amassed treasures of knowledge.

On the top floor, I turn left and take trailing steps, as though mesmerised, to my little spot, my old haunt. The place where Zachary and I spent years navigating the strange battlefield of our relationship.

"Good afternoon, my beautiful nemesis."

His voice is low and gentle and sensuous, and at first, I'm convinced it's an echo from the past, half-ghost, half-memory, rising from the old books and golden lights.

And then my eyes fall to my desk—the desk where I've read so many books and written so many essays.

The old wooden chair is angled away from the desk, and Zachary Blackwood sits upon it, his body relaxed, his long legs crossed at the ankles. One elegant hand supports his face, the other dangles with careless grace off one armrest.

There's an easy smile on his handsome face, and a beam of warm sunlight, refracting off the bronze railings of a nearby shelf, makes his eyes glow like amber.

It's a gorgeous smile, warm as a caress. I pull out the chair near to his—the chair where he would sit for so many hours, his arm pressed against mine as he worked at my side—and sit down facing him.

"Good afternoon," I answer. "My august adversary."

Chapter 51

Effective Method

Zachary

The more I see it, the more I adore Theodora's short hair. The natural waviness of it, like ethereal wisps; the way she pins the tip back in a hair clip shaped like a moon crescent.

When I didn't see her after our literature exam, distracted by Evan and his lovesick puppy antics, I assumed she had gone back to her room to get changed, but she's still in her school uniform. Unlike everybody else, she's still wearing the winter uniform, with its long-sleeved shirt.

But of course, she still manages to look ethereally beautiful even in her uniform. She looks better now than she ever has, and there's a new confidence in her movements that makes my heart catch whenever I glimpse it.

Which I do when she slowly, calmly pulls out the seat next to mine—the seat I always occupied during our many hours spent in this very place. She sits straight in her chair and crosses one leg over the other, lacing her fingers around her knees in that prim way of hers. It sends a hot rush of mingled affection and desire through me, and I have to resist the urge to spring up from my chair to sweep her into my arms.

She sits, and her gaze rests on mine, her expression neutral but relaxed.

"Good afternoon," she says, "my august adversary."

"A compliment, Theodora? How unexpectedly generous."

She gives a small, gracious smile. "Yes. A final compliment to add to your piteous list."

"Final?" I say in a light tone. "I don't think so, no."

"I see you're in one of your arrogant moods."

"Aren't I always?"

She laughs. "Unfortunately, yes. I take it the literature exam went well?"

"Exceedingly. I stole Evan's precious tutor from him; her help and your absence might have given me the edge I needed to match you in getting full marks."

"How can you possibly know if I'm going to get full marks? I might have done terribly in that exam for all you know."

I tilt my head and soften my gaze. "Except you haven't."

"I envy your certainty."

"You are just as certain as I am that you excelled in that exam."

She laughs, almost reluctantly. "I forget. You know me better than I know myself—isn't that so?"

"Not at all. I know you quite well—very well, even—but I suspect your nature is as complex and unfathomable as the deepest ocean, and I look forward to spending much of my future pondering its mysteries."

"You might find more interesting things to do once you leave Spearcrest."

"No, Theodora. You will always be the most interesting thing in my life." I keep my tone light when I add, "Whether or not you choose to remain in it."

"Well, you'll have the summer to ponder over me, I suppose, since your sister has kindly invited me to stay at your house."

"Did she also tell you she will be holidaying in the south of France with our parents?"

"She did." Theodora gives a little shrug, a gesture of calculated carelessness. "I told her I would rather stay at Blackwood Manor and rest."

"Did you?" I murmur. "What a coincidence. So did I."

"Interesting," she says.

"Isn't it just?"

We stare at each other. Outside, in the distant trees beyond the cupola, birds sing the lazy songs of spring evenings. The sun, as it sets, grows more golden by the minute, turning the sky peach and pink above us. A dreamy silence rests like a heavy blanket upon the library.

Theodora is the one who finally breaks the silence.

"Why didn't you tell me it was Inessa? Why did you let me believe it was you?"

Even though her tone sends a twisting ache through my heart, I keep my eyes firmly on hers and my voice light when I answer her.

"I didn't *let* you believe it was me. I told you the truth about me and hoped you would believe me. I didn't tell you about Inessa because I knew it would hurt you to know the truth, and your pain is something I cannot abide."

"You can't protect me from everything," she points out.

"I've not protected you against anything at all," I tell her. "I didn't protect you when I *should* have—when you needed me—no matter how much I wanted to. I failed in my sacred duty, and I'll spend the rest of my life trying to atone for it."

"It was never your duty to look after me," she says, shaking her head.

"It was. Mr Ambrose gave it to me the first time I ever met you. I made a vow I would never fail. In the end, I did."

"You didn't fail. You tried as best you could—I'm the one who pushed you away, remember? Always one step removed from a stranger?"

I sit up, narrowing the distance between us.

"I only ever wanted to love you."

"I only ever wanted to be loved by you." The sincerity in her voice is heartbreaking. "I was just scared this whole time."

"And I was too blind to see your fear for what it was." I give her a wry smile. "You call me arrogant, Theo, and you think I believe I'm better than everybody else. But I don't—I always believed *we* were better than everybody else. I put you on a pedestal at my side, and it never occurred to me that fear could reach you there."

"And now?" she asks, echoing my earlier movement and leaning forward. "Do you still believe you're better than everybody else?"

"How could I?" I let out a laugh. "Look at my friends, those air-headed, stubborn idiots. Sev laid his heart on his sleeve and professed his love for his fiancée in front of everyone during the Spearcrest exhibition. Even Evan, after spending so many years trading barbs and blows with his Sophie, has managed the impossible feat of making her fall in love with him. What use is it being the smartest amongst my peers if they are happier than I am?"

"Being less happy than someone doesn't make you inferior to them."

"No, I don't believe that. I don't believe that at all—not anymore. I rather think the opposite, actually. Happiness is the true marker of superiority—not wealth or power or status. Not even intelligence."

"We'll see if you still believe that," she says with a cruel curl of her lips, "when Mr Ambrose announces the winner of the Apostles programme on Friday."

"Yes. We will."

I smile, my lips tingling with all the kisses I want to lay upon hers. Her eyes flicker to my mouth, and I wonder if she senses the strength of my desire. Unlacing her fingers, she cradles my face in her hands. A tremor runs through me, half-anticipation, half-dread.

She doesn't kiss me.

Instead, she says, "I'm so sorry, Zachary."

I widen my eyes. "For what?"

"For doubting your loyalty when you've never been anything but unwaveringly devoted to me. For mistrusting you when you've never given me any reason to do so. For punishing you for a crime that wasn't yours. For—" Her voice breaks. She swallows and continues to speak in a quavering voice. "For not letting you love me—for forbidding myself from loving you back when it's all I've ever wanted to do. For wasting all this time."

"I forgive you," I answer straight away. "I forgive you for all of it—even though there is less to forgive than you think since you are not to blame for most of the things you've spoken of. I forgive you everything there is to forgive—I would forgive you anything at all. You could plunge a knife in my chest right now, and I would still forgive you."

She gives a warbling smile, and nascent tears glisten in her eyes. I've never seen Theodora cry; I should've known even her tears would be beautiful.

The sun has almost set now, and the library, without us noticing, has grown full of red light and shadows.

"I might grow tyrannical," she says, "if my transgressions are so easily forgiven."

"And I would love you still, my exquisite despot."

She laughs, and a tear falls loose from her eyelashes, rolling like a pearl of dew down her cheek. I kiss her laughing mouth, stealing her breath away. I kiss her with the anxious reverence of a first kiss, the desperate devotion of a last kiss, and the ardent hunger of every kiss I've wanted to give her.

I kiss her until her tears cease to fall and until her entire body is warm and trembling under my hands.

And then we're standing and embracing and stumbling through the crimson blades of fading sunlight and the soft shadows of the library. I pick her up into my arms, crushing her to me before pinning her back in a dark alcove of bookcases as she whispers a frantic string of words into my ear, an incantation of desire.

"Oh Zach, I've missed you, I love you, I need you, now—now."

I swallow her incantation into my mouth, wrapping one arm around her waist and reaching under her skirt with my free hand.

My mouth is hungry on hers while I stroke between her legs, finding her hot and wet as ripe summer fruit. She wraps her thighs around my hips and reaches between us to yank at my belt, murmuring commands into my ear.

And I obey her—my lustful tyrant.

I hold her tight and kiss her raspberry mouth and drive my hard cock deep inside her, swallowing her rasping moan. One hand clutching my neck and the other holding on to the bookshelves for purchase, she arches against me, sliding herself up and down the length of me, forcing me to bite down hard on a moan.

"What are you doing to me," I groan, burying my head in her neck.

"Making you mine," she says in a husky sigh.

"I'm already yours." I thrust deep inside her, burying myself to the hilt and grinding against her. "I'm already yours—I've always been yours."

"Yes," she hisses, and I feel her pleasure in the tautness of her neck, the strain in her voice, the tensing of her thighs. "*Mine*. Oh, please—"

"I'm yours, my love." I kiss her neck, her jaw, her mouth. Reaching between us, I brush my thumb over the tiny bud of her clit, slippery with her wetness. "My Theodora. My love. Come for me, angel."

She comes with a startled cry and writhes against me, clenching around my cock. I pin her hips, forcing her to stay still, her orgasm calling to mine as I fuck her with abandon. Her cries become loud, ragged wails, and I'm forced to stifle them under one palm as my thrusts become faster, harsher, harder, until I have no choice but to come, hard and dizzying, inside her.

We stay entwined, pressed against the bookshelves, my head against her throat, hers resting against the books. Our panting breaths are the only sound in the library, and we wait until both our heartbeats have calmed to finally pull away from each other.

I set Theodora down gently, fixing her underwear and skirt, tucking her hair behind her ears. She lets me, closing her eyes and leaning into each gentle touch. When I'm done, I fix myself, and we stand gazing at each other with sheepish expressions.

"I came inside you," I whisper, covering my hand with my mouth. "We need to find a pharmacy, or—"

She laughs and pulls my hand away. "Don't be so dramatic. I started taking birth control pills the moment I got back from the Christmas holidays."

"Oh."

Her face is flushed from pleasure, still, and the confidence in her laughter is enough to send blood rushing back to my cock. I grab her waist and kiss her hard—a greedy kiss.

"I really fucking love you, you know that?"

"Such a dirty mouth, Lord Blackwood." She laughs, but she answers me back with a kiss just as greedy.

"Lord Blackwood is my father," I tell her. "Technically speaking, you should be calling me the Honourable Zachary Blackwood."

She pulls away from me with a mocking laugh. "Not on your life. Not for all the lords in the land."

"Not even in bed?"

"Not unless you find a way to compel me to do so, no."

I smirk. "I'll find a way to compel you."

"Or I'll compel you."

"You always compel me. I've been compelled from the moment I met you. You have a compelling face—and a compelling mouth, and a compelling—"

She shuts me up with a kiss.

It's an effective method.

If only she had discovered it earlier.

Chapter 52

Sublime Fools

Zachary

When Mr Ambrose calls us into his office on our final day at Spearcrest, his face is set in a grim expression I've never seen before. Theodora and I exchange a frown but say nothing as he motions us to sit in the chairs across his desk.

"Right," he says, pinching the top of his nose as if trying to squeeze away a headache. "Where to begin? Well, let's begin with the simplest thing—as you can see, Zachary and Theodora, you are the remaining two Apostles in the programme. So congratulations on that."

"What happened to Sai, sir?" I ask with a frown.

"Sai was offered an internship with Novus and will be studying in America. He came to see me last week with the news and decided to withdraw for the sake of fairness since he wouldn't be able to accept the Oxford scholarship." He raises his hand to acknowledge the expressions on our faces. "Noble of him—I know. There's a reason why Sai has always been a particular favourite of mine."

"Favourites, sir?" I murmur disapprovingly—and, yes, somewhat bitterly.

"Of course. Any teacher who claims not to have favourites would be lying—even if that lie was to soothe a student's ego. Now. The programme. I have, of course, received both of your final assignments, which you both submitted, as usual, in a timely manner. Since then, I have been trying to solve the dilemma—no, the conundrum—of who should be chosen as my Apostle this year."

I throw Theodora a sidelong glance. She's biting into her bottom lip, worrying it.

She seems a little anxious—but I know why Mr Ambrose is being so strange, and I know it's no fault of hers.

"Common sense would dictate that you, Theodora, should receive the prize. You have been the front-runner through the entirety of the programme. Your work has always been incredibly conscientious, thorough, well-researched and marvellously written. You have proven yourself to be an incredibly academically gifted young woman, but also committed, determined, and admirably resilient."

He pauses, fixing Theodora with a stony look.

I frown. Everything he's saying is lovely enough, but why does it sound as if it's about to precede a significant but?

"Unfortunately—" I freeze in my seat at his words. "I was disappointed to find that your final assessment, while a fascinating read, did not meet the criteria of the assessment nor, in fact, attempt to answer the question set. You didn't even submit an essay. Am I correct to assume this was purposely done and not a grave administrative error?"

He cocks an eyebrow at Theodora, who nods sheepishly. "Yes, sir."

He sighs. "Just as I thought."

"What did you submit?" I ask, staring at Theodora.

"Miss Dorokhova submitted the opening chapter of a highly engaging, if rather... rambunctious story—a rousing and bawdy adventure on the high seas."

Theodora's face is now bright pink.

My mouth falls open.

"Not a... not a pirate romance?" I ask, torn between horror and amusement.

"Ah, I see you are a fan of *The Buccaneer Captain's Stolen Fiancée*," Mr Ambrose says in a completely serious tone.

"He ought to be," Theodora says lightly. "It's his book."

Now Mr Ambrose gives a thunderous frown. "You surely don't mean Zachary authored it?"

"No, sir," Theodora answers. "I wrote it, he owns the intellectual property."

I bury my face in my hands with a groan.

"This sounds like a complicated personal—and perhaps legal—matter," Mr Ambrose says. "The fact remains that, whilst an excellent read—if rather bolder than the books I am accustomed to—your work, Theodora, cannot be said to be discussing the statement you were given. Now." He looks from Theodora to me, and I drop my hands to my lap, watching him. "I can only assume, Theodora, that you submitted this particular oeuvre in the hope, perhaps, to sabotage yourself and allow Zachary, here, to be crowned victor of the Apostles programme. Am I correct in my assumption?"

She doesn't say anything, but Mr Ambrose reads her answer in her wide-eyed silence.

"Ah—just as I thought. A bold gambit, assuredly. I can only imagine you must have had compelling reasons to do so—to gift Zachary a victory he has, no doubt, desperately wished for, and you were, after all, terribly close to snatching that victory away from him." He points his hand at me in a courteous gesture. "I'm sure you could not have predicted, however, that Zachary would best you in a different arena."

Theodora and I exchange another look—this time a frown.

"Zachary might not have bested you academically, Theodora—but in the field of self-sabotage, he emerged the uncontested victor. For his final assessment, he submitted a single blank piece of paper."

Mr Ambrose sits back, steepling his fingers and resting a heavy look on us.

"Why would you—" Theodora starts, her cheeks now bright red, her eyes an angry flash of blue.

"Don't you even start—" I counter, starting upright in my chair and answering her glare for glare.

"Thank you," Mr Ambrose booms, cutting us both short. "It is the final day of the school year, and I am a busy man with more important things to do than to listen to the excuses and arguments of two lovesick young fools. Keep your reprimands and remonstrations to yourselves, you two. I've thought this through long and hard, and I have made my decision, with which neither of you will be given an opportunity to argue."

We watch him, rigid and nervous in our seats.

"This year, there will simply be no victor. Neither of your portraits will sit in the great hall as Spearcrest Apostle. You two, although my most promising candidates yet, have managed to break my programme. Perhaps it is the boon and burden of teaching such bright young minds. Or perhaps it is the risk I took when I chose you two and hoped that sublime love between you would help you reach greater heights instead of sending you both crashing into an abyss of despair and self-sacrifice."

My face is so aflame I hardly dare look Mr Ambrose in the eyes, and when I sneak Theodora a glance, her lips are pinched shut and her cheeks are crimson.

"Now—although there is to be no formal victor this year, this programme and its partnership with Oxford is a long-standing tradition which I respect too much to dismiss or ignore. The Oxford scholarship, therefore, I have chosen to award to you, Theodora."

She opens her mouth, but he raises an imperious hand.

"I'm not finished. You will receive this scholarship because you were the front-runner of the programme for most of its duration, because you have worked exceptionally hard in the light of extremely trying circumstances, and because I personally believe you deserve this scholarship. My decision is final and has already been communicated to the university and to my excellent friend Lady Ashton. That is all—that is my decision."

He waves a hand. "You may now respond—and it need not be any more complicated than a heartfelt thank-you."

Theodora lets out a weak puff of laughter. "Thank you, Mr Ambrose."

He nods graciously. She glances at me and then adds, "And thank you, Mr Ambrose, for asking Zachary to look after me back when I first started."

Mr Ambrose smiles. "I believed he was the right person for the task."

"He was."

"Well—you are most welcome." Mr Ambrose stands briskly to his feet. "You are both welcome. And before you go, I should also like to thank you both. For being exemplary students and admirable captains of our debate team. Theodora, for being a resolute and dedicated head girl, Zachary, for representing our chess team so impressively. Thank you both for everything you have given Spearcrest. It has been an honour and a pleasure, truly, to be your headmaster. I doubt I shall soon teach students like you two again."

At the door, he shakes my hand, and my throat is suddenly dry and hard.

"Thank you, Mr Ambrose. For everything. You've been the best role model I could have asked for or wanted."

Mr Ambrose nods. "Write me from Oxford, you two, will you?" He smiles. "I shall await your letters most impatiently." His smile widens. "And as for the inevitable wedding invitation, please address it to Mr Bellamy Ambrose."

"Sir!" I exclaim, throwing Theodora a look.

But she smiles and takes Mr Ambrose's hand to shake it. "We wouldn't dream of not having you in attendance, sir."

He grins. "I should hope not." Releasing Theodora's hand, he waves at the door. "Now off with the two of you! I believe there is a terribly secret lake-side end-of-year party you two should be headed to."

Since we're both late to the party, Theodora and I grind out a surly agreement to save our argument for later. We part ways outside the Old Manor, both headed for our own buildings, but I turn around at the last minute to catch Theodora's arm.

She whirls around, and I catch her in my arms, pressing a hot, needy kiss to her mouth.

"Be nice at the party," I mutter against her lips.

"I will if you are," she retorts.

"I'll be as gentle as a lamb."

"Probably a wolf in sheep's clothing."

"If I were a wolf, Theo, I would have devoured you a long time ago."

She laughs. "Deviant."

"Temptress."

Chapter 53

Luminous Sound

Zachary

But of course, we argue at the party.

Even though it's a hazy spring afternoon and the air is calm and fragrant and full of the splash of water and the sound of music and laughter. Even Evan and Sophie are in a good mood, having traded their warring for playful flirtation. Luca sits at the edge of the lake, uncharacteristically pensive and taciturn, while Iakov lounges in the grass, tapping a cigarette lazily against his phone.

In the distance, Sev chases his strange, adorable fiancée through the trees like a mortal chasing an elusive naiad.

There's a mingled sense of satisfaction and nostalgia that permeates the air. The wind blowing across the lake shifts the fluffy cattails and spiky reeds at the edges.

Everything feels peaceful, almost magical.

But still, we fight.

Theodora wears a summer dress with a pale floral pattern and thick shoulder straps tied into bows. Her short hair floats in the wind, tickling her cheeks and lips. Sometimes, the wind tugs at her skirts, revealing more of her legs.

Theodora looks gorgeous, and once I draw closer, she smells gorgeous too, and her eyes, in the hazy golden sunlight, are a dreamy blue. And all of this gorgeousness makes it impossible to be gentle as a lamb.

"What was the point of self-sabotage?" I ask, drawing her into the treeline for some privacy. "I didn't want you to hand me the win."

"And yet you wanted to hand it to *me*."

"That's different and you know it."

"And how?" she asks.

"Because I didn't *need* the win."

"Neither did I."

I clench my fists and take a deep breath, to still myself. "Let me rephrase. I didn't *deserve* the win."

"How could you possibly know? We only found out today I was the front-runner."

"Mr Ambrose had already told me."

Her eyes go wide. "He did not."

"When you left. He told me."

"Then why did you self-sabotage? Why didn't you just hand in your essay?"

"Because you were gone for so long, and if I won just because of what happened—because of what you had to go through—that's not the kind of victory I wanted."

"So you thought you would simply hand me the trophy?"

I shrug. "You tried to hand it to me."

She gives me a haughty look. "Make no mistake, Blackwood—I demand a rematch. You and I, in the arena of the greatest academic institution of the country."

I give her a solemn nod. "I'm for it. Oxford, three years, one rematch. A fair one, this time. No self-sabotage, no sacrifice of love or show of devotion."

"It's agreed." We shake hands. "Just try not to submit any blank pages this time."

"At least I would never submit a chapter from a salacious pirate romance."

Her lips quirk. "How could you *possibly* know whether or not it's salacious?"

"Because it's a book about pirates—and we all know how you feel about those."

She smirks and steps closer, hands behind her back. "Still jealous over a fictional character, Zachary Blackwood? It's a bad look."

"Still in love with a villainous pirate from a children's book, Theodora Dorokhova? That's a bad look." I stretch out my open palm towards her. "And I want my copy of *Peter Pan* back."

She bats my hand away. "You're not getting it back. Ever." Her smile widens. "And to answer your question, I don't see myself in James Hook—and I don't like him because he's like you."

"I never asked you that—I would never ask such a nonsensical question."

"You asked it black on white in your annotations."

I clench my hands into fists. "Theodora. Those were my *private* annotations."

"Yes, and I'm answering you *privately*. I don't like him because he's like you. I like you because you're like him."

"What—*cadaverous and blackavised*?"

"*A man of indomitable courage.*"

I laugh and shake my head. "Because it took me so much courage to hand in a blank piece of paper for my assignment?"

"Because it took you so much courage to love me when I was so difficult to love."

I take a step closer and capture her gaze with mine, daring her to look away. Our height difference is significant enough now that she has to tilt her head back to look at me.

"Listen to me, Theodora Dorokhova, and listen well. You are not difficult to love—you have *never* been difficult to love. Whatever happened in your life to make you believe you might be is a tragedy and a betrayal, a crime against truth. Whoever told you or made you believe you're difficult to love is a liar. You're not difficult to love. You are so easy to love that I fell in love with you without even meaning to, I fell in love with you even when you wouldn't let me, and I keep falling in love with you every day. I don't even think I'll ever stop falling in love with you. In fact, I fell in love with you earlier, when I saw you in that summer dress, and I fell in love with you five minutes ago when you were talking about James Hook. And I believe I shall fall in love with you in a few minutes when I take your hand and take you into the tree to kiss you where nobody can see us and get on my knees to worship you the way I know best. And I'll fall in love with you this summer, when we go swimming in the lake and take road trips to Oxford, and I'll fall in love with you every night when I take you to my bed or when you decide to be stubborn and take *me* to *your* bed instead. And I'll fall in love with you when you finish that damnable pirate romance book, and I'll fall in love with you when we're in university and you'll be angry at me for looking down my nose because I'm studying philosophy and you're not. I'll keep falling in love with every part of you because every part of you is perfectly, utterly lovable."

Tears blossom in her eyes. Deep inside my chest, my heart aches because I know that a part of her needed to hear that.

Theodora has probably always believed she wasn't easy to love—and I suspect part of her will always believe that insidious, foul little lie.

It doesn't matter. I'll attack that lie every single day, I'll fight it tooth and claw until it's completely gone, until Theodora has forgotten it ever even existed.

"Maybe *you* should become the writer," she says in a small voice, smiling through her tears.

"I'm going to throw my life away on academia and education—remember? Besides." I swipe away her tears with a thumb and take her hand, drawing her deeper into the treeline. "I don't need to become a writer—I already have a writer girlfriend."

"A writer girlfriend?" she asks, following me. "Since when?"

"Since forever. Since Christmas. Since today." The wind blows her hair across her face, and I push it away with a laugh. "She's a little elusive, this girlfriend of mine."

"But I think she loves you very much." Theodora holds my arm in hers and stands on her tiptoes to whisper in my ear. "I think she loves you and has wanted to be your girlfriend for a long time."

"She loves me?" I ask in a casual tone.

"Oh, she's ridiculously in love with you."

I whisper back. "Do you think she would like to be seduced amongst the trees?"

"Yes. Often."

"Then I must begin at once."

I catch her in my arms like a princess in a fairy tale, and she throws her arms around my neck with a surprised yelp.

"I can walk, you know!"

I kiss her lips. "But why would you when I can carry you?"

She laughs and kicks her legs, throwing back her head. "Now I really feel like an innocent maiden being captured by a handsome pirate."

"Who would have thought my girlfriend would have such frivolous fantasies?"

She taps her finger over my lips. "Less judging, more ravishing."

"Yes, my beautiful darling."

"Thank you, my handsome love."

I stop, and we stare at each other for a second.

"Too much?" she asks.

"No. Never."

She laughs, and I kiss her laughing mouth, and my heart is full of that perfect, luminous sound—the sound of Theodora Dorokhova laughing.

THE END

DEAR READER

Thank you for reading my tale of love and academia. Don't worry—this isn't the last of Zachary and his Theodora. Just like the other Spearcrest couples, they'll also be back for a bonus story set sometime in the future.

In the meantime, if you enjoyed this book and wish to support me while I write the next one, please consider leaving a review. Without the support of a publishing house behind me, most of my support comes from readers just like you, and the best way you can support me is by posting a review—no matter how short or brutally honest!

All my love,

x Aurora

Acknowledgements

Thank you to all the darlings online who supported me, encouraged me and made me feel as if my writing actually matters. You have no idea how much anxiety I felt writing this book because I was so afraid of letting you all down. Thank you for inspiring me and motivating me in equal measures.

Thank you to R, as always, for all the love and the help.

Thank you to my beta-readers, but in particular Danni, for your notes and your voicenotes, for all your support and emotions, for your gorgeous edits and for actually doing homework and for being so very wonderful.

Thank you to my wonderful brother, for sending me a picture of the Waterstones in Picadilly Circus saying you can't wait to see my books in there one day. Thank you for believing in me even when I struggle to believe in myself.

Thank you to my family, as always, and to my mother, for every night you spent reading me books as a child. My love of reading made me who I am, and my love of reading was the best gift you ever gave me.

Thank you to M, my number one.

Last but not least, thank you to R. I write romance because I believe in love

—and I believe in love because of you.

Annotation & Study Guide

Themes to annotate

- The Themes of **Expectations** and **Responsibility**
- The Theme of **Beauty**
- The Themes of **Family** and **Friendship**
- The Themes of **Longing** and **Desire**
- The Themes of **Education** and **Academia**
- The Theme of **Freedom**
- The theme of **Love**

Critical Thinking Questions

- Explore the connection between Zachary's love of academia and his love of Theodora.

- Ultimately, is Theodora who is she is *because* of her parents or *despite* them?

- What is the significance of the library as a setting?

- How is religious imagery used to explore the relationship between Zachary and Theodora?

- What is more important: intelligence and the pursuit of knowledge, or love and the pursuit of happiness?

About Aurora

Aurora Reed is a coffee-drinking academic who is fascinated by stories of darkness, death and desire. When she's not reading over a cup of black coffee, she can be found roaming the moors or scribbling stories by candlelight.